THE QUEEN CON

ALSO BY MEGHAN SCOTT MOLIN

THE GOLDEN ARROW MYSTERIES

The Frame-Up

The Golden Arrow Mysteries, Book 2

MEGHAN SCOTT MOLIN

Text copyright © 2019 by Meghan Scott Molin
All rights reserved.

Published by 47North, Seattle

www.apub.com

Amazon, the Amazon logo, and 47North are trademarks of Amazon.com, Inc., or its affiliates.

ISBN-13: 9781542004190 (hardcover)
ISBN-10: 1542004195 (hardcover)
ISBN-13: 9781542004183 (paperback)
ISBN-10: 1542004187 (paperback)

Cover design by Danny Schlitz

Printed in the United States of America

First edition

To Sawyer, my little sequel in so many ways.

CHAPTER 1

"So, we're still on for *Game of Thrones* Sunday night, or should I sell your tickets?" My best friend Lawrence's voice carries over the stack of fabric I'm carrying into the downstairs closet-turned-costume-haven of his salon. It's already so packed with garments I have no idea where these are going to fit. I've successfully skirted the rusty back door and bypassed the folding metal chair and 1980s-era metal desk that serves as L's back of house. His office still hasn't gotten the same upgrade as the rest of the shop this summer with all the new clients rolling in, but I know it's on the list. In fact, I'd parked my beat-up brown Aspire right next to L's "new" but shiny black 2008 Dodge Challenger. My poor Millennium Turd looks even sadder next to it. Matteo has been bugging me for a month about starting to save for a "safer vehicle," but I just want something pretty like L's.

Which is never going to happen unless I figure out how to make more money. Dropping down to part time from my job as a comic book writer to do part-time costume design has been amazing, but a labor of love. L is my biggest—and, let's be honest, *only*—consistent client. I've had a ton of inquiries after winning the Miss Her Galaxy contest last year at San Diego Comic-Con, but actually *getting* the jobs once I send a price quote has proven more difficult. My new plan is to continue to hone my skills and streamline my process through L's looks and then take on other queens, rather than internet randos, as clients. I keep telling myself that if I put in the time, hustle, and love, the universe will bring it back. I just hope it's in the form of Benjamins and/or a newer, running car.

"Yes, we're still on for Sunday; Matteo is going to try to come too . . . can you help me here?" A strap of glimmery silver hangs dangerously near my foot as I shuffle forward to the door across from the stairs. I use my feet to sweep blindly for the chair that sits in the closet and, upon finding it, drop the fabric onto it with a grateful sigh.

"Girl, you look beat." Lawrence reaches for the pile just as I set it down, and I shoot him a "too little, too late" look.

I pluck the first costume off the stack, a gold-and-black, circus-inspired number that took at least twenty hours last week to finish. "Well, *someone* has a drag revue this weekend and needed *four* costumes updated. So. Pot. Kettle." I know he's been burning the midnight oil too, balancing his blossoming business and his true love of stage performance.

The chime of a bell overhead makes the point for me, and I roll my eyes. "I thought you said you didn't have an appointment right now, L." I try not to sound too snippy. L's success both on and off the stage is funding a lot of my side work. If I need to come back after work tonight, I will.

"I don't. Or at least I shouldn't." L frowns and looks over his shoulder, peeking through the doorway. "Hopefully it's a walk-in. I'll go look and see if someone is scheduled."

"I have a meeting with my Genius team in two hours. I can come back."

"Be right there!" he calls to the front before crossing to his desk and flipping open the large-scale paper calendar on it. The guy seriously needs to move into the digital age with his planning. "This new part-time assistant thing is more headache than it's worth, I swear."

Even from behind I see his shoulders straighten. L has, for lack of a better term, come to full military attention. Whatever is on that paper has him either upset or excited, and by the way he jogs back to the doorway to the salon, I'd guess upset. He peers around the doorjamb, so I join him from the closet.

Forcibly reminding myself of *Prisoner of Azkaban* Stan Shunpike, I stage whisper, "What'cha lookin' at?"

L stares so intently at the figure at the front counter he literally jumps when I speak.

"Geez, L. What's up?" I ask, a chill running down my spine. I turn back to the front of the store, fingers itching to grab my phone. Our case is too fresh in my head, and I start to worry about boogeymen. "Do I need to call Matteo?"

L rolls his shoulders like he's loosening up for a game. "No, don't be silly. Do I look okay? Don't answer that; I don't have time to do anything if I don't."

"What. A. Weirdo," I say to myself as I track his progress across the dark studio and up to the front counter. After a moment, I see his usual posture return, so I shake my head, mystified, and make my way back to the closet by way of his office.

I'm curious about his reaction, so I just *happen* to glance at the calendar for today. There's nothing else for this afternoon except L's fitting. But underneath that is a yellow sticky note in foreign writing—I assume his part-time assistant's—that says,

Someone named Stevie came in to make an appointment but wants to talk with you personally. He'll stop by again to schedule.

Is this what weirded L out? This note? I cast an eye up front as I cross back to the closet. L seems perfectly at ease now, selling the man a few bottles of hair product. I shrug, plopping back down against the nearest rack on the floor next to my stack of costumes and resting my head against the soft pouf of a pink taffeta skirt. Exhaustion floods my body instantaneously, and I'm not surprised that I'm already half-asleep in the few minutes it takes L to return.

He hunkers down next to me, his dark-brown eyes on a level with mine. "Are you sure you want to keep doing this? I know everything's been a little light speed–paced."

"And let you hire a hack? Or, worse yet, sew your own?"

"I don't sew. I bedazzle. And pin things. And I can hot-glue with the best of them."

I stifle a yawn but straighten. "I'm just living the dream, L. Let's get you fitted."

After a few minutes, I poke the Wookiee in the room. "So, was that Stevie?"

Underneath my hands, L tenses. *"What?"*

"I saw that note in your calendar. Who is Stevie? Your number-one fan?"

I laugh, but L basically freezes in place.

"Oh come on, L, loosen up; I'm only teasing . . . wait—are you *blushing*? Okay, now you really do have to tell me who he is."

"No one," L says. "Just a friend from a long time ago. Lots of them coming out of the woodwork when you've been on late-night TV. Now can we get going?"

It's obvious he doesn't want to talk about it, so I oblige him but make a mental note to ask Ryan about Stevie the next time I see him. I wouldn't want someone taking advantage of L after his local *célébrité*.

Halfway through my pulling the circus costume over L's head, my phone chimes twice from my purse. I pause, wondering if it's Matteo. I really should give him his own text tone so I can know from across the room. I've waffled on it because it seems like such a momentous step in a relationship to give your significant other their own ringtone. Was I ready to commit a favorite song or phrase to forever remind me of Matteo? I'd been pondering the classic *Captain America* show opener, the one about when Captain America throws his mighty shield, but wondered if that was too on-the-nose—

"A little help here?" L's voice is muffled by the beaded cummerbund.

"Yeah. Sure. Sorry." I yank down and uncover a disgruntled L. His hair, grown slightly into a short afro these days, is mussed, and I can see a red mark on his cheek where a sequin scratched him. "I—ah—guess I'll add another zipper on the side."

"I hope you and Hot-Lanta get over the honeymoon phase soon. I swear, you two are—"

My phone rings. L rolls his eyes and motions for me to answer it, so I leave him standing straightjacketed by the costume and grab the phone. Instead of Matteo, it's my supervisor, Andy. It rolls to voice mail, which I don't mind, since I prefer to read the message text instead of taking phone calls—so much simpler that way.

"Huh," I say after reading the message and trying to help L's arm through the sleeve with only one hand.

"'Huh,' as in these arms are way too damn tight?"

"Well, it's *obvious* you've been working out more since I took the measurements for these, L. How am I supposed to plan for how stacked you are getting?"

"That sounds like a line, but I'm going to take the compliment. Please plan for this level of stacked-ness for this weekend."

"Deal." I *had* made those armholes *waaaaay* too small. Not quite sure what I had been thinking.

"So, it wasn't your ladylove breaking your heart?"

"No—Andy."

"Andy . . ."

I smack L's arm with my hand. "Andy my supervisor, Andy."

"And what did my good friend Andy want?"

"Actually"—I yank the zipper, only now partly surprised that it won't go all the way up; I am going to have to let out the seams across his shoulders—"he wanted to let me know"—I tug again and then give up and turn my attention to the frilled tail across the back—"that they're hiring another artist to help out our team now that I've dropped to part time."

L grunts, though it may be because he's partially strangled by the corset-tightness of the costume. I let down the zipper a little, and he shakes his shoulders. "Is this a good thing?"

"I don't know. I hope so. Kind of weird to add to the family, but I'm losing my mind trying to balance everything, so I think it's necessary."

The next piece is a much closer fit, a drapey, silvery cocktail dress with accentuated hips and a cameo closure at the tie neck. It's my favorite of the bunch, the one I'm most proud of. Ironically, it took less time to make than the circus one, but whatever.

Halfway through the fitting, L's phone chimes. And then again, and then again. He reaches for it and swipes through several messages, his eyebrows drawing down in a scowl.

"Everything okay on the home front?" I ask around a mouthful of pins, sticking one carefully into a tuck.

Without responding, he shuffles to the right and, despite my protest, reaches for the remote and flicks on the old wall-mount TV.

I follow along as best I can. "You haven't used that thing since our *Firefly* binge night . . . what? Five years ago?"

No response from L. He just flips through channel after channel of fuzz and weird daytime free-access programming like a man possessed. *What on earth?*

I wonder if he's looking for a replay of his interview with Jimmy Fallon on *The Tonight Show* . . . he's been on cloud nine, having checked off *that* bucket-list item last week. News traveled fast that an already-popular local drag queen was instrumental in locking up a double agent, and the media was eating it up. L is reveling in the attention, but L isn't the only local celebrity to come out of our summer. The Golden Arrow, a secret vigilante citizen, helped us catch Agent Sosa—DEA agent turned drug lord—in a chase through San Diego Comic-Con *and* link her to the thirty-year-old, unsolved murder of my boss's father through my favorite comic, *The Hooded Falcon*. The Golden Arrow planted clues, sprayed white rabbits on suspects, left notes in my personal notebook, and tied up drug dealers in an effort to point the LAPD to the link between the drug-ring crimes and a similar drug ring in my favorite vintage comic.

Between the clues and my knowledge of the old comic, I was able to discover that Edward Casey Senior—my boss's father—had actually been writing about a *real* drug ring, and a *real* villain, before he died. A villain who'd discovered that Casey Senior planned to out him in the comic book, and had murdered him, covered it up, and gone scot-free as a DEA agent for more than thirty years. Putting the murderer of my childhood idol behind bars should have been the highlight of my *life*. It brought my oddly normal boyfriend to me and clinched Lawrence, Ryan, and me as family and partners in crime solving, and as a bonus, I didn't have to spend even a night in jail. And yet, as much as life had settled down to a wonderful new normal, the mystery identity of our masked helper rankled deep in my soul.

Lawrence takes my silence as an unasked question about his sudden TV obsession.

"Cleopatra is on the news," he answers, not taking his eyes off the TV.

My eyebrows lift in response. "Cleopatra your nemesis, Cleopatra?"

"The one and only." He grimaces. "She hasn't taken my . . . er . . . newfound success well. It's only gotten worse. She'd better not be throwing shade on the drag revue this weekend."

Cleopatra is Lawrence's main competition on the drag stage in our little corner of the world. And while Lawrence has acclaim from his appearance on *Drag Divas* (the superpopular reality show and TV drag competition), and recently with the Golden Arrow stuff, Cleopatra has managed to mostly hold her own despite being a homegrown queen with little to no big-star airtime. And now her face fills the screen, completely done up.

"That's right, this weekend at the Pink Boa on Santa Monica, starts at nine p.m." She pouts prettily at the reporter. Her makeup is over-the-top glam—big feather false eyelashes, heaps of glittery pink eyeshadow to match her Barbie-pink sequined gown, white feather boa, tall wig—the whole nine yards. Truth be told, she looks good for a queen in the middle of the day, but I'm not about to say anything to Lawrence. The reporter starts the wrap-up of what I assume has been a brief interest-piece interview about drag.

L grunts at the screen. "Well, at least it was just promotion. No clue how she got on there, seeing as I'm the organizer. I didn't even know the news was doing—"

Cleopatra leans in over the front of the reporter, cutting her off midsentence, same as Lawrence. "I didn't get a chance to tell you about the theme of the evening." She raises her hands and wiggles her fingers in a bangle-and-overdone-nails jazz hand. "Capes and costumes, it's superhero-themed, and it's going to be magical."

"The fu—" Lawrence starts.

I glance at him, being fully aware that the theme is currently set as the "Queen of the Night Circus." Tension grows in the pit of my stomach.

Cleopatra fairly drapes herself over the reporter now, who, in truth, handles it as well as one can on regional-access TV. "Yes, there will be superhero numbers. Mine will be the best, of course, so bring your tip money, darlings—and I'm throwing a themed after-party at the Zebra Lounge. Attendees are encouraged to come in costume, *and*—"

I have to physically hold L back from charging the television at this point. He's uttering curses and words like "self-promotion" and "sabotage" as well as several very creative ways that one queen might use pantyhose to kill another.

We miss her next few words in a scuffle over the TV remote, which L attempts to throw through the television. We hit the volume control instead, and suddenly the reporter's voice is so loud we both clap our hands over our ears, remote falling to the floor.

"Did you say a 'special guest' as in who I think you mean?"

"That's right. A *golden* opportunity." She coos a fake laugh and then levels her gaze at the camera. "Let's just say I've developed an inside contact with one of our city's most popular . . . icons . . . and he'll be coming to one or *all* of my parties this fall. There's no way to know other than to come find out for yourself."

The reporter looks at the camera as if this has suddenly become her payday. "Well, folks, you heard it here first. All about this weekend's drag revue and then, even more interestingly, maybe our first public appearance of the Golden Arrow. Joy? Andrew? Back to you."

Even as the anchors back in the studio gape a little at the transition, L is dialing his phone. Within seconds he's yelling something unintelligible as I stare at the TV.

The Golden Arrow.

"There's no way," I say, more to myself than to the room.

"Of course there's no way—this is all a damn media grab. That *basic* bitch," L yells, disentangling himself from the rest of the costume and throwing it to the floor near the chair. "We're gonna have to finish this later; I have a mess to clean up."

I gather the garments into a pile, eyeing my phone warily. I can only imagine Matteo's phone ringing off the hook already. "Yeah, me too," I answer, leaving without a goodbye as Lawrence rants and raves in his closet.

CHAPTER 2

It's not often L wants to dress himself for a show without last-minute adjustments, but Friday night arrives with me sitting in the crowd like an everyday Joe. The room is packed, and not with the typical crowd—it looks like Cleo's media stunt was successful. I don't know whether to be happy or mad about it, so I settle for eyeballing the obvious newcomers near me. There's a tall, dark guy with some seriously beautiful hair to my left, seated with a table of men dressed in various shades of business casual. Definitely not the usual. And it's no wonder . . . with the promise of a possible Golden Arrow sighting, Cleo got the world's interest.

While the attention is perhaps ultimately good, the interview with Cleopatra hasn't just pissed Lawrence off. It's caused a domino effect, the result of which is a brand-new number involving several of L's queen friends, last-minute choreography, and updating the revue information on the website to include "superhero" night. In fact, up until Wednesday, L was an utter stress case, but . . . then something switched. He said he'd had a stroke of good luck and talked about a "secret weapon"—right before he forbade me from attending either the dress rehearsal *or* the pre-show rehearsal tonight so I wouldn't spoil the surprise. I was glad to give up Thursday night to be with Matteo, but . . . my eye twitches with the thought of all the little fixes I *won't* get to do tonight. In a normal runway show, maybe not so bad. But queens *use* their looks . . . I foresee a bunch of hem repair in my future.

"There are a *lot* of people here," Ryan mutters, looking from our crowded little round table to the nearly SRO room. Over Ryan's shoulder, I catch sight of Simon, Kyle, and Tej at a table near the back, rubbernecking unabashedly. Since Simon's divorce finalized last month, Kyle has been taking him out as often as he can, in admirable best-friend fashion, to prove to him that there are more fish in the sea. And from what I gather from limited office gossip, one hopes that this next fish doesn't run away with an accountant.

I have a brief flash of shame that I didn't do the inviting, which in itself is new to me. Up until this year, I haven't exactly been the friendliest or most open officemate. I'm happy to see them here, even if I *know* the reason isn't a love of drag. It's a fascination with the Golden Arrow—something most of LA shares, if the attendance tonight is a good measurement. The Pink Boa isn't big to begin with, but crammed full of a buzzing crowd hoping to see a *real* superhero in their midst? The place feels like a mosh pit.

A martini clinks down in front of me, the harried waitress not even apologizing for the slosh that follows. *A mosh pit that serves martinis at least*, I think, taking a sip, then immediately grimacing. *Watered-down, not-their-usual-quality martinis.* I sigh.

"The crowd? Or the drink?" Ryan asks, casting a baleful eye over me. Sure, it's a million gigawatts of sound in here, but he hears my one sigh.

"Both."

"You've been mopey lately. I thought *true love* would take an edge off your surly side. You know. Twitterpated. Joined at the hip. All that."

"You're one to talk," I say, leaning back in my chair and turning my own glance on the empty chair across the table from me. "Your partner in crime doesn't seem to be here either."

Ryan gives such a start that the table is rocked from beneath, further demolishing my martini. My *twelve-dollar*, barely drinkable martini. "What the hell, Ryan?"

"I'm so sorry I'm late." A voice comes from behind, and while I'm mopping up a dollar's worth of alcohol with the inadequate cocktail napkin, I see two arms slide around Ryan's chest from behind. Even before I see her face, I recognize the effortless elegance of Genius's VP and Ryan's current girlfriend, Lelani. "I didn't mean to startle you; I thought you heard me call your name," she says, leaning over and dropping a brief peck on his cheek before seating herself in the third chair.

Overhead the lights dim once, signaling the show is shortly to start. "Yeah, well, Mr. Jumpy here owes me another drink," I grouse. The glass is definitely half-empty, not half-full, and the olive is gone. I direct my stare at Ryan and attempt to Magneto-lift his wallet from his pocket with my mind powers. Nothing happens, but he gets the point anyhow, raising his hand to flag down a waitress. When one fails to materialize, he sighs in resignation and wades against the tide of people toward the crowded bar, leaving Lelani and me alone.

I sip at the dregs of my drink for a full two minutes, and Lelani studies her nails after making a production of removing her jacket. I never know if we should talk about work or . . . . not-work. It's not like I know much of what she does with her free time, and the only thing I *do* know about her outside of work—that she and Matteo were once engaged—I don't want to talk about. "So, uh, traffic?" I ask finally when the silence has stretched to an unbearable thinness.

"Hmm? Oh, no. I was backstage. I've been here for a few hours."

I set my glass down and eye her critically. In all the din, maybe I misheard her. "Backstage . . . here?" Specifically, *the backstage where Lawrence asked me not to be tonight?*

Lelani flashes me a Cheshire cat smile. "Yes, I've been helping Latifah put the finishing touches on tonight's surprise performance."

"You've been helping. Latifah." It's so nonsensical all I can do is parrot her words back.

"I'm just a minor part of the team; I don't want to spoil the surprise," she says with a smirk. I get the distinct feeling she's enjoying holding something over my head.

"The . . . team?" I mutter, unsure of what exactly that means. She's not part of the *usual* team of Latifah, Ryan, and me. Why did *she* get to go backstage when I was expressly forbidden? I don't have to wait long to find out. Just as Ryan shoves back to our table, the lights dim for good.

In almost no time, Latifah appears on the stage, stunning in an all-white bell-bottom suit. I blink rapidly to clear my vision. It's *not* one of the costumes I made for this show. *What the hell.* Totally tuning out Latifah's greeting in favor of studying her costume, I finally relax a little, recognizing an early effort of mine—an Elvis-esque suit that has been pinned, tucked, bedazzled, and most likely hot-glued to look like a full seventies disco suit. But who did it?

"You've been promised a superhero-level show," Latifah purrs into the cordless microphone, "and we thought we'd have some fun with the theme. So tonight, we're serving up capes and costumes and sequins and sexy crime-fighting in a super-special head-to-head Queen Superhero versus Queen Superhero lip-sync spectacular! It's all the glam and glitz and booty and—well, you know the rest—that you're here for, but now with kapow!" Latifah leans over and gives a suggestive wiggle of her cleavage before snapping up in a fairly impressive karate kick specifically designed to show off her dexterity.

The crowd claps appreciatively, and Latifah takes a moment to smooth her suit back into place over her curves, bantering with one fellow up front. "Did you like the view, honey? You never know what you're going to get with Latifah; my gentlemen have to be ready for *anything*, if you know what I mean . . ." She raises her gaze to the next tier of tables as the audience gives the expected chuckle. Latifah is such a show-woman, and only I catch the slight bobble in her persona as she scans the grouping of tables that includes ours. Her witty banter trails off; I see her eyes dart around and a little "oh" of surprise hit her lips just before she pastes a big smile on her face, does a little shimmy, and turns to smile at the next section of people. It's maybe a few seconds, but *something* has thrown her off.

I crane my neck around, looking for something out of place, but the only thing I see amiss is the table full of business-casual Muggles. True, they're not the normal cuppa, but nothing Latifah hasn't seen before, surely?

Onstage, L has recovered nicely, and no one except me is the wiser. "We've broken into two superhero teams, and we'll battle to the *death*—well, no, not actually. Do you *know* how hard it is to get blood out of white leather? And honey, I just got this suit cleaned. We'll call it Battle to the Shade; we'll use applause and tips as a measure, and the winner gets this!" Latifah brandishes a silver sequin cape, twirls it, and settles it around her shoulder before placing a huge, fake dollar-store crown on her head and winking broadly at the audience. "*And* the rights to host the Halloween Drag Revue. Bragging rights, hosting rights, *and* a crown. It's looking good for Team Latifah."

"Uh-uh, girl." Cleopatra sashays onstage and plucks the crown off her head. "Not until the fat lady has sung."

"Wasn't that last week?" Latifah banters back.

"I believe you're thinking of your rehearsal," Cleopatra cuts in, and the crowd laughs. "Team Cleopatra is more than up for this battle of the Super Dupers, but let's not forget that *I* am the only one who has a connection to the *real* celebrity—"

"Your mama doesn't count as a celebrity," Latifah jokes back, always game, though I notice she's quick to cut Cleo off from expounding on the Golden Arrow. "May the best queen win!" They shake hands with the jingle of bracelets and the swish of white fringe, grinning with a perfect mixture of theatrical drama and good-natured competition. Only I note the steel in Latifah's spine. To her, this competition isn't just some campy superhero battle; it means something—this is *her* ground, and she isn't going to let Cleopatra win.

The crowd breaks into wild applause. Queen versus queen is the norm, but *this* twist—the team approach—both sounds fun and promises fierce competition. Latifah and Cleopatra make a big show of flipping a huge, joke-size coin to determine who will go first. The audience eats it up, everyone scrambling to verify which, heads or tails, has surfaced.

"Tails!" Cleopatra says in triumph, reaching into a pocket of her sleek black catsuit and producing a classic superhero mask. She hands the cordless mic to Latifah, ties the mask on, and does an elaborate ninja jump off to stage right.

Only seconds later, a guitar riff tears through the small lounge space, and I recognize Prince's "Batdance" from teenager-hood. What transpires next can only be described as grunge-superhero hip-thrusting, with Cleopatra playing a sexy, vixen Catwoman to a strapping Batman, dressed all in glitter and tights. A third queen joins them, dressed as a campy and sexy, gender-bent Robin (Grayson, of course, pre-Nightwing—she has *good* taste), complete with mask. The song shifts to "Iron Man," and the group of glittery superheroes end their number in a wild, head-banging, thrash air-band cover. It's good. It's really good. Half the crowd is on their feet, cheering as the song ends on the iconic refrain, "I am Iron Man."

I can't help but cheer along, despite my allegiance to Latifah. It's *different* enough from a typical drag number to be refreshing and captivating. The head-thrashing isn't exactly high-level choreography, but the heavy music and fun costumes are compelling, to say the least.

Cleopatra gets up from playing air-guitar on her knees and yells, "Golden Arrow forever!" to the crowd before exiting stage left, waving to an honestly adoring crowd. Money pours onto the stage and into the hands of designated collectors. A pit of worry starts in my stomach. Latifah is a gifted performer, but . . . that's a tough act to follow. And since I've literally seen *nothing* of what she's cobbled together in the past few days . . . I certainly hope it won't fall flat. I want my friend to *win*, not go home with consolation prizes.

I shouldn't have worried. The second ABBA's "Super Trouper" starts, I'm hooked. Even more so when not only L but also a *dozen* white bell-bottom–clad figures march onto the small stage—four queens, whom I recognize as close friends of L's, and about eight people I've never seen before in my entire life.

The choreography unfolds deliciously. First from military-precision marching onto the stage, then to baton-twirling, sexy *oompah-pahs* to the music, and L standing out front like a shining general of a disco superhero army. The music shifts to an electric version of "I am Superman," and things break into an all-out dance party. Someone swings in on a rope—a *rope*—suspended from the ceiling. This person is dressed all in white but wears a golden cape and mask, an arrow painted across the front of his leotard.

The audience gasps, and my heart stutters to a stop in my chest. Is *this* L's secret weapon? The Golden Arrow? Surely the GA wouldn't agree to be a part of a drag revue.

"Oh, there's Daniel!" squeals Lelani. Squeals. I cannot imagine this woman doing anything that bubbly, but there you have it. She catches my eye and smiles. "He's part of the act."

The audience and I figure it out around the same time, but the amp in excitement has added to L's performance. "Daniel" brings down the house by fake-fighting all the backup dancers onstage as if they're criminals. Latifah and the two other queens join in, using some fairly impressive kicks, given the general tightness and elaborateness of the costumes. Latifah and the queens form the classic *Charlie's Angels* pose, and the montage concludes with Daniel doing a roundoff back handspring right into Latifah's arms as the music ends.

It's unlike anything I've ever seen. I'm on my feet. Lelani's on her feet. Beside me, Ryan is standing on a chair and whistling. A bra lands up onstage. Latifah tosses Daniel's considerable bulk up into the air, and he lands spryly on his feet before removing his mask dramatically, taking Latifah's hand, and taking a bow as if this whole thing were an elaborate stage production. Coins and dollar bills rain down on the stage as the whole group executes another bow and exits the stage.

I have no doubt who won this competition. The amount of money Latifah collects *far* outstrips the amount thrown onto the stage for Cleopatra, but *how on earth* has she pulled *this* off? I've never seen half the people onstage. And the guy who swung down on a rope, fought some criminals, and then flipped into Latifah's arms? He wasn't a queen, or wasn't dressed as one, at least. Latifah has *backup dancers*. This is a whole level of production that baffles my mind.

"How did you like it?"

I blink, finding Lelani wearing a "cat who ate the canary" smile on her face.

"It was . . . phenomenal," I answer, still struggling to understand *how* this was achieved.

"Wasn't it, though?" Lelani smiles, cheering again. The crowd is still going crazy, though most of us are finding our seats. How could the drag revue continue after this? "Of course, all the credit goes to Daniel and L for putting it together so quickly."

I bristle slightly at her use of my pet name for Latifah, but I don't have time to stew. A moment later, L's back onstage, wearing an enormous grin. "You are all so generous. Details will emerge at the end of our show, but it looks like preliminary results say that you'll be attending *my* Halloween Revue." The crowd cheers. Latifah waves and laughs. "Now, now, *all* our superheroes did an amazing job, and don't worry, the show's not over yet. Keep those wallets available and your spirits open to enjoying more of our talented performers!"

The rest of the night goes off more or less how I expect it, albeit more amped than usual by the utterly electrified atmosphere from the show opening. It's one of the best drag shows I've ever been to—and *that* rankles because it's one I've been least *involved* in. As the last number ends, all the queens come back out onstage, wearing little plastic Zorro masks. I clap and whistle wildly.

"We'll see you all in just a few weeks; stay tuned for details!" Latifah says, leading everyone in a theater-style bow. Despite the cheering crowd, Cleopatra is wearing a face that I'd describe as "Lemonhead-level bitter" instead of pleased. She's not happy she's lost.

"And *I'll* see you tonight if you're headed to my after-party," Cleopatra calls as everyone at the tables starts to gather their things. I wonder how many of these same folks will show up to the Zebra just to see if the Golden Arrow materializes. My gaze catches on my coworkers making a beeline for the front door. I know at least three supergeeks who will be there. My allegiance to L says I shouldn't go . . . but my curiosity about Cleopatra's claims to know the Golden Arrow are of equal strength.

I lead the way against the crush of people heading for the door, like a salmon swimming upstream. Largely, it looks like everyone is tired and ready to go home or headed to the party; we're among the few headed for the door to the back.

I'm delayed at the stage for a few minutes while queens catch up with a few friends and fans; the door to the back is crowded. Ryan and Lelani peel off after a moment to go grab one more drink, and I wave, intent on making it backstage to see if Latifah needs any help with the costumes.

I finally manage to squeeze myself through the little door. Just down the short hallway and to the left, I can hear all manner of whooping and yelling. The queens are still amped up over their show, as they should be. It was amazing, and I'd be surprised if it weren't a record tip night for nearly every single one of them. I poke my head into the changing room briefly, searching the sea of people, wigs, and clothes for Latifah. I can't find her in the crush, so I turn my back to the wall, content to wait. It's our usual routine; Latifah will know I'm here if she needs help.

I'm now facing the "green room" for the bands that play here, and usually its only occupants at this time in a show are, well, me, or queens who need more space than the dressing room provides. Tonight, however, the room is pretty full of people. I check my phone—nearly midnight—and no way there's another band playing tonight, right? I push off the wall and poke my head into the room.

It takes catching sight of a white tracksuit for it to click. These are the backup dancers that took the stage. Everyone is stuffing their costumes into bags and picking up shoes and coats. Several of them have matching black duffels emblazoned with "LA Dance" and an address down on Third Street. My eyebrows raise. No wonder these folks had been good . . . they're part of a dance school of some kind.

I gawk, even as the group starts filing past me. I'm still trying to figure out just how everything came together. Where have these people come from? As the room empties, my eyes alight on someone I recognize. It's the guy who flipped right into Latifah's arms. His lithe and muscled form is dressed in a simple white tank top and black soccer pants, black dance shoes still on. I hadn't realized onstage that he's barely taller than I am. Several dancers clap him on the shoulder as they leave, but he's intent on his phone, texting with a ferocity I usually reserve for fights with Ryan about who would win in a showdown: Black Widow or Poison Ivy.

"Daniel, isn't it?"

I don't realize I've spoken out loud until his head snaps up at the sound of his name. His eyes meet mine, and I have some sort of flashback to being thirteen and prank-calling someone. Only this time I can't hang up the phone.

"I—er—" Stammering was *exactly* how one should follow this up. Here I am, standing in the doorway, ostensibly *ogling* him changing. And creepily knowing his name.

"Can I help you?" Daniel makes it seem perfectly normal that a crazy lady is talking to him from a dressing-room doorway.

"I'm friends with Lawrence—Latifah—and I just wanted to say that tonight was . . . wow. I mean, it was so good. You were excellent."

I want to melt right through the floor. He probably thinks I'm hitting on him, especially given how red my face probably is right now. How would he know I'm just socially inept?

"Thanks." He offers me a smile.

I smile back.

"Well, nice to meet you," he says with a small chuckle and turns back to his phone. Only this time, with his back a little more firmly toward me. With a few last clicks, he stows the phone in his pocket. He scoops up his own duffel and tosses in the gold cape, which jogs just *why* I am standing here.

I nearly hit my forehead with my own hand. What a *creeper* I was being. "MG," I say before he pushes past me. I make myself stick out my hand. "I'm sorry I didn't introduce myself before."

Recognition sparks in his eyes at the mention of my name. "Ah, MG. Yes, Latifah did mention you during rehearsals. You make the costumes, right?" He slings the bag over one bare shoulder, brushes a lock of his dark hair out of his almond-shaped eyes, and reaches out to shake my hand.

Oh, thank Thor, at least L had mentioned me. I glance down at his hand, so tan against my own translucently pale one, surprised by the strength of his handshake. Most men give me a pretty wimpy version, but this one is perfect. There aren't any zings or tingles, but his hand feels . . . comfortable. Known. Like we've been friends forever.

"It's nice to meet you, MG."

"You too—hey, is that an Alliance tattoo?" I flip his hand upright and immediately bring it to my face to scrutinize. There in the web of his thumb is indeed a small black Rebel Alliance tattoo. I raise my gaze to meet his bemused one. "That's so cool. I've never had the guts to get a tattoo." I stop myself from adding, *They use needles*, but can't stop the shudder that runs through my body at the thought of that kind of torture.

Daniel laughs outright, allowing my scrutiny of his hand. It's like he reads my mind. "It wasn't that bad."

"How did you pick what you were going to get?" I want to suss out if he is really a fan or if he just thought the symbol was "cool" after the movie came out. Vital difference in possible friend factor.

"After a rough time in my life, I just needed to be reminded daily that 'the simplest gesture of kindness . . .'"

"Can fill a galaxy with hope," I finish for him, my eyes widening. His do the same. Not a lot of people are steeped enough in Jedi lore to know the core philosophies behind the movement. True nerd status achieved.

It's around the time I hear a familiar voice behind me that I realize that Daniel and I are still holding hands.

"Sorry, I'm late, MG. I do hope I'm not interrupting something?" Matteo.

I drop Daniel's hand like a hot potato and spin to face my boyfriend. Afraid I'm going to find him glaring at Daniel, I'm relieved instead to see him appraising us with genuine curiosity. No sign of jealousy; I relax my shoulders. My own reaction probably puts me in the "guilty" category more than what he actually walked in on.

"Matteo!" I force a normal smile on my face. "Glad you finally got off work. I'm just meeting Daniel." I motion, though it's obvious, given the two of us are the only ones in the room. "He did backup dancing for Latifah tonight, and it was *amazing*. I'm sad you missed it."

A shadow passes over Matteo's face, but he covers it well as he reaches for Daniel's hand. "Sorry to miss it, man. Any friend of L's is a friend of mine. I'm not fully off work yet, I still have to go back to the station tonight—"

"Oh, good—everyone's met," another voice purrs from the doorway beyond Matteo's shoulder. Lelani gives Matteo a small smile before stepping around him and approaching Daniel and me. In fact, upon further inspection, Daniel has garnered quite the hallway audience. Ryan and Latifah both stand behind Matteo, lurking for who knew how long.

"Wonderful performance, though I'm not surprised," Lelani says, leaning in and giving Daniel a kiss on the cheeks, pretentious European-style. "I knew you two would get on."

I furrow my brows, thinking she means Daniel and me until I realize she means Latifah. So, *this* is how Lelani has been helping L all week. She knows Daniel and introduced them.

"It was a blast, we've talked about teaming up again," Daniel answers. "It's great work for my adult classes."

"Well, we'll look forward to seeing you in *and* out of the office then," Lelani agrees with a smile.

Cue the vinyl-record screech—what now? In and out of the *office*?

Noting my confused look, Lelani smiles her Cheshire cat smile.

"We'd just barely introduced ourselves," Daniel explains. "No time to talk business as of yet."

My eyes dart between them. I feel like I've been set up for a bad joke, but who has the punch line? "I, uh . . . that's cool." *Sounding pretty intelligent here, MG.*

"Of course, we'll have plenty of time to talk this over at the office. Tonight isn't about work; it's about celebrating a job well done." Lelani covers my response smoothly, all her executive superpowers firing with precision. It's stuff like that that reminds me she's the VP for a *reason*. As much as I can never quite get a read on her, I do have a lot to learn from her. She's the Obi-Wan to my Luke, the Luke to my . . . well, if she *is* Luke, let's hope that *I'm* Rey and not Kylo. That mentorship didn't end up in an edifying manner. I squint at her, totally able to picture her standing over me with a lightsaber, ready to strike.

Lelani quirks an eyebrow at me, and it's not the first time I've wondered if she can read minds. But I'm saved from having to explain whatever expression I'm wearing by my favorite fashion superhero.

"Heck yes, job well done," L agrees, pushing into the room and offering Daniel a handshake and a shoulder clap. "That was *perfection*."

They start to rehash the opening dance number, so I allow Matteo to pull me into the little hallway, his face drawn into what I think of as his "stewing" face.

"What's wrong? You're not upset about"—I push aside my guilty conscience and resist mentioning Daniel—"missing tonight, are you? There'll be other shows. I promise."

"No, that's not it." He puts his hand on my back and pulls me close in the hallway. To anyone else, it looks like a lover's tête-à-tête, but I feel the steel beneath his easy move. This isn't Matteo. This is Detective Kildaire. "Can we go somewhere and talk?"

I pull back slightly, trying to gauge his expression, stomach dropping to my toes. Talk, as in, *We need to talk*, or just talk-talk?

My not quite fully formed freak-out must have shown all over my face because Matteo's arms soften a little, and he pulls me in for a *real* hug and a kiss on the cheek. "It's about the case. Nothing else."

My eyes flick to his. The case? The Golden Arrow. It's the only "case" I could have any part of, the investigation I helped him solve this summer at San Diego Comic-Con.

Ryan must sense something is amiss, because he eyes us warily. I give a small wave, trying to indicate that everything is fine, and lead Matteo out to the now mostly deserted café area. We pick a table that's already been bussed and sit down.

"Detective Kildaire" still looks back from across the table, assessing me. This isn't a date—it's an interview.

"So, the case?" I prompt, raising an eyebrow. "Has there been a breakthrough?" I'm picturing a fantastic chase scene, filled with a vigilante hopping rooftop to rooftop and eluding police helicopters.

"Nothing major, but . . . the first real movement we've had in weeks," he confirms, leaning his elbows against the table. His hands land near mine, but as this is apparently a "business meeting," I don't take them. "I've got to get back to the office, but I wanted to come check with you while you were still up. Earlier tonight, patrol picked up two dealers."

I wait for the punch line about as patiently as Bruce Banner. *Hulk smash, Detective Kildaire.* It's been quiet—too quiet, as they say in crime novels—since we arrested the double agent responsible for a thirty-year-old local murder of my boss's father, and more notably, the original artist of *The Hooded Falcon.* We snagged an ex–police chief and his DEA-agent daughter red-handed in the local drug trade and exposed their long-term cover-up of the murder. I've been *itching* for news of our local vigilante hero—the anonymous citizen who used *The Hooded Falcon* comics to help lead me and thus the police to the killer. "And?" This seems tame fare, but I'm hopeful for something juicier on the page flip.

"Well, I should say patrol got a tip about two drug dealers."

I take the bait, despite my growing impatience. "Okay . . . a tip from whom?"

"From the Golden Arrow," he answers quietly, eyes on my face.

I gasp. "Really?"

Matteo holds up a hand. "*Or* an imposter. We've had a rash of them following the media circus at San Diego Comic-Con."

"An . . . imposter," I parrot back. I know the Golden Arrow has emerged as a cultural icon, and even that some people are dressing like him for cons . . . but it's the first time it dawns on me that Matteo might be dealing with *real* copycats. Hasn't anyone ever watched *Kick-Ass*? Vigilante justice rarely works out for normies.

"If it is, it's a very, *very* good one." The seriousness in his eyes speaks volumes. "My gut says not an imposter at all. Patrol brought them in for us to interview because of the . . . uniqueness of their circumstances when they found them."

Goose bumps chase themselves along my arms, and I dart my eyes around before leaning forward, just like in a cheesy movie scene. They found something at a crime scene. Something Golden Arrow–related. "He's back?"

And immediately I want to know *why*. Part of me believed he'd just never be heard from again, that he did his civic duty. The bad guys were caught. The trial was scheduled. I've made as much peace as I can with never *knowing* who the Golden Arrow is. But if the Golden Arrow is back . . .

"We're in the middle of investigating, so hopefully I'll know more soon. All I know right now is that routine patrol of a common dealing corner found two dealers tied to a lamppost with rope. And this." He reaches into his pocket and produces his phone. Flipping to the camera roll, he scrolls back a few images and slides it across the table to me. "This is what was holding the rope knot secure."

It's a picture clearly taken in evidence, given the presence of a plastic bag, tagged and numbered. Inside the bag is a literal golden arrow. Well, more accurately, *several* small arrows with golden shafts and tiny golden fletching, connected by a ring to make some sort of throwing star.

I squint at the phone. "Okay. That is . . . elaborate. But not canon. The Golden Arrow never used real arrows before, right?"

"True." Matteo sits back in his chair. "But in his statement one of the guys calls the assailant a ninja."

I snort.

Matteo waves off my laughter. "Competent. Not just an average 'Nerd in Spandex,' if you will. Everyone else we've seen has been utterly *incompetent*. This is new. It reminds me of the busts from the summer."

Nerds in Spandex. I *love* that visual and make a mental note to start referencing NISs in my next comic. But back to the matter at hand. "And was the person wearing a cape? Insignia? Something that makes you think it's really the GA? Something more than just a ring with arrows in it; anyone could have bought this." Truth be told, I'm a little afraid to get my hopes *all* the way up lest I have to go back to the sad world where the GA rode off into the sunset, never to be seen again.

Matteo sighs at my cynicism. "I know there should be more solid tells, but I don't know . . . There's just *something* about this one that rings true. I wanted to show this to you in case you had any insight, and to ask you to be present when we interview these two."

A tingle starts in my stomach, spreading upward. Matteo's got a good gut, so if he's sure enough to interview the dealers, it's enough for my brain to start moving to the pieces about the Golden Arrow that remain unknowns. The writer in me desperately wants a resolution to the mystery as to what it contains—it's a completely and utterly selfish desire. "You want me to come into the station?"

Matteo notes the change in my expression. He's learning to recognize when my writer's love for story takes over my brain. "Yes, but it's too late tonight. We've scheduled it for Monday afternoon." He pauses to check his phone and then tucks it back into his pocket. "I have to get back to the office, I'm sorry. You'll have to sign back on as a consultant to the LAPD. I have clearance from the captain and will go print the paperwork tonight to bring to you."

For a moment my mind races to all the things I'm already committed to. But would I miss the chance to be a part of the case if the real Golden Arrow has at last emerged again? No way, no how. "I'm in."

CHAPTER 3

The crush of bodies inside the Zebra's small lounge feels, if possible, worse than the crowd at the drag show. It's not exactly the venue I would have chosen for an after-party, but then again, I hate parties, so I am far from an expert. I bob and weave, searching for either a familiar face or an open seat. *Not likely*, factoring in the sheer number of people here. We've got to be coming up against fire code.

At the far end of the packed foyer, I show my ID to a She-Hulk tank of a front-desk bouncer and fork over the outrageous cover of twenty dollars to get farther into the cramped nightclub. There's a wall of people just inside, and as I try to skirt the mob, I end up knocking into a table. It's covered all in black—a great choice for a black room where the *lights are out*. A basket filled with little glass flasks bounces around on the tabletop, and I just manage to keep it from sliding off onto the floor, the ultimate party foul narrowly averted. That's me, always filled with grace and etiquette. I right the card in the back of the basket, a handwritten little thing that says something like DRINK ME in black-light-responsive ink, and shiver. Go ahead and drink some college kid's version of bug juice that probably contains a date-rape drug? *Nothankyou.* Whether Cleopatra means it as a welcome gift or an attempt at entertaining, unattended drinks are creepy.

The room is dark, but the strobes and the laser lights that flash through the space light it up to almost midday levels every other second. I'm going to have a headache in no time flat, but it'll be worth it if the Golden Arrow does indeed make an appearance. The very air feels charged with electric waiting; everyone else is here for the same thing. I eye the crowd, wondering if any of Matteo's team is here to keep an eye out, given the rash of imposter Arrows they've had. No one seems to lend Cleopatra's claims much credence, *and yet*. The "and yet" is a big one. I contemplate texting Matteo to let him know I'm here and to ask him if I should poke around now that I'm officially a consultant again, but figure his answer will be no, and I really don't want to leave. Ask forgiveness rather than permission, right? And if I *do* see the Golden Arrow, I promise myself to call the police directly. Up until that point, I'm here in a purely social manner—nothing that requires official-police anything.

I skirt the dance floor—the area in the center where people have about point five extra inches in which to attempt to dance. Several people already look three sheets to the wind. They wouldn't know if the Golden Arrow walked up to them and asked them for a waltz. It's such a mixed crowd it reminds me of a con. I see several queens still in their superhero getup from the show, glittering like miniature disco balls among all the lasers and strobes. And in the crowd, some Muggles are sporting costumes too. Zorro masks, and a few capes. A few tees with arrows printed on them. There's even a tall man wearing a top hat, wading through the crowd toward the back near the bar.

I'm knocked sideways as a young man stumbles into me, obviously inebriated, off-balance, and reeking of some sort of sickly sweet alcohol. I right both of us through some small miracle.

"Sorry about that," he slurs.

"It's fine," I say, avoiding the urge to wipe my hand off while he's still watching. I swear his clothing is sticky from . . . whatever . . . too.

"You're pretty. Care to buy any? Limited supply; only have these left." He speaks as if I've won some sort of prize, leans in, and shows me a baggie he has clutched in his hand. I see the flash of some sort of pill before he palms the bag and sticks it back in his sweatshirt pocket. They aren't the typical "white" pill that sometimes comes around a party. Gelcaps.

Call me the girlfriend of a narcotics detective, but I'd bet the Lasso of Truth that I've just seen something illegal laced with other illicit things mixed together in a homemade capsule. The refreshments on offer at this party suck, and I again briefly contemplate alerting Matteo.

"No, thanks," I say.

The guy shrugs, a clear "your loss" in his attitude, and moves off into the crowd. I have no doubt he'll get rid of his wares. Indeed, some people are here just to party. Such is part of the drag scene. Rock stars and drag queens. I equate the love of partying with both groups of people. Some rock stars are clean and just love a good time. Some can't have a good time without chemical assistance. The difference tonight is the ring of Muggles that surround the typical attendees of a drag show after-party. These poor folks clutch their small drinks tightly and peer into the darkness, hoping to see a real-life superhero.

I join them.

I've never been much of a partyer, and thankfully neither Lawrence nor Ryan like the pastime either. Not to say we don't crash parties sometimes and hang out together, but it's more about being together than it is the party. L is particularly prickly about drug use, given his background.

So instead of making my way to the dance floor to look for any of L's friends I know, I stay in the outer ring, eyes darting around. Would the Golden Arrow really show up? I'm probably one of the only people in this room who has ever seen footage of the vigilante, not to mention seeing the Golden Arrow *in person* as he hopped out a second-story window and vanished. I feel this should give me an advantage, but I end up watching every masked figure from the drag show as hard as the person next to me.

Unless the GA stands up onstage and proclaims himself, which seems unlikely, I'm probably out of luck picking him out of the crowd.

Cleopatra's media stunt definitely worked, though; this place is packed. With resignation in my heart, I make my way to the tiny black bar in the back of the room. I order myself a whiskey and Coke, which comes in the tiniest plastic cup I've ever seen, and roll my eyes when my card is charged twelve dollars. Highway robbery all night long, and either the drinks are getting smaller or I'm getting larger. I suppose it's the price of admission to this theme park, and a small dollar amount if our vigilante shows. Not only is my drink a tiny thing, but my cup must have been the first one in the stack. It still has the packaging sticker on the bottom, and I'm forced to peel it off—some gold foil thing—but at least I can rest assured this is one drink that wasn't tampered with if the bartender just opened the sleeve of cups.

Deciding to patrol the perimeter of the room, I turn around, clutching my tiny drink, and run smack into the person behind me. "Sorry," I mutter before realizing I recognize the shoes I'm staring at. White, old-school Nikes so bright they could only belong to my roommate. I raise my eyes to meet Ryan's half smile. Busted. Caught red-fisted, attending L's nemesis's party.

The guilt must be written all over my face.

"We were never here," he agrees. "I told L that I was going over to Lelani's."

"I told him I was going home." We both laugh nervously. "Let's hope L doesn't show up and bust us."

"Nah, he wouldn't. Principle of the thing." Ryan orders a beer—an eight-dollar Coors Light—and we slide to the side of the bar, deeper into the shadows behind the strobe lights. My already-pounding head thanks me.

"I almost didn't come; I shouldn't have come, I just . . . can't help thinking, 'What if,'" I admit as we stare into the sea of people.

"What if the Golden Arrow shows, you mean?" Ryan's voice is muffled, and I see him take a huge swig of his beer.

"Yeah. I mean, Cleopatra is probably making up the story. But . . . what if . . . ? You're curious too, or you wouldn't be here."

He grunts and takes *another* swig of beer. I eye him closer. Ryan's not usually a "down a bottle of beer in three gulps" kind of guy. His gaze turns from the dance floor and finds my critical one.

He sighs. "More than a little curious." He's been through quite a bit with the Golden Arrow too. The chase through San Diego Comic-Con. The questioning, the hearings. He probably wants a glimpse at the person who turned his world upside down. "I'm sure she's making it up, but like you said: What if . . . ? My guess is that someone is pretending to be the Golden Arrow, using Cleopatra to gain some star power and media attention."

"Or it's the real Golden Arrow," I argue, sipping at my own drink.

He grunts again, though foregoing the beer this time.

"Is this caveman hour?" I ask, poking his shoulder.

"I just . . . people are good actors, MG." The look he gives me is surprisingly frank, and serious, especially while we're just shooting the breeze. "You don't know what some people will do for fame. Or money. Or to get even." Another swig, and I see that the beer is almost gone.

It makes me think of the crime scene Matteo just told me about, and I shake my head back and forth. "True. But . . . maybe someone *is* out there, imposter or . . . not."

Ryan shrugs, looking back at the dance floor. "It's a possibility, I suppose. Either way, whoever is here tonight, I get the sense it's the former. Cleopatra probably wouldn't have gone on television with something completely made up. She probably even believes it. The question is, why someone would go to the trouble of convincing her they're the real one?"

I can't help myself. "Or it's the real one."

"Why would the real Golden Arrow come here?" He waves his hand around. "Be involved with Cleopatra?"

31

"I . . . I don't know," I say honestly. My eye catches on a few of the dancers at the center of the dance floor. A young queen, wig totally askew, stumbles around. If possible, these people are getting more drunk. My bet is on friends supplying them with drinks; I haven't seen any of them wading through to the bar in the last ten minutes. Or they're on something else, and the alcohol is exaggerating the effects. I note the man in the top hat still mixing with the dance crowd, and I briefly wonder how he's keeping it on with all these people around. This party does seem a little out of taste from what I know about the GA. "The Golden Arrow stole a journal from Lawrence; maybe he likes queens," I point out.

"Lawrence and Cleopatra are not the same," Ryan says as if he's the authority on the matter. "Lawrence is directly related to the case, remember? The Golden Arrow is interested in something more than these parties, I'm sure of it."

He's so certain about it, something strums a chord deep inside of me. A ripple of suspicion threatens to break the surface of my mind. Ryan has a solid alibi; he's been questioned by the police, but . . . could he know something about the Golden Arrow I don't? Harbor a suspicion he's not sharing? Could he be an *accomplice*? Lightning strikes my imagination, and for a moment I ponder the possibility that the Golden Arrow could have been gathering information from multiple inside sources, including my very own roommate. Which is so ludicrous I decide to shove that thought away entirely. Well, almost entirely. I have a feeling I'll have a hard time forgetting the pebble that caused the ripple in the first place.

Ryan doesn't seem to notice my imagination spinning out of control. "Let's just take a look around and then, want to share an Uber home? It's late."

I stifle a yawn at the mention of the word "late," and I feel my brain coming back online and into the present. My default setting seems to waffle between tired and tired-er these days, so I nod. "Sounds good.

This is probably a waste of time anyhow. Though they're making a killing on concessions while everyone waits," I add in grudging admiration of the sheer extortionary power.

Ryan pulls out his phone, presumably to order us a car. A flash of light and the squeal of a microphone interrupt him. Our heads snap to attention as the room brightens from the glow on the dance floor. Every spotlight centers on the middle of the space, where Cleopatra basks like a fallen angel in red sequins. Her red wig must be four feet tall, shaped in an elaborate updo, reminiscent of Marie Antoinette.

My heartbeat accelerates, and I exchange glances with Ryan.

"Hello all," Cleopatra says, waving into the crowd. "Thank you for joining me for my first party." There is some mixed cheering and whistling, then a hush falls over the crowd, and Cleopatra smiles broadly.

"I know you're not just all here for lil' ole me, but I do throw a good party, am I right?" More cheering, though it drops off quicker this time. Everyone, like me, is wondering if the impossible is about to happen.

Cleopatra's lips fall into a dramatic pout. "Unfortunately, though our friend was here for a brief time, he decided that a more intimate gathering would be his preference . . ." A mutter so loud arises from the crowd, Cleopatra's voice is drowned out momentarily. After a few moments I hear the microphone levels boosted up again and Cleopatra saying, "I know, I know, I know, my darlings. I can assure you, though, he was here. You probably brushed sleeves with him and didn't even know."

Beside me, Ryan snorts. I share his derision. Media stunt, through and through. I make a move to the door, and Ryan follows.

"To prove to you that he was indeed here, I have a special offer from our masked friend."

"Buy seventeen drinks, and the eighteenth is free?" I ask Ryan. He laughs as we join the herd of people headed toward the small door at the front of the house.

"Our illustrious friend has extended several secret invitations to people in attendance right now," Cleopatra goes on. She knows she's losing her crowd. "And I assure you if you find one of the invitations and attend the special party just for those with invites, you will meet our masked friend. The delightful thing is, it's all up to chance who gets to meet him, and the invitations are already distributed. You may have one and not even know it." She cackles and claps, her fingernail polish and bangled bracelets catching in the light of all the spots.

That stops me in my tracks, and I turn toward the stage, along with fifty or sixty of my closest lemming pals. We start looking around—at the floor, at the walls, at each other—trying to discern if this is indeed true information.

"Because we appreciate so much your support of our hosts tonight, we've decided to reward those of you who have enjoyed our refreshments. Several of the flasks, several of the glasses and cups, and several of the plates have secret seals on the bottom of them. Simply check your drinks and food, detach the seal, and keep it. There are a limited number out there, and I know for certain they've all been given out. Our bartender has been told specifically to flag any that were returned and redistribute, so they're all out in the wild right now. Have fun, darlings. Watch my website for more information!"

Her last words are drowned out by the sheer volume of one hundred people diving for the plates closest to them. I catch Ryan's alarmed gaze as we're forced apart when someone dives between us to get at the stack of plates left for a waitress on the tall table directly behind us.

"Holy hell," I yell over the din. Ryan and I manage to get near enough to the front of the panicked crowd that we're not at as much at risk of being carried off.

From over my shoulder, I hear a crow of victory. "I found one!" Some woman is our first victor. *Veruca Salt, ladies and gentlemen.* The scream is met by, if possible, an increase in the volume as people ransack the basket of flasks by the front door.

"So, it's real, then," I say to Ryan.

His face is unreadable. "I guess some part of it. I'd like to know what game she's playing." He perfunctorily lifts his beer bottle and glances at the bottom, then shrugs. "Guess I'll never know. You?"

My heart races inside my chest, having nothing to do with the fervor of the crowd behind us—several fistfights have already broken out from the sounds of it. I resist the urge to stick my hand in my pocket to feel for the gold sticker I'd removed from my cup earlier. I can't tell if I'm glad or physically ill I didn't throw it away. How do I keep ending up in these situations? Something stops me from showing Ryan. Maybe it's the fact that I'm secretly already planning to go to this party and see if the GA really materializes, and I know Ryan won't approve. Maybe it's that telling Ryan would essentially be admitting to Lawrence that I went to his rival's party. And *maybe* it's because now just a sliver of me isn't sure Ryan is telling the whole truth and nothing but the truth, so help him Thor. I make a show of lifting my small plastic cup and finding it empty.

"No one would reward such a girly, small drink," I joke.

Ryan laughs, though my joke wasn't that funny. We push toward the door and break through into the slight chill of the California evening. A hint of fall is on the air, and I cross my arms over myself, goose bumps breaking out after the mad, hot crush of the nightclub.

Ryan glances at me. "Don't worry. I'll ask around; maybe Lawrence can find out what's really going on." His phone dings in his pocket, probably an alert that the car will soon arrive.

"But you don't think it's the Golden Arrow?"

Ryan hesitates a moment and then shakes his head.

A small sedan pulls up, and Ryan opens my door for me before crossing around the back of the car. I slide in, and I can't help singing, "I've got a golden ticket," to myself quietly. The question is . . . where exactly does this ticket take me, if not farther down the rabbit hole?

CHAPTER 4

"All right, L. Your call." I look Lawrence in the eye over my red Solo cup and squint, channeling every ounce of my Cumberbatch Sherlock mind meld. "Death, or boobies?"

L's face doesn't change, even with the swell of the orchestra below us. Truthfully, we should be focused on the gorgeous music, the beautiful amphitheater, and the magic of experiencing live orchestration to *Game of Thrones*, but in true "us" style, we've decided to nerd out—in the form of a drinking game.

L's eyes flick to the large screen, then back to me. "Both." Totally deadpan.

Ryan sighs and squishes his cup, making a crinkling noise. "Both isn't an answer. It's either death *or* boobies."

It's the only drinking game I'll play these days. Tonight we're playing the version where the person in charge guesses whether we'll see death or boobs first in the scene. If the person is right, the others drink; if they're wrong, they drink twice. "Look, you have like three seconds before—"

We all turn at the sound of gore and screaming, and my eyebrows shoot up. "Well, I'll be damned." I turn to L, who has yet to crack a smile but is wearing a smug air. "They killed the freaking prostitute! L, you are a stinking *genius*. It's totally both."

Ryan sets his nineteen-bazillion-dollar beer, *Thank you, public-LA-venue prices*, down on the ledge of the stadium-style seat in front of us, and throws up his hands. "It is *not* both! Boobs clearly came before death!"

I hold up a hand, pointing at the scene, which is just about over. "No, it showed her from *behind*, right before . . ." I mime getting stuck through the chest with an arrow.

"We need parameters. A time frame. It didn't happen *right* at the exact same time."

"Drink up, loser." The beer has loosened my mind and my tongue, and I gulp down another sip of Coors Light. This stuff is awful, but I'm not about to spend the money for craft stuff here. "L, are you *sure* you haven't seen *Game of Thrones* more than once? You're awfully good at this."

I narrow my eyes again, suspicious. "Ah-ha!" I declare, swiping his phone from beneath his thigh on the seat. "I bet you've been looking it up on *wiki*!"

L rolls his eyes. "I'm not cheating. I just have a good sense for the dramatic." His eyes flick over my shoulder. "Like how right now would be an appropriate moment to make a dramatic entrance."

I frown. "What—"

"Hot-Lanta! How's it?" L cuts me off, waving.

I spin around to find my "sexy as hell, even in a rumpled work shirt" boyfriend climbing over the laps of people to get to the empty seat next to me.

"I thought you weren't going to make it!" I say, delighted he's here. My spirits lift with the promise of an evening in his company. "They only just started!" I salute the screen with my cup, sloshing beer over the side.

Matteo gives L a fist bump. "Any more late-night TV gigs?"

"Nah, just Jimmy Fallon's show last week, and *Kimmel* the week before. I'm collecting Jimmys. What I really want is a call from James Corden for the trifecta . . . Guess I might need an agent to accomplish that, though." He laughs off his own remark.

It's been an interesting few months after our SDCC escapade, what with L getting recognition from the lieutenant governor for heroic service to LA. He has a gold key to the city and everything—I've seen it, mounted up on the wall in his little cramped office at the salon.

"L is a proper *celebrity*," I drawl. And he is. While I've gotten a few interviews and Matteo's division received an award from the station, Lawrence and his stage persona, Latifah, are the media darlings—Drag Queen Catches Killer and all that. I get why they're all the rage. L makes a sparkling, witty, and entertaining guest, perfectly at home on the late-night circuit couches.

Matteo eyes me. "Are you drunk?"

"Nooooo," I draw out the word, rolling my eyes. "Not drunk. Happy to see you, and happy to share Death and Boobies with you as a rite of passage."

Matteo blinks his hazel eyes at me as he sinks into the folding seat. "Uh . . . in public?" He runs a hand through his dark hair. Seven Gods, his hair looks *so* good. I want to put my fingers in it and give it a tug.

I lean in, smacking my lips in what I hope is an entirely coquettish way. "Right here. Right now." And before he can say anything else, I shove a red cup of beer right under his nose. "Now." I sit back, prop my feet up on the seat in front of me, and motion to the screen. "The point of this game is simple. You guess which you see first in a scene. Death. Or boobies. If you're right, we have to drink, but if you're wrong—"

Matteo sets the cup down, longing flicking across his face as his eyes graze my lips. "I can't play a drinking game tonight; I'm on call."

I forego my first impulse to yell, *Boo, you whore*, in an homage to *Mean Girls*. It's how I know I'm wandering into tipsy territory; I'm starting to think and speak in movie quips. "Oh, right, I forgot." Stupid adult job—it's a buzzkill.

"But, uh, you guys can still play."

"Hells yes, we can; I've called the last three in a *row!*" L hoots.

I try gamely to recapture the buoyant feeling. "No, that's okay. If you're not drinking, I won't either."

Despite Ryan and L booing and hissing, I set down my cup of beer and turn to face the screen.

"So, who is this?" Matteo asks, taking my hand. He laces his fingers with mine, his tan hand sure and warm against my own. I squeeze. It's not his fault his job overwhelms sometimes; given the events of this summer and the pending trial, he's been so busy. Unthinking, my hand starts to stroke his forearm, admiring how it looks with his sleeves rolled up. Matteo's grip tightens in mine, and I look up to catch him watching me with a smoldering look.

Oops. I guess this is hardly the place. I clear my throat and turn to the large screen.

"This is Prince Joffrey, and we do *not* like him," I say decidedly. "He's the son of the queen, but not the son of the king. It's a bit complicated, but you'll get it. Well, okay, you missed the first part. You see, his dad—who he thinks is his uncle—was in his bedroom and tried to kill this *other* kid . . ."

It takes a beat for Matteo's distracted, "Mmm-hmm."

I cast an eye over at him, noting the cell phone in his lap. "Are you even paying attention?"

Matteo lets out a breath and glances up at me, guilt lurking in those gorgeous eyes. "I'm sorry, it's work; you know I have to respond to all texts and messages when I'm on call. So, son of the king. Kills a kid. Got it."

I give his hand another squeeze. "Well, now this isn't Joffrey *or* Jaime; this is a whole 'nother part of the world. This is Khal Drogo, and we *do* like him."

"Yes. We. Do!" agrees L from beside me.

Ryan salutes the screen with his cup.

"We . . . like . . . this guy? Isn't he . . . trying to buy that girl?" Matteo asks several moments later.

"Well . . . yeah, okay—"

"This one is *easy!*" Ryan says. "Boooooobies! I remember this scene!" He and L clink cups and take drinks in celebration when Daenerys bares her top.

"—yeah, he's trying to buy her, but it's not her fault her brother is a jerk. He gets what's coming to him, and in the end, Khal is a good guy. Well, as much as you can be a good guy in this world."

No response from Matteo.

"Everything okay?" I ask.

He glances up. "Yeah. Well, no. I thought I could do this over email, but I'm going to have to go into the station. Patrol is trying to chase down a lead on these new dealers. I'm sorry."

He stands, brushing off his pants, and leans in to kiss me. It lasts longer than it probably should and elicits a catcall from a seat somewhere above us.

"But you just got here. Are you sure you can't stay for even just a little bit?" I murmur as he pulls away. "There are giant wolves in the next few scenes."

"You siren." Matteo's eyes flash with humor, and he squeezes my knee, his hand lingering. "Alas, even with giant wolves, I have to go." Ryan and L salute Matteo's departure much more enthusiastically than I do, and turn almost immediately back to the screen.

"I'll text you when I'm done. Do you want to come over tonight or your house or . . . ?" He glances at Ryan and L. Matteo is always respectful if I want to spend time with Ryan and L, and I appreciate it.

And I do want to spend time with Ryan and L, but not enough to throw over this sexy detective standing in front of me. "My house," I agree. We haven't spent many nights apart in the three months since San Diego Comic-Con if we can help it.

He smiles his secret smile, and I return it, willing him to throw over his entire career and stay with me. Sadly, his responsible side wins out, and he exits our row for real this time.

The Queen Con

I stew in my thoughts until a cup of beer appears under my nose, proffered by Lawrence. "The current vote is boobies."

I take the cup automatically and flick my glance to the screen. "It's a direwolves scene."

"Exactly!" Ryan chortles from beside L, a little too enthusiastically. They're both tipsy at this point. When nothing happens in the scene—death *or* boobies—L and Ryan clink their cups together and take matching chugs.

Swiping a hand across his mouth, Ryan leans across L, his backward hat giving him all the impression of a frat brother instead of a successful gaming entrepreneur. "Where did Matteo go?"

"He had to go to work. Something about Golden Arrow imposters and these new dealers on the street, I guess." I bite my lip, knowing Matteo is touchy about sharing police stuff. "I don't know; something is up, and Matteo thinks it may be connected with the case."

Ryan frowns. "What things?"

We're shushed from the people behind our seats, and I turn to glare at them, despite being fully aware that we've totally given up watching the event we were here to watch. I guess our general merriment was acceptable as long as it was *GoT*-related. Our off-topic foray is clearly not as tolerable.

Ryan's visage sours before he raises his glass. "*You* need a drink and a pick-me-up murder scene."

Sounds like a legit remedy. "Okay. Who's up?" I ask, refocusing on the screen.

But . . . even as I sit and watch, I can't bring myself to be fully present. I find myself rehashing the case, like I'm preparing for my testimony. The Golden Arrow's clues *do* plague me. They feel *so* personal, intimately tailored. Like someone I know is passing me the answers to a test that only I know how to take. Maybe I've time-traveled to the future and back again. Or maybe . . . maybe the story isn't done. I can't

41

help hoping that Matteo's hunch is right and that we're standing on the edge of knowing who the Golden Arrow is, and everything they know.

Ryan and L either don't notice my mood or refuse to acknowledge it, because they joke and push each other the entire way out of the building.

"Here, let me *hold the door* for you, m'lady," L announces with fervor as he swings open the glass exterior door ahead of me and bows deeply. He wobbles on his feet, rights himself, and then tries to bow again as I walk through.

Ryan snickers. "Hold the door."

Then they *both* snicker, and L throws himself against the door and starts chanting, "Hodor! Hodor! An homage to the greatest door holder of all time!"

It's all I can do to keep walking out of the building. Usually I'm up for geek jokes. I'm in a serious funk. "Okay, guys, we've all had several too many. I'm going to call an Uber, okay? Ryan, give me your phone; I'll call you one too. You're headed to Lelani's, right?"

I roll my eyes as I have to yank Ryan's phone out of his hand—he and L are fake sword-fighting too intently to answer. I open his app and order one for him—thankfully, Lelani's address is saved—before ordering one for myself to go home.

More giggling from behind me. Now they're smashing their faces on opposite sides of the doors to see who can make the most grotesque mosquito corpse. At the sound of ripping paper, I turn back to see that Ryan's "mosquito" has slid down the glass far enough to dislodge at least three flyers from the door.

"Seriously, you two? You're like toddlers right now. Trogdor is better behaved in public . . ." I trail off, leaning over to pick up the closest flyer on the ground just as a gust of late–September wind catches it. Two words on it stand out to me immediately: GOLDEN ARROW.

I hurry to the nearest knee-high path light and bend over to examine it further. It's a simple green photocopied flyer, but by no means amateur. Stylish block lettering proclaims REWARD FOR INFORMATION across the top. Underneath is a well-drawn comic panel of a caped superhero, tying two guys back to back and lacing the rope with an identifiable arrow. Across the bottom of the flyer, words fill the rest of the space: $50,000 CASH REWARD FOR THE GOLDEN ARROW'S EXCLUSIVE STORY. It has a phone number and email across the bottom, but that's not what stops my heart. It's the name above that email.

"Guys. Guys, get *over here* and look at this," I yell, not tearing my eyes from the page. "I know why there are so many imposters."

L is the first to trip up to me, grinning and still laughing like an idiot. "Because imposters are fashionable?" He holds his arm over his face like Dracula and waggles his eyebrows.

"That's *vampires*, dude," Ryan chimes in before snatching the sheet from my hand. "What're you on about, MG?" His eyes scan the page and his eyebrows shoot up.

L whistles, reading over his shoulder. "Fifty Gs is a lot of money."

"Like I said, now we know why there are so many people anxious to prove themselves as the Golden Arrow. And this"—I point to the bottom of the page—"only means trouble."

Ryan and L take a few moments to soak in the seriousness of the situation. Finally, Ryan's eyebrows furrow in thought. In the distance, a siren wails to life, a sense of foreboding filling my mind.

The phone in my hand blares, announcing the car's arrival, and I silence it before handing Ryan his phone back. I snatch the page back from Ryan and stalk toward the main drive of the Performing Arts Center. My own ride is pulling up just behind his, and I don't wait to see if Ryan gets in his car. I climb into mine, already texting Matteo that we need to talk later before staring again at the name—Edward Casey Junior—scrawled across the bottom of the page.

CHAPTER 5

Something rustling in the kitchen wakes me from a dead sleep. I groan, my hand groping in the dark for my cell phone. Blue light burns my eyeballs, but I make out the digits on the lock screen. A quarter past one in the morning.

Beside me, Matteo's light snoring stops; he crawled into bed only an hour ago, and I think he might still be fully dressed. I was too tired to do much other than pat his lovely behind over the covers and roll over to sleep off my four beers.

"You okay?" he asks. He's sleepy, but alert. I'm so jealous; it's one of the superpowers he's developed from being on the force and on call for years. The second he's awake, he's ready for anything.

I'm so sleepy I think for a moment I must have imagined the noise. After another long moment of silence that makes me doubt my own consciousness, I hear what I think is the freezer door open. Down by my feet, the little log that is Trogdor gives a tiny *woof.* He's heard something too, but the fact that he doesn't go full-on alert means that it's Ryan.

It's a little odd that he's home from Lelani's, but I decide that maybe he's hungover and looking for ice cream. And yet . . . something about the noise bothers me, so I swing my legs over the side of the bed. Trog takes my cue and jumps down with a jingle of collar tags. Patting the lumpy form of Matteo, I whisper, "I'm going to go to the bathroom and check on why Ryan is home, okay?" Hopefully he and Lelani haven't had a fight. Matteo pats my hand in return, and I pad out my bedroom door with Trogdor close on my heels.

The house is dark, quiet, and decidedly *chilly*. Fall is definitely on its way in, and I remind myself to turn the furnace on in the next few days. Trog runs ahead through the dark living room and toward the kitchen, so I follow suit to find Ryan sitting at the kitchen table, lit only by the light from the open freezer. He's slumped over the kitchen table, resting his head in his hands, looking for all the world like he fell asleep mid–ice cream raid.

"Ry?" I ask, hesitantly. Maybe he's drunk; this is completely bizarre behavior.

Ryan sits upright with a start, and by the wan light, I see that he's not hunched over asleep—he's hunched over because he's holding a bag of frozen vegetables against one side of his face.

I hurry the last few steps to the table and crouch down at the foot of the chair he's in. "Ry. Are you okay? What's up?"

"I'm fine," he mutters from behind the veggies. "I didn't mean to wake you up. I was trying to be quiet."

"Trog has bat ears, you know that," I say. I reach up to remove the bag of frozen whatever from his face. "Did you hurt yourself? Why are you here? I thought you were at Lelani's tonight."

"Really, I'm fine," he says, pressing the bag back to his face.

"Fine people don't put frozen stuff on their face. You're like Hagrid and a dragon steak in here; please don't tell me you've been fighting giants. Let me take a look." I can't see much by the light in the freezer, so I reach out and swing open the refrigerator door too, a slice of bright-white light stabbing across the dark kitchen. It's enough for me to see that his face is puffy and bruised on one side, and that he has a trickle of blood smeared from one nostril.

Involuntarily, I suck in a breath. "Ryan, *what happened?*" I eye him and his conduct in a new light—literally and figuratively. "And don't you dare tell me you fell on the front stairs. Did Lelani do this?"

He can't help the snort of laughter at my suggestion, though. "MG, that imagination of yours. It's either I'm fighting giants or Lelani beat me?" He puts his free hand over mine and pats. "It's way more mundane. Some dude tried to take my phone or money or something; we got into a fight. I didn't want to get blood all over Lelani's floor, so I came home. It's no big deal—"

"No big *deal*?" I hiss, cutting him off. "Ryan, that's *mugging*; did you report it to the police?"

"I didn't need to—I got my phone back."

"Look, Matteo is here; tell him, okay—"

"Stop, MG. I'm *fine*, I didn't want to disturb you and Matteo, it's why I'm in the dark anyway, just leave it—"

We both spin and flinch as the kitchen light flicks on above our heads. "What on *earth* is going on?" Matteo asks, rubbing his eyes and pinching the bridge of his nose like a father who has discovered his kids making a mess instead of watching cartoons. "Why are you two arguing in the refrigerator?" He pauses when he sees the vegetables and Ryan's face. His eyebrows raise questioningly.

Ryan kicks me with his sneaker, but I tattle anyhow. "Ryan got mugged—"

"*Attempted.* I told you I still have my phone and wallet." Ryan digs in his pocket and produces his phone, waving it in the air. "The guy landed one solid punch, that's it—"

"And didn't *report it*," I finish, running over Ryan's words again. But by this time, Matteo has already crossed the kitchen floor and inspects Ryan's face for himself.

"Where did this happen? This is a pretty good punch, and some road rash. We should probably wash it out. Can you describe the person who did this? What time was it?" Detective Kildaire is in full presence now, basically frog-marching Ryan through the hallway to the downstairs bathroom, phone in hand.

"You don't need to call it in," I hear Ryan arguing as Matteo pulls him into the bathroom.

"You're damn right I *do*," Matteo answers. "This is how hoodlums stay on the street. No one reports them, they continue to harass people, and it goes downhill until they really hurt someone . . ." Their voices fade out as the water turns on, though I can make out that they're still arguing.

Trog and I meet gazes, and I give a little laugh. He and I are left alone in the kitchen, crouched in front of the open refrigerator and freezer. "Did he just say *hoodlums*?" I ask Trog.

He sneezes in response.

"I thought so," I agree, reaching to close the doors. Gooseflesh pricks my arms and legs, the cold air from the fridge not helping the already chilly house. I stop by the linen closet on the way down the hall, grabbing a stack of towels.

Inside the bathroom, Matteo has Ryan's shirt off, and he's dabbing at a long scratch on his ribs with a cotton ball of something. I didn't realize we even *had* cotton balls in this house, but I'm pleasantly surprised that at some point in the past five years I bought something useful for middle-of-the-night first aid. "I thought you said you guys just exchanged punches."

Ryan sighs. "The guy surprised me, and I ended up on the ground first. *Then* I got up and punched him. I didn't really feel like broadcasting that a skinny little twerp almost got the best of me." He's clearly embarrassed that he nearly got his ass kicked. Stupid male ego. But I kind of get what he's saying, noting that without his usual slightly baggy T-shirt on, Ryan has a considerable amount of lean muscle mass, thanks to his current obsession with CrossFit.

Matteo sets his phone on the counter, the speakerphone already ringing. Within two rings, a female voice barks, "Captain Massuda."

In short order, Matteo fills his captain in on Ryan's fistfight, and grudgingly, Ryan fills in the blanks. He decided to let Lawrence take the Uber straight to his house and call a separate one for himself, since Lelani's was in the opposite direction. Lawrence had departed, and while waiting for the next car, Ryan decided to walk around the Performing Arts Center. Near the back entrance, a person grabbed him from behind, demanded his phone, and held something against his ribs. Ryan apparently reacted out of instinct and threw an elbow back; the person punched him in the back, dropping him, but Ryan managed get back to his feet quickly enough to throw a punch as the guy tried to grab his phone. The assailant decided it wasn't worth it and ran off.

"I wish you'd called it in right away. Fighting back like that was dangerous, but if he was incapacitated, we might have been able to apprehend him."

Defensiveness for Ryan rises in my chest. "It's not like he's a damn superhero, Matteo. Ryan almost got beaten to death, so let's lay off the shoulda-wouldas." Ryan looks intermittently defeated, embarrassed, and worried, and I deem him the party worth consoling at this moment. "I'm so sorry this happened, Ryan."

"I guess I was asking for it, wandering around by myself at night," he says, shrugging. But his eyes are downcast.

"Still scary, though," I push, in case he wants to talk about it.

He doesn't.

He waits until Matteo hangs up the phone, then pulls his shirt back on. "Anything else?"

Matteo shakes his head. "No, but rest assured this helps us. If we catch someone doing this to someone else, we'll have a reason to detain and question them. If we can link them, prior offenses lead to jail time and get these people off the street. It sends a message to others that this isn't an acceptable way to make a quick buck. You're doing your civic duty."

Ryan gives Matteo a look that clearly says *he's* doing the civic duty for him, and that Ryan would really rather not, but whatever. "Can I go take a shower, then?"

Matteo nods, though for the first time, doubt creeps across his face. And a touch of guilt. Detective Kildaire gives way to shades of

Matteo, and I think Matteo may feel a little guilty for forcing the issue of reporting it. "Are you sure you're okay? I could take you to the ER."

"No, definitely not," Ryan says, exiting the bathroom.

I join Matteo in worrying that we've really upset Ryan.

At the door, he turns and gives a grudging nod. "Thanks for helping with the scratch, though. I appreciate it."

"Anytime," Matteo answers, and we stay in the bathroom until we hear Ryan's feet tread up the stairs and down the hallway to the bathroom above our heads. A moment later, the water turns on, spurring me into action.

The pile of towels on the sink is easy to wad up, and it takes next to no time for me to stick them in the washing machine. There's no setting for "blood and various gross street chemical stains," so I spin the dial at random and press "Start." They're cotton, so hopefully with enough detergent and warm water, they'll come clean.

Matteo lurks in the doorway, thumbs moving quickly over his phone. Follow-up with his captain, I'm guessing. I grab his hand on my way out of the laundry room and drag him back to my room, turning off lights as we go. Trog has already taken up residence in the bed—right in Matteo's spot, as if he has a point to prove. "No, sir, you know the rules. No dogs under the covers," I say, sliding his furry form to the bottom of the bed. It's bad enough I have to wash my comforter so frequently; I couldn't afford the water bill if I had to wash every piece of bedding that often.

Matteo and I climb back in bed. This time, Matteo takes the time to strip to his boxers and T-shirt, and I battle briefly with whether I want him more than sleep. Sleep wins tonight, thanks to my slight hangover, so I settle backward into my pillows, now as chilled as the rest of the house. Matteo's warm arm comes over me, and the chill is instantly banished. Maybe winter won't be so bad after all. I'm just about to drift off when Matteo's phone chimes from beneath his pillow.

I sigh but know this is what I signed up for, dating a detective. There's no such thing as "silent mode."

Without comment, Matteo lifts the phone, squinting against the light, and then half sits up to type a reply.

"What's up?" I ask, blinking myself back into awakeness.

"Rideout says that patrol picked up a dealer tonight. They had *two* suspects, but one got away. Their report states that this second suspect was injured."

I half sit up with him, my mind going directly to Ryan. "Like it could be the guy who beat up Ryan?"

Matteo pushes a hand through his hair, types another response into his phone, and then lies down again. "Maybe. I'll look into it tomorrow. It seems like more than a coincidence, but . . . these guys weren't anywhere near the Performing Arts Center."

"Maybe they were up to pre-work hijinks?" I guess, lying back down too.

"Maybe," Matteo agrees, though he doesn't sound convinced. "What bothers me is that these new dealers are getting more aggressive. I mean, to just mug a guy like Ryan means they're either on something or they're ballsy. Looking for trouble. Or . . ."

"Or . . . ?" He's silent so long I assume he's fallen asleep, and my own eyes start to close of their own accord.

"*Or,*" Matteo says on a sigh several long moments later, "it wasn't random, and these people targeted Ryan."

My eyes pop back open. "Targeted him?"

"Forget it; I'm tired and paranoid. It just seems . . . off, somehow. And I can't help thinking that you, Ryan, and Lawrence may have made some inadvertent enemies this summer."

A cold trickle of foreboding starts at my head and wiggles its way down to my feet. It's a chill that has nothing to do with early fall. Matteo knows nothing of my suspicion that Ryan knows something about the Golden Arrow, but it *could* be a reason someone might target him. "You think this has to do with the trial?"

"Like I said, I'm tired, paranoid, and seeing ghosts where there probably aren't any," Matteo says, wrapping his arm over me again and pulling me back against his chest. "But it's enough I'm going to look into the guy patrol arrested tonight in addition to the two from yesterday. And, MG?"

"Yeah?"

He squeezes me. "Promise me you'll be careful, okay? Until we know."

"I will," I agree, squeezing back.

"Good night," he says with a quick kiss to my temple.

"'Night," I answer, though now I'm not sure there's any way I'm going to fall asleep. Now the seed has been planted in the fertile soil of my late-night imagination, and it's not going anywhere. *Could* Ryan have been ambushed *on purpose*? Targeted? Could this be connected with the drug lord we just put in jail? And if this is related to the case . . . does it mean that Matteo's hunch is correct and that the Golden Arrow has unfinished business? That he's really back out in the world? There are a lot of little coincidences—the arrow pin, the dealers, the party, and now Ryan's ambush. I am awake long after Matteo's breathing evens out, thinking. One thing is certain, I decide as dawn breaks outside my window: if there is a vigilante out there in Los Angeles who knows something I don't—something that could keep my friends safe—I'm going to find and confront him once and for all.

CHAPTER 6

The next morning, Genius Comics fairly buzzes with Golden Arrow gossip. Between the TV spot, the drag show, and the secret party, the lobby fills with conversation of nothing else as I wait for the previous conference room attendees to exit and this week's team meeting to start. I wince as I rub my eyes. Burning the midnight—make that two a.m.—oil has *got* to stop soon. And today isn't short. I have this meeting, an office workday, and then I'm meeting Matteo at the station for the interview.

Andy, my not-so-fearless team supervisor, catches me stifling a yawn and raises his eyebrows. He motions to the coffee maker in the corner with a "help yourself" gesture, possibly noticing that my usually ever-present coffee cup isn't in my hand. In other words, the end of my arm is naked. I eye the tiny machine warily, balancing the short pro-con list in my head. On one hand, *shudder*, pod coffee. On the other hand, falling asleep in a team meeting won't prove to my coworkers that I'm handling this new part-time work responsibly. So, I force myself up, grab a cheap paper cup, and brew—if you can call forcing coffee through plastic "brewing"—the coffee.

Kyle and Simon are, as per their usual workplace bromance, paired at the hip and gabbing like schoolgirls. "There's no way it's real. Definitely a media stunt. Why would the Golden Arrow show up at a drag revue?"

Simon nods. "Yeah, but that party was insane, and I'm going to watch the website just in case, you know?"

I'm sorting through snarky responses in my head while stirring an alarming amount of sugar into my tiny cup when my vision is filled by a tweed pantsuit.

No man in this office is this fashionable, and the gleaming black hair confirms that this is none other than Lelani. I blink twice, startled to see her. As far as I remember, this is a team meeting, and not an executive green-light meeting. That's *next* week, right? I stifle the urge to grab for my iPhone to check my calendar. If this is a green-light meeting, I'm screwed.

"Ah, MG, I was hoping to grab you before the meeting started. How are things?"

I have no idea if Ryan told Lelani about his attack, so do I mention it? Do I play it cool? Is this about Ryan or work, or am I in trouble? I do my best to stifle my panic. "Um, fine," I respond, ever my eloquent self around her. I never know what to expect from our interactions, and though I've never had proof, I always feel like Lelani tries just a little bit *too* hard to be nice to me. Like she secretly hates me but is too good to show it. Or *maybe*, I reflect as I meet her dark, expectant gaze, she doesn't *like* me because I've been staring at her and overanalyzing my feelings and she thinks me a half-wit. Today, she's not all that far off.

"Well," Lelani continues as if I haven't just made an awkward mess of this whole thing, "I'm just stopping by to announce a new project that your team will be working with, and I want to see if you are interested in being the liaison."

I blink. "New project?"

"A Hooded Falcon movie. Normally we don't have *anything* to do with this, but Mr. Casey sold the rights specifically with the caveat that he's got a say in aesthetics, story lines, everything. We need a team member to help consult on things like backstory accuracy and costume aesthetics."

I blink again, my mind a swirl of questions. "And you think *I* could help with that?" Part of me hates that my voice comes out breathless and giddy like a fifteen-year-old reliving a first kiss. The other part of me doesn't care at all . . . *Dream, meet silver platter.*

Lelani studies me for a moment, and I regret all my half-witted blinking. "You're the first I thought of, but it's your choice, of course. It may mean some additional hours specifically for this project, both in and out of the office, but you have the availability, yes? I assume you can fit something like this into your busy schedule?" She smiles, but it doesn't quite reach her eyes.

"Oh, yes. Of course—"

Lelani holds up a hand. "No need to decide fully now. Come by my office tomorrow for more details before you agree. I wanted to see if you had interest. I know you've discussed having a passion for work outside of your normal arena. Andy agreed your skill set would be the best fit from the team, if you were up for it. See you tomorrow, then."

Without waiting for me to respond, Lelani strides to the front of the table and greets Andy, presumably to tell him I'm a total wackadoo, and I make my way back to my chair. A *slosh* of hot coffee from the little clown cup confirms it: I'm awake, and somehow I've managed to start designing costumes part time, continue writing comics, *and* get what I consider a huge résumé-and-dream-building opportunity.

My attention shifts when Lelani clears her throat. I've missed Andy's opening remarks, apparently. I also missed tasting the first half of my scalding-hot cup of awful coffee, which I consider a win. "Thanks, Andy. I'm only here for a few minutes. I wanted to let you know that Genius Comics just signed our contract for a Hooded Falcon movie!" She pauses and the rest of us politely clap, even though we've been expecting something like this after the huge buzz this summer. The timing seems perfect: Casey and his comics are back in the news, the Golden Arrow hoopla has been nothing but good press, the special-edition comic I helped develop drops this month, and the video game is set to roll out near Christmas. *Not* making a movie would be dumb.

"Yes, we're all excited," she continues. "Anyhow, I just want this team to know I've already talked with MG, and she's preliminarily agreed to operate as Genius's liaison for the production and art direction teams. Unless anyone else feels strongly about doing it? Production won't tic up for many months, but planning starts soon." Lelani looks expectantly around the room, and when no one voices a dissenting opinion, she nods once and makes her way to the sliding glass doors at the back of the room. "Wonderful, we'll keep you apprised of developments; have a good meeting!"

Andy waits until after she's left and then looks at the four of us. "Okay, is everyone *really* okay with this?"

I brace internally, waiting for my team to say that it was completely unfair that I—the girl who had just dropped to part time—get this opportunity.

Instead, Simon nods enthusiastically. "Do they know when the movie is going to be out?"

"Do they need extras?" This question from Tej, who removes his dark glasses and poufs his thick, wavy hair up in a comical boy-band way.

"No idea when the movie release date is; I guess we'll probably know soon? We'll see what we can do about the extras thing, Tej, and, MG, looks like it's a go. Okay, on to other matters. We'll touch on *The Hooded Falcon* first, since we're already there." He smooths back his overly long, curly, blond surfer hair and peers down the table. "We need to start drafting ideas for the next issue; it's going to be an important one, so close after the release of the special edition. We've hired another artist for the team now that things are ramping up, and MG is switching some of her gears. They'll be starting next week. As far as our team goes, maybe we can start a story line that is big enough for the movie producers to pick up threads to?"

I nod along. We *will* need more help, especially on the art end. I know how hard Kyle has been working—though Simon and I can help in a pinch, it isn't the same as having another full-time artist. Contract work is always a possibility, but I'm glad we'll be getting a real team-mate. This is one of Genius's biggest comics, so I assume they can afford the salary.

The boys jump right in with ideas. I don't love-*love* anything thrown out: new alien overlord, the reboot of an old nemesis. It's long been my lament that the most recent reboots turn into flash-and-bang comics—all about the weapons and insane gadgets, and less about the heart. Less about why *THF* exists in the first place. I feel like a broken record, but it has to be pointed out again.

"What about a social-justice plotline? Something that recalls the originals." I've spoken without thinking—right over the top of Kyle's pitch for a change of location, something the movie people may be into. I frantically rewind his words in my head as everyone turns to stare at me; it's unusual for one of us to just completely railroad another team member. I *think* he was talking about going back to the island that the Hooded Falcon had come from for some tropical change of pace.

"Uh," I flounder, my face flushing. "I'm so sorry, Kyle. Your idea just . . . sparked something for me. Continue."

Kyle sits back, not looking too pissed, *thank goodness*. "No, by all means, I'm basically done. It's all yours."

Crap. Now I'm going to have to flesh out a nonexistent idea *and* try to tie it into what Kyle has been saying. *Double crap*.

"Er . . ." I pause for a sip of my horrendous coffee as if it is liquid gold and stop short of faking a refreshed "ah" noise at the end. "So, Kyle brought up the island that the Hooded Falcon trained on." To my relief, everyone nods.

"And it got me thinking about the original series." I *do* have a brain for plots, and it seems like even crappy coffee can fuel it for me. "I like Kyle's idea, but I think we should push it even more. Nostalgia is running high right now. Could we do a throwback story line if we're visiting the island? Not a literal throwback, no reincarnated villains, but . . . something that addresses social injustice, and not just random

56

bad guys?" I feel like this is my go-to idea with *THF*; call me a purist, but thankfully no one says anything.

"Like . . . smugglers?" Simon definitely still looks dubious.

"That's not super pertinent to social justice these days." I fish around in my memory of recently viewed Reddit forums. "I don't know, how about trafficking? Like sex or human trafficking?"

Andy's eyebrows draw down. "I hardly think that sounds like something that could fit in with our current story line."

"We could make it work," I argue, not about to let my push for *real* content get brushed off again. This is why I'm still here, fighting for what I feel comics *could* do for society today. "Historically, human trafficking involved pirates. Pirates could be a new and different thing to write, but they could represent the real-time struggle in our real world. Expose the underbelly, as it were."

Andy and Kyle perk up. "We've done the smuggling thing before, as did the original. But . . . pirates. Pirates could be fun."

"And we can use this to help raise awareness that human and sex trafficking still exists. Maybe list some resources on a blog post about what inspired this issue." Even though I'm not sure it still exists on the high seas . . . Baby steps.

"Yeah!" Simon chimes in. "I do like it. The Falcon could use his old island to stage a booby trap or something. Maybe the movie crew *will* like the idea of tying in to an island scene."

And they're off and away, crafting the idea into a slightly ludicrous but at least partially socially aware story line. We all agree to come up with some material for the green-light meeting, and I relax internally slightly. Crisis averted.

"Okay, well, moving on to the smaller projects." Andy shifts uncomfortably in his seat, and my focus narrows on him. "Tej? Want to fill us in?"

My heart starts to crumple like a slo-mo sequence of Superman nearing kryptonite. That doesn't sound . . . uplifting.

Tej straightens in his seat and tosses out a few single sheets of printed paper to each of us across the table. I take a quick glance, and my heart crumples further. At the very bottom of the list—ranked by sales totals—is my personal pet project, *Hero Girls*, a comic book aimed specifically at teen girls.

"As you can see, we have two projects that are exceeding projected numbers. One of them is *Adventure League* super specials"—Tej nods to Simon, who's been illustrating for that—"and the *Mighty Destroyer* middle-grade limited run. That one is scheduled to end in 2020 but has been enough of a moneymaker Genius would like to consider other ideas for limited-run middle-grade comics."

Tej shoots me a furtive glance, and my eyes flick down to my paper from his face.

"Er, and we have two projects that aren't necessarily doing as well as expected. One is the web series, *The Great Kaching*, and *Hero Girls*." Both Kyle and I level our gazes at Tej. Kyle's been working on *Kaching*, a web series about a magician who discovers that his tricks can be used to fight crime. It's quasi comic strip and seems never to have found its niche audience, I guess.

"Now, I know we *just* did a special edition of *Hero Girls*, but I think we'll need to start thinking about wrapping up the current story line. Same with *Kaching*. Sorry, guys."

I swallow.

"Any questions?" Tej's gaze is frank but kind. He knows what this project means for me. It's my little corner of the world.

"No," I mutter, and Kyle shakes his head. I don't think he cares one way or the other, but I do. We've all had little projects fail. But this was the first heart project. Not a spin-off. My own characters, drawn and conceptualized by *me*. And now, well, my first personal failure of a project. It means I need to analyze why it failed and come up with a new personal project. It'll be *more* time and *more* effort on top of my already full load. I guess maybe it's okay if this one falls off. I'm struggling to keep up as it is.

As I clean up my papers and head to the elevator to our second-floor work area, I nurse a growing sense that maybe I *can't* pull all this off. Having my cake and eating it too. The costumes, *The Hooded Falcon*, my side projects—all the ideas I have for little comics . . . and I realize Matteo's on that list too. I may be forced to pick where my energy goes, and I don't love that thought. The trick is, which ones are my cake, and which ones shouldn't I eat?

CHAPTER 7

The police station smells like burned bean burritos when I arrive later that day. Maybe Matteo's not the only one basically living at his desk recently. Glimpsing a travel pillow thrown casually on top of one workstation confirms my suspicion.

Not having my credentials as a consultant for the LAPD anymore—they'd been understandably revoked while I was under investigation for the SDCC mess—means that Matteo has to meet me at the door, sign me in, and escort me back to his desk. At least until my paperwork is filed and accepted, I don't have a badge. His desk piles teeter with manila folders, loose papers, receipts, and several Lego helicopters and toy police cars. I grab my favorite one—a stress-ball police car where when you squeeze the car, the siren lights bulge entertainingly—and smoosh it in my hands.

"I think I just want you to watch from the booth," Matteo explains. "Detective Rideout and I have developed our list of questions already. You can listen, and take note of anything that sets off comic book alarm bells in your mind."

"Okay." I shift my weight from foot to foot, trying to determine if I'm allowed to hug him hello or not. I decide that since he's clearly at work, and currently channeling Detective Kildaire, that I won't. Matteo catches me studying him and gives a quick smile before leaning in for a kiss on the cheek. "I'm glad you're here; thanks for helping out on this."

"Oh, get a room, you two."

I turn to find Detective Rideout approaching the desk, but he's not wearing his usual scowl. In fact, for how much I know he disapproves of my relationship with Matteo, he seems downright . . . tolerant of my presence today. "Ready to go interview some suspects?" He all but rubs his hands together.

Matteo nods and gathers up a few papers, his notebook, and the earpiece he'll wear during the interview. In a practiced choreography, both men don their small mic packs, Rideout reaching to secure Matteo's wire under his old-school leather suspender straps. They both shrug into their jackets, check their cuffs, and nod at each other. It's obvious these two have done this too many times to count, and it's not the first time that I get the feeling that Rideout knows more about Matteo than I do.

"You just let me know if we need to jump script," Matteo says as Rideout nods. "I'm not expecting a link, but you never know."

"My instinct says these are just nobodies, but I'll let you have your fun before we process them," Rideout responds.

"Okay. We'll play it like normal, then," Matteo says with a nod, and they both roll their shoulders before turning toward the hallway.

At first, I think of them as an old married couple, one indulging the other's hunch. But it strikes me that I'm witnessing a team preparing for battle. Two warriors who love what they do or, at the very least, are very, very capable together. They *are* a team—their job is to support and protect each other, intellectually as well as physically. It's a new look at Rideout I haven't considered before. Matteo's other, *other* half. Most of the time I just lump him into "pain in my ass" territory. I don't usually get to see them working together as the well-oiled partners they are.

"Okay, and MG, you let Detective Rideout know if you hear something critical, okay?"

"Okay," I agree, falling into line after Rideout. While Rideout is *tolerating* me, when he looks at me, there's no spark of warmth in his eyes the way there is when he was talking to Matteo. I helped with the last case, so he's grudgingly allowing my presence in the office. And he'll tolerate my dating Matteo because he has to. But by the set of his shoulders as we file past the open desks, I'm here to *watch* and *listen*. Not to interfere. This is their turf, and while I may have had the edge with the Golden Arrow stuff before, this isn't my territory anymore. He's basically peeing on Matteo, and I'm reluctantly allowing it.

We walk through a series of cubicles, down a short hallway, past the kitchen that is the culprit of the burned smell, and through a set of doors to rooms I recognize from the last time I watched an interview. This hallway has a series of dark metal doors with tiny little windows in them, interspersed with friendlier wooden doors that lead to the booths between interview cubicles. Some are plain rooms, containing only a desk and three chairs. Some are a little roomier, with a bench under a large window, and some—like the one we approach now—have actual two-way glass into a booth so someone can monitor the interview. Casey Junior's interview had been given in a comfortable one; these guys . . . not so much. Without a word, I follow Rideout into a booth—a scrunched room with a desk facing the glass, while Matteo proceeds to the door directly beyond.

It takes a moment for my eyes to adjust to the dim light of the observation room, but I finally make out Matteo's back as he joins two youths at the table. The one on the left looks twelve instead of eighteen and is short and fat with brown curls framing his pudgy face. He looks so much like Augustus Gloop from the old-school *Willy Wonka & the Chocolate Factory* it takes everything in my being not to make a crack about chocolate being his drug of choice. He's about as far from standard-issue stereotypical drug dealer as you can get. On the other hand, the boy on the right looks tall, gaunt, and like he's no stranger to sampling the drugs he's been selling. His teeth are dark, his eyes wary, and his pale head shaved. I kind of can't believe the two were working together; they're complete opposites.

The initial questions are met with sullenness and one-word answers from the shorter boy—silence from the taller. It's clear that though neither has a lawyer present, they've watched enough TV to know that they shouldn't blab a lot before their hearing. And yet . . . Matteo works his magic. He's firm, businesslike, and polite, and *dang* can he work a room. Latifah would be impressed. Even just with his body language and simple-to-answer questions, Matteo slowly changes the temperature of the interview. Soon, they're answering with two- and three-word sentences, and finally, even I can see they're relaxing a bit.

"What we're really interested in is what happened when you were caught." Matteo says, maybe ten minutes into such mundane routine questions that I'm starting to nod off in the dark. "We're interested in the information enough to offer you significant . . . help . . . reducing your sentence at your hearing if you're willing to talk about it."

That got the attention of the two boys. Well, one of them in particular. The short fat one sits up like someone'd rammed his back with a red-hot poker. "Seriously? Could I get out of this? It was my first day, dude. There's no way I signed up for this; I didn't mean anything by it. My parents just wanted me to get a job, and I should have applied at In-N-Out. I'll tell you whatever you want if it means I don't have my chances at going to college killed by one stupid decision."

Singing. Like a bird.

He seems to belatedly realize he's spilled the beans—maybe from the side-eye the taller boy gives him, or maybe from the cough Matteo covers up.

"Allegedly," he adds, as if that could somehow undo his bean spillage.

"Okay," Matteo drawls, with no real change in his demeanor. "Let's start from the beginning. What's the first thing you remember?"

Beside me, Rideout is leaning up near the glass, his face in a tense scowl. If I were him, this would be Christmas, not a moment for scowling. Unless you're Scrooge, and that fits Rideout to a *T* in my head.

"Shouldn't you be happy? He's not holding anything back," I whisper because I can't help myself.

Rideout's eyes don't even flick to me; they're trained on the table in the room. "He's not the one I want information from. First day on the job." He puffs air through his mouth in something closely resembling an old-timer's "feh." "Not reliable. Knows nothing of the business he got into. Completely useless for knowing where the bindles came from." He falls silent as the shorter boy opens his mouth to answer.

"Well, it was dark," the boy hedges, his glance flicking to the taller boy, who in turn stares at the tabletop as if it holds the secrets of the universe. What little ground Matteo has gained with the second kid is gone. "So, I couldn't see much. I was standing there, watching a car drive by. You know, hoping they'd stop." He thinks a moment. "All of this is allegedly, okay?"

Matteo nods, keeping his eyes on his own notes.

"I heard a noise from behind me, and a big thing of rope slid around my middle. I tried really hard to turn around to see who had grabbed me, but the rope was pulled tight and I was yanked backward into . . ." He motions to the boy next to him. "We sorta clunked heads and sat down really quickly. So, I didn't see much. But the guy had to come around front while he was tying us to the light pole."

"So, you saw *him*? You're sure it's a man? Can you give a description?" I hear the note of hope in Matteo's voice.

"Sure. Maybe about six feet tall. Maybe shorter, I don't know. I was sitting down—hard to judge. But he was strong. He coiled that rope around us real fast even though we were struggling pretty hard."

"Okay . . . so somewhere near six feet. Hair color? Eye color? What was he wearing?"

"He was wearing all black," the boy answers, doubt creeping into his voice at this point. "Black mask over his eyes. Black jumpsuit."

"Jumpsuit."

"Yeah, sorta like a military parachute outfit."

"Anything else? Did he say anything?"

"Nope, completely silent. He finished putting the rope around the light pole, pulled something out of a bag across his back—I guess it was that arrow thing—and stuck it in-between us. Then he just . . . walked off."

"That's the entirety of your recollection?"

"That's it." The boy sounds more than nervous now. Even I can tell he's spent his information. Shown his whole hand.

"Get the spare out, see if the other one will talk," Rideout growls into his mic.

Matteo gives the briefest of nods. "Okay, thank you so much for your cooperation. It's been . . . useful, and we appreciate your willingness to help our investigation. It will be noted in your file."

"So, do I get a plea deal? Or get out of my charges? Or what? Can't you just let me go? I helped you."

"We'll discuss with your lawyer," Matteo promises, his voice warming slightly, and I know from his tone he means it. He presses a button on the wall, and almost instantly a policewoman opens the door to the room.

"We're finished here, thanks," Matteo says, shuffling his papers. He helps the larger boy to his feet and ushers him to the door.

I frown in confusion. "Wait, I thought he needed to talk to the other—"

Rideout holds up a hand.

I turn my attention back to the room, where the taller boy studies Matteo's movements over the table the way one studies a hand of poker. The second officer pauses at the door, her hand on the larger boy's cuffs. Matteo motions her on with a wave. "I'll take the second one myself," he says as she nods and exits, closing the door behind her.

Matteo waits in silence.

"So, what happens to me?" the taller boy finally asks.

"The same as before the interview. You'll be processed and heard according to the drugs we found on your person." Matteo flicks open his file and glances through. "Looks like your second offense."

No judgment in the tone, but the kid's eyes drop to the table before coming back up with more certainty to Matteo's face. "This wasn't my crew."

At first, I think he's denying that he's done anything wrong, but Rideout sits forward so fast you'd think this kid just confessed to dousing the Human Torch.

Matteo stays silent.

Shuffling his feet nervously, the kid rubs the top of his head and then sits forward, decision made. "This wasn't my crew. I was just . . . in the market for a job, since my old crew"—he pauses, searching for words—"a lot of them recently went on . . . vacation. It wasn't my first day on the job, but I didn't know them all that well. I'm not willing to do jail time for them."

You can practically hear Rideout clacking his mandibles in excitement. This is obviously a Good Day on the job for him.

Matteo nods. "So, do you have information to trade?"

The kid presses his lips together. "Maybe. But I need more assurances than that loser got." He motions to the door, indicating the fat boy. "I've got something useful. I have friends who went to ground, but know . . . stuff about stuff. I have something you'll be interested in, but I need a promise first."

"If your information is significant enough to develop a lead from, I *think* the judge would let you off with community service," Matteo says after a pause and a glance through the file again. "If you'll share, I'll do my best to make sure you don't serve more than a night in jail."

The kid nods, and Matteo scratches a note in the file before motioning him to continue. "First, the only thing I noticed—the only thing that there *was* to notice about the guy—were his kicks. This was a rich dude, maybe around thirty?"

"What makes you say that?" Matteo asks, leaning forward.

"They were nice running shoes, not all scuffed up or anything. Not ones that kids are buying, but still hip so not old man either. This wasn't your Walmart Asics. New Balance 2040v3, if I had to guess—they are like $350 a pair."

I've never even *heard* of those shoes, and apparently, neither has Matteo.

The kid shrugs. "Just because I do what I do . . . *allegedly*, doesn't mean I don't take care of my body. I happen to like running, so I'm into shoes. I'm not one of those users that waste their life. I'm in a tough spot maybe, but I'm saving for a better future. I work out, plus it comes in handy to be in shape sometimes, y'know? Anyway, these shoes aren't that mainstream, you should be able to figure out who has bought a pair in the past few months that fits your profile."

Rideout snorts derisively. "As if he's interested in health while he's dealing drugs."

"Okay, that's an interesting detail, and definitely worth pursuing," Matteo says, and I can see he means it. "Anything else? Not sure that's enough to get you a reduction in sentence or keep you out of jail, although I can try."

The kid looks at Matteo as if he's about to play his trump card. He's only been warming up. "My friends—the ones who told me about this new crew—said while this is new turf, the distributor *isn't* a new one."

Rideout sucks in a breath, and I swear if he could have pushed himself closer to the glass, he would have.

"A known entity? Operating under another name?"

Maybe Matteo *had* been right, and they'd missed some of the Muñez crew.

"Not exactly . . . they're new to the region. Expanding into empty territory. The bust has been all over the news—the field was left wide open."

Matteo nods, making a note. "Okay, do you have a name?"

The kid snorts. "Names. Never mean as much as cops think they do, but yeah. Or at least rumor."

We all waited with bated breath.

"My friends call her the Queen . . ." He visibly hesitates.

"The Queen," Matteo prompts, sensing the same.

The kid laughs before standing up, a mirthless thing. "Yeah, either it's the Queen, or it's—it's a stupid-ass name in my opinion, but you wanted to know *all* the info, so some people call her . . . the Queen . . . of Hearts."

"So, what do you think?"

We're seated in a different interview room just a few minutes later, the kind of interview room I'd sat in before I'd been a part of the case. Matteo and Rideout sit on one side of the table while I'm relegated to the small couch.

"I'm not sure," I stall. "What do *you* think?" I'm not quite ready yet to let my thoughts out.

Rideout sits back and crosses his arms across his chest, a smug smile playing around his lips. "See? Even your girlfriend agrees this has nothing to do with the Golden Arrow."

I grit my teeth. Rideout refuses to acknowledge I'm here as an *expert* and not as a *girlfriend*. He's nothing if not consistent in his misogyny. "I never said that," I fire back, my inner Janet van Dyne rising within me. "I just asked what Matteo thought. I trust his instincts."

"Like I don't?"

"Apparently not, or you'd have asked him yourself."

"I don't need to ask him, I already know what he's thinking," Rideout responds, complete with a teenage eye roll. We've devolved into arguing about who knows Matteo better. Immature at best. Peeing contest at worst.

"Okay, Beast Boy—"

"Okay, *you two*," Detective Kildaire cuts in. "This is an investigation. An important one. We *are* a team—like it or not—and we need to communicate like one instead of making assumptions." He shoots Rideout a look.

My mouth snaps closed and my cheeks heat. With the glance I sneak, Rideout doesn't outwardly seem fazed, but then I hear him uncross his arms and sigh.

"I'm not sure there's a connection," I offer to break the uncomfortable silence. I sense the victory rolling off Rideout and am quick to jump in again. "*Other than* the name of the new distributor is . . . odd."

"The Queen." Matteo sits back, running his hand over his chin. "It's not the first time we've come up against a woman distributor. Usually they're all-woman rings, though, running through an escort service. He seems pretty convinced she's new in the neighborhood, but established elsewhere."

"I'll check with our counterparts in San Diego and Santa Cruz," Rideout offers. "Maybe they're moving up the coast."

"That's not what I mean," I continue, stopping Rideout short of getting up to leave the table. "I mean, sure, it's probably a *she*. But the Queen of *Hearts*?"

"Does that mean something in *The Hooded Falcon*?" Matteo sits forward.

"He said it's probably just 'the Queen,'" Rideout adds.

I shake my head at Matteo, completely ignoring Rideout. "No, not *THF*, unfortunately. But. It's a character in *Alice in Wonderland*."

They both stare at me like I'm wearing a Captain Obvious sign around my neck, so I sigh. "Okay, I agree it's a little out there, but there's a slight tie-in to your case if you're looking—*from* THF *to* Alice in Wonderland."

Matteo sits back, catching my train of thought. "The White Rabbit."

"Exactly so."

Matteo thinks for a minute, his eyes on the ceiling of the small room, his pen tapping his notebook intermittently. Which gives me enough time to ponder how hot it is in these small rooms with three people—it's Jakku-level *stifling* in here. I shrug out of the cardigan I'm wearing.

"So . . . now dealing with drug dealers who are naming themselves after stupid book characters?" Rideout asks Matteo as if he can't believe he's considering my suggestion. "This had better not be a new 'thing.'" He mutters under his breath about young people and stupid trends.

"I asked MG for her opinion, and she brings up a valid point."

Rideout's eyes goggle at the word "valid." "Well, *I* am going to run with the same assumption that the drug dealer had, that it was a kid calling the distributor a stupid-ass name. The next step is to go ask my connections farther south about the Queen." He stands and strides from the room. I give his back a silent salute of departure.

Matteo chews the side of his cheek for a moment, then gives his head a small shake before turning his gaze back to mine. "Okay. So. Let's pretend this connection *could* possibly be there. Extrapolate. What could this mean?"

I tap my chin. "Well, I guess we'd have to assume, in this situation, that this really *is* the Golden Arrow acting again for some reason. That the arrow is a real tell."

"Otherwise it's just a rich kid out to try and get that prize."

I think about the shoe comment. "Yeah, true. But you said yourself that this one felt different. This guy tied together two people without much trouble, stuck a golden arrow in-between them, and then left. No attempt at publicity."

"No public statement, but also no note. No indication as to *why* the Golden Arrow would have done this. We need to figure out the *why* before we figure out the *who*, I'm thinking." He looks to me, hoping I'll take the next volley and toss out ideas. It's what I'm here for.

And truthfully, I love this. It feels like "old times" for us—sitting across from each other, pontificating and what-if-ing about a crime. It's where I'd met and fallen for Matteo . . . it's honestly where we feel the most like *us*. "There's three options that I see, then." I tick them off on my fingers. "This is an unrelated media stunt, and this guy will come forward and try to claim to be the GA—but he's just a good imposter. Option two: this *is* the Golden Arrow and it's unrelated, and he's just . . . I don't know, got the bug for vigilante crime-fighting now. Like he's bored and decided to clean up the rest of Muñez's crew? And option three: this *is* connected. The Queen of Hearts is related to the White Rabbit, the Golden Arrow knows it, and we're meant to follow the trail." *And*, I don't add out loud, *if it's option three, we have to figure out how the Golden Arrow yet again has information the police don't.*

Matteo nods slowly, turning over the options in his mind. "It seems a stretch for the third option."

We've had a conversation eerily like this one before—about the Muñez case. "Agreed." I think for a moment, letting information filter through unfettered as I review what I know about the Golden Arrow. There's plenty we don't know, but one thing we *do*. "We never did find the other half of that journal. We know the Golden Arrow used the journals to catch Muñez . . . maybe there's something in there that informs his actions."

Matteo closes his notebook. "True. Still not enough for me to go on, and my partner *clearly* thinks I'm overthinking this. I can't explain it. My gut says this is related. Unfortunately, until I have more proof, it's just going to be a hunch. Thanks for coming in." All business, so I stand when he does and brush my hands off on my pants. "And thanks for lending your brains to yet another one of my semi-ludicrous ideas."

"Your semi-ludicrous ideas are my favorite." I can't help the grin I give him.

He winks. "Mine too. But don't tell Rideout." A hint of Matteo inside Detective Kildaire. "Are you okay if AnneMarie lets you out?

I need to go help contact our counterparts down south." AnneMarie is the young detective who took the place of traitorous Officer James.

A *hint* of Matteo, but Detective Kildaire is still on the job.

"Sure. Will I see you tonight?"

"Yeah, I'll be in touch." He leans over, giving a quick peck on my cheek.

I leave feeling buoyed, but it quickly gives way to my natural state as of late: anxiety. This case doesn't seem to be wrapping up. In fact, it seems to be going in the opposite direction. And while I love helping with it again . . . will we ever just have a normal life without the possibility of a real-life vigilante hero hanging over our heads?

CHAPTER 8

Trogdor starts barking before I hear the knock at my door.

"Those huge ears have to be good for something, right?" I ask his cute, bread-loaf corgi butt as it sprints off to the small set of stairs leading to the foyer.

I smooth my currently lilac hair back and adjust my fire-engine-red glasses. Even though I saw Matteo this afternoon at the station, it's different than seeing him for a date. Every once in a while, it catches me off guard that I, Michael-Grace Martin, have a real boyfriend. Like an *adult* boyfriend. With a job, and a car, and an interest in supporting my career goals. It feels at once incredibly freeing and like I've crossed some threshold into being *old*.

But I sure don't feel old when I open the door to reveal Matteo in all his work-shirted glory. I never thought I'd love the look of slacks and a long-sleeve button-down—rolled up at the cuffs—as much as I do. But oh, do I.

"Hey," I say, trying to play it cool.

Instead of stepping in, he produces a large bouquet of flowers from behind his back and holds them out to me.

"Oh!" I take the flowers as if someone's handing me a squirmy child. I hold them at arm's length and try to school my features into something like pleasant surprise. "Flowers!"

I've never actually *received* flowers from a guy before. At least beyond the gerbera daisies of my high-school-prom corsage. Though I understand why some girls like them, all I see is dead plants. They're not really my *thing*, and I'm pretty sure Matteo knows that. At least it's not some big gaudy bouquet thing. These tall and slender stalks of green have multiple purple flowers coming off them—thank God, no cliché commercial roses.

Matteo clears his throat, and I realize he's still standing outside, eyes glued to my face. "Ah, they're irises. I thought they were pretty and matched your hair. I wanted to give you something nice because I know I've been canceling a lot lately. A peace offering."

"I'll, ah, go put them in something." I offer a smile that I hope doesn't come out as awkward as I feel on the inside. *It's sweet,* I remind myself. He wants to get me flowers. *It's a completely normal and adult thing to do. Boyfriends get girlfriends flowers.* They remind him of me. It's sweet. Really.

But as I hunt through my cabinet for *anything* resembling a vase— finally settling on a Batman stainless steel water bottle—I hit upon the thing that's bothering me. I don't feel like a *normal* girl, I'm not sure I want "normal" things, and I'm waaaay overanalyzing this, but do these flowers reflect that Matteo thinks of our relationship—of *me*—as normal? Mundane? *I'm definitely overanalyzing,* I tell myself, filling the water bottle with some water. Normal boyfriends don't match flowers to hair, right? That's unique and special.

I lift my eyes to find Matteo watching me over my kitchen table, Trog cradled in his arms like a furry throw pillow. A crease graces his forehead, along with an adorable lock of his dark hair. He really *is* sweet, and I'm being *way* too picky. I've had a long, stressful week, and the meeting today with the *Hero Girls* news has just been a cherry on top.

"It's very sweet, even though you didn't need to. Thank you."

"I know you don't love flowers, but I do. And they made me think of you." He smiles and puts Trog down, while I proceed to internally kick myself. Here my boyfriend is, trying to apologize to me, and I've basically warded him off with my fingers in an *X*. "I got you something else too, besides the flowers."

He leaves the kitchen, climbs the stairs, and then opens the front door. In a moment he's back with a wrapped box.

I sidle around the kitchen table, take the box, and rip open one side.

"I know that sometimes your internet connection is slow when Ryan is gaming," he says by way of explanation. "And I thought since I missed the other night that we could watch it together."

I finish unwrapping the box to reveal the entire Blu-ray set of *Game of Thrones*. I manage a genuine smile this time. "This is incredibly thoughtful, Matteo."

And really it *is*. The internal sinking feeling I have makes no sense. Here's my supersweet boyfriend, who has done nothing except show up looking delicious, bearing flowers and meaningful gifts. And here I am, Eeyore-ing. But . . . it's been years since I bought a hard copy of a movie. I don't even own a dedicated Blu-ray player anymore. Some stupid part of me keeps insisting that between the flowers and the Blu-ray . . . maybe Matteo doesn't get me as much as I thought he did? That we aren't as perfectly in sync as I like to believe.

But then only *totally snobby* people reassess their relationships based on media gifts, so I shove that annoying part of me aside and motion Matteo into the kitchen. "I think it's perfect, and we can start Season 1 tonight. It won't have the full orchestra, but I'll hum aggressively. After I get us something to drink, I'll go call Ryan and see if he can walk me through using his monstrosity of a gaming station to play the disc, sound good?" Truth be told, I'd touched Ryan's gaming machine *once* and basically had my head bitten off for it. I now avoid his corner of the living room; he might as well have peed a circle around it.

Matteo nods and slides his jacket off, hanging it on the back of a kitchen chair. I start to rattle around for a few glasses for beer, but Matteo catches one of my hands and pulls me to him again. He wraps his arms around me, and leans down, lips in my hair.

"You didn't read the card in the flowers."

I, being entirely unaware that flowers came with cards, shake my head. He nods, and turns me toward the flowers with a gentle nudge. I root around in my bouquet until a plastic stand presents itself, complete with tiny greeting card envelope. One dramatic flourish later, I'm holding a small golden card with Matteo's block lettering basically filling the interior. My eyes scan the interior, expecting, "I care so much about you, yadda, yadda, yadda," typical greeting-card stuff, but stop short at the words "digital versions." My eyes scan backward, and I reread, a slow and happy grin spreading across my face. Matteo has purchased the digital downloads for all the episodes alongside the discs.

"I know you don't play discs, but I thought it would be a good backup in case—I don't know, are there such things as *Game of Thrones* emergencies? Digital blackouts? Internet crises?"

I laugh and throw myself back against his chest. "There may be. And now I'm prepared if there are." I lean back, giving Matteo's chin a quick peck. "Thank you." And I'd been wrong. Matteo hadn't just *known* me; he'd even guessed my reactions. Who in the world has a sweeter and more sensitive boyfriend? No one.

Matteo squeezes me in return, I grab two beers, and we amble toward the living room. I hear the door open and shut, and the telltale clomp of Ryan's running shoes hitting the foyer. I'd told him Matteo was coming over, and he'd promised to stay upstairs for the night to give us some time to unwind. Ryan pauses briefly before his footsteps jog up the small flight of stairs to the second level, and another pause before the shower water starts. Perfect. With Lawrence at the dress rehearsal for his drag revue and Ryan safely upstairs, I can just *be* with Matteo tonight.

"It's been a crazy month," Matteo says, sinking down onto my ugly-but-oh-so-comfortable sofa. He briefly cradles his head in his hands before sitting back against the pillows.

I fold my legs under me, toss my arm across the back of the couch, and study Matteo's face. He looks *tired*. "More about the case?"

"I think I've chased down Ryan's assailant."

I sit forward. "Well, that's great news, right? Good work!"

Matteo holds up a hand. "I don't *have* him yet—I still need to arrest him. But I questioned the two we have in custody about it when you left, and I got a name of someone who purportedly was in a fistfight with a stranger two nights ago. Claims he was jumped, but the boys just thought he didn't want to admit to a customer getting the better of him or something. The timeline fits, even if the story doesn't quite."

I am missing something here; he sounds so morose for having a win coming in his direction. "Okay, so? Not in custody yet, but you have a name."

"He's connected with this new ring, no priors, no history of assault."

I'm still stumped and Matteo must read that. He shrugs. "No known ties to the Muñez ring bothers me. It just made *sense* that this wasn't random. I can't shake it. This week is just . . . getting to me, I guess. Even when I have an answer, it doesn't satisfy me. I'm constantly having to worry about yahoos putting on spandex and getting hurt or killed trying to prove they're a hero. And now with the Queen stuff, and Ryan's assault, and the dealers who know each other but aren't connected with anyone . . ."

We lapse into silence, and when it becomes clear he's not offering more information, I decide to probe a little. "And now . . ."

"Well, I can deal with the imposter stuff—it's media attention, that will die down. But I was expecting the drug scene to cool off a little, given that we just took the major players out. Now I'm wondering if either we created a hole in the market that someone jumped to fill or we didn't get everyone. It all feels connected, but I can't figure it out. My gut says one thing, the paper trail says another thing. And if the GA is involved . . . well, and we already *know* we didn't get everyone technically connected with the case this summer. He's just the only open end I *know* about."

"But the Golden Arrow helped *catch* those guys, right? And if it's him again, he's still tying up dealers? Maybe he suspects the same thing you do. The GA is a good guy."

Matteo scrubs at his eyes again, and sighs. "In theory. A good guy who won't share his inside knowledge and is working outside of the accepted channels still isn't a good guy in my book."

"Batman . . ." I interject, fully equipped for this debate. Though admittedly, I'm not usually on the side of defending the Bat. Somehow in this instance, though, I get it, and it's a hill I'll die on gladly.

Matteo reaches over and pats my knee, effectively stopping the argument before it can begin. "All I know is I don't want to talk about work anymore, and I want to snuggle with my girl and watch something with big wolves."

"Direwolves," I correct him, and I let the work topic slide. It's obvious Matteo has his hands full with work, and I hate seeing him this stressed. With one hand, I flick through my phone to my online video library, happily push the icon for Season 1, and stream it to the television. *This* is why I love technology. It's magic. My own little corner of Harry Potter's world.

I snuggle into Matteo's side, the frosty moors near Winterfell in the opening scene sucking me in instantly. For a few moments, I let the worries fall away, and do what I love best—lose myself in another world.

CHAPTER 9

"Hey, Kyle," I say before I've even put down my messenger bag at my desk. It's Wednesday morning, and I spent all yesterday busting my rear end at home to catch up on work stuff after the ridiculousness that has been my past week. "I finished those story lines to be inked; do you want to take a look at them . . ."

I cut off, catching sight of Lelani and Daniel standing in the back of the office near the conference room. "Oh. Hello."

"Good morning, MG; I'm just introducing Daniel to the rest of the group. He works for the production company, and he'll be their representative liaison for the movie project. Your counterpart, if you will," Lelani explains. "I know you and he spent some time together the other night, but I wanted the rest of the crew to know who you'll be working with."

Her comment raises eyebrows for both Kyle and Simon. *I* know what she means, but she certainly makes it sound like Daniel and I have been on a date or something. All of a sudden, her aside about seeing Daniel in the office makes sense, though I wish she'd just been blunt about it so I didn't have to wonder. It's not the first time I feel like Lelani is sometimes playing a game I'm too dumb to realize I'm even playing.

I frown but force myself to attempt some of Lelani's charm instead of my normal fluster. "Ah, yes, Daniel. It was nice to meet you at the drag show, I'm looking forward to our work together for the movie." I stop short of being overly elaborate about how we'd met, steering clear of "she doth protest too much." It mostly works; Kyle and Simon turn back to Daniel while I finish putting down all my things at my desk.

"Daniel and I are longtime friends," Lelani explains with a smile. "And Genius is excited about teaming up for this movie with the production company. MG, when you're ready, I'll meet with you and Daniel briefly to get you started."

"No problem," I say, adjusting the hem of my black T-shirt over the Millennium Falcon skirt I'd chosen for that day. It *is* a problem; I'm behind in getting this dialogue and beat outline to Kyle, and I had a ton of work to do besides today, but I'm not going to say no to Lelani. I need her to see I'm up for this new commitment.

I follow Lelani's suit-clad form into the conference room, shoving my folder of work into Kyle's hands as I pass. Daniel is dressed more casually in dark jeans and a button-down white shirt, the effect being very "John Cho in *Selfie*." He cleans up amazingly well; I'd be hard pressed to recognize him on the street as the same man I'd met at the show.

I choose to sit across from Daniel with Lelani at the head of the table. Mere moments after sitting in our chairs, Lelani's phone begins to buzz. With an irritated look, she silences it and turns to us.

"MG, I have some paperwork for you to sign for the production company." She pulls a sheaf of papers out of a neat leather folder and pushes them across the table to me. I dutifully pretend to read them while secretly eyeballing Daniel across the table. So far, zero weirdness for how we met the other night, which is a relief.

He and Lelani make polite chit-chat while I sign my life away on several dotted lines. Nondisclosure *blah blah blah*. Basically, I won't be able to tell anyone outside my immediate team anything that comes of my work on the movie until the movie is released.

Lelani's phone buzzes again, and she growls. I pity that phone for the look she throws it. "I've got to take this, I guess. I'm so sorry for my rudeness." She stalks from the room with all the predatory grace of a pissed-off lioness.

I watch her go with fascination. It's rare to see Lelani with any feathers ruffled. I have to wonder if it was more than just a persistent phone. Maybe a text from a secret ex-lover. *No, wait.* I frown. A secret ex-lover could be Matteo, and *now* all I can think about is how Matteo has been distant and cranky. And then all I can do is imagine what sorts of texts Matteo would send to Lelani.

"Earth to MG." Daniel waves his hands in front of my eyes, and I start.

"Oh! I'm sorry," I say, sitting back and rubbing my arms. "I totally spaced out."

"Happens all the time. I work with writers, I know the face."

"The face?"

"Yeah, where you're dreaming up stuff out of the ether."

I laugh. "Any guy who uses the word 'ether' must be a writer himself." And he's right about making stuff up. Back in my real mind and body, I know my suspicions of Matteo and Lelani are completely unfounded.

"Nah," Daniel smiles, and I find myself watching the crinkle of laugh lines in the corners of his dark eyes more than I should. "I just work with a lot of them. In fact, that's our first meeting."

I force my attention back to the table as he slides another few papers in my direction. It's a schedule. Correct that—pages and *pages* of scheduled meetings. I try not to let my panic show on my face as I stare down at a column of days and times that are suddenly eaten up with this new project. What was I expecting? To keep my current schedule and just magic the work for this project? But staring at the list of dates makes my palms sweat, and I'm in serious danger of having a full-on early–Radioactive Man internal meltdown.

Daniel must think I'm studying the list to be thorough and plows on as if I'm *not* having an internal come-to-Jesus meeting. "So, this week we'll start the writers' meetings. Most of the storyboard and screenplay is set, but they're still tweaking, and I'd like to have you present for feedback on some of the critical story lines. Canon checks. Stuff like that."

I glance at the top of the list. These start *this* Friday. No rest for the wicked, I guess. I pull out my phone and start frantically entering dates and times.

"And then here"—Daniel leans across the table, and I catch a waft of subtle cologne—"are the dates for the costume meetings, and then on the second page are the set-visit dates for the iconic scenes where we want to have someone on hand familiar with the franchise to catch big mistakes."

I'm still thinking about the cologne. Not *woodsy*, exactly. Something familiar. I can't put my finger on it.

"Don't worry," he says, again misreading my silence for contemplation of the topic at hand instead of his cologne. "You won't need to do a lot, basically just listen to what we're doing and be available for questions. Costumes in particular are a place where I'm involved quite a bit at work, and Lelani thinks that's a particular interest area as well for you."

My eyebrow raises. "Costumes are of particular interest to your job?"

"Well, yes, I need to make sure they can function in a fight."

I am intrigued. "I just realized I have no earthly idea what it is that *you* do for the production team," I admit. "Is it terrible I assumed you were just a liaison? Like administrative? Check-the-boxes kind of guy?"

Which, as I look at him, relaxed in his jeans and work shirt, is utterly ridiculous. I'm usually great at reading people, and Daniel is *not* a sit-behind-a-desk person.

"Production assistant and specialist in combat choreography," he answers, smile still in evidence, with a mock mini bow and flourish. I refuse to acknowledge the dimple in his left cheek that has emerged. I'm too busy picking my proverbial jaw off the floor.

"*Combat choreography?* That. Is. *Awesome*," I manage. "The coolest." And then I realize that I sound like a fourteen-year-old girl, and I snap my mouth shut for a moment. "Er, I mean, what a fascinating line of work. How did you get started in it?" I shove aside the schedule, so as better to rest my elbows on the table.

"This is actually only my second film on my own," Daniel admits. "I came to the silver screen by way of the theater. Worked for a big-name choreographer for years out of college. My first movie solo— indie movie, probably nothing you've heard of—is actually where I met Lelani. And it's through her I landed this gig, actually."

Lelani, the patron saint of careers, apparently. Interesting. "What other movies have you done?"

"I mostly do *stage* combat choreography. Dance routines, fencing demonstrations. I did a pretty sweet combat scene for New York Comic-Con once, but the *Star Wars Experience* for *Rogue One* was maybe my favorite I've worked on."

I can't raise my eyebrows any more, so I just gape at him instead. "You do . . . *Star Wars* choreography?"

"Lightsaber duels, that sort of thing. It's my specialty, but I don't always get to use it. More often it's pirate sword fights, or mixed martial arts for camera."

"You have the best job ever."

"It is pretty cool." He smiles.

"Where did you learn all that? You look so young!" I flush, hoping he won't take this as impertinence or overt personal interest.

"Not as young as I look, but I started dance and martial arts when I was little, in Seoul. When we moved to California, it was a way for me to develop a community, so I kept dancing. The break-dancing movement was pretty strong at the time, and my high school had like five thousand kids, where my dance studio had only twenty. Way better odds for developing friends. I just never . . . stopped."

"I always wanted to learn to dance," I confide. "I'm hopeless. I have seven left feet. Truthfully, my dog is more graceful than I am, and he's—"

"A corgi! I know. I love those little dogs," Daniel finishes.

I must look alarmed because he continues, "Lawrence has a picture of you guys in his apartment."

"Do you have a dog, then?" This was a subject I could bond over. My love for Trog ran true and deep.

"No, my mother had Jack Russells when I was growing up; I always wanted a corgi, though. She's a horse lady. All the barn women have Jack Russells or corgis. I hated how those terriers dug, though. Ruined the carpet in my room."

I laugh. "That's amazing, I've never seen a horse in real life. How lucky you grew up with them! I can't quite picture you as a cowboy, though. Or cleaning up horse poop."

He shakes his head. "My mom boarded the horse at a stable. Luckily, I never had to do much more than go to the shows, pretend to be interested in her going around and around in circles, and then hug her and take pictures with her and her ribbons. Horses are large, smelly, and entirely time-sucking. I much prefer dogs."

My smile broadens. Friendship status achieved.

At this point we're gabbing like old friends, and I don't even hear Lelani sweep into the room. I give a start as she enters my peripheral vision. Her eyes dart between the two of us, and a look of satisfaction passes over her face.

"Making headway?" she asks, motioning to the schedule on the table.

"Yes, we were"—*just talking about our childhoods, no big deal*— "going over the dates for the writers' meetings," I finish, willing myself to keep the blush that threatens to rise at bay. We've strayed *way* off topic, but it was so easy. Daniel has an effortless charm, so it's like we've known each other forever.

He clears his throat and passes me another sheaf of papers. "I know you have things to do this morning, so now that the paperwork is signed, I'm allowed to give you these to study and provide feedback."

The stack of papers includes rough sketches of various superheroes in costume, and I flip through them like a starving woman choosing from too many restaurant menus. I don't know where to start, I'm so excited.

Lelani gathers up my signed documents and sticks them back in her folder, addressing Daniel. "Thanks for stopping by; I'll scan these and then have a courier deliver a copy to your office. MG, did you have any more questions for Daniel? I don't want to keep you."

I have *so* many questions for Daniel, most of them about *Star Wars* lightsaber duels. But I can't tear my eyes off the sheets in my hands for the time being. I get a chance to review costumes. For the Hooded Falcon movie. Here they are. In my hand. Awaiting *my* response. It's like Christmas has come early, without any of the family baggage. I simply shake my head, eyes trained on the first sketch, already formulating my thoughts.

"It was nice to meet you . . . again," Daniel says, rising and holding out his hand.

A genuine happiness I haven't felt in a long time rises in my chest. I feel suddenly like I'm right where I'm meant to be, and that isn't something I take lightly. I grasp his hand and give it a firm shake. "You have no idea how much I'm looking forward to this."

We follow Lelani from the room, but not before I think I glimpse that strange Cheshire cat smile one last time.

CHAPTER 10

"It's Friday, right? Office day? You're going to be late if you're riding your bike," Ryan says without preamble as he jogs into the kitchen, heads for the fridge, and pulls out an Odwalla green smoothie. The swelling on his face is totally gone, the bruise mostly faded, and he has just a few little nicks that remain from his encounter. And he's entirely too chipper for a man who narrowly avoided a mugging this week.

My gaze snaps to the clock from my iPad, where I've been reading up on Michele Clapton—the famed costume designer behind a lot of *Game of Thrones* looks. Rewatching the series has reminded me just how *amazing* the costume work is.

Damn. Ryan's right. Not much time. I hit the button for the Reddit home page, planning a quick perusal of the daily highlights before I go.

"Shopping for an upgrade?"

"Hmm?" I look up to see Ryan over my shoulder, reading my screen. I follow his gaze to where the front page of Reddit has a feed about whether or not *People* magazine's "Sexiest Man of the Year" really is *all that.* "Uh . . . no. Eyes on your own paper, Ryan. I was just reading the news."

He gives me a dubious smirk. "Sure."

I roll my eyes. "Like I care about"—I scan the preview of the comments—"Whalon Fox-Stevens. Whoever that is."

Ryan chokes on a laugh. "Wait, you haven't heard of Whalon Fox-Stevens? Do you live under a rock? Who do you think the tech guru is that basically runs your smartphone?"

"I prefer not to answer that question," I say loftily. My interest is piqued, though, so I do a quick Google search and *voilà*. There's the *LA Times* article proclaiming Whalon Fox-Stevens LA's most eligible bachelor. And then *People*'s Sexiest Man Alive. "But, uh, they're not *wrong* . . . hot damn, that's a beautiful man." Whalon's coppery skin and dark eyes hint of Middle Eastern descent, but it's his long lashes and tousled curls that momentarily halt my perusal. I catch Ryan's amused look.

"Which"—I say as I click the cover of my iPad firmly shut—"doesn't matter to me at all, because *I* have the best boyfriend in the world. And besides, as you've pointed out, I'm going to be late to work." Today *is* chock full. Work at Genius, and then my first writing meeting with the production team. And then *if* I have energy left, sketch out a few cosplay costume ideas I have to see if they seem marketable. I'm toying with the idea of launching my own geek-couture line in my imaginary spare time, and for that I need a collection—sample garments that show my unique vision.

"Did you sleep at all last night?" Ryan sips his smoothie and regards me over the bottle. "You look tired."

"Gee, thanks. Love you too." I scowl at him. "But thanks, *Mom*, I'm doing okay. I got at least five hours."

"You're really pushing; I'm worried you're not taking care of yourself," he observes. There's no malice or judgment in his tone, just concern.

"Says the dude who came home bleeding after being punched by a mugger?"

Ryan pointedly ignores me, so I change streams.

"I need to take a few pieces back over to L's this weekend. Do you want to come with me? Hang out a little?"

"Yeah." Ryan's eye roll is evident in his tone. "How's he doing?"

"Pissed," I answer, shoving the rest of my avocado toast into my mouth. I thought about my afternoon there. "Plus, he was all weird about this note from some guy named Stevie. My theory is that this assistant won't last much longer. I don't know that L is cut out for expanding his business bookings—he hates giving over control to someone else."

Ryan casts a quizzical eye over me, reaches for the remote on the table, and turns on the news. "Weirder than normal, or weird just because of Cleopatra?"

"Weirder than normal, and I think it was because of that note. L says he and 'Stevie' were friends a long time ago, but he didn't really seem happy about it. Maybe an old boyfriend who suddenly wants to rekindle something now that L is famous?"

Ryan's thinking face is on, gazing off into space.

My own brows furrow, sussing out his reaction. Ryan should have just shrugged this off. "Have *you* heard him talk about a Stevie before? You've known him longer." I wonder if this is some torrid affair I don't know about.

Ryan slowly shakes his head. "It sounds familiar, but I can't place a face." He gives a comically overdone shrug like he's trying to convince himself. "Did L say how long ago?"

"Nope." I stand and head for the door. "Just one of those things where I realize I don't know everything about L. Maybe he's got a secret life as an ex-spy or something. The Casey stuff certainly came out of nowhere. They say you never know people fully, even those close to you."

Ryan's expression flashes through several emotions I don't understand. I'm about to question his odd reaction when I realize he's not even really watching me; he's looking over my shoulder at the news. I turn to see what's captured his attention. The local news. I'm just in time to catch the flash of a picture on the screen—a Latino man—before it disappears. Something seems familiar about the face, so I grab the remote from Ryan's hand, and with two pushes of the buttons, the volume booms through the kitchen.

"Investigation is ongoing, but the victim from a party this weekend has been identified as Louis Castilla. The coroner reports that this is an unusual case of a drug overdose—the drug in question is one of the new designer drugs whose popularity is sweeping the nation. We'll have more about this story at nine tonight, along with ways you can talk to your teen about avoiding these dangerous trends. The mayor of Los Angeles is expected to give a statement later this morning about the emerging epidemic in the United States, and LA's response to the ongoing war on drugs. Back to you, Rosa."

As the camera pulls out, I suck in a breath in recognition—they're the windows of the tiny nightclub where Ryan and I attended the party. My gaze flicks to Ryan.

"They said 'party.' Like the party we went to?"

Silence from Ryan. He obviously just saw the same report; he doesn't know any more than I do.

I glance at the television again. I'm too late; the little scrolling information thing on the bottom has already disappeared, and the anchors are back and talking about the weather. "I never heard about someone OD'ing, did you?"

"The news rarely reports on drug overdoses," Ryan replies. But his eyes are still glued to the screen. He appears to be thinking. "Not unless there's something about it that makes it newsworthy. They love a good scare story. Remember that case of the guy who did bath salts and tried to eat people's faces?"

"Okay . . . well, they reported on this one. And it was at the Zebra. So, I'm guessing it happened after we left." I'm already opening my iPad up. Instead of going to my usual Twitter and Reddit feeds, I do a specific Google search. None of the mainstream news outlets picked the story up, but a local paper has a small blurb about it.

"Private party attendee found dead in lounge parking lot." The date on the piece was yesterday, so I *hadn't* missed it being in the news. It hadn't been reported until today.

"Well, that's unfortunate," I say, scrolling through the rest of the article. "It just states that police were called after someone checked the car in the morning, and that no foul play was suspected after they confirmed a drug overdose. I guess it was sort of business as usual until the coroner discovered it was a designer drug they hadn't seen before." The same picture used in the news lurks at the bottom of the page with a brief description of Louis.

"Hmm," Ryan says, still staring blankly at the screen. It's like he's not even listening.

"It's sad," I say again. Drug overdose. My mind flashes directly to the strung-out guy at the party. And then the face of the dead man clicks into place too. The young queen out on the dance floor who had looked so, *so* drunk. "I think I saw him. What if it was those drugs from the party?" What if I'd *seen* the guy who sold that poor kid the drugs that killed him?

Ryan's gaze focuses on me, sharp and intent. "What do you mean?"

"There was this guy peddling pills at the party. He ran into me, tried to sell me some. I turned him down—obviously—but my guess is that he found someone who *didn't*." I motion to the screen. "It's just sad that this is what drugs do to people."

"Agreed," Ryan says, eyes back on the TV.

The news shows that today's weather looks like a good day for my bike; I have to get going *now* if I'm going to make it to work on time. Looks like my coffee habit is going to have to sit out a day again. I down the rest of my juice and head out of the kitchen. "Truthfully, if it's the pills I saw, they looked homemade. Just like Mom used to make. Yum yum. Who knows what was in them?"

Ryan doesn't laugh at my halfhearted joke.

"Okay, *welp*, have a good day," I say, heading for my room. Tough crowd.

Speaking of, I know I should be thinking about work this morning, but as I grab my shoes and bag and head out the front door, I just can't shake the mental picture of the young queen out on the dance floor. If I'm right, and that queen was Louis, then a call to Lawrence is warranted to make sure he doesn't need a shoulder to lean on.

"Great, thank you, Tejshwara, for the update on our sales figures," Casey Junior says from his relaxed position in the deep leather chair at the head of the conference table.

Tej sits just to the left of Casey, across from Lelani. I'm farther down the table, near the back of the room—mostly because I went to the bathroom to try and tame my fading-lilac mane into some semblance of a polished executive style. No one at the office ever cares that my hair is colored—I love that about my workplace—but I try to draw the line at looking like a ragamuffin. I make a mental note that I need a color, because while I'm #grayhairdontcare, I don't like to let it go too long.

Casey nods to Lelani in some prearranged signal, and she stands to address the room. "We also have a new team member to introduce. I'd like to welcome Paige DiGregorio; she'll be assisting on art for *The Hooded Falcon* part time. Mondays, Wednesdays, and Fridays, when MG is here at the office, at least for a bit, so that she and MG can work as a team."

The large double door at the back of the room gives a creak, and we all turn dramatically to watch the entrance of our newest bunkmate.

Paige rolls into the room, and I hear someone suck in a breath to my right. The chair is a surprise for those of us in the room, but Paige seems to expect the reaction and her face remains carefully neutral.

Blonde hair, icy eyes, fierce blue eyeliner, and *damn*, that girl is wearing sequined, fingerless gloves. Any person who wears sequins on their first day is an automatic friend of mine.

"Hello, everyone," she says, rolling to a stop at the end of the table and waving.

Silence.

I look to my left and to my right. Every single pair of eyes in the room is set to "goggle," and you have to wonder if anyone has ever seen a person in a wheelchair before.

Lelani is the only one aside from me who seems to just take Paige's appearance in stride, though she obviously had a heads-up, given she conducted the interview. "Paige joins us from San Diego; she's a graduate of the Art Institute and did work with Pixar until her move to LA. Anything I missed?"

Impressive résumé. We pivot as one, our chairs squeaking, to peer at Paige again.

She seems unaffected by the examination. "Nope, that about covers it. I'm excited to be working for Genius."

Casey Junior coughs, and several of the executives shuffle some papers in response. "Welcome, Paige. All right, then. We'll move on to our green-light meeting. We've got Hooded Falcon business . . . Andy, why don't you fill us in first, and then Michael can report on the movie."

While Andy presents our story line for the next issue, I feel Paige's eyes on me. I turn and offer a small friendly smile, but it's met with cool acknowledgment instead of a returned smile. Her ice-blue eyes are lined with the neatest cat eyeliner—L would adore this girl.

Casey's voice breaks into my thoughts. "Michael, please share with the team about your involvement with the movie team."

I swivel my chair back to center, where I find everyone else at the table looking at me. As I rise to give my report, I note that Paige's eyebrows rise. She'd been staring expectantly at Kyle, seated to my right. It's not unexpected—my boss *insists* on calling me Michael. It's either call me that or admit that he thought I was a man when he first agreed to interview me off my résumé. He makes a point of leaving off the

"Grace" and *never* calls me MG. Not even Ms. Martin. Michael—every bat time, every bat channel.

I fill the room in on the meetings planned for the week and promise to give a full report back for the next executive meeting. It feels nice to have this unique responsibility.

"Okay, moving on," Casey Junior intones, shuffling his papers. "New project proposals."

My heart starts to beat a little faster. The feeling of "all is right in the Universe" evaporates immediately.

"Andy, why don't you give us an overview, and we can look specifically at Kyle and Michael's proposals since their series are wrapping up this season."

Andy shoots me a look. He has no idea what I'm presenting. Heck, *I* have less than a full idea of what I'm presenting. My heart hammers inside my chest now. This is so far away from the woman I was six months ago at Genius. When I worked hard to "stick it to the man" by being perfectly prepared in every way. Now I've got too much going on. Not for the first time I briefly wonder if deciding to pursue my passion for fashion and costume design—to have *everything*—was the wrong choice. I listen as Andy presents the overview of the smaller projects that are rolling right now. And then everyone is looking at me.

"Michael?" Casey prompts, and I swallow. How am I going to get out of this? I haven't actually prepared *anything*. Nothing. Nada . . .

"Space monkeys versus robots." The words are out before I can stop them.

"Space . . . monkeys?" Casey asks, meaty brows pulled down over his eyes.

"Chimpanzees," I clarify. I guess if this is the hill my brain has picked, I am going to die on it.

Kyle and Simon look as if someone stuffed live goldfish in their mouths, and Lelani frowns at me in an uncharacteristic break from her typical serene polish. I brace for the torrent of disappointment sure to follow my stupid proclamation.

"Elaborate," Casey Junior says.

My eyes fly open. *Elaborate?*

"Er . . . ," I stammer, fishing around in my brain for something. Anything. Go-go-gadget imagination. "It would be a smart satire of all the smash-and-bang comics out right now. Ray guns, spaceships, galactic duels. But tongue-in-cheek, so playing off tropes and acknowledging it. That sort of thing." I pray to all the old gods and new that somehow he'll move on and not ask any more detailed questions. Usually I have sketches, story lines.

Casey Junior considers me at great length over the glossy top of the table. It takes everything in me to maintain eye contact. Here it comes; I see the words forming in his eyes before they reach his lips: *Michael, you've lost your touch. Schedule a private meeting with me to discuss your future at this company.*

"I like it."

I blink. *What?*

Casey misses my surprise, though, and starts to shuffle through his papers again, already on to the next agenda item. "This one is something I can see taking off."

And then it hits me. Of course he can—I first had the idea because I was bemoaning mainstream comics. It's robots, monkeys, space, and ray guns. *Okay, fine,* those sound awesome independently. But those are the sorts of things that drive me crazy working on the new *Hooded Falcon.* There's only action, no heart. Panic rises in my chest. Now I have another personal project—one I haven't thought through at *all*— and it doesn't even fulfill my goal to reach a different market. At least I'd slid the satire thing in there—*maybe* this could work. Maybe. Or I'd be drawing space monkeys for years to come, because Murphy's Law says that this will be the first project of mine to be long-lived.

Casey glances up at me one last time and offers a rare . . . I won't say smile, but a lift of the corners of his mouth. It doesn't do much to improve his "bald and large pro wrestler in a suit" bearing. "Usually your ideas are more touchy-feely; it's nice to see you stepping outside your comfort zone. Well done."

Touchy-feely? Excuse me? Comfort zone? What the hell now? He thinks that just because I care about the world and I'm a woman, my ideas are touchy-feely?

Lelani and I connect gazes approximately point three seconds before my mind implodes and something comes out of my mouth that will terminate my employment here. He can take that *warped* "attagirl" and stick it right where the sun don't shi—

"I *think* what Mr. Casey is trying to say"—Lelani must sense the impending detonation, or the impending lawsuit—"is that we appreciate that you always have an eye toward innovation and progressing our industry into new markets. And that this project is different from your previous projects, but no less a possible vehicle for social change or the furthering of our business. I can assure you we admire our employees who are so flexible in their creative endeavors."

Dead silence in the room—everyone is quiet, now having figured out that Casey Junior has taken a severe misstep in his language. Probably waiting for the show, since I'm not exactly known for my ability to contain my less-than-proper thoughts in the boardroom.

"Er. Yes. Yes, I mean that." Casey throws Lelani a grateful look, and she matches it with a steely one of her own. Just because she's bailed his ass out of this one, it doesn't mean she didn't pick up on the sexist slight. My previous projects—though aimed toward a female readership—were less than "touchy-feely," and I like action as much as the next guy.

And yet, after Lelani's compliment—no matter the reason she had to give it—my mouth clicks shut and my inner laser beams power down. How does she *do* that? Her cool demeanor and words, even though I *know* they're meant to de-escalate, soothe the beast inside. I'm now resolved to making this little slip-up work for me. I'll make these monkeys "touchy-feely social-justice warrior" if it's the death of me and wrap them in space-opera flashbang. That's what it's about, right? Lelani said it herself. I'm not a one-trick pony. I can take *anything* and make it mine . . . including, apparently, space monkeys.

The meeting moves on, and I hardly pay attention. My brain is already stressing about this new project. Beside me, Paige is studying me like a riddle. And not one she particularly enjoys. I offer her a small smile again. Nothing.

When the meeting wraps up, everyone shuffles for the door, and I'm surprised that no one stops to talk further with Paige. She tosses her folder of meeting materials into her lap and spins to follow Kyle out the door, but I stop her.

"I just wanted to introduce myself; it's nice to have another woman here." I can't help it; I'm excited our numbers are increasing.

Paige turns slightly back to study me again. "I heard your name in the meeting. Michael, right?" She doesn't seem overly excited that I'm following her out the door and into the elevator lobby.

"Michael-Grace, but seriously don't call me that. MG, please."

"MG," she confirms. "Pronouns?"

I blink. "Er, 'she' works fine for me. You?" I've never actually been asked that before at work, though it's a common question at Lawrence's shows.

"She/Her." Paige hesitates. "With a name like Michael . . . well, I figured I'd check."

Touché. "Well, it was really thoughtful of you. Are you on your way to the office?"

"Yeah, you?"

"Yep."

Silence descends, and we stare at the polished stainless-steel doors of the elevator. I glance down, and her gloves catch my attention again.

They are lovely; I can tell from here that they're handmade, or really high end. The cuffs look hand stitched.

Paige catches me looking, and her face sours.

"I hope I'm not overstepping here, but—"

"Go ahead and ask," she sighs. Her tone is acerbic, and it catches me by surprise.

"Er . . . okay. Where did you get those gloves? They look handmade."

It's Paige's turn to goggle at me like she's never seen a girl with purple hair before. "What?"

"Your gloves," I ask again, motioning to her hand. "The sequins. They're amazing, and they look hand sewn."

Paige laughs, a sudden lightness flooding her face. "That's the question? About my *gloves*?"

"I sew. Design, really," I say in defense. I hate getting laughed at. "I just—"

"No, it's fine. Really refreshing, actually. I made them myself. I sew in the evenings." She pauses and studies me again as the elevator dings. "Thanks."

I let her enter the elevator first and then follow, pressing the button for our floor.

"So how long have you worked here?" she asks when the elevator doors close.

"Oh, about five years."

"And Andy?"

"I think about eight. Simon and Kyle were here before me, and Tej was hired the same year. Lelani was just hired this year."

"So, I guess you're sorta the OG. Woman, I mean."

"Yeah, I guess." I offer her a small smile again. "It's really good to have you here. It's almost even numbers now on our team, and that's unusual in this business."

"Yeah, I'm not so sure everyone's happy about that." Paige rolls her eyes.

"It's almost like they fear it's going to stop being a comic book company if the majority shifts. Like we'll start publishing stories about tampons instead of comics."

Paige snorts.

"Here's the final question, though: Bat or Supe?"

She doesn't hesitate. "Batman. Is there even a question?"

"Hey now," I say, wounded to my very core. "Superman is a social-justice warrior—"

Paige snorts again. "He's a picture of patriarchal domineering. Damsel in distress. Pearls and vacuum cleaners."

"Just because he's a product of that time, doesn't mean he buys into it . . . Okay, fine. He's ridiculous sometimes. But I admire his moral fiber, and the golden age when a superhero was a *superhero*, you know? Batman is just . . ." I waggle my hand back and forth.

"Morally ambiguous? Yeah, but that's what I love about him. He's not afraid to let a little revenge get in the way of good crime-fighting. It makes *such* a better story."

I could discuss this all day, and frequently have. "I'll agree to disagree for now. I suppose it doesn't matter if you are misled about the best superhero; what matters is, can you *draw*?"

The smile that flashes across her face is genuine, and blinding. "You bet your ass I can."

I smile back as I disembark the elevator after her. "You'll get along *just* fine here then. Kyle and Simon are cool. Andy's a bit of a tool"—I wince at my flagrant abuse of my supervisor, but Paige just laughs—"er, but he's nice enough."

We pass reception, and just before we reach our portion of cubicles, Paige turns to me. "Thanks for being welcoming."

"No problem, I'm not really doing anything for you I wouldn't do for another team member, though. I'd warn *anyone* that Andy is sort of a tool . . ."

She makes another derisive noise. "Well, I appreciate that attitude. Not everyone is that . . . progressive. I didn't really think about it before I left Pixar. I just wanted to do something new; I didn't think about the interview process."

I groan, sympathizing. "This industry is rough. Try doing it with a name like Michael."

Her gaze flicks down to her chair and back up, and she raises an eyebrow in challenge.

Point taken. "Fair enough. All I'm saying is that I had a rough time, too, even though it was a few years ago. If mine was that tough, I can imagine yours was worse." I ponder a moment. "Was it really that bad?"

"We'll just say not many of them liked my . . . outfit."

I sigh. "I keep thinking we're making headway in this industry, and then sometimes I wonder." I really want Paige to feel welcome. No, more than that, I want to talk to her about gloves and sewing, and super-fierce makeup. I want to be her friend for real.

An insane thought fills my head, and I'm speaking before I can even think it through fully. "I'm having a party next weekend at my house. Work people. You should come."

Another small smile. "Okay. But only if you tell me more about your designing."

"Definitely." *As if she could stop me.*

Kyle and Simon have apparently been waiting for our entrance, because Kyle elbows Simon so hard he falls off the desk where he's been sitting with his Converse Chucks on his chair.

"Oh, hey . . . Hey, Paige. I'm Simon. I just wanted to introduce myself," he says once he jumps to his feet with more grace than someone like him ought to have. I suppose all the LARPing is paying off.

"Hi, Simon, it's nice to meet you." The icy mask of indifference is back over Paige's face when I glance down.

Simon looks like the thirteen-year-old who has stopped the cheerleader in the hallway of the school to ask her to the dance but now can't do anything except clutch his book and stare at her.

"Uh . . . are you coming to MG's party?" Paige asks, and the statement goes along so well with my high school metaphor, I have to blink.

Kyle gives a chortle. "MG's . . . party?"

Simon and Kyle have turned to stare, and I twitch uncomfortably.

"Ah, yeah, I mentioned it to you guys. Next weekend, I'm having work people over, remember?" I never have parties. Ever. I've attended exactly one non-work-function party in all my time here, and that was because Matteo accepted for me. "I thought maybe Paige might like to come and hang out and get to know her new coworkers," I say, nodding exaggeratedly.

"Oh. Yes. Definitely." Kyle says, with as much good acting as the original Power Rangers. "Er, what time . . . again? Can you remind me—us?"

Okay, fine, we're not going to win any Oscars.

I nod. "Six o'clock next Sat—"

Kyle shakes his head vehemently, so I change tactics. "Friday? Definitely Friday after work. I'm ordering pizza, movie night. Totally what I'd already planned."

I look at Simon next. Everyone nods like little bobbleheads.

Paige suspects this is some sort of pity invite—it's written all over her face. I start planning a defense when Simon saves my rear end.

"So, Paige." His awkwardness hasn't faded, and his gaze is riveted to Paige's chair. Silence stretches as Simon fumbles for words, and I close my eyes, waiting for him to blurt out what I know is coming.

"Alligator," Paige says, voice back to frosty.

My eyes fly open, and I turn to look at her. Simon and Kyle are already regarding her with horror. "What?"

"I know that's what you're all wondering."

Simon's jaw literally drops open. *"Really?"*

Paige snorts. "No. But it sure is fun. You can tell people *anything* and they believe it. I just try to have fun with it when people stare."

Simon's ears redden. "I wasn't . . ."

She shrugs and heads for the empty desk. "You were."

Kyle coughs. "You were, dude."

Simon reddens further if it's possible. "Okay, I was, but not for . . . not for that. Well, I mean, I was *looking* at that but—"

I cut him a look that I hope clearly communicates that he should stop talking.

He takes a deep breath and steadies himself. He rolls his shoulder and walks over to where Paige is unloading a messenger bag of pens and a notebook onto the desk surface. He sticks his hand out. "Okay, I'm sorry, I was unintentionally rude, and I apologize. I'll try again. Hi, Paige, I'm Simon. I'm sorry I'm an idiot when I meet pretty girls, but I'm looking forward to working with you."

Paige's face whips up to meet his like she's afraid he's making fun of her, but her face softens when she sees his obvious distress. She reaches out and shakes his hand. "Nice to meet you, Simon. Y'know, for a geeky dude, you have a pretty good grip. I hate when people give me the limp-fish handshake."

Preach, sister.

Simon takes his hand back, and rubs the back of his neck. "I mean, I work out. A little. Training, really—"

"LARPing," Kyle supplies helpfully.

"—yeah, LARPing." He coughs, then decides to just own it, and shrugs. "I'm training to do sword combat stuff. It really is cool. Better in person than me explaining, I promise."

Page looks at him like he's declared his ambition is to play for the band in the Tatooine cantina. And then she smiles slightly, not missing the implied invite. "LARPing, huh? Never got into that. I like to rock climb on the weekends, and any of you are welcome to join me anytime."

Simon looks like he's not sure if it's a joke or not. "Really?"

Paige: "Yes, really. Upper body strength—"

"No, I meant, really, I—we—could come?"

Paige laughs outright. "Yeah, any of you are welcome to come. You guys are all a little weird, but I think I'll take it."

Simon flushes. "Cool. Now. Let's talk business. What are you currently reading? And what do you think about the current run of *The Hooded Falcon*?"

Paige's eyes light up. "I'm a huge fan of Oracle, or anything Gail Simone draws."

I leave them to their conversation and sit down at my own desk, finally taking a moment for a breath. I'd been nervous about adding another person, but Paige seems to be awesome. I smirk as a line from one of my favorite Netflix binges surfaces in my mind. Maybe things are finally lining up for ole Liz Lemon. I have to only hope that things with the case will resolve this nicely.

CHAPTER 11

By later that afternoon, Lawrence hasn't returned my calls or my texts—a bad sign. I probably should swing by to make sure he's okay. I don't think my coworkers will notice if I cut out a *little* early, though I feel somewhat guilty that it's to pay a personal visit to a friend.

I'm also not getting a lot done at my desk at work, anyhow. My Hooded Falcon stuff is coming along okay; I'm on autopilot with the dialogue, but it's not bad. What I'm struggling with is the end of *Hero Girls* and any sort of idea for the new pet project I accidentally pitched at the meeting. It's like the creative well inside of me has gone still, dark, and silent, receding down to a winter level. Each time I try out an idea or a set of possible characters, it just feels flat. Off. Trite, tried, or tired. The three *T*s of death, in my way of thinking. What I really *want* is to reach a new audience. An audience for whom I can open a world to the wonder of comic books. And that certainly isn't going to happen with robot aliens versus cowboy chimpanzees, or whatever. *Actually, maybe something outlandish could be fun to write, if I can make it* me . . . I mentally smack myself on the head.

It's bad when I'm actually considering writing about cowboy chimpanzees. There's no true inspiration there. No message. No target audience other than "guys who like robot aliens versus random things." Sure, I can stick social justice and satire in it, but how many people will get the deeper heart of that satire? *That's* what I show up to work for. To wrap a deeper truth in a good story and awesome art. To inspire. To change the world, one *fun* page at a time.

I shove away from my desk and growl.

"Good day at the office?" Kyle asks, not even lifting his head from his work. "I swear you've growled more today than Simon's stomach."

"Shut up, dude. You know I'm following a timed diet this week," Simon shoots back.

I look between them.

"Simon is trying to *get fit*"—Kyle uses air quotes—"for LARPing." I think it's a pretty accusatory tone for someone who *actively* did the same thing.

"It requires stamina *and* strength," Simon argues back. "People who do real combat are *athletes.*"

It devolves into a conversation about knights and the different types of armor and whether or not someone had to actually *be* fit to kill someone with a sword.

"Okay, well, I'll leave you to your *work*," I say maybe five minutes into the debate. "I have that meeting with the production crew this afternoon."

Andy, who has largely been ignoring the arms discussion, turns around at his desk and flops blond hair back over his shoulder. "Let us know how it goes. And don't forget Ms. Kalapulani wants a report about the project next week, so keep notes."

"Ms. Kalapulani?"

Andy flushes, and I can tell he's embarrassed by my catch. Usually we call her Lelani—both to her face and within the team. She's never insisted either way, so I am surprised he's changed.

I don't press him on it. So, he's trying to kiss ass. Or feels awkward calling his boss by her first name. Fine, whatever. His deal. I have no problem addressing Andy as *Andy.* My body will be dead and cold before I call him Mr. Dermot.

"See you all later." No arguments, just some generalized waving, so I head out.

Outside, the day is gray and blustery; fall is on its way. I'd prefer bright sunny skies and crisp temperatures to the slightly damp threat of possible rain in the air. Rain makes things cold, and I hate being cold.

I swing my messenger bag over my back, thankful it's waterproof, and settle my helmet on my head with the smallest pang of sympathy for my hair. It will suck to arrive at my very first meeting with helmet hair, but it would suck worse to end up with no brain. And if you've ever cycled in LA, you know that you can't count on drivers being any sort of merciful to a bicyclist. If I play my cards right, I'll have enough time to check on Lawrence and either bike to my house for my car or call a car to get to the meeting.

I try to be ultra-alert while I'm biking. Someone once likened commuting by bike in LA to a roller derby, and they weren't far off. In truth, it's a bit of what appeals to me. I don't like feeling like I might get squashed at any moment, but the *reactivity* of it versus the stop-and-go grind of traffic. I can go around a jam, take a shortcut, double back—to me it's worth the risk for the flexibility. But today my mind barely registers the red-painted curbs or white pylons of the bike-safe area as they flash by. On autopilot, my brain races as I pedal. The constant motion sometimes shakes loose my best ideas. I often have breakthroughs on my projects during my commute. Instead of working on a new comic, my brain has gone straight back to its current obsession: the Golden Arrow. Specifically, the party I'd gone to, the queen I'd seen dancing, the drugs, the flasks, the golden stickers . . . and the sense that I'm living in some sort of *constructed narrative*. I can't come up with any better way of describing what I feel. As a writer, I sense the presence of *story*, and this all feels like one great big setup, an elaborate . . . something. *But what?* Is the Golden Arrow really this bored that he's planning parties and attending them? Is this *all* a media stunt—a ploy to increase his celebrity status? Why not just go to Casey Junior and take the reward if this is about recognition or money?

And then there's the report from the two drug dealers. One *could* conclude the Golden Arrow is indeed back at the tie-up-bad-guys game. But why? Why tie up guys in secret if at the same time you're attending secret parties to gain cachet? None of it makes sense.

The blaring of a horn brings my attention fully back to the road, and I stop just in time to avoid running into a car parked at a stop sign.

"Sorry!" I yell, getting a middle finger in response. Ah, California. Land of the eloquent.

With a quick glance around, I pedal forward, determined to watch more carefully. I'm not any help to the case if I wind up Ron-Karr all over the pavement.

I'm just about to cross the street when I catch sight of a figure I think seems familiar. It takes a moment to place the easy stroll, compact build, and dark hair, but finally it clicks into place: Daniel Kim. The very same Daniel Kim I'm about to meet in an hour at a meeting on the other side of town. On instinct, I slow my advance, eyes scanning the street. He's walking south, a few blocks from Lawrence's, but pretty far from both the office and his dance studio on Third. It's none of my business, I know this, but . . . there's a strum of *mystery* deep in my soul that sounds as I peruse the scene.

Abruptly, I pedal back to the corner I've just left and dismount as much behind a trash can as I can manage. From here I can watch without being detected. I nearly laugh out loud at myself. *Watch what,* though? Watch a guy from my office walk down the street, apparently. I've officially crossed into stalker territory, and I've made my mind up to get on my bike and go say hello when Daniel does something that sets the alarm bells off in my head.

He looks around him, scanning the street—I drop back down behind the trash can—before turning and ducking into a narrow alcove just beyond a little shop's windows. The neighborhood here isn't bad, but it's not the greatest, and the set of bars over the window prevents me from really seeing what he's doing. His movements seem furtive. But what could Golden Boy Daniel Kim possibly be doing that requires stealth?

I have to get a better look. Before I've thought it through, I've locked my bike to the light pole and crossed to the opposite side of the street, straining to keep eyes on Daniel the entire time. He seems to be waiting outside a tiny door, intermittently talking into a buzzer box. The store across the way has a useful sidewalk rack out, so I flip idly through a display of men's secondhand blazers, keeping myself concealed.

I really shouldn't be doing this. This is insanity. This is me, reading too many graphic novels and thinking too much about the Golden Arrow. *This* is the crap that gets me in trouble with Matteo when I decide to play detective on my own. Daniel could just be visiting his girlfriend, or his mistress. Or his mistress's girlfriend—you know, normal American stuff. *Or*, I note with intense alarm, *he could be handing someone something gold and glittery through a door.*

I can't quite see the face of the other person; it's obscured by shadow and the only partially open door, but I know my costumes, and I know my fabric. And the little slip that Daniel makes in handing over the pile he's holding is enough for me to identify a mask and cape. A gold mask and cape.

I try and manage the surge of possibilities that blossom to life in my head. This could all be coincidental. This could be totally explained by normal human rationale. *Or* I just stumbled onto something big. And with this opening, my imagination is off and soaring—no chance of me reining it in at this point. Because Daniel Kim isn't just your normal human being. I fairly tick off his credentials on my fingers as I know them. He's athletic, and *acrobatic*. Check. What did those dealers say? They were tied up by a ninja. Seems to me that someone with an advanced background in dance and acrobatics could essentially *be* a ninja. He's a comic book enthusiast, with specific knowledge about *The Hooded Falcon*, and he's out here, skulking about in a shadowy doorway *with a cape and a mask*. My instant suspicion is that if Daniel Kim isn't at the very least in league with the Golden Arrow, he's the Golden Arrow himself. He's handing a cape to someone . . . it could be his teammate!

The person behind the door. The person behind the door could very well be the vigilante I'm looking for. This is critical information if my theory is going to have legs to stand on. There's no way I can go to Matteo with something so flimsy as "a guy I know handed someone a stack of fabric"; I've got to be sure when I throw Daniel Kim under the bus. And more importantly, if I can get inside information, I might be able to figure out what he knows. Everyone will talk to a friend; not everyone will talk to the police.

I stand back from the rack, determined to cross the street and get a look at the face of the person behind the door when I unknowingly back straight into the pathway of someone walking on the sidewalk. I'd forgotten it was the middle of the day and that we were in broad daylight in public.

But as I hurtle toward the pavement, the hands that wrap around my waist to try and keep me upright are surprisingly, and uncomfortably, familiar.

The pair of oxfords on the pavement I dangle mere inches above are familiar.

I've *definitely* taken off the pair of gray work slacks that are cuffed above the oxfords, and as the person slowly helps me back up to my feet, I know exactly who I'm going to see.

I school my features into careful surprise by the time they pass a work shirt, cuffed at the elbows, and lastly, Matteo's rather shocked face.

"Oh, hello, sweetie," I say, as if I trip my boyfriend on street corners outside of secondhand stores all the time.

108

His face wears instant suspicion. "MG. What are you doing out here?"

Damn me and my open-book face. I must look guilty despite my attempt not to. *I am most definitely not out following someone I now suspect to be the Golden Arrow like some crazy person.*

"Nothing," I say and then realize immediately that's a guilty-person answer. "Shopping, I mean. Not *nothing*, that would be stupid. I'm not just standing on some random street doing *nothing.*" *Shut up, MG, shut up.*

Matteo's eyes dart around, first to the glass table with bird figurines on it that I wouldn't be caught dead buying and then to the tub of five-dollar shoes that aren't any more my style than the birds.

"Blazers," I say, waving at the rack. "You know, for"—*think quick, MG*—"one of Lawrence's costumes. Halloween. Costume." Maybe a quick smile to cover my complete inadequacy as a liar?

Matteo's not buying it. He nods slowly, gaze passing over the rack of decidedly dowdy and unbedazzled old-man blazers.

I force a cheery laugh. "You know us fashion designers, always looking for something boring to change into something amazing. I'm planning on adding a double breast with some sequins and stoning the back like an Elvis jacket, what do you think?" I'm full-on *rambling* now, but I'm hoping to throw enough sewing jargon into my explanation that I lose Matteo.

It works; he nods again, this time a little more convinced. "Oh, okay, that sounds great. You always do good work. Anyhow, you okay? You didn't hit the sidewalk, did you?"

"No, I'm okay." I rub my middle, where being caught has caused some major chafing under my shirt, though. He looks like he's going to start asking more questions, so I decide to flip the tables. "What are you doing out here in the middle of the day?"

It's Matteo's turn to smile, though his looks forced too. "I'm not a vampire, I do most of my work during the day."

"Not lately," I remind him.

"No, not lately," he agrees with a sigh. "I'm actually out for some reconnaissance on Ryan's assailant." His gaze narrows suddenly, and he looks me up and down as if a light bulb just popped on over his head. "You're not out here following me, are you? MG, I've told you *so* many times to let me do my job. I don't like having to worry about you *and* the case at the same time. You promised—"

"I am definitely not out here following you," I say with conviction. Take me to a lie detector; I'd pass that. "You tripped over *me*, remember? And anyhow, if I were following you, I'd be doing a pretty bad job if I knocked you to the ground, right?"

The suspicion abates in his expression, but not fully. That gut of his is telling him I'm up to something, and unfortunately for me, he's right.

"Ryan's assailant, though. In this neighborhood?" I look around but don't have to feign the look of unease. "This is so close to L's."

"I thought that too." Matteo frowns. "Anyhow, I've got to get going. I'll see you later, okay?"

"Okay," I agree. We sort of awkwardly hug—I'm never sure what the protocol is when he's on the job—and he heads off down the sidewalk.

I instantly turn to the opposite street, only to find it completely devoid of Daniel's form. *Rats.* Somewhere in the five minutes I've been talking with Matteo, he's gone, as is my chance to see who lives there. I note the address and make a point to peruse the blazers for a good five more minutes in case Matteo checks my alibi. I contemplate following *him* but decide against it. I've done enough of my own sleuthing for the time being, and it's netted me a fairly interesting theory. Now I just need to prove that Daniel Kim is involved. Making a show of deciding none of the blazers work for me, I go and unlock my bike, only just now realizing that I've been "shopping" for the last ten minutes with my helmet on my head. Brilliant. No wonder Matteo suspected something was up.

I sigh, hop on my bike, and pedal hard for Lawrence's.

CHAPTER 12

A few streets down, I turn right, Lawrence's little shop within view.

And just in time too. The threatening humidity starts to morph into more serious mist, and my clothes are absorbing liquid at an alarming rate. I pray I make it to the shop before I'm soaked or struck by lightning. As if in response to my thoughts, a low rumble of thunder rolls through the gray clouds above me. *Okay, or both. Thanks, universe.*

I screech to a stop on L's sidewalk and two-step my bike around the back, through the gate to the parking area. It takes me but a moment to secure the bike in my standard place—the gas meter pipe—and try the door. Locked. I spin around, verifying his car is parked by the trash can, then pull out my phone.

Hey L, Let me in.

I type, hugging the building in hopes the small overhang over the door will protect me from the big fat raindrops now falling perilously from the sky.

Came to check on you. I'm out back. Starting to rain.

I wait, staring at my phone for a response. Droplets of cold water threaten to form on the end of my nose while I wait. Finally, three dots appear and my shoulders relax. "Thank God," I mutter even before the words *hang on* show up on my screen.

Another rumble of thunder, and the skies open up. Gone are the big raindrops, and in their place a shower of cold rain. Seconds later, I hear the lock of the door rattling.

"Saved by the—" Usually L opens the door and I barge in. It's our thing. But somehow our typical dance steps are reversed, because instead of stepping aside to allow me in, L steps out onto the concrete pad I'm standing on. I bounce off his muscled chest and ricochet off the brick around the doorframe into the rain.

"Sorry. You okay?" L's hand shoots out to steady me.

"Yeah, just . . . wet." I look down at my pants, which are basically soaked through. "Maybe out of the rain would be good?"

Lawrence hesitates a moment, which is either rude or *weird*. "Come on in; let's get you dried off. I guess you probably can't bike in the rain."

I eye him skeptically as I follow his retreating back into the shop. Given I've just arrived, I find it an affront that he's planning my exit—or noting the lack of it. "Yeah, I guess not," I agree, trying to keep the sarcasm out of my voice. I ditch my helmet just inside the door, shivering as icy rivulets skate down the back of my shirt. "Especially since I came here specifically to check on *you*. You haven't answered my texts. I wanted to make sure you're okay."

L pauses just past the little nook of an office and reaches inside the closet door across from the stairs. He produces a pile of white, fluffy towels—usually reserved for drying hair, but in this case, a whole person—and tosses a few my way. "I'm okay. I've been really busy today. Just headed out, actually."

I pause in mopping to glance over his shoulder. The shop is dark and quiet, no hum of lights, no OPEN sign on in the window.

"Oh." I refocus on L. "Sorry to keep you, then. Can I borrow a T-shirt? I guess I'll just call an Uber from here and stop by my house."

"When are you going to get that car of yours fixed?"

"I'm close to being able to afford it," I answer.

"Why don't you just look into a newer one?" L asks.

"You and Matteo," I grouse, reaching down to my shirt, undoing a few buttons in preparation of removing my sodden button-down from my person, when L's hand snakes out to stop me. "MG, I wouldn't."

It's like he's grown six heads, and I might as well call him Hydra. "Wouldn't do what . . . take my completely soaking shirt off in your empty shop?" My question trails off as the sound of feet on the stairs fills the quiet, and L steps away from the doorway. The door that leads to his apartment.

"Ah," I say, a light bulb going off. "L, you just had to tell me you have *company*, no problem. I'd have waited until later to stop . . ."

I lean around L with a bit of a grin to see who is coming down the stairs, but my humor—and words—dissipate as Daniel Kim emerges from behind Lawrence. I blink. Twice. *This* is unexpected in so many ways, I'm at a loss.

"Oh, hey, MG," he says offhand, like we meet in my best friend's dark stairwell while my shirt is half-unbuttoned all the time.

"Hey . . . Daniel," I answer, quickly buttoning my wet shirt again. I shoot Lawrence a look, and he studiously avoids meeting my questioning gaze.

"Raining, huh?"

"Yeah," I agree. "Sure is." We all stand for a long stretch, listening to the *splat splat splat* of water dripping from my hem.

"I'm actually headed to the meeting now; is that where you were headed?" Daniel breaks the silence at the same time I grab for L's arm and ask, "L, can I possibly borrow a T-shirt? Upstairs? Please?"

Daniel laughs. "Oh! Right, you'd probably want to clean up from the rain. I'm sorry, I wasn't thinking." As if this is no big deal to him. As if my "goods" aren't fully visible to anyone who looks an inch below my neck. Maybe I've gotten a wrong read on Daniel and he likes men. Or maybe he's *really* cool, and way better about handling awkward situations than I am.

"How about you go get dried off; I'll wait down here, and you can let me know if you need a lift?"

"That sounds good," I agree, dragging Lawrence up the stairs behind me. We don't talk until we're at the top of the stairs in his little apartment bedroom.

I raise my eyebrows at him. "Daniel? As in the Daniel I work with, Daniel? You and Ryan sure are keeping it in the family." I realize the moment the words are out of my mouth that they sound judgmental, and I bite my lip as I watch L's expression shutter.

"It's not like that," he says.

"I know, I'm sorry. It just caught me by surprise that he was here, you know?"

I finish peeling off my shirt and reach for the tee he's holding out. I pull it over my head and instantly feel less prickly. "Sorry, L, that came out wrong. It's not my business. You can see whomever you want, obviously." And I'm *dying* to know what he was doing before he was here. I will not ask, *I will not* . . . "Did, ah, did he say where he was before he stopped here? By chance?" I should just go to jail, I'm a chronic meddler.

L looks completely baffled. "No, the office, I would assume? Or the dance studio? Why?" His tone says he thinks I'm being rude and nosy. Which I am.

Abort, abort. My theory isn't even formed enough to share with L. "Oh, uh, just wondering, since we have a meeting and I didn't see his car. But enough about that. I'm here because of you." I step over to him and offer a small hug. "I'm just worried about you. I saw the news, thought you might need a friend, came to check on you. Honestly. I didn't mean to crash your party."

"It's not a party, it's a business meeting. Consultation, really. And you weren't interrupting," Lawrence insists again, though he returns my squeeze before stepping away. "I think you left a pair of shorts here this summer; I'll go look in my closet."

Lawrence is gone a few moments but returns carrying not shorts but a fluffy skirt. Think, Carrie Bradshaw in *Sex and the City.*

"Seriously?" I ask him. "No shorts?"

"This is at least a wrap-around, and won't leave your . . . er . . . *assets* exposed?" He waggles his perfectly penciled eyebrows.

I grab it with a grumble, shimmy out of my soaked, salmon-colored pedal pushers, and wrap the skirt around myself. "Well?" I ask, presenting myself to Lawrence.

"Fabulous," he says without batting an eye. "Work, girl."

"Liar," I deadpan. "But at least I'm warmer." I slip my soaked flats back on and sigh. "Where are you headed off to?" I tactfully avoid asking any more about Daniel's presence.

"Down to the dance studio, actually." L shuffles his feet. "I'm taking a class to help with my performing."

"Oh! That's great!"

"And thanks for stopping by," Lawrence reaches out and hugs me again. "Helena Bottomcarter was one of Cleopatra's family, but it doesn't mean we didn't know each other. The news has been hard today."

I gather that Helena was Louis's stage name and nod. "Yeah, I know you all are a close community. Let me know if I can do anything."

He gives an empty laugh. "Keep drugs off the streets?"

"I'm trying," I say, meaning it. I am doing my part. Or more than my part, given I just followed a coworker out of pure curiosity and plan on attending a secret soiree to meet the Golden Arrow. Lawrence doesn't even know that I attended Cleopatra's party, or that I may have seen the drugs that killed Louis. This doesn't seem to be the time to come clean, given we both have places to be and the Golden Arrow himself may be downstairs.

"Sorry I didn't check in earlier; you should have texted."

"I know you've been busy, I didn't want to bother you," L answers, and my heart sinks a little. Here was one of my BFFs, who has been hurting, and I'd not been there for him. Complete friend fail.

"I'm here now, and in fine form." I wave at myself. "I'll throw over my meeting if you want to sit and talk."

"Nah," Lawrence answers, turning for the stairs. "I really do appreciate it, though. Maybe soon. Right now, I think dancing might clear my head. Plus, I want to drop off the flyers Daniel brought. I've been meaning to call about seeing if you want to help with costumes."

"*If* I want to help with costumes; L, do you know who you're talking to? It doesn't even matter what it is, I'm there." I take the printed sheet he swipes off his banister and holds out to me. Man, I must really be putting out the "I'm too busy for you" vibe if L hasn't been able to ask *me* about something that involves costumes. It's a staunch reminder that my friends' lives were happening with or without me.

I read through the flyer as we descend the stairs back to the shop. "*Drag-cula Spooktactular.* Halloween parade and party," I read out loud, then fall silent, my eyes scanning the rest of the page as we make our way downstairs and through the door at the bottom. "L, this sounds like so much *fun.*"

Beyond fun. It's a talent call for queens of all ages who want to be involved creating and running a float for West Hollywood's Halloween Carnaval Parade, to be followed by a huge pageant, revue, and drag-themed bash for the rest of the night. I can't imagine anything *more* up my alley.

"Seriously," I say, grabbing his arm as we reach the bottom. "This is a genius idea. You just let me know how you want me to help, and I'll be there. Promise. How did you come up with this?" The flyer mentions sponsors; this wasn't just something thrown together on a whim.

L preens with the praise. "Daniel has been helping me come up with some new ideas for how to push my businesses. It's been really amazing. *He's* been really amazing. I want to top whatever stunt Cleopatra has going on *and* help other queens in the process." He motions to Daniel, who waves self-consciously.

It takes everything in me to stop short of crowing about my suspicions of Daniel. Getting in with Lawrence. Conveniently working with me. Volunteering for drag events. Seemed like a perfect setup for the Golden Arrow to me.

"No need to thank me; I'm enjoying my foray into new worlds," Daniel says with an "aw shucks" motion. "My dancers are loving having a new and fun place to perform, and I get to share business ideas with another talented entrepreneur. It's win-win-win."

L smiles at Daniel like he owns the sun.

"I didn't realize you were an entrepreneur," I say by way of inserting myself back into the conversation. *Or a vigilante hero.*

"I own the dance studio," Daniel answers, again like this is NBD, and checks his watch. "Speaking of, you'd better get going if you're going to make class, L. Give my regards to Harrison."

"Harrison?" I ask, but my attention is pulled from L's face to his front door where something white flaps in the glass.

"Harrison is my business partner, and he teaches all the hip-hop classes," Daniel answers, peering around my shoulder.

"L, your mail is going to get soaked." I motion to the front of the store.

"I'll go grab it," L says, pulling on a jacket. He eyes me. "Are you going to be okay? Do you want me to call you a car?"

"If it's acceptable to you, I'm happy to drive you to the meeting." This, from Daniel.

I dither only a moment. Another rumble of thunder from outside decides it for me. Plus, this might give me time to pry, and him time enough to slip up. I need *proof* before I go to Matteo with my suspicion. "Yeah, a ride would be nice. But, um, do you think we can swing by my house? It's not far from here, and, well . . . ." I motion to the skirt and tee.

"No problem. I'll just go grab my keys." He heads to the back office, and I speed-walk to the front.

By this time, L has returned from outside, his jacket spattered with droplets.

"L, what's wrong?"

Lawrence stares at the paper in his hands like he's holding a baby viper.

I shuffle around behind L, since he's obviously not going to show me on his own. I see what has him rattled—I *know* these pages. One more glance confirms it; we're staring at pages from the Casey Senior journal.

Immediately, my gaze flies to Daniel. No. Possible. Way. I almost don't care that this is too much to be coincidence, and my brain fixates on the immediate concern. The journal. It's here, manna from heaven for my mystery-obsessed soul.

"Is this all there was?" I ask, grasping the back of the short sheaf of white paper and feeling for a black paper cover. There's nothing. These are just copies.

"I don't know, I guess so. Unless more blew away?"

"How long have they been here?" I'm almost manic now. Had the Golden Arrow been *here?* Right here under our noses? While I was here?

Lawrence and I sprint for the front door at the same time and create a jam in the jamb that would have been comical in a movie but is incredibly painful in real life.

The street is empty. Empty of people, empty of blowing pages, empty of lurking vigilantes.

We retreat into the store and pore over the two photocopied pages. I definitely recognize the hand and vaguely remember seeing them in the journal, but the pages are . . . boring. There's a scribbled note in one corner and a few doodles of gadgets on another. Some sort of throwing star, a gun that shoots arrows like a crossbow. There's nothing meaty— no big *Hooded Falcon* scenes. No finished panels, even. This is a page of straight-up doodles and personal jots. Why on *earth* would they have arrived on L's doorstep? The Golden Arrow is losing his touch, or I'm losing mine.

"Why now, why these?" I demand as if Lawrence isn't just as surprised as me.

"I—I don't know. Stop shaking my arm, dammit; I can hardly see *what* we're looking at," Lawrence whispers. We're huddled around the front door, and Daniel is already making his way to the front of the store.

"Everything okay?" he asks.

"Oh yeah, you know. The usual," I say brightly, not sure what *the usual* is.

"People pitching me for money," Lawrence answers, blithely. I see him start to fold the paper, then think better of it. I'd call the way he tucks the pages under a stack of papers on the front counter *loving* or *tender*. L's rattled about the pages arriving, but as I cast a critical glance over him, he's also *overjoyed* that they've shown up. Something about these pages—or maybe that it's any piece of the journal at all—is important to him.

I think back to our conversations about his previous journal—the one stolen out of his home, the one that was his last gift from Casey Senior before he died. L mourned the loss of the journal, his only connection with a man who gave him a start in life. It's easy to see that its return in any form—the only existing half of it still being in police custody—means the world to him. I'm instantly heartbroken for L and what he's had to endure for this case. Sure, he caught a killer, but he lost the only keepsake he ever had of the man who took him in off the streets.

And yet. Because the pages have appeared, Matteo is going to need to know. Not to mention my theory about who I suspect delivered them. So as Daniel and I head for the back door, I try to lob L the softball in a way Daniel won't recognize.

"So, are you going to call Matteo about that thing we were talking about earlier? Or am I?" Hey, I never said I was *good* at acting, but Daniel just keeps walking, so it must be enough.

L sighs. "I will."

I offer him a small smile as the door shuts between us.

CHAPTER 13

Once we've stopped at my house, the majority of our ride to the studio is quiet. I can't figure out a way to drop into a conversation about the Golden Arrow without giving away my suspicion. *Hey, do you like to play vigilante?* seems a little too on the nose. Daniel has an eclectic mix of music streaming from his iPhone to fill the silence instead of trying to draw me into conversation—something I appreciate. Usually I can't stand other people's music. But though not my usual taste, it's easy to listen to. It goes with his down-to-earth vibe, despite his apparent achievements of being a studio executive, dancer, business owner, and business coach.

"So, you are a busy guy," I voice my thoughts out loud. This is good, get him talking, see where I can press further. We've hit a little traffic, probably due to the weather, and I determine that I can't stew in silence the *entire* way to the meeting.

"I hear you're the same," Daniel answers with a smile. Cagey answer. On purpose?

"Two peas in a pod," I agree. "Thanks for helping L. The parade idea is . . . well, it's going to be amazing."

"Lawrence is passionate about his performance and his businesses. It's something I admire in other people and help foster where I can."

"Admirable," I observe.

"I spent a lot of time in life chasing stuff that didn't matter," Daniel answers with a glance my way. "I'm over that. I only look for genuine people and experiences now."

Something in the way he says it flips my stomach. It's not . . . butterflies, exactly. It's more an intensity. Most people aren't this unguarded or candid with people they hardly know. Despite my suspicions, I'm drawn into genuine conversation with Daniel. "That's a really amazing way to live. One I aspire to as well. Only I like to draw guns and fights and stuff too."

Daniel laughs. I love that he thinks I'm funny. Usually only Matteo finds my geekish humor entertaining.

"Don't get me wrong. I do stage combat. A good old-fashioned fistfight is sometimes a genuine experience."

I chew on my thoughts for a moment, trying to find a tactful way to sleuth for answers. "Thanks for the ride; I really appreciate it. I, er, thought I saw you driving earlier, before I got to Lawrence's, but I wasn't sure what you drove so I wasn't going to wave wildly at a stranger. People in LA have been killed for less." I try to laugh in a totally natural way.

Daniel smiles. "True. Well, it probably was me; I think I got to Lawrence's about fifteen? Twenty minutes before you did. If you were biking, we were probably sharing the road."

"Yeah, it was just a few streets down, near some shops."

He throws a sidelong look at me I can't decipher, and my heart starts to hammer. "I stopped to, ah, browse this little secondhand store on my way to Lawrence's. For costume stuff," I say. The key to lying is to lie consistently, right?

Understanding dawns. "Ah. Yeah, that was probably me. I made a stop on Curtis Street."

To pry or not to pry. Who am I kidding? "Too bad; we could have coordinated blazer-shopping efforts," I joke. Joking was the right way to go about this, right?

"Nah, though good to know the next time I need one. My brother lives on that street. I swung by to drop something off on my way to L's."

Oh. Well, that's decidedly boring. And plausible. I contemplate the reality in which Daniel's brother is the Golden Arrow, but decide to table my suspicions until I have more data.

Daniel's car inches forward, and he flips on the turn signal, though we're nearly a mile from the exit we need. He glances at me one more time. "Your turn. MG Martin. Genius comic book writer, costume designer, and now consultant for a movie."

"Yep," I agree.

"And some sort of semifamous bad-guy catcher. It's been fascinating to hear Lawrence's story."

I'm not sure how much to divulge, so I just smile and nod.

"So, what do you *do* exactly?" He navigates the exit ramp, and we're heading through a wash of rain toward Valhalla. I can only barely make out the rows of residential houses that pad the slightly industrial area where several studios sit near Hollywood Boulevard.

"What do I do . . . ," I muse, trying to figure out if this is polite interest or him fishing for info. "Well, I got the job because I know comic books, and the Golden Arrow seemed to be recreating comic book panels. So, I guess I am a professional consultant of the comic book variety." I see his eyebrows quirk up, and I laugh. "Niche field. Sorta like *Star Wars* lightsaber choreography, I assume."

"Touché," Daniel's voice rumbles with laughter. He steers into a lot and stops at the attended gate, offering his badge. Once we're through, he parks and turns to face me in the car. "So, what you're telling me is that you're the real-life Gwenpool?"

I stare at him for a few seconds. "You know what, I've never put that together." I hit myself on the head. "Seriously. I actually am. I can't believe you actually know who Spider-Gwen is." Though I lacked Spider-Gwen's actual superpowers, Gwenpool is a little-known reference to an alternate character, and it is an apt comparison. Gwen had claimed to come from the "real world," hired a designer to make her a costume, and had *become* a superhero. I just helped catch them instead of wearing the spandex myself.

"I read a *lot* of comic books as a kid. I loved the idea of becoming a superhero, who didn't? I guess so does the Golden Arrow, whoever they are."

"It's a little surreal," I agree. But he'd hit it right on the nose. Daniel just *got* it. We grinned at each other for an extended minute until his watch chimed.

"Okay, meeting time. You ready for this?"

I sigh and gather my messenger bag up, ready to dash from the car to the building through the downpour. "Ready as I'll ever be."

I don't know what I expected from a script-writing meeting, but what greets me is far more informal than my vision. I thought maybe writing for movies was more . . . glamorous than writing for comic books, but it looks to be about the same. Daniel leads me through an open office and into a large conference room full of people. A huge, heavy table dominates the space and is littered with everything from index cards and markers to cups of coffee, Danishes, and several tiny action figures.

The general din of the room doesn't even diminish as we walk in. It seems several conversations are happening simultaneously, and along one wall, a man in a coffee-stained button-down motions at index cards posted to the wall.

Daniel clears his throat. "Everyone, I'd like to introduce you to Genius's liaison, Michael-Grace Martin."

The din quiets somewhat, and I get a few curious glances and half-hearted waves. I'm *not* prepared for the more-than-several irritated looks thrown my direction. I get the impression that I'm crashing a party I'm not one hundred percent welcome at.

"MG, please," I correct and paste a small smile on my face. "I'm not here to interrupt the magic. I'm here as a resource, and I'm looking forward to working with you."

A few of the men—and I spy no women around the table at this particular moment—relax a little at this, and I sense a small victory. Maybe they worry I come with the expectation of steering the story. In truth, I have no *real* idea what to do here.

Daniel addresses the room at large again, since it's devolved back to the same conversations. "I was thinking maybe we could start by giving MG an overview of where the screenplay stands right now in development, key plot points or scenes we're excited about, and let her ask questions and point to areas that she thinks we may need to look at."

Though there's some grumbling, the large, padded rolling chairs gravitate back to the huge oak table, and I snag a spare chair from near the door and sit. Someone produces a storyboard—something I definitely recognize—and my nervousness fades a little. I'm in situations like this all the time at Genius. I just need to do my thing.

The explanation offered by the first guy on my left—thick-framed black glasses and trimmed beard and mustache touched with gray, so maybe a senior writer—is sporadic at first. Several people jump in from around the table to explain problem areas or the awesomeness of a certain fight sequence. Overall, I gather the main plot is the Falcon and Swoosh defending their city against the takeover by an antagonist that uses cell phone towers to transmit mind-and-sleep-altering brain waves. It causes mass hysteria and mass hallucinations, and he basically holds the city's infrastructure hostage since no one can think straight enough to defeat this guy or call for help.

I'm not *wild* about the "typical superhero plot" vibe of the whole thing, but I wait until they've run through the basic framework of the movie to make any comments.

"Well," I start, "from a Genius standpoint, there are only a few critical issues I can pinpoint. From a purist and fan standpoint, though, I'm going to add a few of my own thoughts in." I completely ignore several of the eye rolls I see. "Since I *write The Hooded Falcon*, I feel these viewpoints are grounded," I remind them. Writers hate feeling critiqued by armchair experts. I get it, but that's *why I am here*. I'm an expert, even if I constantly have to remind people.

"So first off. The villain—"

"He's not canon," a man from the back cuts me off. "We know that."

"No." I suck in a breath to calm the flood of anger that fills me. "He's not. I'd appreciate if you'd let me finish my thoughts, though." I don't point out that I let *them* finish theirs, but I am damn proud of myself for doing it. "So, the villain. I think that he appeals to the current readership of the Hooded Falcon universe. I also think you could come up with a simple way to make him appeal to the fans of the older works. Remember, the original *THF* is going through a revival of sorts right now."

Silence greets my words, which I take as a good sign. "What if you don't *change* your villain, but give him a little more of a social agenda. Rather than generic 'big bad,' make him either related to the Falcon's origin story or an original archnemesis? A spin-off?"

Again, no one interrupts my thought flow, so I go with it. "The Hooded Falcon started largely as a socially conscious vigilante. He addressed real people within his community that were bent on harm. Everything from drugs, mental health, weapons, trafficking, preying on innocents. Really, it wouldn't be hard to tie it in to something like that. Just change your villain's backstory a little. Make him someone related to the story of the city. Perhaps the protégé of a previously defeated antagonist, and give him a little more of a social agenda—maybe he's even targeting the Falcon or trying to draw him out for some reason. For destroying his mentor, or maybe because he resents that the Falcon has become so popular when he lost his living. I think if you ground this character a bit *more* in true canon, it will work for both audiences."

There's no call to burn me at the stake, and in fact I note more than a few thoughtful faces in the crowd. Good. "Okay, next point. This cast is all male." I hold up a finger to forestall the arguments I see brewing. "The *protagonist* cast is all male. Yes, Swoosh's sort-of love interest is in there. She's being fridged." Blank stares meet my gaze, and I sigh inwardly. Time to womansplain some current culture to them as nicely as I can. It's such a common theme in superhero movies, people sometimes fail to even recognize it exists or the stereotypes it perpetuates.

"You all know what that means, right? When a woman only serves to heighten the stakes for the men. It's all she does. What I'm seeing here in general is—forgive me for putting it this bluntly—a very generic superhero movie setup. The Hooded Falcon has had several woman antagonists over the years, and historically the Red Canary has served as more than a love interest. She's fought alongside Falcon. She has her own story arcs. We need a more balanced team"—I avoid pointedly looking around the writing room at the male-only cast of writers—"and all players need to play a critical part in solving the conflict."

This silence is stonier. Or at least on one side of the table. The side I assumed were the more senior, die-hard-superhero-movie, "we've written so many of these" fellows. On the other side of the table though, a few younger men jump in with ideas.

"We could make Swoosh a girl," one throws out. "Gender-swapping is super popular right now. Look at the Thirteenth Doctor."

"But what about the love-interest line?" Another asks the first. I follow the volley like a tennis match.

The first shrugs. "It'll be more progressive if we leave it?"

"Yes, but *why* would Swoosh be a girl?" I ask.

The first guy looks at me like I have tentacles. "Because you said it would be a good idea to have a—"

"Don't just put *stuff* in because it is popular, or just to put a girl in. It has to be vital to the story," I say, not even caring I'm cutting him off. "If you just toss a girl in there to fill some sort of checklist, she's not going to *do* anything. Make her as complex and as vital as any other secondary character. Maybe add a subplot about another vigilante who is trying to take down the same villain? Make her plan at odds with Falcon's, but no less smart or viable. Make them have to work together or compromise in some way. I'm just pointing out a lack of balance, and today's viewers are so much more aware of it than they used to be."

Grudgingly, I see nods, and beside me I think Daniel wears a pleased smile.

The rest of the meeting passes in a more companionable manner: the balance of the issues on my list are minor and easily flagged for the team to work on. They promise to think about the villain and gender balance, and all too soon I'm hailing an Uber home while Daniel chivalrously waits with me.

"Well, how was the first day on the job?" he asks.

"Y'know, I think I kicked a little ass." Inside my pocket, my phone dings. "Oops, sorry, gotta check this, it's probably Andy asking for my pages."

His lopsided grin confirms it for me. I return it, digging out my phone.

I expect an email notification, but not this one. It's a flag I put on Cleopatra's website, which has just been updated. I hastily click through to read, even though the mobile capability of the site is awful.

Saturday night. From 11pm-2am. Anyone with a golden seal is invited, plus one guest.

My eyes scan the online invite for more information. It looks like they'll be raffling off four more seals *at* the door, which means that it's going to be a complete zoo outside the venue. A quick Google search reveals the venue is a black box theater downtown. My heart skips inside my chest. Am I really going to attend? All by myself? Something about this seems risky, but . . . Cleopatra isn't going to all this trouble for a ruse, surely? What if I can actually meet the Golden Arrow? Ask him his intentions. See if I *recognize* him—more specifically, see if he's a dead ringer for my current work companion. Ask if he's been the one tying up the drug dealers again, and if he knows anything about the Queen of Hearts.

"Everything okay?"

My eyes snap up, registering Daniel's concerned face and the waiting car.

"Yeah, totally," I lie. "Work stuff . . . *other* work stuff," I amend, seeing his confusion. He can tell something's up. But I offer a cheery wave as I slide into the car, even if I'm anything but cheery on the inside. This could impact the case I'm working on. And *that* makes me realize that it's time to come clean to Matteo about what I've been up to.

CHAPTER 14

Usually I'm just glad to see Matteo, but tonight I'm nervous. It's my turn to go to his house, and I sit in my car, staring at the neat little modern desert house far longer than I need to. I have no idea under what set of circumstances my car decided to work again today—the ambient temperature? My lucky T-shirt? Mercury's astrological alignment?—but I'm grateful. I tried it on a whim; maybe it just needed a vacation. The drive out here has helped clear my head, and I've determined that I *have* to tell Matteo about my intention to go to this party. And reveal that I've been chasing the Golden Arrow on my own. Which . . . he's not going to like. Not only because his girlfriend has been at wild parties where people end up OD'ing, without telling him, but more so because I'm an active consultant on this case and withheld information. Again. Old habits die hard, I guess.

I push through the unlatched gate and cross the courtyard, noting that Matteo has been gardening. There are a few black plastic pots piled to the side of one of the beds and a smear of dark dirt still on the usually pristine pathway. It's getting dark fast, so I can't make out what he's planted, but I'm struck by the difference of what Matteo does in his free time versus what I do. The man gardens. At a house he owns, in a location he picked specifically because it calls to him and his design aesthetic. He drives a paid-off Prius twenty years newer than my Aspire. Though we haven't talked at length about it, I assume he saves for retirement. I'm at once both intensely jealous and insanely intimidated by his level of *adultness*. I can never seem to have it this together. Matteo and I are roughly the same age, and here I am, still attending midnight parties with my roommate, staying up at all hours trying to launch a new career, running on coffee, failing in supporting my friend Lawrence, and . . . well . . . what exactly is Matteo doing, dating a mess of a person like me?

I contemplate that sentiment as I step up to the beautiful red door—an addition in the last few months; I like to think it's some of *my* design aesthetic rubbing off on him—and knock. It's not that I don't think I'm a catch. I think I'm awesome. I'm happy and loving this scrappy chase-your-dream phase I'm in. I'm funny and smart, but I still feel . . . young and unfinished next to Matteo's polish. It's not the first time in as many months that I've wondered, though I'm definitely drawn to him, if we're just too different to make it work. Unbidden, a flashback to my conversation with Daniel rises to the top of my brain like cream—or impurities—rising to the surface. Daniel knows who Spider-Gwen is. In a million years, no matter how hard Matteo tries, he's never going to be a fully immersed *nerd* like me. Like Daniel. Should I be with someone more like myself? *Wait. Am I really wondering if Daniel is a better match for me when I'm standing on my boyfriend's doorstep?* Steps sound near the door, and I shake myself.

Seeing Matteo's face light up when he opens the door goes a long way to soothing my ruffled feathers. Any guy—any *person*—who looks at you like that can't be *that* wrong for you, right? I step in and take a deep whiff of whatever it is that Matteo is cooking.

"Chicken cacciatore," Matteo answers without me having to ask. "And *yes*, I bought that ridiculously gross ranch dressing you love for the salad."

"Ryan doesn't let me keep it in the house," I explain. But my shoulders ease by degrees. It's all this time away from Matteo that messes with my head. *He knows me.* When we're together, it's wonderful. I don't know why I get myself all tied into knots about it. I know one of my weaknesses is getting too far into my own head.

"You've been gardening." I mean it as an observation, but it comes out as an accusation.

His dark eyebrows lift as he helps me out of my coat. Whereas I would have slung it over the nearest chair, he takes the time to hang it in the tiny coat closet near the door. Then he returns, wraps me in a hug that I gratefully return, and kisses my head.

"Is that a crime?"

"No." I take a breath. I'm still trying to shake my sudden attack of internal Jessica Jones. "No, of course not."

Matteo pulls back and looks at me, his brow slightly wrinkled. I give a gusty sigh. "Don't mind me, I've had a . . . weird day."

"Trouble at the office? Didn't you have your first production meeting today?" He leads me into the kitchen where the smells of dinner are even more delicious. "Did none of the blazers work out?" A pot of tomato sauce bubbles on his stove in the neat little kitchen. I sit down at my customary spot at the little island and watch him putter around, stirring things and setting plates at the two-person table.

"Blazers were fine, the meeting went okay. That's not what's bothering me."

"Maybe this will cheer you up." Matteo knocks a spoon against the pot and reaches for something on his counter. It's a manila folder, and inside I find two photocopies of journal pages.

"The pages!" I squeal, flipping through the set and wishing it contained new material. But it is the same—scribbled note, weapon doodles. I glance up at Matteo. "Did you find anything?"

He shakes his head. "No fingerprints, nothing. The copies were made on a home inkjet printer, so basically impossible to track. But what interests me is *why* they were delivered at all—it's where we need your and Lawrence's help."

I sigh and close the folder. "I'll look at it in more detail, but to me it looks like a note about a meeting and a bunch of doodles of weapons for the comic. There's nothing here about the Queen of Hearts, nothing about pills; I have no idea why the Golden Arrow would have left this for us."

Matteo turns back to his sauce, and I scan the drawings, pulling them out of the folder one by one. In the corner, one doodle tugs on my memory. I hold up the paper and point. "This one kind of looks like that throwing-star thing you found with the drug dealers, doesn't it?"

Matteo approaches and studies the loose sketch. "Hmm . . . maybe? Yeah, I guess the general idea is the same."

We exchange glances. "So, this could be proof that it's the real Golden Arrow?" I debate about sharing my suspicions about Daniel.

Matteo nods. "I'll compare the drawing and the throwing star; good thinking. Anything else on the page?"

I squint back down at the paper. The rest of the doodles bring nothing to mind, and I turn my attention to the personal note. It's hard to decipher, but the scribble looks like: *meet with D about garbage, poss. fund from Svenie.*

No, wait. I squint my eyes and turn the paper slightly. Not garbage. Gadget, maybe? Given the content of the doodles on this page, I'll go with gadget. Okay, so he was meeting with someone named D and Svenie? What kind of name was that? The initial *D* was useless, but there should only be a handful of Svenies in the world, right. I squint again, and the drag of the pen strokes shifts again. Not Svenie.

Stevie.

A thrill runs through me.

Is *this* Lawrence's Stevie? The friend he talked about? What are the odds that the Golden Arrow would have dropped off pages containing the very name L and I had just talked about? Or did it have to do with the reason that this Stevie visited L's shop? Could Stevie be our Golden Arrow, and these pages were meant as a sign for L only?

But . . . how would Stevie know we'd talked about him? I frown. Is L's place bugged? Coincidences are piling up like gamma radiation in a warp-drive failure. The idea makes me uncomfortable.

"Penny for your thoughts."

"Well, it's just this note says something about a meeting with 'D and Stevie,' and a Stevie came to visit L this week. L said he hadn't talked to him in years . . . I'm wondering if it's more than coincidence."

Matteo straightens. "Maybe. We can ask him about D and Stevie, see if he remembers anything. He's never mentioned him before? I know you guys tell each other everything."

I hesitate before shaking my head. "No, and Ryan couldn't think of a Stevie either. And we don't tell each other *everything*." Case in point: the party. It reminds me I'm here to tell Matteo something specific.

I sigh, and Matteo raises his eyebrow at me. He doesn't make much comment but continues to putter, letting me choose how much to share. I love that about him. He rarely pushes, ever patient. Whether it's just his nature or the job training, it's everything I'm not. It makes him a good detective—the ability to wait people out. Eventually people like me just talk to fill the void.

"I have a few more things to tell you. First off, I think you should look into a guy I work with, Daniel Kim. Or his brother."

Matteo's eyes widen. "The guy from the dance troupe?"

"Yeah, I don't know. Something he said makes me think he's interested in the case. Coincidences, like I told you. But maybe follow up on him, and his brother."

Matteo nods, and I can tell he's making a mental note. "Okay, what else is on your mind?"

This is the one I'm really worried about. I was able to not quite admit to sleuthing on my own with Daniel, but not really any way out of it with this one. "So, Ryan and I went out a few nights ago. After Lawrence's show."

Matteo pauses, his shoulders tensing a little bit. "Okay."

I know him well enough to recognize we are bordering on Detective Kildaire; already, I've put him on his guard.

"I didn't tell you—or Lawrence—I went to the after-party because I didn't want L to know I'd attended his nemesis's shindig."

"This is the person claiming to have inside knowledge of the Golden Arrow."

"Right." I take a grateful sip of the water he puts down in front of me, trying my best to avoid his penetrating gaze. He doesn't move away, even when a timer on the counter starts beeping.

"And the party where that kid overdosed."

"Yeah." My mouth goes dry.

"And?"

My gaze flickers to his and then drops back down to the glass of water. I spin it in my hands. "I should have told you about this earlier, I'm sorry. I felt stupid for going. I ran into Ryan there, and he basically felt the same. It would break L's heart to know we'd gone to try and see the Golden Arrow."

Silence from Matteo.

"It was a bust anyhow, no Golden Arrow, but I should have told you," I finish, knowing he's concerned about the case. I'm still working up to Part Two of the conversation.

"Is that it?" he asks when I don't say more. "You went to a party last weekend and didn't tell me? MG, I'm not your keeper. I thought—never mind. If that's all that this is, I appreciate you telling me, but you don't need to be worried that I know every move you make. I suppose since this has to do with the case, you should have told me, but no harm done."

The absolution both helps and hurts. "Well, there's more."

"Okay." He draws out the word and pivots to turn off the timer and the stove, then back to me.

"Well, at the party, there was this Willy Wonka golden-ticket-type thing. If you found a seal stuck on the bottom of your cup or plate or whatever, you got an exclusive invite to the next party. And Cleopatra said that the Golden Arrow arranged this limited party specifically to meet a few people in the public." I watch his face as I reach into my messenger bag and produce the seal, putting it on the counter. "I didn't tell Ryan I found one. I didn't tell Lawrence."

"Or me."

"Or you," I agree. "And today, I got an alert about when and where the next party is. So." I wait for him to pounce all over me for withholding information pertinent to the case. Why, for all we know, I could be holding one of fifteen tickets to see our searched-for perpetrator in person. I could get an ID. I could crack the case.

Matteo's face is unreadable as he studies me. "And that's it. That's what you needed to tell me?"

"Yeah?" I'm still waiting for any shoe to drop.

"Nothing . . . else."

"No?" I'm not sure what he's fishing for, so I clam up and return his stare, willing him to see my truth.

"When is the party?"

"Saturday night, eleven p.m." I give him the location of the theater and the details I'd garnered from the limited publicity release.

He lets out a breath; truth be told, he looks immensely *relieved* despite the tight timeline. "Okay. We can work with this. I would have preferred to know earlier, of course, but we have time to plan."

"We do? You're not mad?" I ask, hesitant.

"No, of course not. Do you think the Golden Arrow will really be there?"

"Maybe? I don't know. Ryan seems to think that this is all a media stunt. But. This is a lot of trouble to go to if there's *nothing* behind it."

Matteo's brow still pulls down over his eyes, but now it's in a more thoughtful, less defensive way. "Kind of what I'm thinking too. I think it's worth pursuing. I'll need to check with my captain about what sort of surveillance we'd offer you. Are you okay wearing a camera?"

I swallow. I hadn't thought of that aspect. "I . . . guess?"

"And you can't go alone; maybe I could, or Rideout . . ."

"There's no way they're going to let us in if you're with me, you're becoming as well known in LA as Muñez was in his day. You're the *face* of the Golden Arrow investigation."

He gives me a look that says, "You're one to talk."

"Yes, I know some people know I'm involved, but I'm not on the TV, talking about the case. What if I take Ryan? He's useful. And large, if you're worrying about safety."

A strange look passes over Matteo's face, but his words are even when he speaks. "No formal training; I can't be sure he wouldn't be a liability in a nasty situation."

I give him a look that clearly states what we're both thinking—that I *would* be a liability in a nasty situation. I'm not known for my grace under, around, or near fire.

"How about Lawrence? He's had formal training." Matteo references L's stint many years ago as Casey Senior's security guard.

It's a solid suggestion. But. That means confessing to Lawrence that I not only went to the first party but also intend to attend the second. "Cleopatra might recognize him. And besides, Lawrence may not *want* to go."

"Can he not invent a disguise? I thought that was the name of the drag game. You're probably going to have to wear something too, right?"

"It *is* another costume party," I allow. And then give in. "Fine. But I'll ask *both* of them and see which one can go." I hold up my hand to forestall his argument. "I'm not going to force L to go if he doesn't want to."

"Fair enough." Matteo turns to the stove and dishes the chicken, vegetables, and sauce over pasta. I follow him to the table, sling my messenger bag over the back of one of the chairs, and slide in. He sits down across from me, and we both pick up our forks.

"So, did you see the kid that overdosed while you were there?"

I swallow my first mouthful of hot chicken a little too fast. "Yeah, she was pretty out of it when I saw her, though I wasn't all that surprised that it ended up being the same person. Lawrence is upset about it; queens are a tight community when it comes down to it, even if they're competitive with each other."

"I bet, and I'm sorry for his loss. No matter how many young people I see OD, it never stops being a stupid, pointless, tragic loss of a life. Out of it, how?"

I shrug as we eat in silence for a little while. One thing is certain about dating a police detective: our dinnertime conversation is rarely banal. "Out of it, like loopy. Drunk. There were these flasks on a table, probably something homemade, and combined with drugs . . . well, it didn't go well."

Matteo's eyes narrowed. "He seemed drunk?"

"*She*, since she was in her drag persona's costume, but yeah." I try to remember how the queen was acting. "I guess *maybe* it seemed like more than alcohol. Well, and we know it was, right?"

Matteo hesitates and then nods.

"Actually, I got offered pills while I was there; I'm supposing it was a combination of the pills I saw and whatever was in the flasks."

"You *saw* pills?"

"Yeah. But they weren't your normal white, pressed pill. These also looked . . . homemade, for lack of a better term. Gelcap-looking things with granules in them. Maybe someone crushed up the opioids and packaged them together—"

"Pills. Filled with powder?" Detective Kildaire is in full residence now, his semirelaxed posture gone. He doesn't even apologize for cutting me off. "You didn't think to tell me this?"

"Well . . . no, not really. Matteo, drugs at parties like this aren't exactly unusual. It wasn't until the kid OD'd that I even thought about it again, honestly. And the police are talking about opioids, so I figured that's what he OD'd on. Which, I know, thanks to being the girlfriend of a narcotics detective, isn't what the Queen of Hearts is dealing, right? It wasn't a baggie of white powder I was offered. Pills." I describe what I saw in as much detail as I can recall.

"Red and yellow?" Matteo mutters, sitting back, his *thinking* face clearly on.

"Kill a fellow," I answer grimly.

"That's . . . unusual. It's valuable information; I'll do some checking. If you see anything like that again, get a sample if you can."

"As in buy the drugs?"

"Better yet, text me, get a picture, we can arrest the guy and hope for a legally seized sample."

We eat in silence for long moments. The cacciatore is delicious; the man can cook. He's not enjoying his dinner, though; his brain is on high. I let him get lost in his own head. I wonder if his brain ever gets tired of this aspect of his job: just when they think they've made big headway against a drug ring, something else pops up. Always trying to be one step ahead, but always one step behind. It would drive me batty. It's why my heroes always conquer evil in the end—if you didn't have that hope to look forward to, how would one go on day after day?

"So, do you want to know what I planted in the garden?"

"Huh?" We've been eating in silence, and my brain has taken over for who knows how long. The problem with being a writer. Give me silence, and I fill it with stories in my head.

"You accused me of gardening. Would you like to know what I planted?"

"Sure?"

"Irises."

I blink. I'm terrible with flowers in the first place, but this seems to mean something to him, so I try on a smile. "That's . . . great! I'm happy for you."

Matteo laughs, seeing straight through my act. "It's the same flower I brought you the other night. Yellow irises. I have a bit of shade right near the roof overhang, and I dunno." Matteo turns slightly blotchy, and it's endearing. "They remind me of you."

It's my turn to cough, my throat strangely tight. "You planted a flower that reminds you of me?"

"They're colorful. Bold. I picked yellow because of those shoes you like to wear. I love the idea of being reminded of you each spring."

That stops me cold.

I look at this man like I've never seen him before. No one has *ever* done anything semipermanent regarding our relationship before. And this is a far cry from a ring, or a proposal, but he's changed his garden for me. To include me. And I was on his doorstep not an hour earlier, wondering if we were a terrible match.

"Are . . . you okay? I don't have to keep them?" And he seems so reduced, so *hurt* by the fact that I might not be pleased, that I immediately shove aside my horrible inner self.

"I've . . . just . . . no one has ever done anything like that for me before." It's the honest answer.

Matteo hasn't moved, still trying to decide if he's somehow offended me.

"It just took me by surprise is all. It's so sweet." And here I was thinking in the past month that he was ready to dump me, or that maybe I should be dating someone like Daniel instead. I'm an ass. But I'm not lying. I *do* find it sweet. Incredibly sweet. Overwhelming, new, and a bit alarming—just call me Belle, I guess. But I'm definitely flattered. Something rises up in me, as tender and delicate as a little baby plant. "No one's ever done anything lavish like that before," I say again, trying to send home the point.

I see him debate and then decide to take me at my word. Almost absentmindedly, and partly to himself, he justifies, "It's not lavish. In my thinking it's the least you can do for the girl you love. You must have dated some really interesting people if this takes you by surprise."

Time stops.

I stare at him.

He continues eating, unaware of the bomb he's just dropped.

My palms itch.

Panic rises inside my chest.

Matteo just said he *loves* me. Not in passing, but like. *Real* love.

First comes love, then comes marriage, then comes . . . MG strapped to a lifetime of babies and mortgages and annoying cartoons with no plot.

But again, from within the war-torn battlefield that is now my thoracic region, that baby plant of something new and tender and delicate doesn't wilt. Is it possible that I'm both terrified and *happy* about this?

It's a good thing he's focused on his plate, because I don't even know what my face looks like. Sheer panic? Utter joy? Imminent vomit?

Do I love him?

Is it possible to both question if we should be dating when we're apart and for it to feel so perfectly natural, so homey, so *forever* when we're together that I *could* be in love—*love* love—with him and not have realized it? It's only been, what, a few months? Granted, basically my longest, healthiest relationship ever, but . . . can someone *know* that fast?

"Do you want wine?" he asks, standing and heading for the kitchen, totally blissfully unaware of my plight.

"I—uh—I shouldn't. I'm driving." Words. I need to form words.

"You could stay if you wanted." And after the last piece of conversation, his totally *normal* offering of his house to me is more than I can bear. I wolf down the rest of my food while he's pouring himself wine and barely can contain myself. I'm crawling out of my own skin. "I also bought you your very own pillowcase so that you don't have to put a towel down every time you dye your hair. It's all warm and cozy on your side of the bed."

He means it to sound tempting. He looks so proud of his thoughtfulness.

He should be—the pillowcase is perfect. But it's the linen version of my own drawer at his house. It will be *my* pillow. In *our* bed, not just his pillow in his bed that I use sometimes. It's the MG equivalent of asking me to move in.

"Thanks for the offer," I say, hoping that my voice sounds normal to him, unlike the I-just-huffed-helium sound I hear in my ears. "But I need to get home tonight after dinner. I've got that stuff to finish. And ask Lawrence and Ryan about tomorrow. So." I trail off, unsure of how much to blather on, lest he get a whiff of my panic.

Matteo studies my empty plate with surprise as he reenters the dining area. "Oh, well, yeah. Of course. I know *we're* busy right now, but I appreciate you coming out here for dinner. I miss seeing you, but this is a season, right? The Golden Arrow can't stay at large forever. Things will calm down. Maybe around Christmas we could go on a long weekend and relax."

"Relax. Together." A trip. He's thinking of a trip several *months* in the future. I'm seriously about to lose it.

He takes my near-hyperventilating words as dubiousness and laughs, setting his wine down and coming around the table.

I stand at the same time, unable to stay sitting.

It surprises him, but he reaches out and pulls me to him again. Instantly, my heartbeat slows a little and my body relaxes an inch, though I'm still basically frozen in place.

"I know. You don't relax well, but I'm hoping I can convince you that it's nice to do every once in a while. Hey"—he must suddenly realize how wooden I feel—"you okay? I know you're stressed about all your deadlines. I'm fine, okay? It was so nice to see you tonight, but why don't you head back so you can work? You can stay next time?"

He kisses my head and lets me go, and I stumble gratefully away. At the same time, I miss the warm glow that is present whenever we're pressed together. How can one person feel all this at once? "Okay." I manage a weak smile.

Not three minutes later I'm stumbling out the door, gulping crisp fall desert air on my way to my Aspire. If I didn't think my life was full before, now I have several things to add to my freak-out plate. The fact that I am going to have to come clean to Lawrence about the parties and go undercover for the police, *and* that Matteo just said the three words I've spent a lifetime avoiding.

CHAPTER 15

Saturday night arrives with a heavy dose of anxiety, topped with jitters. I skated through with barely two hours of sleep. The morning involved trying to track down Lawrence, who was increasingly hard to get ahold of with his new Halloween idea coming together, and convincing both him and Ryan that it really *is* a good idea to go to this party. Surprisingly, L was cool about the party thing, if a little surly . . . Truth be told, I guess that he's just downright *curious* about Cleo's activities, and this gives him an excuse to gate crash. Though Lawrence agreed to be my date, Ryan insisted on walking us to the door, having heard the media frenzy that had arisen from the lottery.

"There are way too many people here," Ryan mutters as we make our way to the building that houses the black box theater. The street is filled to the brim like an iPhone release week. We started passing people in clubbing clothes and costumes in the last block—people like *us* who were forced to park a million miles away.

"It's that damn lottery spot," Lawrence answers as we make our way across the last little alleyway and approach the actual entrance.

"You're mad because it's, yet again, a brilliant PR move," Ryan shoots back.

"It *is* brilliant," Lawrence grouses. "What I want to know is why suddenly my nemesis is such an evil genius."

"Late-night infomercial webinar about growing an underground following the old-fashioned way?" I quip.

"Playing to the sinful trifecta: Sex, drugs, and rock 'n' roll?" Ryan asks.

"Precisely," I answer. We're now abreast with the end of what is clearly designated with velvet ropes as the "lottery pool." A teeming line of humanity, smashed against the side of the building. I spot Muggles in and among costumed queens, party girls squashed up against people with press badges. It is a damn zoo.

"Okay, so. One last check, are you sure we look okay?" I turn to L, who looks about as basic as I've ever seen him. Gangster jeans, probably borrowed from a friend, baggy black tee, backward black hat with do-rag underneath. No bling, no sparkle, no queen. It is disconcerting to say the least, but it's how he says he'll be least recognizable. He's fully in character now, complete with swagger—though that might be the baggy pants' fault.

"You look fine," L answers without so much as a glance at me. I fidget with the zipper of my black pleather jumpsuit—a total hack job on my part. I'd sort of stitched together leggings and a slinky black mock turtleneck dress shirt, and then added a quasi-vest over the top of it. From far away the effect is one of "Kill Bill goes clubbing." Close-up, I look like I'm wearing Joseph's monochromatic dreamcoat. What my auburn wig is hiding, though, is the thing I'm worried about: I have a mic pack on the top of my collar and a wire that's running up to my ear. The buttons of my fur vest are also imbedded with a wireless camera setup. I'm a damn spy, and I feel like anyone who looks at me is going to know. I adjust the sunglasses on my face—we're all wearing them, despite it being ten forty-five at night. Something I typically find annoying and stupid but just feels . . . right . . . when you're going undercover against the enemy.

"Stop fidgeting. That's what's going to get you caught," Ryan agrees, slapping my hand down from my wig and wrapping his own around mine. I'd be tempted to call it sweet, except his grip is anything but comforting. It's a band of iron meant to keep me from outing us before we're in. Ryan is dressed in what I can only describe as a Bruno Mars look: slim pants, open front blazer, fedora. He looks so far from the typical gamer guy I live with that I wonder how he even came up with the outfit.

"Lelani," he answers, catching my gaze.

Dammit. My friends know me too well.

"So, she knows you're here."

Ryan gives me a look that says, "Duh."

"I mean she's cool with this? All of it?" I didn't think Lelani had been too keen on Ryan's involvement with the police after our little debacle at SDCC.

"She and I both think it's a . . . fascinating opportunity to see what's going on," Ryan answers cagily.

Not for the first time, I'm getting the sense that Ryan has his own agenda, but I don't have enough time to pursue the course of conversation. We're almost up to the three bouncers at the door, and I use my one free hand to reach into the top of my shirt and produce the seal. I'm careful not to do it in view of the waiting crowd. Just this week in the news, a major film actor offered not a small sum of money for getting a seal. Rumor has it that someone showed to take advantage of the dollar figure and several other people jumped the seal possessor. One person critically injured, several arrested, and no one's sure exactly who ended up with the seal.

The crowd hushes as we approach, and I get my first taste of what it would be like to be famous. The scrutiny. The palpable jealousy. The feeling of crazy, immense "I have it all" that washes over me. Like a scene in a bad movie, I palm the seal and reach out to shake hands with one of the bouncers—a big, beefy Samoan-looking guy. Quite frankly, it looks like he could pound me flat with one swipe from his ham hand.

He squints at me and then turns the seal over in his hand. Next, he puts a jewelry loupe to his eye and inspects it before waving several wands over it. Apparently my golden ticket passes muster, because I'm ushered forward.

"One guest."

Ryan starts to peel off while Lawrence steps in behind me when another bouncer lays a hand on the first guy's arm. They have a brief conversation that I can't hear over the rustle and mutter of the crowd behind me.

"You're on the list, Mr. St. Claire. You may all go in," the first bouncer says to Lawrence after the hushed tête-à-tête. He then steps aside, bringing with him the red velvet rope that grants all three of us access to the theater.

My eyebrows shoot up immediately. I turn to Lawrence, who looks equally surprised. And suspicious. In his nondrag look, it's pretty hard to recognize him. And this does more than raise my eyebrows. Something cold and slimy takes root in the pit of my stomach.

"List?" I ask, glancing around. His podium is empty. There's no list I can see anywhere up front.

The bouncer doesn't answer, just holds the rope open.

Something is definitely *up*. Lawrence is well known enough to get in, I guess, even if someone were looking specifically for him in any dress, but *why* is another matter. Cleo isn't supposed to know L is coming. In fact, we solidified that plan only this morning, and the police are the only other people privy to that info. Add to it that this list seems to be something of an oddity, given the grumbling of the people closest to the door. No one else on this imaginary list has been given entry yet tonight.

"L . . . ," I start, planning on telling him that he can leave, that something doesn't feel right.

"It's fine. I'm *not* leaving you alone here; we need to stick together, capisce?"

"Aye aye, Captain," Ryan agrees as we cross out of the glare of the streetlamp and into the dark foyer beyond.

Just beyond the main doors, a heavy curtain hangs across the room, blocking our view of the theater. As we shuffle forward, two figures clad all in reflective black sequins—I suspect queens, but no way to tell in this dark—step forward and execute mirroring, neat bows before each pull aside half of the curtain to admit us to the room beyond.

I'd use the word "party," except maybe the word "landscape" fits better? The curtain parts to reveal a completely surreal setting. So much so the three of us stop on the threshold just to gawk. Around the exterior I assume I can make out rings of seats, sitting silent and empty. Rather than feeling abandoned, the empty seats, half-shrouded in darkness, seem watchful and malevolent. Like an unseen audience is judging our performance.

And what a *set*. Literally. The entirety of the floor of the black box theater is overtaken by a hulking, human-scale neon-lit chess set. More than that, the "white" pieces, which tower over my small form, are clear glass or acrylic and transmit the colored light from the squares on the floor. Only a few other occupants wander around the pieces, looking as thoroughly disconcerted as I feel.

"What. The. Actual. Eff," Ryan mutters as we move among the pieces, studying them in the changing lights from the floor. Everything is given an unearthly appearance, lit by greens and pinks, turning them into what are essentially glowing ice sculptures.

"What. The. Actual. Eff," Ryan again mutters from my left.

"About where I'm at," I agree. I've spotted what I think is a bar on the far side of the chessboard, shrouded in black cloth but bearing decanters of smoking liquids. The glasses—no, test tubes?—are lit from within, the same eerie lighting effect that the chess pieces give on the floor.

I'm about to suggest going and checking out the glasses when I realize that Ryan isn't even looking at the bar; he's watching the figures of the people walking among the chess pieces. I assumed all of them were seal-bearers like myself, but upon closer inspection, the figure closest to us seems to be wearing a catsuit lined with glow sticks and carries what appears to be a snake.

In fact, as I look harder around the room, it's easy to pick out that nearly half the people attending the party are . . . performers, for lack of a better word. The one that crosses closest to us is a queen in high-fashion, high-art drag. Much closer to a "Sasha Velour meets Cirque du Soleil Club Kid" than most of the camp/glamour queens that I hang with. This queen is juggling what looks like a spinning lighted ball, balancing it on each hand and then passing it off to her foot. I'm mesmerized, watching the lights swirl and dance inside the piece.

She moves away, and I'm tempted to follow her. I'm not sure if it's to study her play on mime makeup and her perfectly tailored catsuit, or to see where else she plans to balance the gyrating orb.

Instead, Lawrence pulls me across the floor, and we move toward the bar.

"This is beyond crazy," Ryan says, trailing us, his eyes following a small group of people—I assume regular Joes like us, though they're dressed up in clubbing clothes—who are trailing the snake woman.

"It's . . . oddly *beautiful*, though?" I'm searching for words. "Beautiful" isn't the right one. "Otherworldly," I add.

"Hmm," is all Lawrence will concede. "But how on earth did she pull *this* off?" He waves around the room, and I get what he means.

This party is on a different level. Even from the pretty avant-garde party at the Zebra. And truthfully, it smacks of some pretty high-end taste that I wouldn't have necessarily attributed to Cleopatra before this. Media stunts? Yes. High-art fashion queens, glowing chessboards, and snake women? Harder to reconcile.

"Refreshments?" a smoky voice inquires from our right.

We swing as one to find the party's version of a cigarette girl—a queen in a black dress made of bubbles that Lady Gaga herself would be jealous of—carrying a tray of drinks.

No.

Flasks.

There, on the gold-plated tray, sit tiny glass flasks. One filled with red, one filled with the liquid the green of absinthe, and one filled with a deep amber liquid. All three bottles have colored, cut-glass stoppers, and a hand-scripted placard in the center of the tray reads, simply, Drink Me.

Reflexively, I grab for Lawrence's hand, willing him to remember what I told him about my suspicions that the refreshments at the last party played a role in Louis's death.

Beside me, Lawrence stiffens visibly. He's gotten my message. "No, thank you," I answer, flashing a smile.

"Are you sure? I insist. They're on the house." This to Ryan.

Small alarm bells go off in my head.

"We're good for right now," Ryan agrees. The queen moves off without another word. As one, we step closer to the bar. I'm getting the sense that I won't be eating or drinking *anything* at this party. Call me paranoid, but there is something I don't trust about it, whereas I'm usually all over the party food at gatherings. The more artichoke dip, the better.

The bartender steps forward, black towel over arm. He's dressed all in black and sporting a rather impressive silk top hat.

"Do you have anything bottled?" I ask. "Red wine, or beer?"

"I have the soda water for the mixes," he answers in a lilting accent. Eastern European, maybe? "But our drinks are of the highest quality liquor, each one a piece of art, I assure you."

That's basically what I'm afraid of. I eye the dazzling array of drinks in front of me. This bar *looks* professionally stocked and manned, but . . . the flasks have me rattled. And his mention of soda water has me wary of even that; it could be spiked.

"Er . . . bottle of water, I guess," I say, immensely saddened. I could really *use* a drink, truth be told.

"Same," Lawrence says.

148

Ryan, on the other hand, picks up the red-lit glass in front of him. "What's this one?"

"Ah, that's the Red Canary. Vodka, cranberry juice, lime, and a hint of jalapeño."

My eyebrows raise for a second time that night. "And this one?" I point to an amber one.

"The Golden Arrow. Walnut-infused whiskey, brown sugar, muddled orange peel."

"Interesting." So, the drinks are named after Golden Arrow characters. This party is insane, down to the smallest details. I'm about to keep quizzing him about the green drink next when Lawrence cuts me off.

"May I ask which bar service you are with? I'm hosting a party on Halloween, and I'm impressed with your presentation. Would you mind getting me contact information?"

"No problem, sir," the waiter says, producing a black card out of thin air and handing it to Lawrence.

"Thank you for the drink," Ryan says, saluting the bartender with the glass after a long pause. We slide to the side of the table and continue to look around while I sip at my water. *Yuck.*

Beside me, Lawrence flicks the seemingly solid black card over twice in his hand, then tosses it on the table. "What the hell? Who hands out blank cards? This shit is weird, the whole thing."

We both nod in agreement, and I note Ryan hasn't even touched his drink. He juggles the glass back and forth across the table top, letting the alcohol slosh out the top. The glass lurches into the center of the table after one extra-hard push, the little circle of colored light from the bottom of the glass spilling onto the black card. Before Ryan can snatch his glass back, Lawrence's hand whips out and grabs the glass.

Lifting the glass, he peers at the bottom. "Do you think this is UV?"

Ryan and I exchange confused glances, and Ryan shrugs before answering, "Uh, black light? Maybe?"

Something about the ambience of the room pulls my attention away from Lawrence. Everything around me glows a bit *more* than it did before; have the lights dimmed? I look up, squinting at the rafters of the theater, then have to stifle a gasp. Lawrence and Ryan respond to my surprise and turn their attention to the ceiling as well. Suspended above us are two fabric dancers. They are dressed mostly in black, but little lines of glowing fabric are sewn down their sides and the outside of their legs and arms. The fabric itself looks to be flecked with something glowing. Were they there when we walked in? There's no way I missed them. Unless they weren't visible before, all dressed in black against the black of the ceiling and the glare of the lights? Maybe they'd just dropped down?

Either way, I decide that if I see their glowing fabric and costumes this well, the light level has to be dropping. The realization that it probably was happening gradually doesn't do much for my feeling of unease. This whole party seems to exist solely to undermine a person's sense of reality.

"Anyone else realize it's getting darker?" I whisper. I'm not sure *why* I whisper, other than I'm not entirely certain how many of the people mingling around us now are hired performers, Muggles, or seal-bearers. Reality is certainly in question, because in the time it took me to look up and see the dancers, it seems like the number of people on the chessboard has multiplied.

Lawrence seems as unsettled as I feel, and we all exchange glances. The new level of darkness has increased the glow of the glass in Lawrence's hand, and I finally see what has drawn Lawrence's attention. Where the circle of black light from the cup touches the card, a pattern has emerged, revealed only by the light. Where there's no light, there's no pattern.

"Is that . . . invisible ink?" I ask, the slide down the paranoia rabbit hole increasing in speed.

"I think so," Lawrence answers, returning to his perusal of the card. He waves the cup over the card, then flips it over and does the same. One side is blank. The other side is *filled* with a loopy, hand-drawn pattern. We all squint. Within the loops and swirls, it seems like there are words.

"Well, I'll be damned, what does that even say? Seems like a crappy marketing ploy if you need a specific light to read your card." I bend closer, trying to make out the script that has appeared. "Hat-something . . . Here, hold that light closer. Ah, there. 'Hat Trick Entertainment.' And there at the bottom, there's some text. 'Fine purveyors of living art, refreshments, and debauchery . . . ,'" I trail off, not sure I've read that right.

Lawrence goes unnaturally still. "What did you just say?"

It's a stereo of the same question; Ryan leans in from my right, having spoken at exactly the same time.

"Yeah, I can't have read that right," I agree, squinting closer. "It's pretty loopy script, what word looks like 'debauchery'?"

"No. The name."

"'Hat Trick'? Our bartender is wearing a top ha—Lawrence, where are you going?"

Lawrence hasn't even let me finish. He's striding across the dark, glittering chessboard.

CHAPTER 16

Lawrence isn't messing around; he's headed toward the door and quickly, lit intermittently by soft green and red lights. It gives him the unnatural appearance of moving in fits and starts, almost like a horror movie. It gives me the willies.

Around me, the clear chess pieces sparkle like cut crystal, and the lights on the board fade in and out to the heavy drumbeat of the music. I do a double take and hesitate, rooted to the spot, even after Ryan sprints in pursuit of L's retreating back. Heavy drumbeat. When on *earth* did the music start? One of the things I'd noted when we first entered was the silence of the room. Now, it's no soft, faint classical music that accompanies fine conversation at a gala; it's heavy drum/bass of a trance. I cock my head. Is it just the drums, or do I hear the faint tinkle of a melody playing above it?

Ryan and Lawrence duck out of sight, around one of the opaque pieces on the board, and I physically shake myself loose from whatever has hold of my focus. I dodge around the opaque piece, narrowly avoiding running over a cigarette girl and her willing customer, and bowl through a pair of people—possibly Muggles, possibly performers—gyrating to the music beat on the chessboard like it's a dance floor.

"Sorry," I mutter, though they don't even utter a squeak of protest. They just keep dancing.

Finally, I catch Lawrence and Ryan and grab the back of Lawrence's shirt.

"We're leaving," he announces.

"Um, we're here for a *reason*. We can't just leave."

"No, we're leaving." This from Ryan instead of Lawrence, and I throw him a surprised look. He's *supposed* to be on my side.

"No, we're *not*. Ryan, aren't you the one who wants to prove this Golden Arrow is a fraud? And Lawrence, what is *with you?* You *both* know we're here . . ." I cut myself short before I can say, "To get the police access to this party." But I wave meaningfully at my wig and then to my buttons. "To *see the Golden Arrow*." I give each of the last words a verbal punch so he knows I mean more than what I'm saying.

"What does the card mean?" Ryan is asking Lawrence, right over top of my spiel. How freaking rude.

"I'm not talking about it," L answers, his voice short and clipped.

"Well, it obviously means *something* to you."

"Not here," is all L will allow.

"Agreed, not here," Ryan says, looking around like he's just seeing this place for the first time.

Ryan, too, seems spooked. I look back and forth between my brave champions. "Okay, well, either *both* of you just realized that the party we're at is *really weird*, or we're going to have to talk about this afterward?" The hairs on the back of my neck stand up. Neither of my BFFs are easy scares, and if they want to leave, something is up.

I'm about to insist someone tell me *something* when directly next to us, someone turns on the sun. I'm not the only one who immediately covers their face with a hand to block out the *immensely* blinding light that emanates from a single spot from the ceiling. It's like a helicopter has silently flown above us and pinned us with a searchlight. Everyone freezes.

Lawrence moves to my side and wraps an arm around me. I'm not sure if it's brotherly protection or if it's instinctual, but L isn't messing around. He's wound as tight and hard as a spring. This isn't a comfort hug; he's one hundred percent ready for an attack—to push me out of danger or throw me over his shoulder and run.

"Welcome, welcome to my Drag-Night Cirque," a familiar voice purrs over a sound system.

My eyes water against the light. I manage to stand upright under the weight of L's arm and squint against the glare, determined to figure out what on God's green earth this light is illuminating. Directly ahead of us, maybe six or seven feet, the lip of a simple black box stage is lit to daylight levels by a single spotlight. I drag my eyes up, but there's . . . no one onstage. My eyes continue upward. Is that . . . dust? No. The light is *glittering*, and now looking back at the stage, I see a dusting of it on the black. There's glitter falling from the ceiling. A murmur runs through the crowd—because there's a legitimate crowd of maybe fifty people shoving around us now—as we all glimpse a figure at the same time. Cleopatra, dressed in a dazzling white body suit with gorgeous geometric cutouts and wearing a tiara and white boa, floats through the air. Every inch of skin that is showing is glittering—glowing—in the light. She's seated on a fabric swing, and the swing is being lowered by unseen means—Wires? Motors? Zombie monkeys? The hand of God?—toward the stage.

"I do so hope you're having an amazing time and enjoying our entertainment and refreshments to the utmost."

I exchange looks with Ryan.

"I'm so glad to see so many of you tonight, and so glad that I can extend this once-in-a-lifetime opportunity to those present here."

Polite applause rings out, and I golf clap along with them, though Lawrence's grip on my shoulders makes it difficult.

Cleopatra alights on the stage with more grace than I typically see from her. She's in her element, completely. Her tiara shines brilliantly in the light, throwing disco-ball lights across those of us in the audience, and in her hand is a sequined baton that she wields like a scepter. She twirls it, more glittering light dancing across the stage and onto those present like a gift of holy water from the pope.

"My lovelies tell me I'm not the only queen in the house tonight. In fact, we're among royalty. Won't you all give a nice round of applause to our distinguished guests—we have several of Peter Wu's queenly court among us, and I just want to say thank you for the support from our reality show celebrities." She blows a kiss directly to us, and my gaze slides to Lawrence. He hasn't been called out by name, but he *is* one of Peter Wu's court, having been a runner-up on *Drag Divas* in his younger days. In turn, he's gazing around the room, I assume trying to figure out which of the other queens here we'd recognize.

L may be trying to figure out *who*, but I am trying to figure out *how*.

How has Cleopatra vaulted herself from second-rate queen to this creature I see holding court in front of me, hosting an expensive party that attracted the cream of the crop of both queen and non-queen attendees?

"We have noted those of you with seals, our valued guests, and will be approaching you individually for your audience with the Golden Arrow," she purrs.

The crowd stills.

"Oh yes, he's here and will entertain visitors as long as he wishes. I can't promise you all will see him this time around, but I promise some of you *will*. Until then, enjoy the refreshments and the show. Let the celebration begin!" She gives a dramatic snap of her glitter-painted fingernails, and we're plunged into instant darkness.

Startled gasps fill the air around me. L and Ryan and I grope for each other's hands and hold fast, unsure if we should make a move for the door or if this is intentional. It brings forcefully to mind the black-out on the night of the auction at San Diego Comic-Con, and hair rises on the back of my neck.

The darkness persists, but something changes in it. Perhaps the lighting on the chessboard has begun to glow dimly again? I squint and . . . yes. There. A faint flash of green. And there. Above the chessboard, the glowing costumes of the fabric dancers. I can't even make out their forms among the blackness of the ceiling, so it comes across as two writhing, glowing snakes, or an odd interpretation of the aurora borealis above our heads.

The low drumbeat has emerged again as well, and along with the slow swell of the black-and-glowing lights from the chessboard, I think that I hear a man whistling. And there! Walking among the hulking and sparkling shapes of the chessboard is a silhouette I know I've seen before. It's the man in the top hat I saw at the first party. This time the top of his hat glows in the dark, and his otherwise black suit is piped in glowing material. As he passes through the chessboard, the colors surge to life, rippling out behind him as if he's moving through glowing water. The lights of the chessboard change with his every step, and the cut-glass quality of the clear chess pieces dance with the light. As soon as he's past, the ripples subside. It's . . . marvelous. It's beyond creepy. The performers here are unlike anything I've seen. We're in a living art installation.

"How . . . how did he *do* that?" I whisper to Ryan. "The performances are unreal," I add when he doesn't respond.

Beside me, Lawrence stands stock still, watching the man in the top hat walk across the board like a deer in the headlights. Or perhaps L is the predator, crouched in the dark as *his* prey shows his feathers and walks by without a second glance.

The top hat disappears from view, and we're left with the softly glowing board, the music that thumps with heavy bass. The other performers reinfiltrate the crowd, and everyone disperses again, most headed toward the bar.

"This . . . isn't possible," Lawrence is muttering to himself.

"This is utter insanity," I agree.

Ryan is silent. Maybe he's so wigged he can't even talk. I can respect that.

"Refreshments?" another voice asks us from behind. We spin around, none of us having heard the cigarette queen who snuck up behind us.

The tray holds three cut-glass flasks, just like the last one, glittering in the reflected light. The script on the card glows in the dark, again reading, DRINK ME. But a second card glows next to the first, this one different than the one I'd seen before. EAT ME is printed in the same heavy script. I squint at the tiny round things on the tray next to the flasks. Three discs sit evenly spaced. At first glance they seem like . . . mints. Large mints—small cookies?—the size of a silver dollar. Not cookies, no, they're glittering subtly with red and gold in the muted lights of the room.

"Mints?" I hazard, leaning over them.

"A house specialty, for your enjoyment," the cigarette girl answers. "Limited to one per attendee on the house this evening, with our compliments."

My hairs rise for a third time that night. That sounds an awful lot like political side-speak for, "This is gonna mess you up."

"Uh, no thanks," I say at the same time that Lawrence leans over the tray and snatches one of the flasks and one of the mints.

Ryan and I gape at him, but he motions for us to do the same, so we do.

"Thanks," I say, trying desperately not to drop the mint into my pocket and wipe off my hand in front of the cigarette girl. I don't want to be anywhere near it, whatever it is.

She pauses for a moment, and I see her eyes note Lawrence uncorking the stopper of the bottle before she smiles and moves on. It's almost as if she *noted* that we took *and intended to eat* the snacks. It's all beyond insane.

"You *cannot* drink that. Absolutely not," I say, shoving the mint into the pocket of my vest, and reaching for L's flask.

"Don't be stupid, of course not," he agrees. "These," he continues, pouring the contents into a small plastic vial and sticking his mint into a baggie while we watch, "are samples. And we *need* samples; I have a bad feeling about this."

"Oh." And by "Oh," I mean, "Lawrence, you are bloody brilliant," because I'd already forgotten Matteo's directive to do just that. And I definitely didn't think to pack sterile bags or bottles or whatever to *collect* the samples in. Ryan and I hand over our flasks and discs in short order, and soon they're stowed in Lawrence's pockets for future retrieval.

"*Now* we can go," Lawrence says just as someone clears their throat from behind us.

"Michael-Grace Martin."

"Jesus, doesn't anyone just walk up to someone's face here?" I ask, spinning around for the third time that night. "That's me."

The queen who greets me wears a smirk that says "I know" on her black-painted lips. The lips that complement the slight *Elvira* look she's got going on, with a clingy black evening gown, long black sequined gloves, and a clove-smoke-smelling, smoldering cigarette holder.

I realize belatedly that I both did *not* give my name at entry and was in costume. My heart skips a beat beneath my own jumpsuit.

"Your audience is granted, if you'll come with me."

Holy shit. "Seriously?" I ask, my gaze darting between the queen and my companions.

She smirks again and turns, wading into the crowd. It's easy to pick her out, as her dress has glowing circles sewn down the length of the gown's back and train. But if I don't follow her, she'll be quickly swallowed by the crowd.

I'm surprised by *how* many people are in here now. Each time I turn around, it seems like it's multiplied. They must have given out a *lot* of lottery passes, or way more seals than they said they did.

I make a move to follow the queen, but a hand holds me back. One look says it's Ryan.

"Are you kidding me? This is the whole reason we're here."

"MG . . ." His face is chalky in the black light, and I've never seen Ryan look this serious. "We need to talk. There's no way this is what it seems. In fact, I'm worried this is *more* than it seems."

"What kind of vague bullshit is that, Ryan? The whole *reason*"—I wave at my person yet again—"we're here is to lay eyes on this guy, and I just got the nod. Now man up and let go."

Ryan presses his lips together. "Only if they let one of us in there with you."

I ignore the last bit of whatever he's saying and stride off after the queen. I assume from the muffled epithets that Lawrence and Ryan follow. She leads me off the chessboard and around behind the stage box, headed for a black-curtained entrance on the opposite side of the theater from where we entered.

At the curtain, she halts and turns to face me again. "Have you been enjoying the refreshments?"

"Oh, um . . . very much." I try to slur my words a little, given that I'm holding an empty cut-glass flask of . . . whatever this was. Chances are it had been potent.

A nod follows my statement; I've given the correct answer. She claps once, and two men appear, as does a black velvet box in her hands. I swear she wasn't holding anything three seconds ago. "You may deposit your cell phones in this basket for the duration of your audience; they will not be touched, and they will be returned. You're also being inspected for weapons. Security, you understand," she says, smirk still very much in place around her lips before taking a long, clove-scented drag from her cigarette holder. I wonder briefly if it's even *allowed* for her to be smoking in here, but bigger things take over my mind in short order.

One of the men approaches, wielding what I assume to be a metal detecting baton, and waves it over my person. It hums quietly as he goes over me once, twice, and then over my hair at length. I'm not carrying anything metal, and I know all the surveillance gear is plastic, but my heart hammers nonetheless. I let out a little breath as the first man steps backward with a nod. The second man steps forward next, carrying a little black box with small green lights on it. As he approaches, some of the lights turn amber. He halts, looks down at the box, then me, and then holds it up and adjusts a dial.

The lights brighten, and he waves it up and down before me. The lights shine amber and then red . . . right as they pass over first my microphone, earpiece, and then button camera. *Shit.* He repeats the action over Ryan and Lawrence, though nothing except green light greets their person.

The second man speaks quietly into his wrist and then approaches me. "Surveillance is not permitted; you are being excused from these premises." His eyes flick to Ryan. "You too, Mr. McCarthy."

Ryan and I exchange glances. They *definitely* know who we are, costumes or no.

He turns to Lawrence and addresses him alone: "*You* are invited to a private audience."

Before I can protest that this turn of events is insane, the man steps forward to block my view of the curtained opening, which is now parted for Lawrence to step through. "I suggest you leave quietly and don't make a scene." He steps back toward me, placing a beefy hand on my back and propels me forward.

"Lawrence!" I hiss, looking back over my shoulder.

Ryan and I are all but frog-marched back past the empty stage and through the chess set. No one in the crowd even looks twice as we pass. Either everyone's been enjoying the *refreshments*, or someone brought their own. Just like at the first party, there are many people here now that seem a little *too* happy to have had just a few drinks in under a few hours.

We're deposited unceremoniously back outside the front door, where a mass of people still waits against the building. As we emerge, a babble breaks out among the crowd, and not a few people start yelling questions at us.

The lights outside are just the standard streetlights, but they're blinding after the soft black-and-glow from inside. I squint up at Ryan as the exterior security guard takes over where the interior ones left off.

"This way, if you please," the beefy man who let us in growls before pulling a hand out of his coat pocket. Something hits the ground between us—a ziplock bag containing our phones. Once I scoop it up, he leads us down the block and ensures we cross the street. He turns and walks back to his post, but something inside me says we're waiting for the other shoe to drop. These people just figured out I'm probably still working with the police, attempted to spy on them, and then . . . what? Held my other friend hostage? The whole thing has an aura of going south very quickly.

I immediately fish my phone out of the bag, and hand Ryan his. Lawrence's is missing, which bodes well for my immediate course of action. I hope he somehow has managed to keep it on his person, though I suspect they confiscated his too.

"We've got to get to Lawrence," I say. "This is too weird, and I have a bad feeling about it."

"No shit, Sherlock," Ryan mutters, jabbing at his phone screen.

"Are you calling Lawrence?"

"Uh . . . yeah. Yeah. I'll call L," Ryan agrees. He's clearly about to call someone else. Maybe Matteo? But that is *my* job.

"*I'll* call the police," I confirm. "You get ahold of L and tell him to get his ass out here as soon as he can." I text Matteo. 911. It's not a code we agreed on, and I'm not sure of the delay on the feed from my camera, but it should be enough to spark him into instant movement. Three dots show up immediately, and I wait impatiently while I watch Ryan dial L's phone several times with no answer.

Get to the station, we have enough on camera, we're headed in. The text comes back.

I look at Ryan. "We're supposed to head to the station, which is gonna be a trick, considering L has the keys to his car. The police are coming."

Ryan's jaw tightens. "I'm not just leaving L—" he cuts off, craning his neck back toward the entrance of the building.

I mimic his actions, trying to see what's caught his attention.

It's L, under his own steam, walking at a measured pace out of the building, down the block, and to us.

He crosses the street, doesn't make eye contact, and continues past us toward the car.

Somewhere in the distance sirens wail to life, and I wonder if this is already Matteo's crew. Are they coming to break up the party and search for drugs? To try and apprehend the Golden Arrow themselves? "Er, we're supposed to go to the station," I announce at large as we fall in line and head to the car.

Lawrence jerks his head in a nod.

Ryan and I exchange glances.

"L? Are you okay?"

"No." The answer is clipped.

"Did they hurt you?" Ryan asks. We cross yet another street, the car within view now.

"No."

"Did you . . . did you see him?" I hate the way my voice sounds hopeful, even after all the shit we've just seen. "Is it real?"

"It's something, but I don't know what this whole circus is. I saw *someone*, but it sure as shit wasn't the Golden Arrow—or at least it better not have been."

Ryan stumbles to a stop, mere feet from the car, and we both swing around to see why he's frozen. "There was actually someone in that room?"

"Yep."

"Did you talk to them?"

"Nope."

"You just *left?*" This one from me, whose internal teenager can't believe Lawrence left without even *talking* to the Golden Arrow—supposed or not.

"Yep."

Lawrence throws open the driver's door of the Challenger and gets in, cutting off our conversation. Ryan and I scramble to get in the car too, and I hazard a look around. The feeling of being followed is strong, and I suspect we're not out of earshot from whomever is pulling the strings at that party.

"So, we're all . . . going to the station?" I ask hesitantly at the same time as Ryan demands more information from Lawrence.

"Can you describe what you saw?"

Lawrence is grim as he finally glances around at us.

"We need to talk. Not here. Maybe not even at the station. I'm going to turn over what I know, and . . . figure out what to do from there. I might need to get outta Dodge for a bit. I'm not safe here right now; I'm going to have to deal with this myself."

Chills seep down my spine. Not only is Ryan spooked about the whole thing, Lawrence is *beyond* spooked.

We drive in silence, Lawrence piloting us toward downtown.

"I have to ask; I can't wait any longer. What did you see?" I'm picturing dead bodies. Murder scenes.

"Someone I think I knew, once," Lawrence answers.

"What did they look like?" Ryan demands again. "Come on, if you're going to tell the police, you can tell us."

"I'm not going to *tell* the police anything," Lawrence spits. "I'm going to show them what I saw, and then I'm going to go take care of some business and do some research."

"Show them," I repeat. "Show them, how? I'm the one with all the surveillance gadgetry stuff."

"Which is why you got *your ass* caught," Lawrence confirms. His hands are tight on the wheel, and he keeps looking in the rearview mirror. "But you weren't the only one with a camera; I just went low-tech. And we'd better pray to whatever deity you choose that they never figure out how smart I was, because if they do, my ass is grass."

We wait.

L steers onto the interstate before he speaks again. "Before they figured out I hadn't had enough of their refreshments to make me loopy, *I* got a picture."

CHAPTER 17

"Well, we can't technically arrest the guy if he refuses to help, but *he* doesn't know that," Rideout growls, sinking into the chair opposite the couch where Ryan, Lawrence, and I are sandwiched like sardines. I shove aside the pile of current magazines and rest my feet on the small table.

"You'd think a photo manager at Walgreens would be happier to help the police in an investigation." From the eye Rideout casts over L, I get the sense he's not too happy at the turn his evening has taken. Well *I'm* not too thrilled to be stuck in a room with him or his boring tan slacks either. *Basic judgy bitch.*

"I doubt he gets many calls at midnight for his expertise," Matteo responds dryly before turning back to L. "Okay, we've done what you've asked. We found someone totally unrelated to the police force to develop the film from the pin thing."

"Pinhole camera," Ryan corrects. "Bloody brilliant. A modified pinhole camera in your necklace. Where did you get the idea?"

"How about that story later? Let's talk about what you *saw*, if you please," Matteo interrupts, steering the conversation back to the party. "You have my word that no one except us can hear us in this room."

My palms sweat again. It doesn't bode well that Lawrence insisted on a private meeting—no cameras, no recordings, no nothing. He's not even allowing Matteo to take notes. I've never *seen* him like this, truth be told. There's a hard edge, a wariness, a *predator* lurking inside the affable exterior of my best friend. I've seen it only once before, and only on film. The finale of *Peter Wu's Drag Divas*, L had this look.

L is talking to Matteo about going away for a while, which sounds a lot like running from something. I think I might be the only one to pick up on the notion that L isn't running. He's going *hunting*. And that's more unsettling to me than almost anything I can think of. L doesn't go looking for trouble without a damn good reason.

"I've seen it before. That 'eat me, drink me' stuff," L says, his body barely moving. It's like someone's cast the Imperius Curse on him, forcing him to speak. It's creepy as hell.

"Okay," Matteo agrees, eyes locked on Lawrence. "Tell me about the last time you saw it."

"I . . . it was a long time ago. At a party."

The hairs on my arm prickle. *A long time ago.* "Like, thirty years ago, a long time ago?" I ask, turning in my seat to face L.

One single nod confirms my hunch.

Thirty years ago, Casey Senior, original author of *The Hooded Falcon*, had been murdered. No one was more familiar with the timeline than the people in this room, since we'd all just tracked down the dirty DEA agent whose father had pulled the trigger, so to speak.

Matteo sits back, grasping the gravity of that comment. He opens his mouth to speak, but Rideout jumps in.

"Okay, so a party thirty years ago. What kind of party? This guy . . . one of your kind? What makes you so sure it's the same person?"

Lawrence's mouth snaps closed with an audible click. All of us pivot to face Rideout.

"What?" he asks when even Matteo raises his eyebrows.

I'm seeing red, and my restraint on whatever modicum of congeniality I attempt to keep when Rideout is present slips off. "I'm sorry—*your kind?*" I ask, attempting to keep my voice level.

Rideout sits back, looking surprised at the venom in my voice. "Oh, uh, I didn't mean—"

"You *meant* what you said, but you didn't think about it before it came out. And L here isn't any one sort of *kind* to have. He's a human, so if you meant, was this other human a *human*, the answer is yes." I'm just winding up for the pitch. I can't keep it from coming out, even though I know it's going to be bad. Bad, bad, bad. "And if you cannot be a *decent* human being and treat your informant with a little more humanity and understanding, you can just *get out*."

I can't stop it. I've just ordered a detective out of his own interrogation. I can't help it. I am always defensive of L. At bars, at shows. It drives me crazy when people try to treat him like anything other than a person whose hobby is dressing up in glitter and prancing majestically to music. People celebrate it when women do it; why get so judgmental when anyone else enjoys it too? Rideout embodies all I hate about the general populace.

You could have heard a pin drop.

Rideout gives a halfhearted cough-laugh before realizing I'm serious.

"Get out," I reiterate, this time with complete composure. "If you want this interview to continue, you may not be present anymore."

"You can't be serious. Kildaire—"

Matteo sorta hooks his head over his shoulder. "Maybe go follow up with the photo guy."

Rideout looks around the room like someone's just spit on his burger and called it a special. No one moves. He puffs up his chest and storms out of the room, slamming the door behind him.

"He didn't mean it like that," Matteo offers after a moment of ringing silence.

I open my mouth, but L cuts me off. "I don't need you to defend me, MG. I mean . . . thanks, girl. I know you have my back, but I can fight my own battles. And I know he didn't think about what he said, but ignorance doesn't absolve anyone of being an ass."

Matteo concedes the point and wisely decides to move on. "Will you tell me about your recollection about the party?"

L nods. "Shortly before Mr. Casey died, he called me into his office and told me he was going to a Halloween party. He wanted to take me instead of whomever else he'd planned on taking. I can't help but wonder now if it was because he suspected someone was after him, but I can't be sure. He just told me he wanted me there in an undercover security capacity. Most people knew at this point that Mr. Casey had taken me in, but not everyone knew I was working for him, or that he'd paid for defense training."

Matteo's fingers twitch, and I just know he's itching to write this down. Respect for L's wishes wins out; he sits quietly until L is ready to continue.

"So, this party—pretty standard fare Halloween party for rich people. Costumes, themes, that sort of stuff. This particular party happened to be a *Through the Looking Glass* theme, so we got all dressed up—Mr. Casey was a playing card, and I didn't have a costume so he just gave me this tall hat that he said the other person was supposed to wear."

Matteo and I exchange glances. This is the second time *Alice In Wonderland* has surfaced in as many days. My Spidey-sense says it isn't mere coincidence; there's more here.

"We arrived at the party, and it definitely felt weird. Off. We didn't stay long. But while we were there, the refreshments were served on trays that looked a lot like the trays at the party tonight. At first, I thought it was coincidence, but now I'm not so sure."

"What about them was similar? Be as detailed as you can."

"The wording. 'Eat Me,' 'Drink Me.' That sort of thing."

Matteo nods. If he were Sherlock, he'd be filing something away in his mind palace.

"So, tonight it weirded me out to see it again, but I told myself it was coincidence. It's in a famous book and all that. But I wasn't so sure after I got *this*." He flicks the card from the caterer at Matteo. "Something about this seems so . . . wrong."

Matteo takes the blank black card and examines it.

"Black light–activated, we think. It says 'Hat Trick Entertainment,'" L explains.

"And what does that mean to you?" Matteo asks, tucking the card in his pocket. "In light of this case, I mean."

"Well, it's just that the tie-in to *that* specific party seems a little too coincidental. I haven't told you the whole story yet. In the parking lot on our way out, a car tried to run Mr. Casey and me over. I'd chalked it up to an accident—it was dark, people had been drinking, that sort of thing."

"But now you're not so sure?"

"I'd already started to wonder after Mr. Casey died. But it was ruled a heart attack, so I put it out of my mind. Then when the whole Muñez thing went down this summer, I thought about it again, but it didn't seem to matter anymore since they ended up wearing stripes. So, this is the third time I've wondered if someone were trying to hit Mr. Casey on purpose that night, and, well, it seems plausible *and* relevant at this point."

"I'm still not following what all this has to do with the Golden Arrow," Matteo says, running his hand through his dark hair. I feel the same; the "ah-ha" moment hasn't hit me either.

"This is where it gets dicey as a theory. I'm operating on pure gut and imagination at this point." L pauses for permission to continue, given this admission, looking between Matteo and me.

"Intersection of pure gut and imagination is where I live," I quip. "Matteo is fully capable of handling the crazy theories, I assure you."

"Well, okay. The party tonight was weird. The refreshments were weirder. But when we got to the back room . . . you know about that part, right?"

"The camera recorded up until MG left the theater."

"Well, I was ushered into this side room. And there was a guy in there sitting in a big chair, like a king taking an audience from his throne. More than that, though, it's like he . . . knew me. Like he'd specifically been looking to come face-to-face with *me*." L sounds rattled all over again, and gooseflesh breaks out on my arms.

"Can you describe him?"

"Not well. He was dressed in this black paramilitary jumpsuit thing, and he had a cape and a mask on—"

"Hold on. Hold on—he had a cape and a mask on?" This is the first time Ryan has spoken. "Like a real cape and a real mask?"

"That's what I *said*, isn't it?" countered L. "Gold. Glittery. But not like those old Batman capes from the TV show that would have gotten in the way. Just enough for . . . I dunno, *effect*, I guess." Only L would critique the fashion of a superhero's cape.

The cape clinches it for me, though. "So, it was *him*," I say.

L hesitates. "I . . . I hope not. I'm pretty sure this is the same person who tried to kill Mr. Casey thirty years ago."

We let that bombshell settle for a few moments.

"What makes you say that?" Matteo asks, voice totally controlled.

"Okay, I told you that this was dicey. The voice. I've heard it before. Yeah, yeah, it's been a hot minute, but it's recognizable. Gravelly. Like he's smoked seven packs a day or had throat surgery or something. He had it even when he was younger. I—I think it was a guy who used to work for Casey. DeWayne or something. I only met him a few times, but that *voice*."

"What did he say tonight?"

"He said he'd been looking forward to meeting me and asked me if I enjoyed the refreshments. He questioned the goons that held my arms about if they'd seen me eat and drink the food at the party and then got really mad when they said they weren't sure. I . . . panicked. I can't tell you how I *know* it, but . . . this guy meant to hurt me. He wanted to talk first, but he definitely meant for me to be out of it enough not to remember much or fight back."

My skin crawls.

Matteo sits back, fully serious Detective Kildaire now. "What did you do? Why did he expect you to be out of it?"

"I snapped that photo so that even if they killed me, maybe somehow someone would see that bastard's face, and then I played dumb. Loopy. Started talking to one of the guards like he was the Golden Arrow. I tried not to play it up too much, not overdo it. The guy in the cape had me escorted back out, was yelling at everyone that they brought me in too early. I think they meant to give me more time for whatever was in the refreshments to work fully, but I pulled the old 'pretend to be a potted plant' thing and walked out of there."

We all stared at him, baffled.

"You pretended to be a *potted plant*?" Ryan asked.

"Not *literally*. I ducked, covered, and walked out like I was any old schmo. I don't think they thought I could move very fast on whatever was in those 'refreshments.' And I don't know if it was in *all* the drinks or just the ones they gave to me. There's no way to know how targeted this was. An entire party just to get to lil' ole me seems excessive when I'm onstage two times a month at Hamburger Mary's."

"L, that was really brave to just walk out." He'd been so cool, so calm . . . no hint of what had gone down.

L snorts. "It was self-preservation. Now. Hot-Lanta. I'd appreciate if you figure out who this guy is."

Matteo's gaze is in parts thoughtful and concerned. He draws in a deep breath through his nose and sits back in his chair. "Just to sum up: the guy who says he's the Golden Arrow somehow allegedly arranged to have drugs slipped to you, requested a private meeting, wanted to talk, and then maybe beat you up for unknown reasons. You've heard him before and saw the same sort of placards at a party thirty years ago where someone tried to run over Casey Senior. We have a picture, but our suspect is wearing a cape and mask, and you have no idea about his current whereabouts."

Even to me, it sounds jumbled. None of the threads line up.

171

Matteo states the obvious. "I'm not going to lie; it's not a lot to go on."

"I know." Lawrence is dead serious.

A thought occurs to me. "DeWayne something? Could he be that 'D' in those journal pages you got?"

L's eyes hood slightly. "Yeah, probably. He and Casey did business from time to time. It's why I saw him in the office."

So just *coincidentally* both "D" and "Stevie" have surfaced this week in L's life. Hard to chalk up to random chance. Maybe the Golden Arrow knows something we don't. Maybe the journal pages aren't *completely* useless.

"And the other name in the journal, L . . . if you look at it, I think it says Stevie. Isn't that the guy who came to your shop?"

At this, L literally clams up as his mouth snaps shut and his gaze goes to the door.

"Lawrence?" Matteo prods. "This is important. Could Stevie be involved in this? He and DeWayne had a meeting together with Casey. That's more than coincidence, right?"

Lawrence's eyes flash up, filled with such a range of emotion it almost takes my breath away. "Stevie would *never* be involved in tonight's escapade. Or the OD. You need to leave him out of this."

Whoa.

I've *rarely* seen L this worked up about *anything*, much less a thirty-year-lost friend.

Matteo seems to sense the same. "Okay, but, Lawrence, you knew this person a long time ago, right?"

L nods.

"And you aren't in current contact?"

Hesitation, but ultimately, L gives a resigned shake of his head. "We haven't talked for years. Not since . . . well, things went south shortly after Mr. Casey died."

Matteo's voice is gentle. "Then how can you be so sure he's not involved?"

Lawrence closes his eyes once and then focuses on Matteo. "Because I know Stevie."

I can tell Matteo is getting annoyed, but he navigates this well. "If this is connected to Casey Senior's case, why have you not mentioned it before? Is there something that needs to be added to your testimony?"

Lawrence's jaw clenches, and then his shoulders give ever so slightly. "There's nothing much to tell, and it's personal. It had nothing to do with Casey Senior. Stevie and I—we were involved. I've never said anything because his father never knew he was gay—*couldn't* know he was gay. If I outed him—even now—it could ruin him. I never wanted that for him—back then he told me he was leaving that part of his life behind and never looking back. But I knew him and the kind of person he was back then. He wouldn't need this sort of production or *circus*. He just wanted to live his life, and our relationship complicated things too much for him."

The pain in L's voice is raw. After all these years, it's obvious L has never gotten over his feelings. It makes sense as to why L has been quiet about this too . . . L's love isn't something one earns lightly. And once you have it . . . well, apparently thirty years isn't long enough to tarnish it.

Matteo is silent a long moment. "Okay, if he's not connected now, could this Stevie help us find DeWayne, since he knew him? This is to find the person who allegedly tried to hurt you tonight. No one needs to know we reached out to him, or that we've made the connection. I promise we will be discreet."

After the longest pause in history, Lawrence lets out a five-hundred-pound sigh. "Maybe."

Victory. Matteo sits back. "So, do you remember Stevie's last name?"

Lawrence gives a hollow laugh. "Stevie's name is a hard one to forget." He reaches down at my feet and plucks *People* off a stack and tosses it at Matteo.

It takes a long moment for the magazine cover to click with my brain. Copper skin, chocolate eyes, tousled curls.

I suck in a breath. "*Stevie* is Whalon Fox-Stevens?"

Ryan nearly falls off the couch. "Tech guru Whalon Fox-Stevens?"

L nods.

"*People*'s Most Eligible Bachelor, Whalon Fox-Stevens?" I ask, just to clarify that the world has, in fact, been turned on its head.

L tosses me a look.

Guess it's not hard to figure out why Whalon might still be single, on that note, given L's admissions tonight.

Matteo blinks rapidly, this twist unforeseen. "I, er, will reach out to his office and see if he'll set up a meeting with us. I'll let you know what turns up . . . given the background, would you like to be invited to the meeting?"

My heart lifts at the thought. Maybe Stevie has pined for L all these years, and that's why he showed up at his shop last week. Maybe L and Stevie will get a second chance. I squint, something about his hair pulling at my memory. The show. I saw Stevie at the drag revue, right when I sat down with Ryan. He had come to see L, I was sure of it now; maybe my theory isn't so far off.

But L's face remains grim. "You work on your end; I'm going to work on mine."

Both Ryan and I swivel to face L. "What does that mean, exactly?" Ryan asked. "L, you should let the professionals . . ."

"This is someone from *my* past. I'm going to do everything I can to figure out who it is. It's personal. I already told you that I don't know his last name, but someone in my old hood must. People talk. If DeWayne is the Golden Arrow, I'm going to find out about it."

Matteo's face doesn't change. "As a part of this investigation, I'm going to have to ask you not to leave the area."

My mind flashes back to a few months ago, when L went underground after receiving a threat. Truthfully, this is probably L's best plan, if what he said was true. If the Golden Arrow is somehow out to get Lawrence . . . well, that changes everything.

"Oh, I'm not leaving the area," Lawrence says, rising from the couch and heading to the door. "I'm just going somewhere they won't talk to cops."

And without another word, L walks out of the station.

"You realize that now we have no ride home, don't you?"

Ryan is the first to speak. We've waited almost ten minutes to see if L will come back, but no dice.

Matteo takes a deep breath and stands. "I'll take you two home; it's late. Rideout will let me know as soon as he has the picture in hand, and I'm not going to bed until then anyhow."

Ryan and I shuffle out of the room behind Matteo, and the impact of the evening hits me like a stack of comic books. The party, L's story, the dire look in his eyes when he walked out that door. I may be exhausted, but now I'm vibrating with anxiety. Not the prize I'd been hoping to win tonight.

As much as I'd guessed—no, *known*—that the Golden Arrow story wasn't over, this is a turn of events I'd never have predicted. Questions tumble around in my mind faster than an X-wing with a critical hit. I hold them in only as long as it takes for the three of us to wedge ourselves into Matteo's pristine Prius.

"Why would the Golden Arrow go after Lawrence?" I ask at large. I operate best when I can either talk out the story problem or do

Meghan Scott Molin

something physical, like throw a ball against the wall—à la House, MD—or bike out the issue.

"He's not the real Golden Arrow," Ryan says from the back seat. After a beat he amends his statement with, "*I* don't think so, at least." And neither do I, truth be told. Daniel Kim fits every requirement, and this guy . . . doesn't. Puzzle pieces of suspicion fall into place, and a picture forms. Ryan knows *something*, but what? Maybe I need to look into whether Ryan and Daniel know each other well . . . it's possible Ryan is passing Daniel information, as much as I hate to think about Ryan lying to me.

"But why now? And why has Stevie suddenly shown back up, too?"

"We don't know that he—if it is even the same D from the journal or the same person from Lawrence's past—wanted to hurt Lawrence for certain. We are going pretty far out on a pretty thin limb here," Matteo interjects before Ryan can reply.

I know he can sense the *look* I'm giving him in the dark.

"What? It's true. All of this is hunch. *All* of it." He means the whole Golden Arrow case at this point, and he's not wrong.

For the second time in as many months, we're hunting ghosts and whispers. Be that as it may, I secretly love it and feel a little salty that he's dashed my questions with the cold water of fact.

"Yeah, okay, Beckett, you can just *detective* over there while I Richard Castle over here," I say, unable to hide my surly side. I swear Matteo rolls his eyes, but I ignore him and choose to flounce instead. I turn in my seat so I'm facing more toward the back and Ryan.

"What we have to figure out," Ryan continues as if he, too, is ignoring the elephant of missing facts in the room, "is why this *someone* is impersonating the Golden Arrow." I gather the inflection is for Matteo's benefit.

"And *why* he's suddenly after Lawrence," I agree. I'm stumped on the actual GA, so trying to come up with why an imposter would be impersonating him puts my writer skills to the test. I nibble on my lip

176

for a moment, letting the story take me. What would I write if this were my villain? The theory that he's somehow related to an existing bad guy seems most plausible. "Maybe this guy works for Muñez."

Ryan sits up in the back seat; I can hear the swish of his jacket against the seat. "True. Like retribution for putting his boss in jail?"

I chew on that a moment.

Ryan speaks up in my silence. "Or . . . he has a grudge against L."

I snort. "A thirty-year-old grudge? Against a person he met a few times?"

"All right fine, it's unlikely. Maybe it's related to the trial," Ryan agrees.

"Why would they want to hurt Lawrence and dismiss the both of you if it has to do with the trial?" Matteo asks, his voice filled with exasperation. "That's what I can't figure out."

"Oh, are you playing this game now?" I ask archly.

Under the flash of the overhead streetlights, I see the dark look he shoots me. I decide to play along instead of antagonizing him further. His brain is just as good at this game as mine. "Theory on the table is retribution," I repeat.

Matteo shakes his head. "Why go after L instead of any one of us? Any one of us is ultimately more culpable and a better target. L may be the face of the story, but MG and I both have much more intrinsic testimony for the trial."

"That's a cheery thought," Ryan intones.

"Yeah, gee thanks," I toss in.

"I'm *saying* that they had an opportunity to have all three of you in that room. They chose L."

"That is a good point," I allow grudgingly.

"So, we're back to, if this is a person from L's past, why now?" Ryan sounds salty. "Why L, why now."

"He knows something." Matteo sounds so sure, I swivel to look at him.

"Knows what?" I ask, my left eye squinting.

Matteo shrugs. "Something. He may not even *know* what it is he knows that is important. It makes perfect sense. L says he knows the voice of the Golden Arrow—"

"*Alleged* Golden Arrow," Ryan chimes in tartly from the back seat.

Matteo ignores him and continues on. "And if they want Lawrence, it must be because he *knows* something important to the case."

"But you've asked him every question under the sun about that case. He's been under oath. *We* know everything there is to know too." Even my writer's brain can't keep up with this, and he sounds *so* sure. The student has become the teacher, I guess.

Matteo shakes his head. "Except we don't. Someone tried to kill Casey the night of that party. Lawrence only just thought to mention it. And the whole DeWayne thing—"

"L said he'd met him three times, hardly something one would think of offhand," I defend.

Matteo forges ahead. "We're forgetting the half of a journal that's still missing. Lawrence knows something, and someone doesn't want him to reveal it. I believe it's connected to this person, the *alleged* Golden Arrow—whomever he is—from L's past."

We all sit in silence, mulling that over.

"I feel a lot like Scully to your Mulder here, but there's no proof that this guy *is* the Golden Arrow. Just because you believe it doesn't make it true."

"The truth *is* out there," Ryan quips from the back.

I snicker despite the serious tone of the conversation. I can't help it; a good nerd joke is a good nerd joke. "Matteo, you're forgetting one thing. The journal pages. Why on earth would the Golden Arrow deliver pages to incriminate himself?"

No one has an answer to that.

"Okay, so we're back to DeWayne being an imposter," I say. "We're still stuck on *why*." I rub my head, suddenly tired. "Here's a recap:

178

Lawrence knows something, the Golden Arrow wants what he either has or knows, *or* wants to keep him silent. It either has to do with the trial *or* the current cases with the Queen of Hearts. And journal pages were delivered by the *real* Golden Arrow, presumably to incriminate DeWayne—a person Lawrence hardly knew—and possibly Whalon. Who, it turns out, is Lawrence's teenage love and now a tech billionaire. This is so confusing it's exhausting."

Matteo slaps his hand to his head. I see the gleam of his eye in the streetlight near my house as he pulls to the curb and turns to face me in the car. I recognize that look. It is the look of catching the threads of a story. A *good* story. When I get that look, I lock myself in the laundry room of our house and don't come out until I've poured my ideas out on a page in some form or another.

"What if we're overcomplicating this? Assuming our current Golden Arrow is an imposter, there's a simple explanation. What if he's going by another name these days—one related to an *Alice in Wonderland* party thirty years ago?"

I got it in the same exact moment that Ryan did.

It makes sense. The person from L's past, the person who is pretending to be the Golden Arrow now, the person anxious to silence the one person who could ID him? Why not masquerade as a vigilante hero while you're secretly a drug lord?

We all speak together, a chill running down my spine.

"The Queen of Hearts."

CHAPTER 18

The Genius lobby bustles more than usual when Ryan and I make our way out the front door after work on Monday. My car has returned to its state of not working, and I'm bumming a ride home with Ryan's Uber so I can change before my movie meeting. Since our little mental breakthrough, I've been on pins and needles, waiting for an update from Matteo on the case. So far as I know, they have a meeting scheduled with Whalon Fox-Stevens for this week, and no one has heard word one from L. Meanwhile, the Golden Arrow has gone to ground again, and I feel like I'm living for the Twitter feed #goldenarrow, hoping for a hint of his next move. I'm so immersed in my thoughts, I narrowly avoid colliding with a woman just inside the foyer.

"Whoops," I manage, pivoting to avoid dropping my messenger bag and sketches. Ryan does a nifty sidestep and actually uses her elbows to execute a do-si-do. It obviously delights her, and she tosses her dark curls back, hoping to catch Ryan's eye. He's so spry, I'm jealous. Maybe I should pick up CrossFit classes.

"Sorry about that," he says. Without another glance at her, Ryan wades through the crowd. I alone see her look of confusion—she's gorgeous; I highly doubt she's often ignored like that. I follow Ryan, studying his bearing from behind. There was many a year I knew him where Ryan would have either stammered and turned red under the gaze of a pretty girl or, in our later life together, attempted to flirt back. Ryan has never had game, and he's never really handled female attention well. It's one of the things I've found quirky, authentic, and charming about him.

But now . . . this cool, assured Ryan is someone almost foreign to me. I suspect a lot of it is Lelani's presence in his life. It's almost impossible for her confidence *not* to spill over onto other people, and maybe this version of Ryan has been waiting to get out. Sometimes I'm not kind about their relationship in my head, but for a moment I can appreciate the metamorphosis that Ryan has gone through in the last year.

I hasten to catch up with him as he disappears down the walk in front of the building, heading for the employee parking. As we shortcut through the landscaping, Ryan's phone dings. And then dings again.

"Man, you're popular today."

Ryan stops and checks his phone. "Just the usual. Hey, do you mind if I return this call real quick?"

"No pr—"

But he's already walking away.

I make a game out of attempting to shuffle pebbles into a soft strip of asphalt paving, and it lasts me for about thirty seconds. I'm trying not to eavesdrop, but Ryan's conversation is heated. He sounds upset? Angry? No, maybe not angry, but definitely urgent. I think I hear something about a test . . . a test run? A sample of a game? I'm guessing this has to do with his meeting. I know he had the last test of his video game before market this week. Maybe the video game still has problems.

"MG." It's Ryan, and I turn to see him shoving his phone back in his pocket, a frown creasing his brow. "I've got to change my plans. Right now. I'm sorry. Can you find another ride home?"

"I—uh—sure?" I stammer, but he's already pulled out his phone again and returned to texting. I've been dismissed.

My first inclination is to call Lawrence, but that doesn't seem like it would be a fruitful avenue, so I tap my Uber app instead. I groan inwardly, thinking about how long it might take to get a car at this time of day, then hesitate. If I throw over the plan of changing clothes, there's one person I know who might be okay giving me a ride last minute.

I feel like a bum, I type. But my car didn't start. Is there any chance you're near the Genius building and you could take me to the meeting? If not, no problem, I'll just order a car.

Almost immediately, a reply pops into the window.

Actually, just wrapped up a meeting here, headed out to the parking lot.

I throw Ryan a thumbs-up, even though I'm feeling awful about having to ask people to cart me around. He only halfheartedly returns it; he's now leaning against the wall by the employee entrance, looking ready to run the second I let him. I can only imagine this is some sort of video game emergency I'm witnessing, he looks so agitated.

"Is everything okay?" I ask him.

"Hmm? Yes. Yes. Work stuff."

He turns back to his phone, so I turn back to mine. I'm not sure if he's going to text me again, or . . . Daniel appears at the threshold of the door behind Ryan, and I wave at him. He catches sight of Ryan to his left and reaches out to clap his shoulder in a "Hey, Bro" kind of move when Ryan startles. He must not recognize him, because the second Daniel reaches for him, Ryan steps back and pivots like someone's trying to jump him in an alley.

In an equally knee-jerk reaction, Daniel jumps back, coming to rest in a position I recognize as a "waiting/defense" position from martial arts. On the balls of his feet, hands up. "Whoa, whoa, whoa," he's saying.

"What the . . . ." It's like a movie. Both of them.

Ryan's face becomes red, and he rolls his shoulders twice before sticking out his hand to Daniel. "Um, sorry, dude. I was really focused on this email, and I thought you were going to take my phone."

Given the fact that his face is *just* now healed, it's understandable. Not to mention we're all extra jumpy right now with Lawrence being MIA.

"Yeah, uh, no problem?" Daniel returns, running his hands through his hair. He and Ryan face off for a moment like rival tigers, and I don't really understand the tension. Ryan's gaze is flitting from Daniel to me, and something like comprehension dawns across his face.

My cheeks heat. I'm fairly certain that Ryan thinks there's something going on between Daniel and me at this point. His look of "ah-ha" unsettles me. There's *nothing* to "figure out" here. Ryan asked me to find another ride; Daniel was the natural choice, seeing as he's going to the same meeting.

I'm about to reiterate something along those lines when Ryan just sort of waves and peaces out, already dialing a number on his phone, leaving Daniel standing alone in the doorway. He's staring after Ryan with a puzzled expression on his face . . . Ryan's weirdness wasn't lost on him either. This encounter doesn't lend itself to my theory that they're working together. There wasn't any familiarity in their interaction, unless they're *really* good actors.

"So how is life, other than your poor car?" Daniel asks as he holds the passenger door open.

"Oh, the usual. Drowning in work. You?"

"I've got some projects that are picking up too. I hear you," he agrees. He shuts my door and comes around the front of the car before picking up our conversation again. "The movie stuff isn't stressing you out, is it?"

"Not too much," I say. "I really enjoy it, and I'm excited to see the sketches of the costumes today."

"How's the case coming along?"

The fact that he even asks raises my suspicions again. Is it coincidence that he asks right after the weekend debacle?

My phone dings in my bag, and I search through the pockets, looking for it. It's probably Ryan, apologizing for his ridiculous behavior. "Slow," I hedge. "We're still exploring several leads." There, that could mean anything.

"Pretty crazy about that reward. I've seen the flyer everywhere and keep meaning to ask you if you knew about it."

I slant a look at him just as I locate my phone. I pull it out triumphantly. "Oh, I definitely know about the reward." Is this him admitting interest in the reward to me? I make a mental note to renew this line of suspicion with Matteo. I assume he'd have told me if his investigation revealed anything about Daniel, but I should check in about it. He'd just *literally* done a ninja move in front of me.

Daniel pulls out of the parking lot and onto the main road. "It's all over the media that some people got to meet the real Golden Arrow at a party the other night."

"Yeah, uh, I heard that too," I fudge, clicking my home button to bring up the alerts for my text messages. Matteo. And it's not a friendly *hello, how ya doin'*.

"Hey, Daniel, do you mind swinging by the shop? I think I'm going to try to borrow Lawrence's car. It sounds like I'm going to need to go somewhere after the meeting."

Daniel glances from me to my phone. "Yeah, sure. Everything okay?" He switches lanes and immediately puts on his turn signal to do a U-turn at the next light.

"Yep. Work stuff. Drowning, remember?" I'm not lying, but I'm not being entirely honest either. I read the text one more time before clicking my phone back off. Looks like I'm not going to have to wait long for the conversation about Daniel.

Need you at the station ASAP. GA.

Driving Lawrence's car is like sipping straight out of a bottle of tequila—all at once a rush and the sensation that this could get you in a lot of trouble. I feel like the heroine in the bad-assest of comics as I speed along the side streets. The engine of the Charger purrs, the steering wheel vibrating slightly under my hand. I can imagine myself as the Golden Arrow, prowling the streets for drug dealers this way. I'd have my cape and mask on the side seat, ready to throw on in a flash, the second my Spidey-sense notices something amiss. Holy hell, why doesn't Lawrence drive *everywhere* with this thing? I've already taken two detours on my way to the meeting just to keep driving. My own vehicle inspires none of these feelings, and I'm loath to ever drive it again—like what Riker would feel if he ever captained a lesser ship after so many years aboard the Enterprise.

Daniel was kind enough to drop me off at the shop, and I just *happened* to know where L kept his spare key set in the back office. Which I used my only-to-be-used-in-emergencies key to the salon to get to. I sent a text saying I hoped it was okay, I was borrowing the car—still no concrete word on where L actually *is* at the moment. The shop held an air of neglect. For now, I have too many other things to deal with before trying again to get L to tell me. First, I have this meeting about costumes for the movie, and then I need to throw on my Sherlock cap and head to the station. A comic book expert's day is far from dull.

Dark clouds start to roll in off the coast, and I'm doubly glad I'm not on my bike as I pull into a parking spot outside the studio office. If it's going to rain, I'm going to leave most of my stuff inside the car—I need very little for this meeting other than my brain and my sketchbook. I make a move to clear L's gym bag and shoes off the passenger seat to make a space to open my messenger bag when something catches my attention.

Maybe it's that picturing my own cape and mask in the side seat put me in mind of the case, but something about his gym gear strikes a chord in my head. There, set neatly atop the black bag that I *know*

L takes with him to the gym are what *I* would consider boring gym shoes. Black, silver and red stitching, but yawn otherwise. Except . . . the insignia on the bottom is a name I've heard before. New Balance. On a hunch I check the shoe's tongue. 2040.

Now. It could be coincidence. It could *totally* be coincidence. You know that thing where when you hear a word for the first time, take note, and then hear it a million times the next day? Maybe I'm experiencing that with men's athletic shoes. But . . .

Lawrence *couldn't* be the Golden Arrow. It's Daniel Kim. Or Daniel Kim's brother.

Right?

We've already gone over this . . . he testified in court. His alibi is solid. He and Ryan both cleared questioning—I've been around this mulberry bush before. But. That was the first case, earlier this summer. Nothing saying it's the *same* Golden Arrow, or that Lawrence hasn't picked up a gig fighting crime on the side, inspired by the GA.

My mind spins out, quick as a wink. L *had* helped me catch Agent Sosa. He has inside knowledge of the journals and access to the investigation. He's an excellent actor, and certainly fit enough for the description we'd heard from the drug dealers. Hadn't he just told Matteo that he was going off to investigate the case on his own? Could it really be that simple, that the Golden Arrow has been *right* under my nose the entire time?

Casting a quick eye outside the car to make sure no one was watching or waiting for me, I slip the shoes to the side of the bag and grasp the zipper. I don't know if I *hope* I'll find a cape and a mask, or if I hope I won't. My heart hammers inside my chest like I'd just run down my thirteenth ubervamp on the *Buffy* series finale.

On the internal count of three, I open the bag and peer in. Black gym shorts and two tees sit on top of a small stack of items in the bag. I really don't want to invade my friend's privacy, so I hesitate at digging any further. From this vantage point, it looks like your average gym bag and shoes. I note the bottle of hair glitter rolling around on one of the sides and smile despite the crucial moment. Only L would think hair glitter a necessary item to take to the gym, and it certainly doesn't scream Golden Arrow to me. I let out a small sigh of relief and zip the bag back up, then carefully replace the shoes on top. I'm not fully convinced L *isn't* the Golden Arrow—the idea has taken root in my mind and merits personal investigation—but for the moment I feel okay to sit on the discovery of the shoes. It wouldn't do anyone any good to call Matteo in on the simple fact that my best friend happens to own a pair of shoes that maybe sorta kinda fit the description given by a teenage drug dealer. One who probably didn't even know for certain that the brand of shoes he'd given was accurate. It would be a big pile of trouble for L, and all for nothing, unless . . .

Unless.

I needed to think about that unless. But I note to myself as my phone dings an alarm for the meeting, that "unless" would have to wait until after this meeting, and after I heard what Matteo had for me.

CHAPTER 19

The moment the art meeting starts, I know that I've found "my place." It's an odd feeling. I'm sitting here, in a room full of people similar to the writing meeting. The same style table, the same group of mostly men in hipster beards and glasses. The same mess of papers scattered across every available surface.

The difference is that, instead of feeling nervous and feeling like I need to prove my worth to be here or navigate some sort of gender-imposed social structure, I just *exist* here. And maybe it's because this group has a few women in it, and the men aren't outright hostile to my presence like the previous meeting. Or maybe it's just that because from the moment I see the sketches for Swoosh's various costumes and the look of the Falcon's cape . . . I'm home. I've sketched these very ideas. Well, not these specifically, but the subject matter. How many times have I reenvisioned what I'd like *THF* to look like instead of the mainstream comics? Too many to count. This is my chance. These are my people. *This* is the place that my journey has brought me, what I've been fighting to find, what I've been looking for without knowing it.

It. Is. Like. Christmas.

It's a buoy in an otherwise stormy sea of my life right now. It's the first thing that I've found to cling to after I unmoored myself from being a full-time Genius employee. For the second time in my life, I have the thought of, *I can't believe they're paying me to do this.* The hour flies by. Daniel and I set up station at one end of the table, and we work through the cast of characters in order of importance and appearance.

There is lively debate about the functionality of "boob armor," and I end up sketching a suggestion for the new female protagonist that doesn't involve seven miles of cleavage and two inches of spandex. Daniel adds his own expertise to the mix, even demonstrating for the artists several of the movements he thinks the actors and stunt doubles will need to be able to accomplish with the costumes on. It's eye-opening, really. To think of not just sketching something that looks good on paper but also needs to actually function like superhero costumes were intended to function: allow our supe to fight, flee, and do magnificent stunts of probably unnecessary but totally cool acrobatics. It's a crossover to my drag costume work, and one that leaves me with this warm and glowy, fulfilled feeling that has been sorely missing in my life lately. Daniel and I play off each other with ease; he and I both take and give constructive criticism in a way that makes it feel edifying and not personal. I feel useful, vital, and a part of a kick-ass team.

I reflect on this as Daniel and I make our way out to the parking lot. Between his working knowledge of costumes and acrobatics, and my design skills, costume work, and background with *THF*, we really are *the* Dream Team for this movie. And beyond that, there's this solid familiarity that is extending into a budding friendship that I'm not used to. Despite my suspicions about his spandex-wearing activities, I *like* Daniel Kim. And now that I'm back to square one, suspecting everyone I know, maybe I can just drop my suspicion and live in the moment. Enjoy life without imagining an agenda behind everything. Just *be* MG Martin, comic book writer, kick-ass costume consultant.

"That was *fun*," I say.

"You act surprised."

"I love my work, usually, but I wouldn't always categorize it as fun. I guess I usually have an agenda to 'stick it to the man' or make a positive change or impact on my industry. Sometimes I think I miss the forest for the trees."

"This role is perfect for your skill set," Daniel confirms. "I'm glad you're having fun. Me too."

The streetlights are starting to turn on in the dusk, and the one overhead casts an orange glow that accentuates the yellow of the setting sun. Maybe it's just because I spent several hours thinking about superheroes and big sweeping dramatic settings, and capes and costumes, but this moment feels a *lot* like the start of some awesome partnership. I feel like reaching out with some secret handshake. In this moment, it's not hard to picture either of us as secret superheroes. In this case, I guess we're teaming up to take on the world of stagnant comic book movies, but I can almost picture us as *real* superheroes, I feel that amped up and powerful right now.

My phone dings in my pocket, and I break the gaze I didn't realize I was holding with Daniel. I offer a small smile, and wave and head to my car.

It's Matteo, wondering where I am, and I almost feel resentful of him for interrupting this triumphant moment in my career. But then I realize this is exactly what I want too. Because even though Matteo isn't interested in talking about the length of a cape ideal for a crime-fighting vigilante, I'm already a part of a pretty awesome crime-fighting duo.

"You look tired." I can't help but reach out and pull Matteo into a quick hug, despite the fact that we're in the lobby of the station. He's got a seven-o'clock scruff on his jaw, and in an entirely un-Matteo-ish fashion, his shirt is rumpled and there's no evidence of a tie. Truth be told, it looks like he's slept in these clothes.

"Have you gone home?" I ask.

My suspicions are confirmed when Matteo shakes his head. "No, we've been on a wild-goose chase, and I needed to be here."

"Wild-goose chase?" I picture him hanging out the passenger side of Rideout's patrol car with a pistol in an old-fashioned car chase and shoot-out. In my imagination he's wearing those vintage suspenders, and his favorite fedora is perched jauntily on his head despite the wind. It would make a fantastic panel in a comic book. "But wait. You said you're working on the Golden Arrow case? Why didn't you tell me? I could have come along!"

"I couldn't tell you until now, because it was an internal investigation." We pause by the coffee pot, and he refills his mug. "We'll wait until we get to the interview room to talk."

Internal investigation. *That* didn't sound good. In fact, that sounded an awful lot like what had gone on at the beginning of the summer. My stomach drops.

"Do you need anything? I can have some dinner brought in." Matteo holds the door open to the same interview room I've been in several times.

"No, that's okay; I'll eat when I get home. Have *you* eaten? Anything besides coffee-bean slurry, I mean?" Though it's obvious I'm here in an official capacity, I can't help but worry about the circles under Matteo's eyes and the drawn look he has on his face. Whatever this is, it's in the category of "not good."

"I think so?" He waves his hand dismissively. "At some point today. I'm okay; I'll head home after this for some rest. I have some leftovers in the fridge."

"Okay, well, let me know if I can help you out in any way." Something almost maternal rises inside of me, and I fight off the urge to pull Matteo in for another hug.

"Well, I'm in desperate need of your brain on this case." He sighs and sits down in the chair across from the couch as if his bones weigh eight million pounds.

I plop on the edge of the couch, hands clasped between my knees. "Okay, shoot, Sherlock. I'm all yours." I'm flattered that he needs *me* in

191

particular in this development, and I'm also desperately curious about what has transpired. "Did you talk with Whalon?"

Matteo nods. "Yes, but that's only half of what this is about."

I frown. "Did he . . . help?"

Matteo sighs and runs his hands through his hair. "He remembers DeWayne, though not really well. He says DeWayne had approached him with a business venture—I guess DeWayne wanted to manufacture gadgets based on Hooded Falcon stuff and sell replicas. They were set to pitch it formally to Casey with Whalon's family as the capital when . . ."

"When Casey was murdered," I finish. "Was that all he said?"

Matteo shrugs. "Overall, he was pretty blasé. He agreed that he and Lawrence saw each other a few times when they were younger, but that his family wouldn't respect that sort of dalliance, so he ended it. DeWayne's business proposition didn't move forward when the estate was turned over to Junior, who was interested in retaining all rights. We know now that Casey Junior wasn't particularly *fond* of his father's— what did he call them?—charity cases. Whalon remembers DeWayne wanted to pursue other business ideas with his capital, but Lawrence didn't like the ideas much and counseled Whalon to decline. Things fizzled with Lawrence, Casey Senior's death was under investigation, and Whalon just decided that cutting ties with the whole company would save him a lot of trouble. He was pretty young at the time and doesn't remember many particulars since the venture never got off the ground. He hasn't spoken to L since. He saw him on *The Tonight Show* and just got curious about how he'd turned out. Went in to get a haircut. That's it."

"Ouch." Double ouch that L's attachment was so apparent, and I guess Whalon's feelings weren't equal. Maybe it was complete innocent chance that Whalon was at his show too. True to L's insistence, Whalon doesn't seem to be a part of this at all.

Matteo sits in silence for a bit, and I shift on the couch. "Was there something else, then? Since Whalon seems like a dead end?"

"We caught Ryan's assailant."

I clap. "That's *great* news!"

Matteo nods, but it's not enthusiastic. "I *am* excited, but it's more questions and not a lot of answers. The guy *insists* that he was jumped and not the other way around. He admits there were several people present and that he was under the . . . influence . . . of his wares, but his statement isn't something we can hold him for, for long."

"So, he's getting released without being charged. At least he's in the system?" I read the droop of Matteo's shoulders. "That's not all of it."

"No," Matteo says, grinding the heel of a hand into his right eye. "His name came up on a list of attendees at the party last weekend."

My gaze flies to his. *Interesting* doesn't seem to cover it.

Matteo nods at my look. "Yeah, more coincidences. More connections. And I can't figure out what the common denominator is." He smacks the desk, and I jump. It's the first time I've *ever* seen Matteo even a little riled up.

"Sorry," he says. "I'm just tired. This is a great win, another piece in the puzzle. It's a clue I'm on the right trail, it's proof that we're making headway, and yet."

"And yet," I agree. "Do you think he and Ryan were attacked by the same person?"

"If it's the same person who attacked Ryan, that's a possibility. But again, I'm left wondering if this is a dealer with connections to our trial whom I can't find. And that's not even the greatest of my concerns right now. It goes without saying that what I'm about to tell you doesn't leave this room. Not L, not Ryan, not your mother. No one."

The sinking feeling returns. "Okay. I agree." This must be *bad*.

Matteo nods. "We had evidence stolen."

I blink. "Evidence . . . from this case?"

"Yes, and we didn't discover it until last night. We have no idea *when* it was stolen, only that it wasn't there when we went to look for it."

Okay, that *was* bad. Definitely bad. "What evidence went missing?" To my knowledge, we only have a few things. The knife Sosa used to cut the canvas at SDCC, the painting, and . . . "Oh no, not the journal?"

"No, not the journal. The sample of drugs from the bust in the warehouse last summer."

"Oh." My pulse slows back down a little. A small sample of drugs, while obviously important, doesn't seem as irreplaceable to me as the thirty-year-old journal. "Isn't that better than having the journal stolen?"

But Matteo doesn't *look* less stressed. He looks . . . harried. Shaken. "Yes and no. Evidence going missing is a big deal, no matter what it is. And drug evidence is one of the most stolen pieces of evidence in our country because of its nature—it's why it was an internal investigation first."

"Okay . . ." I'm still not grasping what he's getting at. It sucks that the drugs are missing, but it doesn't seem like he should be this upset about it.

"It means that someone on our force went into our evidence room and removed our samples specifically. It *means* we're more than likely still dealing with someone working for Muñez."

Ah. There's the crux of it. The sinking feeling completes its run, my heart now somewhere in the neighborhood of my ankles. "More dirty cops."

He nods and sets his forehead in his hands on the desk. I've rarely seen him this undone. "At this point, I don't know what to think. Not after Officer James—he was a close colleague. And then after this . . ."

"Well, how do you know it's not coincidence?" I ask, looking for anything to make this go away. I don't want to ramp up the paranoia quite yet. There may very well be an explanation. "You said yourself that drugs get sold off; it sucks, but it doesn't mean it has to do with this case specifically."

Matteo gives a humorless laugh. "The internal investigation revealed that the drugs were present and accounted for as recently as last week. As far as anyone can tell, they went missing the day after our meeting with you and Lawrence after the party. When we talked, *in private*, about testing the samples. It's not something in a published report somewhere. Only my team knew about it. In the twenty-four hours it took for Rideout to organize the testing with the lab . . . the original sample went missing."

I have no response other than to stare at Matteo in dawning horror. Because if he's thinking what I'm thinking . . . well, there's only one other cop who knew that we were going to test the drugs. And that other cop is Matteo's partner.

"Does Rideout know about the internal investigation?" I ask hesitantly. I don't want to lead my witness, but I have to suss out what he's feeling.

"Yes."

"And?"

"He insists it's coincidence."

"And the police force is just going to take his word for it?" I'm aghast. "It wasn't me" seems like a pretty shoddy excuse when you're one of two people who had knowledge of the sample.

"I haven't told you everything yet. It gets even more complicated."

I narrow my eyes at him. "Okay, out with the whole shebang."

"The internal investigation revealed that there was likely inside *help* but that there was an external perpetrator."

"Okay, so *whomever* was working with someone. And it's a recent development." And by someone, I knew we both meant Muñez. Who else would have been interested in the sample of the very drugs that incriminated Sosa? Especially since they've been in evidence for months? But even *I* found it hard to imagine Rideout—staunch, play-by-the-rules, old-man-Joe Rideout agreeing to work with Muñez *or* Sosa. Their bust had made his career. "So how do they know there was an 'external perpetrator'?"

"Because when Rideout went to pick up the sample for the lab, he found this in its place." Out of his pocket, he produces a small computer tablet. It's like one I've seen before—a tablet belonging to the police department, usually used for victims to review photos of suspects. Stuff like that. The last time I held one of these in my hand was the first time I actually *saw* the Golden Arrow on surveillance tape—the night my life took its biggest and most unexpected turn ever. The night we realized we were chasing a *real* vigilante. And so, when I lean forward, I expect to see surveillance footage. Maybe of Muñez, maybe of the crime in real-time.

Instead, it's an image of a shelf, filled with plastic bins—each labeled with a long string of numbers. An off-camera gloved hand holds a single bin tipped outward. On top of the bin is a sheet of paper with a simple message scrawled on it. I can't read it from the angle of the picture, but the little hairs raise on the back of my neck.

Without a word, Matteo flicks his finger across the screen, bringing the next image up—a close-up view of the note. Our eyes meet over the tablet the instant I read the words.

Follow the White Rabbit.

Unless I've missed my mark, the Golden Arrow has struck again.

CHAPTER 20

"The Golden Arrow." I state the obvious, on the off chance Matteo's thinking something different. He's not.

"I assume so. The writing looks the same as the note we received earlier in the summer; I gave it to the lab for handwriting comparison. But this is where you come in. Help me see how this ties in to our case."

Answers are beyond me; I'm stuck so far in questions, you might as well call me the Riddler. "So, either the Golden Arrow is a cop"—my first thought is Rideout, which is *highly* unlikely given the level of comic knowledge needed to have investigated Agent Sosa—"or a cop is working with the Golden Arrow?"

Matteo shrugs, the defeat weighing on his shoulders. "It makes sense, as much as I dislike it. How else does this person keep getting in front of our investigation? They have inside knowledge of this case."

I bite my lip at my next thought. "And given the cops already involved in this case, and the nature of the evidence taken . . . this cop probably works for Muñez."

"Or his replacement," Matteo agrees.

Our eyes connect, and we just stare at each other in mutual distaste for that idea.

"That would mean the *Golden Arrow* is working . . . for Muñez?"

"Or his replacement," Matteo agrees, again.

This is bad. *Bad*, bad, bad. But if I look at everything that has transpired in the past few weeks: the interview with the drug dealers about a new game in town, the parties where the Golden Arrow is keeping questionable company, and even the very fact that Lawrence laid eyes on the person claiming to *be* the Golden Arrow and didn't think he was a good guy. Maybe even a guy connected to Muñez, given he potentially tried to kill Casey Senior the night of the party thirty years ago.

Everything fits. Except . . . my gut.

"Matteo, this can't be right. The Golden Arrow is a good guy. I know it. I *feel* it. Out of curiosity, did you ever look into my coworker? Daniel Kim? Or his brother?"

"Squeaky-clean background check," Matteo sighs. "Not even a parking ticket. Divorced, one child, part owner of a dance studio. Shows up for jury duty."

"And his brother?"

"Only child, I think."

Well, *that* rankles. "I'm pretty sure he's mentioned a brother," I argue. "Why would he lie about it?"

Matteo eyes me. "Our records aren't complete; I can check again. He's never been booked, so I don't have a lot. Why?"

I guess it is time to come clean. The case has just hit a major snag, and Matteo needs all the information he can get.

"Well, I just . . . one time I followed him and he sorta delivered a cape and a mask to someone on Curtis Street. I asked him about it, and he said his brother lived there."

Matteo's eyes goggle. "When was this?"

"Er, a few weeks ago when I told you to look into him?"

Matteo pinches the bridge of his nose. "So, you went out sleuthing on your own when I expressly told you not to—you know what? It doesn't matter. I'll throw someone onto this, check him out thoroughly. Which I could have done weeks ago *had you told me what you'd seen*—"

"I thought you'd get mad—"

"I *am* mad, but I'll get over it and I have bigger fish to fry. Thank you for telling me. We need every lead we can get right now." Matteo searches my eyes, and I see him warring with the anger and betrayal, and the need to just push forward. "I need you to look through the comics for any clue, *any* similarity to what's going on. I know you know these backward and forward, but I need to be *sure* we've jumped track. This note indicates yet again that our vigilante knows something we don't. What I'm worried about now is their motive."

He doesn't say it, but I'm thinking the same thing. Because if I follow the theory of the dirty cop working *with* the Golden Arrow through . . . what if, now that Muñez is behind bars, this vigilante has turned to clearing the field of people who put him there? The people familiar enough with this case to catch him. Those people are . . . us. Ryan's been attacked, L has been almost attacked.

Though a chill runs down my spine, I'm not quite ready to commit to that narrative. Not when my writer's gut is telling me that we're not dealing with a rogue vigilante. The Golden Arrow is *not* a double agent. He loves the Falcon. The Falcon would break a few laws, sure. But he'd do so in pursuit of the greater justice. We're dealing with someone who has an interest in solving crime, *battling* the bad guys, not joining them. "The other possibility is that the Golden Arrow knows something we don't, *and* he stole the sample all of his own volition."

"In the twenty-four hours when we'd decided to test it?" No judgment from Matteo with this statement, but I can tell he's dubious.

"Yeah, I know. But maybe? Crazier things have happened."

"He stole something from a police department without being caught?"

"That seems less likely, but still possible."

"And nothing rings a bell from the comic books that he could be following?" Matteo looks ever-so-slightly hopeful with this question but deflates again when I hesitantly shake my head.

"Look, I'll do some searching in the comic. Maybe there's something in the journal that would have pointed the Golden Arrow to the sample." It sounds unlikely even to my own ears. "Maybe something will show up if I'm reading the issues with this in mind. And I'll take a look through Casey's journal too—well, the part of it we have."

"Okay," Matteo agrees, though he clearly doesn't expect anything new to come of it. "Now, one last order of business. We need to talk about Lawrence."

Instantly, I'm on alert. My knees jerk together and I sit up straight. *Crap.* The shoes. My suspicion that perhaps *Lawrence* is the Golden Arrow. How on earth could Matteo have arrived at this same conclusion?

"Lawrence?" I manage, trying to play it cool but sounding strangled instead. *Do not mention the shoes, do not mention the shoes. Wait and see what he has first before you rat out your best friend.* I feel immensely guilty for not immediately spouting my suspicion, but there it is. My loyalty to L outweighs my loyalty to this case.

"I'm concerned about him. Do you know where he is?"

I swallow, thankful that for once I'm not lying about this to Matteo. "No. He even let me borrow his car, so I have no idea at all." I shove down the slightly guilty feeling that statement causes. I mean, we've always borrowed each other's stuff, so I'm *almost* certain L would condone my use of the Dodge. I refocus on Matteo. No need to *look* guiltier than I already feel.

Matteo's grim look returns.

"You . . . you think he's involved?" I hedge.

"I guess so. We probably need to get a security detail on him until we've figured this mess out." He runs his hands down his face and over his stubble.

Oh no, oh no. Matteo knows. Matteo suspects. How could this be possible? Hadn't I just talked myself *out* of believing Lawrence could be our vigilante?

"I don't think there's any way Lawrence is the Golden Arrow," I offer, hoping I sound casual.

Matteo shoots me a look so confused I decide you can just call me the Dazzler, I've missed the mark that badly.

"I don't think he's the Golden Arrow; I'm *worried* about him, Michael-Grace." His face plainly says he thinks I'm paranoid. "The only people who knew about that drug sample were my team. My team is also the only team who has seen that photo and knows who took it."

The leak.

I fill in the rest of the blanks quickly. Lawrence went in search of this person, or information *about* this person. If it's really true that our imposter Golden Arrow knows about the drugs, knows about Lawrence, and either *is* or is working for the Queen of Hearts . . . my best friend is in big, *big* trouble.

It's hard not to dwell on Lawrence as I drive his car home. In fact, he's so heavy on my heart that I swing by his shop in hopes of seeing a sign of him being there. We *need* to talk. If he's off wherever he's off to, and in danger, I want him to come home.

I text him for the third time that night. Let me know the moment you're home, we need to talk. GA. 911.

I contemplate camping out in his shop to know the very *second* he walks through the door, but decide that's not wise for a couple of reasons: One, someone may come looking for Lawrence, and I don't really want to present myself as an easy alternative target. And two, I have so much work to do, I really do need to go home if there's nothing I can actively do at L's.

Just as I'm about to pull back into traffic, my phone dings, and I almost hit my head on the roof of the car. I'm so frantic to pick the phone back up, I drop it twice and have to turn on the overhead light to find it between the console and the seat. Expert stakeout-er, I am *not*.

Waves of disappointment sweep over me when I discover that it's not, in fact, L who has texted me, but Daniel.

Have you heard from L? I have sponsors who need info about the Halloween bash, and he hasn't returned my call.

It's almost eerie that Daniel chooses this exact moment to ask about L. I wonder if he and I have mind-melded or something. Maybe he has Spidey-sense too.

I type back a quick response. **No, L is still out of town, I think. Anything I can help with?**

I pray the answer is no, but the three dots that appear on my screen don't go away any time soon. With every passing second, it seems more likely that there *is* something I can help out with, and I almost wish I hadn't volunteered. Almost.

L is my best friend, and I dragged him into this whole Golden Arrow mess to begin with. Now his life is in danger—yet again—because of me, and well, the least I can do is organize some sponsors for his pet project, right?

And that's exactly what Daniel is asking. I read over the list of sponsors that need everything from tax-ID paperwork for the nonprofit donation of their goods and services to schedules for deliveries and descriptions of the event. They need a location for float building, and a timeline for construction. In short: they need everything. I assure Daniel that I'll get to this as soon as I can and that L will pick up from there when he's back in town.

So, as I pull out into traffic, I stuff one more thing into my over-flowing "things to care about" box in my head. The Golden Arrow case, Lawrence's safety, my report on the costume meeting—complete with sketches—Hooded Falcon scene sketches and scripts . . . and that's not to mention that Lelani wants to see some concept sketches for my space monkeys comic. And now helping L plan his party. And we won't even mention my worry that I haven't seen my boyfriend in three days any-where outside of his work, or that he told me he loved me and I haven't really addressed that in . . . any capacity. There are so many straws on this camel's back, it's a wonder it's not flat on the floor of the Sahara.

I pull in behind my own Millennium Turd—nay, I shall now just call it the Hurtling Turd once again, revoking its star cruiser status—and realize there is yet *another* thing I need to do soon. Call a tow company and get my noble steed into the shop.

I drag myself into the house, noting the dark windows. Ryan isn't home yet either. I haven't heard from him since this afternoon, and I frown as I unlock the door. Usually he's home by now or I get a text that he's going out. A frantic Trog meets me at the door, and I hurry inside, tossing my keys and coat onto the floor in favor of hustling my poor dog outside for a pee. Ryan hasn't been home at *all* since I saw him if Trog hasn't peed yet today.

"I'm sorry, baby," I coo as my sweet little corgi lifts a grateful leg on the single tree outside my townhouse. "Life has been crazy, and you are definitely getting the short end of the stick." He probably hasn't eaten yet, so I fill his bowl, laughing at his puppyish bouncing. It's hours past when he normally gets fed. Me too. I totally understand his enthusiasm.

Unfortunately for me, it's cabinet-cruising time and then straight to some sort of work. In short order, I make my way through the downstairs and past the bathroom to the converted utility room in the back of the house, a plate of crackers and a jar of peanut butter balanced in one hand. Sure, the utility room still houses our serviceable washer and dryer, but it also has my sewing machines, dress form, drafting table, and approximately three square inches for my rolling chair to go between these things.

Ryan hates coming back here.

I kind of love it.

It's my creativity nest. Plus, I always point out to Ryan, I can't fit this stuff in my bedroom, and I don't begrudge him his corner of the living room for his pile of gaming paraphernalia.

I set my dinner down on the dryer and look around the room. I have no idea where to start on my list, but I have to start *somewhere*. Maybe something mindless like hemming? That way I can ponder the case. Better yet, I could even go get my copies of the early *Hooded Falcons* and glance through them while I sew.

I detour yet again back through the dark house, Trog padding at my heels. He's not happy unless I'm sitting stationary and he can lie where he can see me. Or preferably, if I'll let him, lie directly on my feet. It's herding-dog mentality; Trog is at his happiest knowing exactly where all his people are at one time. In his younger years, he was known to attempt to herd Ryan, Lawrence, and me into one room together for his own peace of mind.

It takes less than a minute for me to locate my stack of Hooded Falcon comics—still left handy from our case earlier in the summer because I suck at putting things away—and I head back to the utility room with them. It's fully dark outside now, and I settle in at my smallest sewing station directly under the overhead light. I try several positions to prop up my comics so I can see them while hemming, but end up having to use my phone flashlight to illuminate them separately. I add another note to my junk-pile-to-the-sky to-do list in my head to look for a brighter bulb for this room. If I'm going to be working this many nights in the near future, I need better lighting.

Luckily, I don't have to read the comics so much as glance at the page so that I recall it in my head. Then, I spend time thinking about the panels I know are in that sequence while I hem a pair of slim tuxedo pants for one of L's forties-throwback looks. Latifah had put a heel right through the hem in her last performance.

Somewhere around Issue 14—the one where Falcon is fighting the Brain on a secluded mountaintop—I hear a noise outside.

At first, I think I've imagined the soft scraping noise along the side of the house. Truth be told, I started to nod off, I think. Caught in that weird state of consciousness between sleep and awake where my hand is still technically sewing but I'd also been thinking about how ranch dressing seemed like a panacea for all the world's ills.

I'm about to chalk it up to something in my quasi-dream state when I note that Trog is sitting forward, ears perked, Wonder Bread body alert. He gives the lowest of *woofs*, and I know he's heard something too. That's when the goose bumps rise on my arms. A quick glance out the door shows me that the house is still completely dark. Ryan isn't home yet.

Please let this be Ryan.

But . . . why would Ryan be skulking about his own townhouse? He usually just gets a ride with Lelani or Ubers home. This certainly wasn't the sound of an Uber.

I rise, debating whether I should flick off the light in the utility room. I can't help but picture any number of *bad guys* related to the Golden Arrow case sneaking around my house with ill intent. Deciding against turning off the light, I instead make my way to the front door, Trog on my heels. The best way to know exactly what that noise was would be to catch the person who made it still in the act of . . . whatever. It's the first time in my life I've prayed to find your average teenage hoodlum out for a nice night of breaking and entering at my neighbor's kitchen window.

"Okay, boy, go for the Achilles if we meet anyone," I say, clipping his leash to the collar. I have little confidence that Trog will *actually* be of help with a perpetrator. A herd of hair dryers or vacuums maybe, but not humans. Nevertheless, it makes me feel better to have him with me. I whip my phone out, pull up Matteo's number in case I need to call him with the push of a button, and silently count to three.

On three, I flip on the exterior light and at the same time push out the door and onto my porch, brandishing my phone and my corgi with as much daredevil drama as I can manage.

"I'm calling the cops right now," I say in a sure voice to cover the moment when my eyes are adjusting from the dark of my entryway to the light just off my tiny railed porch.

While the night seems to be totally ordinary, I catch the snap of a twig off to my right that doesn't sound like your average bunny or squirrel. *Crap.* There really is someone out here.

"I have a gun," I add for good measure, holding my cell phone out in front of me the way TV agents do.

Trog starts to strain against the leash, and my heart hammers in my chest in response. It suddenly dawns on me that all that stands between me and this potential threat is my brave—but not very imposing—dog. And I don't want Trog to get hurt.

I press the number to call Matteo and whip my cell phone back in the direction of the noise. It's at that moment that Trogdor starts to bark. It's a deep sound, not the little warning *woofs* he does sometimes that just puff out his cheeks. This makes him sound like he's mastiff size.

"MG?" The voice comes from alongside the building, out between the landscaping and the wall to the townhouse, and just beyond the reach of my phone's flashlight or the porch light.

It takes me a moment to place it. *"Ryan?"*

"Yeah, hey, sorry. I didn't mean to scare you." He appears slowly from the vegetation, hands held aloft in surrender. He's dressed in black workout clothes, making him extra hard to see in the dark. If I didn't know better, I'd say that was his intent with his outfit, and my Spidey-sense tingles.

"If you didn't mean to *scare me*, then what the hell are you doing in our bushes at night, dressed in black?"

I'm prickly. I should feel relieved, but all I feel is mad.

Ryan hops over the railing—actually quite an impressive feat—and passes his gaze over my phone and Trog. "Thank God you're not actually armed." Trog moves forward, sniffing Ryan like he, too, is suspicious as to why we're having this meeting on our porch in the dark.

"What does *that* mean?" I ask, intercepting him as he makes a move toward the front door. "And *what* are you doing out there?"

Ryan looks reluctant to say, which is infuriating.

"Ryan! You scared the living daylights out of me. I thought . . ." He doesn't know about the L snafu or the missing evidence, so I cut myself off just in time. "I thought you were a burglar. I almost called the cops."

No, wait. I *had* called the cops. I look down at my phone. It's been connected to Matteo's number for almost thirty seconds. I whip my phone up to my ear. "Matteo?"

"MG?" He sounds either alarmed or incredibly annoyed. Maybe both. "You *called me*. Are you okay?" Usually I text, and he might have heard the part about burglars. Or about calling the cops.

Ryan's eyes widen as he realizes Matteo has been on the phone. He makes another move toward the door, but I move to block him again.

"I'm perfectly fine. Pocket dial. Call you later," I say into the phone, hanging up before Matteo can argue with me. I barricade the door with my body, leveling my gaze at Ryan.

"Geez, MG, it's my house too. It's not like I need a warrant to be in my front yard."

I cross my arms.

Ryan realizes he's not getting around me, so he sighs. "Okay, fine, but don't be mad okay? I had an errand to run for L while he's gone. I borrowed your bike because mine needs a new chain. And I didn't want to make Trog bark by locking it on the porch, so I locked it to the gas meter back there. I know I didn't ask to borrow it; I'm sorry, and I meant to put it back in the morning before you found out."

I crane my neck around him and peer into the landscaping, then look back at him, question evident in my face.

"I didn't want to take an Uber," Ryan says, defensively, correctly guessing my question. Then his shoulders deflate. "Look, money is kind of tight right now, until I find out if this next contract gets picked up, okay? I'd have asked to borrow your car but . . ."

I feel awful for being suspicious of my roommate—of *both* of my best friends recently. I'm seeing spooks around every corner, grasping for any round peg that fits the square hole of this case. Of course, I totally understand the whole empty-pocketbook thing. Too well. So well, in fact, I'm not sure how I'm even going to pay to get my car towed. I might very well be the one locking my bike to my porch at—I glance at my phone—11:34 p.m. next time.

"I thought you'd be in bed," Ryan says sheepishly as we push through the front door together, Trog trotting happily into the darkness now that his humans are both home and the crisis is over.

"Nah, work," I say, stifling a yawn.

"Are you finished?"

"No, I'm going to work a bit longer." I don't needle him by pointing out that I have my adrenaline rushing despite my yawn, and there is no way I'd be able to sleep, thanks to his antics.

"Okay, 'night." Ryan makes his way up the stairs, and I head back to the utility room. It's only after I'm back in the room and seated at my desk that I remember that his *antics* included an errand for L. It's tempting to go grill Ryan in case it's important to the case, but just as I rise from my chair, I hear the shower turn on upstairs. I sit back down. I don't want to know *that* badly.

With a sigh and one last longing thought about my bed, I turn back to the comic books and the pile of sewing. It's going to be a long night.

CHAPTER 21

I wake up the next morning, quite literally drowning in my work. It takes me a moment to fully gather my bearings, but the indent of sequins on my cheek goes quite a long way in informing me that I never made it to my bed last night. All around me are the remnants of my attempt to catch up last night—sketches, thread, bolts of cloth, several rumpled garments, my sketchpad, and a stack of comic books.

This should distress me. But it doesn't. The dream I had just before waking is still fresh in my head—a glistening jewel of inspiration and creative energy.

It's as if communing with my work in a very real way has led to osmosis. Instead of feeling the same bitterness and disappointment with my comic sketches that I feel when I think about the space monkey project, I feel buoyant. I could reach out and hug my creative nest. It's done its job, melding all the things I love together. It's given me an *idea*.

I open my Moleskine, jotting down several key words before starting in on the sketch of the panel I woke with burned into my imagination.

That's how Ryan finds me.

"Did you sleep at all?" he asks, taking in the wreck that is my nest.

I peer at him with manic glee over my stack of comic books. "Some, but it doesn't matter. I know what I want my pet project to actually be! Screw those chimpanzees in space."

"Pet project?"

I bite my lip, trying to think back. "I guess maybe I didn't tell you that part. *Hero Girls* got canceled."

Ryan frowns in concern. "Oh, I'm sorry, that's awful."

"Yeah," I agree, then shake myself. "But it's okay, I guess. Not really, but it is what it is. Anyhow, I accidentally pitched this robot versus space chimpanzees idea—"

Ryan's eyes goggle.

"Yeah, yeah, I know. Anyhow, it was a placeholder idea, because I had this crazy dream last night about L, and well, I can't say too much until I talk to him, but I feel *really* sure this is the right project for me . . ." I break off again, eyeing the weird posture Ryan is standing in. It looks like he's looking for the earliest opportunity to interrupt my victory speech, which is unlike him, and ultimately why I trail off. "What?" I ask.

Ryan holds up his phone. "It's Matteo; he called me because he was worried when you didn't respond to his texts or calls."

"Oh!" I rush forward, dragging half a bolt of cloth with me and tripping over my stack of comics that has slid onto the floor. I distinctly remember *not* plugging my phone in to charge, so it must have died. Given that my boyfriend heard only a snippet of conversation last night, most of it about burglars, before I essentially hung up on him, I get that he might be a *teensy* bit worried. I grab the phone from Ryan.

"I'm sorry, I'm sorry," I say before the phone has even hit my ear. I bump the speakerphone button, and fumble unsuccessfully to reverse it. Great. Now Ryan will be present for my imminent dressing down. "My phone died."

"Michael-Grace, I was up half the night worried I needed to come check on you," Matteo admonishes. "I know you're resourceful, and I didn't hear any calls come into dispatch to your address, so I didn't. But after the conversation we had at the station, I can't believe you thought I wouldn't worry about your safety."

Ryan's eyebrow quirks up in curiosity before I finally get the speakerphone button pressed and hold the phone back to my ear. I wave him off. Matteo said *no one* could know about what he'd told me, and that includes Ryan, unfortunately.

"Look, I really am sorry. I had so much work to do last night, I just plain forgot to call you back. I promise I'm fine. In fact, I'm headed out the door right now for a meeting; maybe we can get together later?"

Matteo lets out a sigh. "My turn to beg off for work. Can we make it Friday? I could bring over some soup and salad, we can watch another one of those ridiculous shows you love."

"Sure—" I start, but then something wiggles in the back of my brain. Friday after work. Paige. "Oh . . . actually, yes to Friday but ixnay on the soup and aladsay. I'm having a work party."

There's silence on the end of the line.

Which I deserve because I never have uttered those words together in all the time Matteo has known me. "We hired a new girl, and I want her to get to know the team better. And I should ask Daniel to come too, since he's a part of the team. Paige is pretty cool . . . Plus, she *sews*, and I want to pick her brain about that."

Matteo seems to be attempting to form words. "Ah, that's all rather unexpected, but it sounds wonderful. I hope you have a good time."

"What, aren't you coming?"

"Am I invited?" There's an edge to his voice that I don't recognize.

"I told you yes for Friday night. Of course I want you here if I'm hosting a party. Can you get off work? I know the case is crazy right now."

When he answers, his voice is a little softer. "Yes, I think so. I wouldn't miss *you* actually hosting a work party."

The man knows me well, and I snort. "I know. And I'm actually *almost* excited about it." Truth be told, I feel a little like a thirteen-year-old hosting a birthday party. I just hope, now that I've committed, that people will come. I glance at Ryan's watch since he's still standing in the doorway. "Hey, I gotta run to work. I'll call you later? I'm still looking through the comics for . . . those things," I hedge, trying hard not to meet Ryan's gaze. "I'll call you if I find something."

We disconnect, and I hand the phone back to Ryan. "Thanks."

"A party?" he asks, eyebrow still raised.

"Yeah, can you make it?" *Crap.* Would that mean I'd have to invite Lelani? Somehow, I picture her being a buzzkill at a work function.

He hesitates. "I think I have something Friday night. I'll let you know if I can make it. Doesn't L have a show, though?"

I shrug and push Ryan out into the hallway, closing the door on my precious mess. "No, not this week. Speaking *of*, what were you doing for him? Do you know where he is? He's not answering my texts." It rankles that Ryan has been in contact with L when I haven't.

"Dropping off a check," Ryan answers promptly. Almost too promptly, like he's been rehearsing. "For the space to rent for the float construction."

"At eleven thirty?"

Ryan shrugs. "They asked for the payment before midnight; I don't know L's bank logins to do an e-transfer."

I squint one eye at him and open my mouth to question him further, but he beats me to the punch.

"I don't think he'll be gone much longer, though. He said he'd be coming home soon."

That shut me up in a hurry. "Did he say if he found anything?"

Ryan seems bored with the conversation now and glances at his watch again. "He didn't say specifically, but I'd guess not. Hey, it's time to get going to work if you're going to make it. Do you want me to unchain your bike for you?"

Ugh. Thank God for short hair, I don't have time for a shower. "Yeah, thanks. I'll be out in a minute."

I dash into the downstairs bathroom and scrub the mascara out from under my eyes. I swipe a handful of pomade through my short locks, noting that the color has faded even more. I'm about to be a member of the #grayhairdontcare club; I need an intervention soon, or I'll be rocking an off-white pompadour.

Next, it's a stop in my room to sniff-test clothes, and I settle on my "I'll send a fully armed battalion to remind you of my love" Hamilton T-shirt, off-white linen blazer, slightly rumpled red tweed pedal pushers—the rumple won't matter after a bike ride anyhow—and red ballet flats.

No time for breakfast *or* coffee, so I stuff my sketchbook into my bag and head out the door.

"I thought you might need this," Ryan says, greeting me at the door with a steaming travel mug.

I sniff, and my hand whips out.

"It's just black with cream. None of your fancy stuff."

"It's the best gift anyone's ever given me," I joke before reaching out and hugging him, the cup sandwiched firmly between us. It reminds me of all I need to catch up with him about. "I feel like I've been so underwater with work lately, I know I've been a crummy friend. Let's catch up soon, okay?"

Ryan gives a hollow laugh. "I think we've *all* got a lot going on; no biggie."

I look up at his face before heading to my bike. "Video game stuff?"

Ryan makes a noncommittal shrug that I take to mean, "That and other stuff."

"Should we carb-load and gossip like schoolgirls this weekend?"

"Deal," Ryan says with a smile.

I buckle my helmet on, glad I didn't spend any more time on my hair, and head off to work.

"Ah, MG, come in."

I've arrived at Genius Comics not two minutes early for my meeting with Lelani, and as I walk in her door, I hastily drop my bike helmet into the nearest potted plant and fluff my hair. Plenty of time to worry about how I look *after* the meeting.

I follow Lelani into her office, fighting the urge to select one thing to move while I'm here, just to see if she notices that her complete and ultimate *order* is upset. The leather desk blotter is literally perfectly centered in the middle of the glossy black desk with two silver pens sitting atop a red folder to its right side.

Does the woman do any *real* work for this company? Who has two pens and a folder on their desk, unless they're a West Elm advertisement? Definitely no one *I* know. If she could see my creative nest, she'd probably poop kittens.

"I have to say," she continues as if she doesn't notice my perusal of her office, "I'm surprised by your proposal for your small project."

I sink into the chair opposite her desk. It's rounded in the back and glossy black like the desk, with a *seriously* comfortable cushion on it.

"This is silk," I state before I can stop myself. I know my fabrics, and I'm more than a little impressed that *anyone* at Genius has anything in their office that's silk. Lelani is peering at me in a positively unreadable way, so I refocus. "Er, but we're here to talk about my project and not your chair cushions."

"Indeed," she says, her face still giving no hint at what she's thinking. Then something softens around her eyes, and she leans forward a bit, elbows resting on the edge of her desk. She manages to look both conversational and proper. I have no idea how she does it. "Tell me a bit about it. It's not what I . . . expected, given your track record for passion projects."

I consider bullshitting her—talking about how I'm taking a stand, using this as a satire platform. How I've carefully crafted my idea to appeal to the very market I feel needs changing. Instead, as I stare into her steady gaze, I decide it's time to be real.

"I panicked. I literally said the first thing that popped into my head."

Some measure of respect and then satisfaction flashes across her face. "Ah. I surmised as much. It lacked your typical style and particular brand of . . . forgive the pun, genius." She sits back in her chair and studies me for a moment like she can see through me. There's something predatory there too, like she's a feline, waiting to pounce on me if I make a wrong move.

"I've since come up with something else," I offer. "If that's okay. I know Mr. Casey approved the other idea but . . ."

Interest kindles in her eyes. "Please, by all means share if you feel able."

"Okay, well, I fell asleep sewing last night—that's not important. Other than to say, it's sort of like all the pieces of my life sort of melded together into this idea. It's really a personal project idea." That last statement takes even me by surprise because I find it to be absolutely true. And suddenly it's like standing in Lelani's office in my underwear. This idea isn't just *any* idea. It popped in my head fully formed. It already exists. It's all the things and people I love, all rolled into one. This is *my* project. I feel it in my bones; this comic and I are meant for each other.

But it puts me in a position of vulnerability with this project. I *care*, which is something I vowed long ago not to do too much of in this industry. *Hero Girls* being the perfect example of this: a comic that hit all the notes for me. Girl cast. Amazing costumes. Social justice bent to the action and plot lines. And yet . . . not enough people wanted it. So, it's on to the next project, the next idea. Wash, rinse, repeat.

Except I don't know that I could *not* care if this project got the axe.

It's as if Lelani can read my every thought. Her dark eyes narrow thoughtfully. "Okay, tell me about your vision. I assume this has to do with the Golden Arrow case? I'm not sure how much we could publish and keep from upsetting the police, but truthfully I think it might make a fantastic comic."

I gape at her. Truthfully, I hadn't even *thought* of an outright Golden Arrow adaptation, and I kind of want to kick myself. Would that be *too* meta? A comic based on a real-life vigilante based on a comic? It's

215

borderline, well, genius. "Yes, well . . . not really. It has some of those elements, but I think the bulk of it is based on Lawrence."

Lelani blinks. "Lawrence?"

"Yeah, I was thinking of the tagline 'Drag by Night, Vigilante Hero by Later Night.'"

"A . . . drag queen superhero?" There's no outright judgment; she's tasting the idea as she says it out loud. Offering the idea to an ethereal panel of judges I can't see.

"Well, I was thinking through this case how much the queens see in the way of crimes and social justice issues. Drugs, beatings, racial profiling, social intolerance. It would be like Queen Eye for the Straight World, if you'd like. But think of how *beautiful* this comic could be. The colors. The costumes, the capes. Not to mention the humor!"

Lelani's mouth quirks up in an uncharacteristic smile. "You are nothing if not surprising, Michael-Grace."

I decide to take it as a compliment. "Thank you."

She sits back and draws in a long breath. "Have you pitched this to Andy?"

"No, not yet. I only just came up with it." I'm pretty sure she's about to smack down my idea. The more we talk about it, the more ludicrous it seems that she'd go for it. This is *completely* outside of Genius's box.

"Well, I like it. I think we should pitch it to Mr. Casey and see what he says."

I stare at her. "Seriously?"

She shrugs. "Especially if you roll some of the Golden Arrow vigilante stuff in . . . it's timely. It's different. 'Different' is good sometimes. Do you have sketches?"

I show her the quickly rendered frame that had lingered in my imagination after my dream.

She looks it over and hands it back with an emphatic nod. "Keep working on it; we'll need some finished panels to show Casey. Now"— she checks her watch, then pulls a slim tablet notebook out of the folder on her desk—"I'm glad we had a chance to talk about your project, but I have a meeting with the Dubai rights subsidiary committee."

"Yeah, no problem." I head back out the door but stop short and turn to look over my shoulder. I kinda can't believe I'm going to do this, but what the hell. "And thanks for listening about my new project. I appreciate it."

"It's what I'm here for. You're talented, Michael-Grace. It's not hard. Sometimes you just need direction."

Lelani is the best mentor I've ever had. And not just because she's a woman—I've had countless terrible bosses over my lifetime of both genders. Lelani believes in calling me on my bullshit and pushing me to do better, to *be* better. At my job as a writer and a contributor for Genius. But also, for my career. She does it without being overly familiar or gal-pal about it—something that is at once both unnerving and refreshing. She would—and probably does—give the same sort of critical and perfectly directed critique to anyone on her team. It's crazy to picture the working world this way, where I'm seen as an individual with interests and a platform that just happens to be female, rather than as a "female comic book artist."

I hesitate at the doorway again, and she raises a brow at me in perfect query.

I brace internally, shoving the part of me that is afraid to have Matteo and Lelani in the same room together right over my internal cliff. "I'm having a party for work people on Friday night. To help welcome Paige to the team. You should come. I mean, well, if you can—you're invited."

Her eyebrow doesn't drop, but the corner of her mouth turns up. "Thank you for the invite. I believe I may have another engagement, but I'll talk to Ryan and see if we can change our plans."

I offer a small smile in return and attempt to convince myself as I head to my desk that I hope she comes.

CHAPTER 22

"Thank you for bringing the artichoke dip!" I yell out the front door as Kyle and Nina make their way down the walk and toward Kyle's car.

Nina waves in acknowledgment, and I close the door behind me with a sigh. This is why I never hostess. Hostessing is *exhausting*. The smells of pizza and artichoke dip still waft from my kitchen, though the shuffle and clanging coming from that room suggest that Matteo is cleaning up, bless him.

"Thank you so much for hosting this party," Paige says, wheeling from the living room and into the hallway with me.

"Hey, anyone who sides with me about the best comic book movie adaptations is welcome anytime."

"*Thor: Ragnarok* forever," she agrees solemnly.

I smile.

"Although . . . I *don't* agree with you on the biggest travesty in adaptation."

I cover my heart, pretending to take a mortal wound. We'd had a rousing conversation following our viewing of several key Marvel movies leading up to *Infinity War* as only a group of comic nerds could have.

I groan. "Don't tell me you side with Tej on that one."

"The gaffes in *Ant-Man* defy the physics set forward in the comics," she says with a shake of her head.

"You obviously just need more convincing." I say. "Captain America's whole shield—his *powers* got changed. Biggest travesty, comics aren't about real physics. Be that as it may, now that all the menfolk are cleaning up the dishes, come into my sewing parlor for brandy and cigars." Her chair fills up the doorway, but it's enough for me to pull up a chair from my desk and show her my work.

She tosses me a look.

"Okay, no brandy or cigars, but there are sewing machines and colored pencils."

"You had me at sewing machines," Paige agrees.

I'm surprised when thirty minutes of geeking out about *Project Runway* flies by like thirty seconds. Paige is easy to talk to and shares so many interests, I have a hard time not making her a friendship bracelet on the spot.

"I do need to go," she says eventually, after laughing with me over my ridiculous sketches for the chimpanzee comic.

"Oh, okay." I feel sad that she's leaving but understand as the hour is getting late. I have the insane urge to continue my "thirteen-year-old hosting a party" fantasy and ask her if she wants to pop popcorn and stay for a sleepover.

Matteo meets us at the kitchen entrance. "Are you headed out?"

"Yeah," Paige yawns. "I'm beat. It's been a good week but a lot, you know?"

I nod. I know.

"Thanks for inviting me. Our team is pretty nice. Kyle and Nina are cute. Almost gag-worthy, but cute. And Simon is . . . enthusiastic. About everything."

I giggle, which draws a look of astonishment from Matteo. Man, I'm really channeling this thirteen-year-old, whoever she is. Certainly not thirteen-year-old *me*, because I'd have been holed up in my room to escape my parents and read comics. I had watched as Simon danced around his obvious growing crush on Paige, mostly by talking alternatingly about LARPing, then deciding that wasn't cool enough and switching to workout stuff . . . which led to talking about LARPing, and around and around he went.

"He's sweet. And single." Look at me. Matchmaker, matchmaker, make me a match. "You know, if you're into the short nerdy boy thing."

Paige shrugs, but I think I see her smile. It's hard to read her body language, so I let it go. "So, I'll see you Monday!"

"Sounds good." She rolls to the patio door and I unlock it for her—I learned the hard way that my front porch was inaccessible for her, but she assured me that she's gone in and out of patios for years for that very reason. I'm humbled by the amount of grace she gives the rest of us, bumbling about to accommodate what should be normal. It's no wonder she's hard to read sometimes.

I flick on the exterior lights and wave as she rolls around the corner toward the street where she's parked her van.

As soon as I hear it pull away, I turn the light back off but continue to stare out into the little greenbelt that backs our row of houses.

"What are you thinking about?" Matteo's voice breaks into my reverie.

I sigh and dunk another glass into the sink. "About how neither Ryan nor Lawrence were here. It's odd to have a party without either of my best friends. I miss them."

Hurt flashes across Matteo's face, and I hurry to patch my unintended wound. "I'm lucky my best *boyfriend* is here, or else I'd be all by my lonesome with these heathens." I put my hand across my forehead dramatically. I suppose Matteo is technically now one of my best friends, though I still think those titles go to Lawrence and Ryan respectively.

"Something tells me you'd be okay without me here, but I appreciate the vote of solidarity," he says, managing a wry smile. "Still no word from L?"

"No." I set the glass on the drying rack. I really should invest in a repairman for the dishwasher too, but Ryan and I have both been hurting for funds.

"And you said Ryan was out?"

"Yeah, I assume with Lelani." Matteo's face doesn't change, so I continue, "I invited them both; I hope that's okay. And told them you'd be here just in case, well, in case . . . ," I trail off, not exactly sure how to finish this thought without either sounding wildly jealous or paranoid. Or both.

"You think she skipped because of me?" He's looking at me with something like dawning suspicion.

I shrug, nonchalant. "She could have skipped because she doesn't like to mix with the underlings."

But Matteo has the picture of me just right in his head. He cocks his hip against the counter, crosses his arms, and places one stockinged foot over the other like I'm suddenly entertaining.

"Michael-Grace, you just told me you specifically *warned* her I'd be here. As if there were something she needed to avoid. Do you think that she and I can't coexist in the same space genially? We're not wild animals; it's not like we're going to get into a fight over the artichoke dip."

I'm indignant. "I didn't think you'd *fight*."

Something in the way I've said it outs me. Matteo's eyes narrow further. "Whoa, whoa, whoa, do you think I still have feelings for Lelani?"

I study the soap suds on my chipped brilliantly orange-painted nails. "No."

Matteo doesn't buy it. "Well, this is the pot calling the kettle black, MG. I promise you if I wanted to be with Lelani, I would have stayed with her. I didn't. It was mutual. I can assure you we're over it. Both of us."

I study his face, and he gazes calmly back at me. My rational brain is telling me that he's being sincere. Matteo is *nothing* if not honest, even to a fault. My lizard brain is telling me that he and Lelani are perfect for each other, and there's no way he prefers me and my hot mess of a life over Lelani's polished *adultness*. She has *silk office-chair cushions*, and a shiny red sedan. It would sit so perfectly in the driveway of his neat and stylish desert house, next to his shiny white Prius.

Something of my thoughts must reflect on my face because he literally throws up his hands, then grasps me by the shoulders. He brings me in for a kiss on the mouth and then sets me back down in front of the sink. "Come on, MG. You're going to have to let it go. Isn't that a song?" He starts to hum, only slightly off-key, a song I remembered hearing a few years ago on every *Disney On Ice* commercial.

"Ah, yes," he says, clearing his throat. He reaches over to the countertop, grasps my drying towel and puts it over his head like a babushka. "Let it goooo, let it gooooo . . ." he sings, twirling around the room.

I laugh. I can't help it. It wells up from my toes, bubbling over my lips like an unstoppable force. Here is my super straitlaced detective boyfriend, singing Disney songs in my kitchen with a towel over his head. Soon I'm bent over my knees, laughing so hard I have tears in my eyes. "So, let me get this straight: you'd never seen *The Princess Bride*, but you can sing a song from a Disney movie on command? Do you have a secret Disney obsession I don't know about? Hidden vault of Mickey Mouse Beanie Babies behind the fireplace?"

Matteo grins back good-naturedly. "Well, I figure it's a good investment in my future. That way I can sing along with my kids."

The picture of Matteo as he is now—work shirt slightly damp at the rolled-up cuffs from doing dishes, face open and carefree, hair mussed from the towel—is so charming, I can completely see him dancing around some future sunny kitchen with two little girls in tow. The picture is warm, sweet, and utterly charming. Matteo as a father seems as natural as Matteo as a detective.

And then something inside me seizes.

My heart catches up to my mind.

That picture of Matteo with children is so . . . vital. So *real*.

And everything that's warm freezes. I turn to a White Walker on the inside, laughter dying on my lips.

Matteo quirks a brow. "What, you don't like my Elsa impression? Okay, fine, I'll do an impression of that caribou thing, but I can assure you it's not very good . . ."

I paste a smile back on my face, and clear my throat. "I—ah, I can really picture you with children."

A smile lights his face, and he returns to the counter, content to continue our conversation. "Honestly, it's the one thought that keeps me going sometimes in my job. I see so many kids who didn't have parents to help equip them for the real world. Who didn't appreciate their joy and innocence. I'm going to soak in that stuff as long as the real world will let me."

"Mmmm," I manage in response.

He notes my odd tone and turns to face me again, taking the glass I've washed automatically from my fingers. "Er, have *you* ever thought about that? A little MG nerdling to raise up in the ways of the Falcon?"

I clear my throat again. I have *no* idea how to navigate this conversation, and not on the heels of having such a good time with him tonight. I feel like Atlas, holding up the weight of a world—our world—only Matteo has no idea. "I've thought about it," I hedge.

Matteo's smile slips slightly as he studies my face. I see the moment he decides not to press the issue and breathe an internal sigh of relief.

"Well, you threw a great party," Matteo says by way of bypassing our awkward topic. His brow is still furrowed slightly, but he sets a determined grin back on his lips. "I'm so proud of you. Who would have guessed that the girl I guilted into attending her first work party would be hosting her own a mere three months later?"

"The pupil becomes the teacher," I agree. "Except that artichoke dip. I can't get it right myself. Nina will just have to be my friend forever."

"It *is* delicious. Maybe you can keep practicing and bring it to the Christmas party. Everyone will love it. I promise to eat any and all efforts."

He pats his stomach in jest, and I give a halfhearted laugh, trying to cover that for the second time in as many minutes, my insides have gone from jelly to something curdled and awful. His statement rings in my head: Christmas party.

"What?" he asks, obviously replaying his words in his mind. "Are you upset I assumed you'd cook? I really didn't think before I spoke. Of course, if you don't feel like making the dip—"

"No," I interrupt, "I'm sorry. I'm just in a touchy mood, I guess."

"Touchy . . . about Christmas?" He looks genuinely puzzled.

Everything I have bottled up starts to boil over and froth like Dr. Horrible in his singalong blog. I can't stop it. Something in my thoughts is going to come out; I'm just trying to do damage control. I wipe my hands on my jeans and smooth back my hair, unsure of how to address this without saying something that sounds insulting.

"You're so sure of what you want."

This doesn't clear anything up for Matteo. "Like . . . artichoke dip?"

I should laugh, but I don't. I square my shoulders, suddenly serious. If this is where we're at, then I'm going to meet it full force. I'm going to ignore the insane pounding of my heart in my ears and the part of me inside that insists I'm about to ruin the only happy thing I have in my life. "No. You're so sure about *everything*."

Matteo isn't laughing now either. He regards me with a mixture of concern and apprehension. "Well, you are too? It's one of the things I love about you. You know what you want, and you're going after it."

This time the laugh that burbles up is hysterical in nature. There's that word again. *Love.* Love. Christmas parties. Babies. Just go ahead and tie my hands, stick the white veil over my face and walk me down the aisle to be chained into tradition. I know my fear is slightly irrational, but at this point Matteo has pushed so many of my unseen buttons, I can't help but unravel just a little.

"I may be going after what I *think* I want, but I'm a mess. A hot mess. If I get any hotter, I'll have to be the Girl on Fire for Halloween."

Matteo nods, and it's clear he's sensing danger. "Well, pursuing goals like these isn't always straightforward. You're not afraid of hard work. You're going after it with everything you have."

"Yeah, all these part-time things that don't even really add up to a whole. I'm barely adulting these days. You have a *real* job, your car is spotless, you want kids—"

Real panic shows on his face at this. "Don't you? I mean not *now*, but eventually?"

My first instinct is to just say that I don't. I've never pictured myself with kids—been terrified of having them since I was in college. The commitment. The *lifelong* commitment. The soul-sucking, completely life-draining amount of work those little creatures are. I much prefer my corgi, whom I could leave with a friend or in a kennel overnight if need be. But. Picturing Matteo with kids—picturing *myself* there with him has thrown me for a significant loop. One I'm not sure I even want to acknowledge. "I don't honestly know."

Matteo's silence is only punctuated by the dripping of my faucet into dishwater. I study his face, and he studies the counter for a long time before raising his hazel eyes to meet mine. "How unsure?"

Sickness invades my lower half. I don't want to have this conversation. But is this a giant Band-Aid that just needs to be ripped off? I've been feeling tension for weeks. I should just be honest and let the cards fall where they may. Maybe we're just not meant to be, and I've been loath to end this happy dream. "I . . . I don't want to be tied down. Trapped. I saw my parents suffocate under all that: monogrammed towels, two kids, gigantic mortgage, picket fence."

I swear Matteo's face has gone a bit ashen, but he still questions me with directness. "And have you felt . . . trapped . . . then?"

No. No. No. This will *kill* him. But in some sort of morbid sense of being honest to a fault, and with about as much horror as I have watching the end of *Infinity War*, knowing what's coming, I whisper, "Yes."

His eyes close briefly, and I scramble to explain.

"But only a few times. I've also felt incredibly *wonderful* and *not* tied down. See? I'm a mess."

Matteo's gaze has gone from searching to a little defensive. "Care to explain so that I can understand just exactly when you felt trapped?"

I bite my lip. "That night you made me chicken cacciatore when you were telling me about the flowers you planted." At his complete look of bafflement, I sigh and flail my arms slightly. "It wasn't the dinner or the flowers. It's what you said *about* the flowers. You said that it's the very least you could do for the girl you *loved*."

I wait for a moment and then see the light click on, and his eyes fly up to meet mine. "You . . . you felt trapped because I told you I *loved* you?"

I study him back. "Well, no, not exactly, I guess. It wasn't the . . . love . . . part." I have a tough time even getting those words out and rush on. "It's the 'what comes *after*' part."

"What comes *after*?"

I realize he thought I felt trapped by physical intimacy. I can't help but give a laugh, though the mirth quickly dies. "No, not *that*, the whole *life* part after that. The part where I sacrifice my dreams for my role as a wife and mother. Where I resent my children for making me give up my career. Where I stop dyeing my hair because the PTA disapproves of my Ariel-colored hair and mermaid skirt. Where I stop going to cons, stop designing for Lawrence, and stop being . . . me."

As awful as I feel, a weight has ascended up off my shoulders like a hot air balloon taking flight.

"I've never asked you to give up *anything* for me," Matteo says quietly. The quiet unsettles me. We're wandering into the tone he uses with suspects. Matteo is slipping into Detective Kildaire—closing himself off. It's terrifying.

I feel like reaching out and holding on to him, anchoring *Matteo* to the here and now. I don't. "I know."

"And I never would. MG, I'd *never* ask you to have children if you didn't want them. And I'd *never* want you to be anything less than fully you, because *that's* what makes you so vibrant. And amazing. And wonderful, and smart, and passionate. Why would you ever think, after I've been supportive of everything you've done and grateful for all you've done for the case, that I wouldn't continue to do that?"

Tears prick my eyes, and I don't know what to say to him, so I sort of just shrug. "Because you're the best *man* I've ever met? And you've got it so together. House, car, job. Suit and tie. Straitlaced. I guess I kind of assumed somewhere in the back of my head I'd end up with someone more like *me.*"

I've finally hit a nerve. I see the fire roar to life behind his hazel eyes like the ignition ring on a spaceship in a movie. "You, MG, are a nerd snob."

My temper flashes, hot and white. "I am not."

"You are. You rail *all the time* about being put in a box. About being afraid of being pigeonholed by being what you are—a woman, a nerd, a geek, a comic book artist, a costume designer. You continually tell people you want to be judged for who you *are* and not what you're into, or what people assume about it. And here you are doing *exactly* the same thing. You're about to excuse me from your life just because I don't fit the picture of who you thought you'd end up with. Even though I've come to every event, dressed up in costume willingly, watched—and loved—your shows and movies, you're holding it against me that I just don't *seem* like someone you thought you'd end up with? You're judging me against a man that doesn't even exist, and I'm found wanting?"

I open my mouth to argue back, to unleash some of the fury I'm feeling, but I can't form words. There *aren't* words, because what do I say?

Matteo's just getting going; I can tell he's mad now, his cheeks pink. "And you didn't even talk to me about what you *thought* I meant. You just went ahead and assumed the worst-case scenario. I was tried and convicted before even knowing my charges."

The shame I feel wars only with my own internal logic. I'm set to disagree, to defend my right to my feelings, but his point still rankles. I surprise myself by admitting that I own a small piece of this mess. "Okay. I'll agree that *maybe* you're right. I could have been a little . . . snobby. But, Matteo, *every* other guy I've dated has wanted to change me. It's not like I just made it up or have rampant paranoia."

I expect hot debate, but what I get is the fire in his eyes banking to smoldering coals. He's still upset but getting ahold of himself. "Did they love you?"

A beat. "No."

Another beat. His point is crystal clear, shining like a beacon in the dark night. But it still takes several breaths for me to develop the support in my abdomen for my next words. Because if this is it, I guess I'd like to know. "Do . . . do you?"

He waits until I've raised my eyes from the kitchen floor's grimy tiles under the dishwasher to his brilliant eyes to answer me.

"Michael-Grace Martin, I love you." His voice is sure. Quiet. Self-possessed and certain beyond shadows of doubts.

My insides rearrange. Tears prick my eyes. I'm silenced by the sheer power of emotion that rises within me.

Matteo watches this unfold on my face, and he sways closer, hand brushing like a feather against my cheek. I think for a moment he's going to kiss me, and I lean toward him, welcoming it.

But it doesn't come. Instead, he holds my gaze, waiting. Waiting for a response.

"Do you love me?" he asks when it's clear I'm not going to offer it without question.

Like a niffler searching for shiny things, I sort my feelings as quickly as I can. The vast majority is screaming *yes* louder than I could have yelled from a mountaintop. But I've never *loved* someone before. And, in among the shiny jewel flowers of my new feelings is a forest full of weeds and dark places—my fears about being forced to change are still there. And my past few weeks with Daniel have thrown some wrenches into my otherwise perfectly spinning wheels.

"I don't know," I whisper, settling on the truth. For it is the truth. My truth, and if the ship is going down, I'm captaining it until the very end.

Matteo seems satisfied by my answer, rather than enraged or hurt. "That is entirely fair, and I appreciate your honesty." His tell is when he runs his hand through his hair, and I catch the fleeting expression of longing and heartbreak that exists on his face before he's back to neutral. It undoes me.

"Matteo, I *think*—"

Matteo reaches out and grasps my hand, stopping my words short. "MG, I love you. That doesn't change. I told you once you were worth the wait . . . you *are*. And I'll wait for you. I'm sure, but you need to be sure too. At least now everything is out in the open, right? I don't want you to do anything you don't *want* to do, and that includes being with me. Maybe a break will help you clear your head and sort out what you want. Just take some time, and let me know what you decide."

Those jewel-bright feelings in my chest explode into shrapnel that pierce my lungs. My heart. My stomach. A break? Matteo was breaking *up* with me? Right after declaring his love? This would *never* happen in a comic book. This is when the hero kisses the heroine and they charge off into battle together. It's not when the hero gives the heroine space to suss out her feelings.

This is all wrong. This isn't what I want, is it? "Matteo, I—"

He silences me with a quick kiss, and then he's gone.

I last all of three minutes standing alone in my kitchen with the drip drip drip of the faucet. The walls have absorbed our fight and keep replaying his words to me.

I love you, Michael-Grace; I'm sure. You need to be sure, so we'll go on a break.

A break.

No Matteo. Right now, I have *no* Matteo, unless I'm all in. And I don't think I am ready to go all in.

Anger flairs, deep and hot inside me. How *dare* he do this to me? Tell me he loves me and then *leave me*? What sort of horrible villain does that? We've been together for three months. How can he possibly be sure? How can he think I could be sure?

But he's not really asking me to be sure I *love* him, he's asking me to be sure about *him*. About his character and his care for me. Which . . . I am. I think I am, at least. Enough to know that I feel a desperate, yawning loss after our fight. I identify with Luke, because it feels like someone I love just chopped off my right hand, and I'm teetering at the top of an abyss.

I'm headed out my own door before I know what I'm doing. And I'm in Lawrence's car, roaring down my street before I know what I've decided to do. I *think* I'm headed to Matteo's house to hash this out with him. To tell him I need time, but I don't want a break.

Out of instinct, I drive through town. Or maybe the car drives itself to its house. I'll never know. What I do know is that just like Ron Weasley discovering the light on in Hagrid's cabin, I spy the smallest of lights on in the shop's apartment as I drive by.

And like I've conjured my closest friend when I need him most, I pull to the side of the street and stare.

L is home.

CHAPTER 23

"Girl, you look . . . faded." Lawrence peers at me, and I get the sense that he means more than just my hair. I'm nestled in my favorite chair in his quiet studio, and even that isn't soothing my ills. There's too much going on, not the very least that L hasn't said a word about where he's been.

I raise my eyes to meet L's in the mirror. "Gee, thanks. Love you too," I retort, my surliness rising full force in my gullet. I can't help myself from studying him in the mirror though—the slightly puffy right eye with healing cut, the Band-Aids on one clavicle beneath his black tank top emblazoned with a Swarovski crystal DANCE across the front. Other than the abrasions, it's like he never left.

Lawrence catches the cast of my thoughts. "I already told you last night and today, I'm *fine*. I was visiting old friends—the type who don't have cell phones and don't drive cars unless they're stolen. I had to hang out for a week to see who would show up on the weekends. Nothing turned up other than some stupid bar fights at a party. I'm going to just lay low, but I have *got* to get caught up with this Halloween event."

I squint my eyes at him. He's been like this since I texted him yesterday. Nonchalant. A complete one-eighty from the "spooked out of his skin" Lawrence who left last week. I can't tell if it's an act or if he's truly put at ease by whatever he did or didn't find. I've thought it before, but this is yet another moment where I realize I may not, and may not ever, know everything about Lawrence. I used to think him easy to read, but right now he's holding his hand pretty close to his chest.

Yes, I'm home, come over tomorrow morning and we'll do hair.

That's what I'd gotten after my seven frantic texts trying to determine if he was home and safe. Well, and my second objective was obviously that once I determined L was safe, I needed a best friend. But I didn't want to explain my fight with Matteo over text, and L was so cagey, I decided to wait until I could see him in person.

We'll do hair. That's all he'd sent, as if he hadn't just been gallivanting off to Lord knows where, doing whatever it was he was doing. As if he hadn't left a police station after handing over an incriminating photo of a man he thought was trying to hurt him—a man either pretending to be or actually appearing as the Golden Arrow.

Then again, he didn't know what I knew—about the leak, the missing drugs, or Matteo's theory about a police leak. *Matteo.*

My heart squeezes so hard I have a little bit of acid burn in my throat.

He doesn't know about that either. About the spaghetti splatter of my love life all over my kitchen floor. He doesn't know that his arrival home derailed my pursuit of my boyfriend, possibly to his house. Possibly to show up on his doorstep a sobbing, wretched mess.

After I'd seen L's light on and determined that he was both alive and not leaving his house until morning, I'd turned around and gone home. I'd sat in the quiet living room for exactly one hour, until realizing that Ryan wasn't coming home either, then cried myself to sleep, hugging a completely bewildered Trog. It's a little known fact that corgi fur sops up human tears better than any other fur.

This morning I'd woken with the determination to text—no, *call*, this was important—Matteo and discuss just what exactly had transpired last night. I felt lost. I felt adrift. I still felt confused, at war with myself, and caged in. But I knew one thing. I knew I didn't want to be apart from Matteo. Did I?

Unbidden, a memory of sitting next to Daniel in his car, the easy humor, the sheer nerd understanding between us, springs to life in my memory. Should I be with someone like that, someone already *my kind*?

Well, add that to the pile of goo in my head, I guess.

Lawrence either hasn't noticed my continued silence, or he's purposely overlooking it. "Speaking of Halloween, don't forget you're basically my walking billboard. Maybe we'll even make you a T-shirt or something. All right, what are we in for today? Electric Boogaloo blue? Hot to Trot red? Oooh, I was thinking we'd do a shaved layer underneath, but lady's choice." He shakes out his fingers and arches them like a classical pianist about to attack the keys.

I deflate. "I don't know. Maybe just a trim."

L squints one eye. "A trim."

"And I'm not sure on the color, maybe let's just put it back to natural?"

L's hands still, alarm growing in his countenance.

My shoulders slump. I'm feeling less than powerful, or sexy. "I guess I could just work on growing it out."

The chair whips around before I'm prepared for it, and I'm brought face to . . . well, chest, with Lawrence. "Girl," he says peering down at me as if I've just declared myself contagious with greyscale. "This is serious. *What* is going on in that head of yours?"

"Can't a person just love what they are born with and celebrate it?"

"Whatever you are selling, I am *not* buying it," Lawrence says, completely deadpan.

I deflate instantly. "Yeah. Me neither. L, I'm a mess." In fact, no one is buying *anything* I'm selling these days. That thought brings tears, and L has to hand me an entire towel—not a Kleenex, a *towel*—to mop up with. I spill the story from Daniel to Zed while L listens patiently.

The story takes long enough that he takes a seat in the swivel chair next to me, chin in hand. He's such a good listener; I don't stop just at Matteo, I regurgitate *all* of what's been going on. How I'm drowning in work, haven't been a good friend, how the case has me tied in knots. I let it all run out, like someone squeezing the last water out of a water balloon that has popped, finally dribbling into silence.

"Okay, first off, boring hair isn't going to help any of that."

I snort.

"Second off, you're being like a sumo wrestler and just *pushing*. Pushing everything. Pushing yourself. And you're up against a pretty big world with a lot of weight, so maybe pushing isn't the way to get what you want."

I blink at him. "Isn't pushing for what I want exactly what we talked about me doing?"

"Well, yes and no. Going after what you want is exactly what you should be doing. But trying to use brute force to get there may not be the best tactic."

"I'm not following."

Lawrence stands and comes behind my chair, running his fingers through my hair. It's meditative on his part, like a reflex. It's soothing on my end, my body instantly relaxing in anticipation of one of L's famous scalp massages. He grabs a bowl off a nearby workstation and starts mixing color while he hums—all normal for him, but I get the sense that he's trying to think too.

"Let's leave Hot-Lanta to the side for right now," are the first words out of his mouth as he approaches my chair, armed with black brushes, gloves, and bowls balanced on his arm.

"Okay . . ." I agree, eyeing the bowls. I'm not sure what color he's chosen, but I guess I abdicated my vote earlier with the trim nonsense.

"So, you're not in love with the Hooded Falcon stuff. But you really love the movie work."

It's a fair summation, so I nod.

L pins my hair and begins slathering the goop onto a brush. "Well, it seems to me that despite you not *loving* the work with the comic right now, it's brought you two jobs that you do love—the movie gig and the LAPD stuff."

I nod again, my nose twitching from the smell of the caustic glop. I secretly love the smell, but it does sting the nostrils sometimes. From the look of the gel before L wraps the foil over it, I'm guessing he's chosen some shade of pink.

"As far as the costuming stuff, girl, you know you can tell me to take a hike any time—"

"Definitely not," I break in. "It's basically my favorite thing to do."

"So which things aren't bringing you joy?"

I frown. "Joy? L, it's 'Which things aren't bringing me money.' I'm so broke I can't even fix my car. No, strike that—I can't even *tow* my car to have it looked at to not be able to afford to have it fixed."

"No, the question is joy. Chérie, when you're drowning, you need to locate shore before you start swimming."

I frown. "In order of joy, I'd say the movie stuff and your costumes are the best. And then the LAPD case, *minus* my broken heart. Then my pet project that I came up with—so we'll say *any* of the comic projects that actually mean something to me bring me joy. I have less joy about taking on more sewing projects, and even less joy about my writing job." *Sorry, Falcon.* Sad to see the day when the *Hooded Falcon* comic was one of my least favorite items on my list.

"Okay, so tell them that you aren't going to write that chimpanzee comic. That it's either your side project or the highway. You can self-publish comics, right?"

"But that's crazy—"

"Okay, so we've axed one of your weights. Then renegotiate or drop those other sewing projects. Finish these and don't take on more. There's more weight. Poof. Gone."

I goggle at L. "You are so fast to just axe those things, but those other sewing projects are literally what is putting food on my table, aside from my *job*, which I'll *lose* if I tell them to take a hike with the project that Casey green-lighted."

"Have you asked that?"

"Well, no."

Lawrence gives a wry grin. "Then ask. Or tell and then basically ask permission on the back end. Same idea: back out of the projects you don't enjoy. Don't take more on."

"That's ballsy."

"Never thought you were a girl to shrink from a challenge."

I press my lips together. Can it really be that easy? Step up to the plate and tell them that I am doing the project I wanted or not at all?

"I'm not, but how on earth am I going to afford to live?"

"You're resourceful. I've been pretty selfish with your time. Maybe it's time to raise your rates and go after some other queen to design for." He holds up a finger. "Just maintain a little discount for your best friend, hmm?"

I just stare at him in the mirror. "Where is all of this coming from? Were you off attending a business conference or something?"

L foils one last piece of my hair before taking up residence in the other chair again. "I'm showing you where you could weave instead of lean. It's something Daniel and his business partner, Harrison, and I have been talking about. Doing more of what you love, less of what you don't, and pricing yourself at what you're worth."

Well, that sounds simple enough. Except not affording my life isn't simple. And yet, there is a grain of truth in what L is saying. I have just been . . . leaning. Trying to do everything. His point stands.

I cross one knee over the other, putting my chin in my hand to mirror his. "Has Daniel been helping you this much with business stuff? It sure sounds like you've recently been over it."

L's eye slide sideways and then back to mine. "Yeah, I'm preaching to the choir about going after what you want, basically. I've been looking to make some changes."

Alarm bells ring in my head, and I sit up straighter.

"Not *drastic* changes, sit yourself down. Hire on another stylist. Open another studio. Brand my own hair care products, stuff like that. And I think I'm going to perform less."

"But you *love* performing!"

L nods. "I do. It's my life's passion. But I don't want to be stuck trying to make who I am fit who I want to be if it's not who I want to be anymore. I think it's healthy to allow yourself the opportunity to grow a new set of passions."

That strikes a chord in me. Is that what I am doing with Matteo? Clinging *so* hard to what I had pictured for so many years that I wanted without really checking in internally to see if I still want it?

L sighs. "Truth be told . . . I'm *tired*. I feel like I'm running around all the time. I want to step back and do more limited performances. Sell-out shows instead of hosting the revue." He shrugs, and I get the sense that he's suddenly bashful. "More time at home, maybe a family."

My eyes widen, and then it hits me. "This has to do with Stevie."

L doesn't answer, and I know I'm right.

"Has he stopped in again? Did something happen? I can't believe you didn't *tell* me—"

"No, he hasn't come by again, but this just has me thinking. Maybe I'll reach out and see . . . well, I don't know. That ship has probably sailed, but it gets me thinking. Stevie and I were a long time ago, but it doesn't mean that there's not someone else for me. I don't know. Maybe I'll ask Harrison out for coffee."

I nod. "That dancer body."

Lawrence returns the nod. "True, that. Anyhow, I guess I realized I picture me sharing this with someone, someday. Maybe I'm ready to take my Grade A buns off the market. Forty is in the rearview mirror; I'm just thinking about the future. It's why Daniel has been working with me on branding and possibly franchising. It's not like hosting a revue is going to pay for retirement. And Stevie showing back up . . . well. It has me thinking about *my* future."

"That's really . . . adult . . . of you, L," I say. I fear he takes that as a criticism by the look on his face, so I reach out and grab his big, warm hand, holding it in mine. "And for what it's worth, if Stevie doesn't still want your Grade A buns, he's crazy. It's worth checking on if it means you gain back your long-lost love. Any way it works out, it sounds wonderful. I'm excited for you. I want to see all those things for you if it's what you want."

He offers me a small smile. "You don't think it's too . . . boring? I mean, I am *still* a queen. I just want the drama to stay onstage, maybe."

I squeeze his hand. "You'll *never* be boring. Even if you find yourself a mister."

Lawrence's face lights up with his smile; it flashes quick as a wink before he peers at my hair. "Let's check these and you can tell me blow-by-blow about your fight with Hot-Lanta."

My heart convulses involuntarily. Matteo. I feel nearly sick, but spilling the tale to Lawrence seems cathartic.

L snorts when I explain how Matteo called me a nerd snob.

I raise my eyebrow in the mirror, and L tries to cover his snort with a cough and then finally gives in to a short fit of laughter.

"Girl, he hit it on the head."

"Does *everyone* think this?" I ask. I'm offended, but I also realize that I thought Matteo could have a point when we fought. The fact that Lawrence agrees with him outright is disheartening. "I try *so* hard to be open-minded."

"You are. About *most* things, but not this one." L is kind when he corrects me. "But up until this point, it hasn't been a problem for you."

I open my mouth several times and then finally land on, "I've dated other people. You never said anything then."

L cocks an eyebrow at me. "Honey, every one of those people deserved to be excused from the game." He spins me around and crouches down so we're eye level. "But you get up in your head, and sometimes you can't see the forest for the trees. And it's been even worse lately because of this work stuff. You're tied up in knots, trying to please everyone and do everything . . . when I think all you need to do is reevaluate. Be honest with yourself. Accept who you are and what you love to do now. Find someone who loves who you are and supports what you want to do now. A wise mentor once said to me, 'If you can't love you, how the hell are you gonna love somebody else?'"

"Amen," I say automatically, which earns me a smile from L.

"Okay, now tell me what happened next."

"What do you mean? I just told you everything."

"No, after that. What happened *after* the fight?"

"I just stood there? And then I sort of just got in the car, and when I saw you were home, I pulled over and—"

L *tsks*. "You should have just driven to Matteo's and left my sorry butt alone. I was safe and sound and told you as much. You worry too much."

I swallow hard. "Yeah, there's been a development in the case you don't know about. That's one of the things I need to tell you—one of the things I was going to tell you last night."

L's hands still, then he pulls the cape from around me. "Come over to the wash sink and tell me."

I follow him over and relate the facts as I remember them—the missing evidence, the note, and Matteo's suspicion that the Golden Arrow may be working with Muñez. The possibility of a leak.

L frowns. "That could be potentially problematic."

"Potentially problemat—L, Matteo thinks you're in real *danger*."

He shrugs, though a tinge of worry has replaced the nonchalance on his face from our previous conversation. "I've done my part, sown my seeds. I need to see what the harvest is, if you will. Tell your Hot-Lanta I'll be careful, but that I'm declining the security detail. It would mess with my own operation."

Warm water splatters my neck and forehead as he rinses my hair, then steers me back to the chair for the trim and styling. "He's not *my* Hot-Lanta; didn't you hear me earlier?"

"I heard you say that he's sure he loves you and just wants *you* to be sure you love him for who he is and not be afraid of who he isn't. That still sounds like *yours* to me."

"And what exactly do you mean by *your* operation?" Unbidden, the thought that L might *be* the Golden Arrow resurfaces. Fear prickles the back of my neck, competing with the aggressive combing from Lawrence to create an overall uncomfortable sensation.

L takes his time blow-drying. He's focused on his work, a master at his craft. And he is too; what is emerging from his handiwork is nothing short of spectacular. Cropped close in at the sides and nape, my hair starts as a deep russet. But the pièce de résistance is the longish top that L is styling into a quasi-messy fauxhawk or pompadour. It's not just russet—it's run through with strands of brilliant pink, bright orange, Ariel-red, and maroon.

"It's absolutely stunning," I say, nearly breathless as I admire myself in the mirror. I preen like a peacock, turning this way and that until I catch sight of L washing up the bowls behind me. "It *also* hasn't excused you from having to tell me what you've been up to."

L stacks the bowls and removes the gloves. I expect more anxiety, but when he turns to face me, he's got a devious smile on his lips. "It's really quite ingenious. Instead of looking for this guy myself, I delegated the work."

"Delegated." I'm not following.

L nearly claps with glee as he starts to sweep up. "I got the idea from watching *Sherlock*. Specifically, his homeless network. I crashed at a few old friends' places, waiting to see who would show up for parties and the like. Asked a few questions, but everyone got suspicious that I was there working for the cops and clammed up. Almost everyone in that neighborhood either has a reason to fear the police or knows someone who does. So I came up with the perfect cover."

"Something tells me I'm not going to love this." Somewhere in the back of the salon, my phone starts to ring in my messenger bag. "That's Ryan; I told him to call me when he was headed home from the gym so he could pick me up." Both of us being without a vehicle was getting pricey.

"I told them I'm working for Casey. Which"—he twirls me in the chair with a flourish—"since they knew I worked for Senior, it wasn't a stretch that I work for Junior now. They accepted it without question."

I check my hair one last time before heading toward my bag, running my fingers over the soft shaved part over my ears. I simply adore it. "Okay, but why would you even tell them you were working for Casey?"

L's eyes sparkle. "You're off your game; usually you're better at this, miss LAPD consultant. *Because* the one person who has a legitimate reason besides the cops to be trying to track down this Golden Arrow is Casey Junior."

The light clicks on in my brain. "The reward."

"Exactly so." L's attention has turned to his own reflection in the mirror, and he leans in, examining his lips. Apparently finding them in want of a lip color, he starts digging through a drawer filled with miscellaneous cosmetics, pulling out lipsticks to read their names before tossing them back. He looks up to find me still watching him as I dig through my bag. "What?"

"So that's it? That's the grand plan? Tell them you're trying to find the Golden Arrow for the reward?" It's good, but it's not *that* good.

L leans into the mirror again, having found a shade that he likes, and starts applying. After blotting and blowing himself a kiss, he turns back to me. "The brilliant part is that I played like I was getting a cut if I found the Golden Arrow—the person who was at the party that night. And I *may* have led my friends to believe that anyone who helped me find this guy for his reward money would get a nice 'thank you' gift from my cut."

"That *is* smart—" I've picked up my phone, and the text isn't from Ryan. My heart makes a trip down to my toes and back up, lodging directly under my larynx. I can't finish my thought.

L cackles. "It *is* smart. The underground knows the underground best, y'know? And a little money always greases the wheels. So, I never asked outright, but I know that several of my friends are looking on my behalf. It's genius, really—what? What is it? Girl, you're about two shades from Michael Jackson's ivory."

I can't do anything except hand him my phone as I dig out my jacket.

He whistles between his teeth. "I guess you'll need a ride to the station."

"Do you mind?" I read the text one more time before dropping the phone into my bag. It's Detective Kildaire. This is no love note, no reconciliatory pining. It's curt and to the point.

Come to the station ASAP. Golden Arrow is in custody, need you for the questioning.

My coat threatens to strangle me as I zip it up—suddenly it's several sizes too small. It's not even the thrill or shock that they have the Golden Arrow in custody; it's that I'm going to have to face Matteo. I have to go in, do my job, and act like this fight isn't killing me.

L, ever the best friend, snatches his keys off the counter where I left them and tosses me the lip color. "We're going together for this."

I'm still stuck in place. L turns, looks over his shoulder, and says the exact thing that helps propel me out of the door.

"Well, if you're going to have to see Hot-Lanta, at least you look dynamite."

True. I square my shoulders. I have my bestie, I look dynamite, and who cares for now if I have a broken heart? I have a vigilante hero to meet.

CHAPTER 24

Daniel Kim sits quietly on the other side of the one-way glass into the interrogation room. This one is a mirror image of the one used for the drug dealers, only the person sitting in the chair across from Detective Rideout isn't a drug dealer. It's someone I know.

Beside me, L stands, a silent sentinel. He almost seemed relieved when he saw Daniel—maybe he has been fearing the man he's been looking for in his old neighborhood. Either way, he's been quiet as an oak since we got here. Given the identity of the suspect, he's been allowed back with me and has signed several sheets of paper that ensures he won't speak at large about this. L is basically a second consultant on the case at this point.

I chance a glance at Matteo—I've purposefully looked everywhere except at him in the ten minutes we've been here.

Our gazes connect, and it's like a gut punch. I feel the urge to say something. Ask how he is. He looks to be warring with the same set of struggles, his eyes flicking from my hair to my matching fire-engine-red lips, then back to my eyes. Emotion uncoils in my stomach at the sheer *longing* I glimpse. He turns away first and shuffles some papers, clearing his throat. "We followed your tip *and* an anonymous tip. We have grounds for the arrest."

Grounds for the arrest. I study the figure I've grown to know well through the glass. So, I'd been right and the Golden Arrow had been under my nose the entire time.

Daniel sits, calmly answering Rideout's questions. Or he's attempting calm. I can tell from the way he moves around that he's agitated but trying to keep his cool.

Truth be told, I'm a little surprised to see Rideout, given the internal investigation. I don't realize I've voiced this out loud until Matteo answers, his voice a little defensive. "He's on probation essentially. He's not allowed to conduct any police business by himself until he's cleared."

If he's cleared, but I decide to let the point drop. Instead after a quick glance at Matteo's stoic face, I turn back to the glass, and clear my own throat. "So, uh, what's going on now?"

"This is the mundane part of the interview, meant to loosen him up while gaining necessary information for paperwork." Matteo bumps the knob up on the control panel, and we can hear more of their conversation. "But I have questions for you both about Mr. Kim."

In the background, Daniel is spelling the name of his dance studio and asking if there is a way to access his online calendar for the dates Rideout has asked about.

Matteo—no, Detective Kildaire—glances through some notes. "We've discovered that Daniel has a black belt in hapkido."

At my confused look, Matteo explains. "It's a Korean martial art. Grappling in nature, by my research." I hate the assured set of his jaw. He's *confident*. And . . . maybe with good reason. We've known the Golden Arrow had impressive physical skill to accomplish what he's done. Wrangling people, using long cords to tie intricate knots—they're not skills your average office schmo possesses.

"The physical pieces fit, but he has to know the pop culture stuff too. Do you believe Daniel would have adequate knowledge of the comic books to pull this off? We're going to question him, but do *you* think so?"

"He's adequately . . . nerdy, if that's what you're asking."

"We're going for facts here, Ms. Martin." Matteo doesn't look up from scribbling his notes.

Ms. Martin. Well, that rankles. My ire rises to meet my impressive new hair color. "Well, *Detective Kildaire*, he's read the comics, he works for the franchise. Facts enough for you?"

At the use of his title instead of his name, Matteo snaps his notebook shut and draws himself up as if I've struck him. Good. Let him see how it feels. "I'm just trying to arm myself for interrogation. He has an alibi, and we'll need to nail him on these other counts to keep him."

"I thought you said you have grounds for the arrest."

"We do," Detective Kildaire says, turning back to the glass. "Here's the first item we found when we searched his apartment."

Lawrence and I pivot as one just in time to see a flash of something gold pass from Officer Montoya to Rideout.

"That's not what I think it is, is it?" Lawrence asks.

"One cape and one mask," Detective Kildaire confirms.

"The same one from the party?" Lawrence asks.

"We're not sure. Recovered from his closet."

And Daniel certainly does *not* have a gravelly voice, per Lawrence's recollection. Detective Kildaire's thoughts seemed to mirror my own, as in that exact moment he leans across me and asks L if he can identify Daniel as the man he'd seen that night.

The scent of Matteo's clean and light cologne meets my nose, and I inhale reflexively. The smell brings with it every good feeling and memory of this man, filling my head. Everything from the time I met him, the day we met on my front porch, sitting across from him in the Genius comic library, sitting on my bed looking at sketches, our first kiss in an alleyway during a stakeout . . . it killed me for weeks, not being able to touch him due to the case. And here I am again, inches from this man and unable to touch him. My fingers literally twitch in an effort to reach out and run themselves through his dark, wavy hair.

My imagination has terrible timing, because now I'm remembering how cute Matteo was, watching *Star Wars* for the first time. How adorably bewildered he was by San Diego Comic-Con and cosplay,

245

but how he never grumbled about dressing up. And how he supports Lawrence onstage every chance he can, not to mention, cheered me on through the terrifying decision to drop to part time with my job and try to costume for part of my living. I'm having a hard time holding on to that caged feeling in this river of thought. If I just let it go, it will float downstream, never to be seen again. Will I be okay with that, though? It will be uncharted territory for me—terrifyingly new, *committed* territory.

I've tuned out Lawrence, though I'm assuming he's saying something along the lines of, "No, Daniel cannot possibly be the person I saw." I think I hear Matteo ask him if he recognizes the cape and mask, and L responds in grudging affirmative. The floodgates of my mind have opened, and I'm standing awash in emotions. If standing this close to Matteo without touching him is tough now, could I let him go for a lifetime? Just because this man wanted a future with me?

I study the side of his face, his profile. I try to imagine waking up next to him for the rest of my life, and then I wait for panic to intrude. But . . . it doesn't come. By slow measures I try a new future on for size. Not all at once, but in degrees. Picturing Matteo and me living in his snug desert house, my colorful items and stacks of sketches intermingled with his straight lines and muted palette. And still the panic doesn't come. I can't picture a traditional wedding, so instead I envision something I never thought I would: a sweet elopement in his courtyard. Just him and me, and a few friends. Again, I wait for the panic to seize me as I picture a ring—plain, thankyouverymuch—sliding onto my finger. And what freaks the *hell* out of me is that this *doesn't* freak the hell out of me.

As if sensing my thoughts, Matteo straightens and catches me staring. No, basically peering into the depths of my very own soul. His eyes widen with whatever he sees on my face, and then ever so subtly, a smolder starts in his hazel eyes.

Crap.

Has he seen too much? Have I let all the cats out of all the bags? *Can Matteo actually read minds?* I'm not ready to share what I've just dipped my toe into. I'm not even ready to share *with myself* what I just pictured, much less the object of my affections. Not until I've decided what it means for sure, and this is not the setting in which to navel-gaze. I frantically reel in my emotions. I let them get wildly out of control internally. I am here, supposedly consulting on a case where a *friend of mine* was just arrested, and I'm picturing getting *hitched*. Paint me red and call me Irma; I'm ready to fire myself.

I cast around with my eyes for anything other than Matteo. Not his luminous hazel gaze, not his touchable dark hair, not the stubble on his kissable . . . *dammit*. I force my gaze into the room, feigning intense interest on the case. Which I'm supposed to have. I study the tableau in front of me, shoving the thoughts about Matteo into an inner suitcase in my mind.

The gold cape and mask sit between Rideout and Daniel on the table, and Daniel hasn't made a move to touch them. In fact, he's regarding them rather like a poisonous snake someone surprised him with. He looks *unnerved* but not guilty.

My little thought dalliance with Matteo must have only taken seconds because Rideout is just now questioning Daniel about the cape.

"Our search warrant resulted in several found items directly of interest in this case—"

Daniel doesn't let him finish. "This isn't mine. Where . . . where did you say you found this?"

"In your apartment, Mr. Kim," Rideout says with all the patience in the world. He's a cat toying with a mouse in his head.

"Yes, but *where* in my apartment?" Daniel is more insistent.

"I—ah, I'm not sure. It will be in the notes; does it matter?"

"Of *course* it matters. That's why I'm asking." It's apparent that Daniel is losing his patience.

I can still feel Matteo's gaze on me, heating my skin. I wish so badly we were alone in this room. Trying to keep myself from succumbing to the mental opening of that suitcase in my mind, I jam it farther under a mental bed and intensify my focus on the table.

"Ask him about his brother. He delivered those items to that property on Curtis Street," I say, eyes on the interrogation room. "Catch him in the lie."

Matteo frowns but passes the message to Rideout. Officer Montoya knocks and enters moments later, handing Rideout several printed sheets of paper. After a quick review, Rideout slides them across the table to Daniel.

"You can see here that the cape and the mask were found in a closet, in a black gym bag."

The sheets must contain prints of pictures from the scene because Daniel responds in a baffled tone of voice. "That's my gym bag, yes. And my closet where I keep my dance costumes, but I lent these to a friend for a Halloween costume. There's no way they ended up back in my bag."

Rideout sits forward. "It's in a witness statement that you claim to have lent these to a brother."

Daniel's eyes widen, and I know in that moment he realizes I must have squealed on him. "I, er . . ."

"You don't have a brother, Daniel," Rideout purrs. He's in his element now. "So, if you're protecting someone . . ."

This gets a reaction from Daniel. "I'm not protecting anyone. Please. He *is* my brother. Ex. Ex brother-in-law. The divorce was nasty; we're not supposed to still see each other by court order, but my daughter— well, my daughter wanted to trick-or-treat with him on Halloween, and I caved. They were going as the Golden Arrow and Swoosh."

There's a long beat of silence.

Well, crap. Now I feel horrible. If that story is true, the entire reason I suspected him is totally explainable. Maybe—just *maybe*—we've got this all wrong and Daniel Kim is innocent as he claims.

"This is not the only item we know to have once been in Mr. Lawrence St. Claire's possession, which went missing. And not the only item we found in your bag."

Daniel looks alarmed at this. Downright freaked out. "What do you mean?"

"I mean it's in your best interest to work *with* us and not against us. We can offer you lesser sentences. We can offer you protection. We just want to know *how* you've been doing it and what you've found in this that has helped."

Matteo leans forward, and I get the sense that Rideout is getting ready to play a trump card. What on earth could he have that cinches up the case this neatly?

"Seriously, this is crazy. I don't know what you're talking about," says Daniel.

Rideout makes a motion through the window, and Officer Montoya appears shortly in the doorway carrying a ziplock bag I recognize as an evidence bag.

She hands it to Rideout, who removes it from the bag and tosses it on the table.

And while Daniel looks completely puzzled, I recognize it.

And it cinches the case for me too. Daniel *has* to be the Golden Arrow, because only the Golden Arrow would have this in his possession.

It's the piece of missing evidence we've been looking for.

The journal.

CHAPTER 25

"Well, what do you think?" L has been quiet the entire drive back to my house, allowing me to pore over the copy of the journal pages Matteo gave me, using the map light in his car. It's the real deal. This is definitely the missing half of the journal from Casey Senior's painting that we lost track of at San Diego Comic-Con.

Lawrence pulls up to my curb and puts the car in park, letting it idle. Usually I'd chide him for destroying the environment, but I feel like right now he and I need some time to decompress, and the safe little cocoon of his car seems the perfect place.

"It's definitely your journal." I hand him the sheets, and he riffles through them, nodding. I note the two pages that we already had copies of from last week. It's definitely the same journal.

"Do you think I'll get it back? The whole thing?"

I sigh. "Probably not until after the trial. We're lucky they gave us copies. Matteo made me swear I'd basically lock them up at night."

Lawrence frowns, leafing through the pages again. "So, you think that this is all true? Enough to go to trial?"

"How can it not be?" I start to gather up my bag and glance at my phone. Ten o'clock, and I'm beat. I hope Ryan is home and has let Trog out—there's a light on in the living room, so I'm confident that's the case. "You saw the cape and the mask. I mean, who else would have this?"

Lawrence props his arm against his window and rubs his eyes. "I mean, I guess it makes sense. He certainly is physically capable."

I nod. "He's adequately nerdy, and he's always interested in the case, which I took to be natural interest, but . . ."

"He might have been keeping tabs on what we knew?"

"Exactly."

"I feel kinda *used*, and not in a good and fun way," Lawrence says.

I laugh feebly. "Well, the only good thing to come of this is that if Daniel is the Golden Arrow, you're in the clear. He has no ties to Muñez, and you don't think he's the same guy you met in the club, right?"

Real worry creases Lawrence's brow. "I've been trying to sort that out as we drive. I guess it's just a coincidence that I recognize the voice? Or he was pretending to be the Golden Arrow for the reward money. Either way, the journal kind of ties it up, doesn't it? Only the true GA would have it."

While he talks, he leafs through the copies, pausing several times to inspect the sketches.

"Hmm," he says, turning back to a page several times.

"'Hmm,' like you see something?"

"'Hmm,' like this sketch looks familiar; I've seen something like it recently, but I can't think of where." He points to an axonometric sketch that looks unlike the other superhero or series-related sketches.

Unease uncoils in my stomach. "Something related to the case? The Golden Arrow?"

L shrugs, rubbing his eyes. "I don't know. I'm pretty tired. I'll have to think about it. I think DeWayne drew it, but I don't know why I'd have seen it recently. Maybe I'm just making stuff up now."

I nod but can't help continuing my processing of the evening. "I still have a hard time picturing Daniel doing it, but maybe that's the whole idea. Be the Peter Parker so no one suspects the Spider-Man. Now we just have to get him to tell us what he knows about the Queen of Hearts." I start to open my door, then stop. "Actually, it's funny . . .

for a few days I really thought *you* might be the Golden Arrow. You seem so much more the type."

Lawrence pauses. "Greedy for a reward and crazy enough to be a vigilante?"

"No, I don't know. Like you had a stake in the game. You loved Casey Senior. You knew the players. You had access to the journal, access to the case . . . it's stupid, but I saw your gym shoes, and they matched the description given by one of the two suspects tied up earlier this month. That's it. It's not like *you* have a cape and a mask and a dark personal secret to make reparations for." I relate briefly what the two boys had told us about the Golden Arrow.

"My shoes." Lawrence looks either amused or pissed. I'm not sure which.

"I didn't go through your bag or anything. Okay, yes, I did. I opened it to make sure you didn't have a costume—a Golden Arrow costume—in there, which you didn't. It didn't make any sense anyhow, given you helped chase the Golden Arrow. It was a really weird thought; I'm just glad it turned out to be wrong."

Lawrence makes some sort of *humpf* noise and hardly says anything as I get out of the car. He's staring through my open door, at my porch.

I lean back down. "Are you okay?"

Lawrence jumps like I've stuck him. "Yeah, of course. It's just been a long day."

I hear that, a yawn appearing unbidden on my lips. "Okay, so tomorrow I guess I'm going to be combing through these journal pages, and then, want to pick me up Monday after my half day in the office? We can look at the pages together and then maybe hang out so I don't realize how utterly alone I am right now?" I offer puppy dog eyes as extra incentive.

L shakes himself, like he'd drifted off while I was talking, and his eyes snap to mine as if he's just now realizing I'm still here. "Oh. Yeah. Monday works. I have some hair and makeup tutorials I'd like to try out for Halloween, if you want to come hang. And now that . . . well. Now that my business coach is in custody, I'll probably need some help with the Halloween project. We can talk about that."

"Perfect. Love you, L. And please be careful. If Daniel is the Golden Arrow, it means that guy may still be out there, trying to hurt you."

"I will." And he means it, I can tell.

He waves as he pulls off. It's normal enough, but there's still something off about his behavior. Maybe the thought of a Golden Arrow and a Golden Arrow imposter unsettles him again. Who *wouldn't* be off after a day like today? This is certainly a twist I didn't see coming.

My house is warm and cozy when I enter, and thankfully has the aura of someone else being home. I don't want to be alone right now for several reasons. I shut the door against the developing chill of the night . . . it's not hard to believe that fall has finally arrived in California.

"Hello!" I call out, pleased to hear the familiar click of Trog's little trot as he comes across the kitchen to greet me at the foot of the stairs.

"Hey," comes Ryan's voice from the living room. "You're home late. Anything interesting?" There's a lack of gaming noise, which is unusual.

Trog graces my face with dozens of corgi kisses before I set him back down and make my way into the living room. Ryan is sitting reading a book. An actual book, not even on his iPad. I eye the curiously silent TV screen and game console. For other folks this would be a cozy homecoming; for me it's on the verge of *The Twilight Zone*. "What'cha up to?"

Ryan holds up the book like I'm daft. "I asked you first."

I sit on the edge of the couch, and Trog dutifully hops up, settling himself in some sort of starfish corgi sprawl on my lap for a belly rub. It's adorably indecent. Trog has no modesty. I indulge him, and he wiggles and sneezes appreciatively.

"Interesting doesn't begin to cover my day." I'm not one hundred percent that I'm allowed to divulge the identity of the suspect in custody so I say cryptically, "There was a pretty big break on the case. They think they have the Golden Arrow in custody."

Ryan sits up comically fast, like he's in some sort of play. "What!"

"Yeah, I know. It's pretty crazy."

After a beat of silence, Ryan waves his hand in a forward motion. "Aaaand?"

Trog hops down and heads to the water dish, his back having transferred a sufficient amount of rust and white hair to my clothing. It gives me a moment to consider how to tell Ryan without *telling* Ryan. "Well, obviously they're still investigating, but they found some items. Some *missing* items and a cape and everything at this person's house. It looks pretty legit."

A flash of triumph crosses Ryan's face, replaced immediately by almost comic-level interest. "Really." He draws out the word.

"Really." Ryan was there the day we chased Agent Sosa through SDCC; he's nearly as invested in this case as I am. I share some of his triumph in finally having some answers. *Some.* We have an identity, but we're a long way from understanding what the Golden Arrow knows or how it could wrap up this case.

"So, is this the guy from the party? The one Lawrence thought he knew?"

"No, they brought L back to see if he could positively ID the guy, but he said it's not the same person."

"But I guess now that they have someone in custody, L can quit searching, right?" He says it like it's a foregone conclusion, one he's relieved about.

I shrug, again hedging around what I know about the case. "I guess. L thinks the guy from the party may be trying to get the reward or . . ."

Ryan frowns. "Or . . . ."

"Or I'm worried that it's someone who used to work for Muñez, pretending to *be* the Golden Arrow. The current suspect has no ties to Muñez or Sosa at all. No ties to *anyone* that we can tell. If we have the Golden Arrow in custody, it means that this other person is a player on the chessboard somehow. If it's someone who wants to hurt L, it could be that they're using the Golden Arrow costume as a cover to meddle with the case or to hurt the people that could identify them."

Ryan's frown deepens. "That's a pretty brilliant theory. Batshit, but brilliant." He doesn't *look* impressed, though; he *looks* disappointed.

I guess I feel the same. Feeling like L might still be in danger doesn't sit well with me either. "Well, we'll hope that it's just someone out for the reward money. I wonder if Casey Junior will come to see our suspect and offer him the reward for his story."

Ryan is silent, which I take to mean he's not all that interested in what Casey will do with the reward money, so I turn my attention to his book. I raise my eyebrow at him. *"The Merry Adventures of Robin Hood?"* The white of a library barcode flashes at me—I wasn't even aware Ryan knew where the library was. Teaches me to pigeonhole my friends.

Ryan glances down at the book. "Research for a new game idea I have."

I perk up. "Is Genius doing a *Robin Hood* reboot?"

"No, I pitched another Hooded Falcon project to them; should hear back this week. Which will be *good* to pay the bills, y'know. But the *Robin Hood* project is personal."

"Well, I admire your . . . dedication." I try to make "dedication" sound like a good thing, and not the "you couldn't make me read that old book if you tried" I felt.

A ghost of an odd smile flashes across his face before his features return to neutral. Almost *carefully* neutral. I haven't checked in with Ryan in a while, and it's been on my mind. Maybe his projects aren't going well, or maybe he's really concerned about finances and he doesn't want to freak me out.

"Are *you* doing okay? You seem . . . off."

Ryan looks at me a moment too long before offering a relaxed smile and leaning back against the couch, opening the book. "I promise, I'm totally fine. Everything is normal and fine."

I squint at him, and beside me Trog gives a sneeze that I take as equally suspicious. "Okay, well, I'll leave you to it."

"Lelani and I were working on my new project tonight," Ryan calls out as I turn for my room.

I turn back. "Oh?"

"Yeah. I'll have to show you my sketches for it sometime; I think you'll like it." He doesn't make a move to go get said sketches, so we stare at each other for a beat before he picks his book back up. "Anyhow, you asked where I was earlier, and that's where I was."

I've been dismissed, and awkwardly at that. What is *with* my life right now? I decide to lean in instead of flounce, because sometimes we need our friends to see through the *fine*. "Are you sure you're okay? Everything okay with you and Lelani?"

"Totally fine. Normal." Impassive. Rehearsed. Total crock of corgi poop, in my estimation. Anyone who feels the need to add "normal" into the description of their relationship *isn't* doing *fine*. I'm about to press him on it when he turns the tables. "And you? How's love in the LAPD?"

The silence stretches a moment. A silence that in my head is filled with *so much*. Daniel. Matteo. Our fight, my feelings, my changing picture of my life . . . that I just can't seem to encompass them in words. Not long ago, I would have flopped on the couch and divulged my every thought. But tonight, I feel stranded. Alone on an island of my own making. Stuck between who I'm trying to be, who I want to be, who I am, and how isolated I've become. Or maybe I'm just too tired. Or my brain doesn't have enough room, or enough capability, to go through everything again tonight. Whatever the reason, I meet his eyes and parrot back with spot-on mimicry. "Totally fine. Normal."

It's on my way to my room, Trog in tow, that I have my pang of sadness over my response. "Hey, Ry?" I don't even get back to the living room; I just call around the corner.

"Yeah." It's not a question; it's a statement. And he sounds way more exhausted than he had moments ago.

"Let's pick a time to hang out soon, okay? Just the two of us—we could look at sketches or watch a movie, whatever you want. I miss you."

It's quiet so long I don't think he's going to answer. But just as I'm going to poke my head around the corner to see if he's fallen asleep or something, he does. He sounds a million years old, and I get the sense that there's just as much behind his "fine" as mine.

"Yeah, that sounds good. I miss you too."

CHAPTER 26

"These are good. *Really* good." The Hooded Falcon panels keep me entranced several moments longer, though finally I tear my eyes away and meet the artist's cool gaze.

"Don't act so surprised. I *told* you I could do my job." There's the hint of a smile playing about Paige's mouth, but I admire her ability to deadpan.

The sheets are crisp and fresh, so I lay them carefully back in the folder before turning to lean against the half wall of her workspace. "It's more than just drawing. You really *get* the writing. Usually it takes me a few months to get to that point with an artist."

"Aw shucks, girl power, yay, rah," Paige says drily, though I note the slight quirky smile still in her expression.

"More like mind meld. I don't think this has to do with girl power so much as shared vision for the comic world."

I resist the urge to open the folder back up. The panels were almost exactly what I would have done. And I appreciate that Paige has a slightly edgy freshness about her pen strokes. They breathe new life into the story, where maybe Kyle, Simon, and I have gotten a little stale. Paige's work is the right mix of edgy and nostalgic. Her hatching, use of the frame . . . something about it reminds me of the original *Falcon*. It may sound silly to anyone other than another comic writer, but it gives me goose bumps. These little details—things you can't train into an artist—these pieces of organic vision reignite my love for this comic all over again.

"Um, are you *crying*?" Paige asks, all sense of quirky smile gone. In its place is true horror.

"No, definitely not," I say, resisting the urge to dab at my moist eyes and give myself fully away. What is *wrong* with me? Getting nostalgic and teary at work over a comic that *I already work on*. "I'm just . . . well, I wanted to say that I love your work, and I can see why you were the best candidate for the job, hands down."

Paige still seems wary, but a small smile makes its way onto her lips. "You're just saying that because you like that I stuck to your script."

Man, is this girl sharp, and a real ballbuster. I freaking love it. A great big burst of laughter launches itself from my belly—something also uncharacteristic of me. I'm just not used to someone calling me on my stuff, or being *right* about it. "Fair," I manage around the fit of coughing I use to cover up my laughter.

A quick check of the room confirms that Kyle, Simon, and Andy all are staring, and all have looks of incredulity on their faces. Given that I'm usually cranky, all business, or, in the past few months, harried . . . I can see where their confusion stems from. Stuck in my ways, *pah*. Look at me, MG: crying and laughing at work. Nary a prickle in sight. I'm turning over all sorts of new leaves. I'm a whole new *tree*, practically. But it doesn't bother me the way I thought it would. My coworkers, other than thinking it's odd behavior for *me*, don't seem to be treating me any differently these days. I still feel like I'm useful and an expert in my field. Really, aside from Casey Junior, no one seems to even note the change. I'll blame it on Matteo and his tea-drinking, Prius-driving, flower-planting ways. That thought sobers me.

"Okay, well, carry on; thanks for letting me peek at the pages." I affect an air of breeziness and do my best to walk to my desk like this is completely normal.

Out of habit, I check my phone as I sit down at my desk. I may be a new tree, but I'm still the intermittent master of procrastination. No one has ever asked about it, but I always figure I'd tell them that Reddit and Twitter offer daily fodder for ideas for ridiculous banter between characters and inspiration for story lines, and I'm checking on our presence online. Mostly I just troll for fan-related drama and fan art, but no one has to be the wiser.

As I'm scrolling, a text comes through.

Hate to bail, but my homeless network netted me some info. Going to meet him right now. Might not be back, depending on traffic. Rain check for Tuesday?

Gah. I've been looking forward to makeup tutorial night with L, but this doesn't seem to offer much in the way of wiggle room.

Okay, but be careful.

I sound like such a mom. The thought makes me hesitate before typing the next line, but I decide to own it. Text me when you get home, okay?

Three dots appear. I wait.

Okay, MOM.

That elicits a giggle from me, and I go back to trolling Twitter. I've just tucked away my phone and reached for my notebook when a throat clearing behind me nearly knocks me out of my chair.

I slowly spin around to find Lelani standing behind me. "Michael-Grace, I was wondering if I could possibly"—she eyes my empty desk—"interrupt what you're doing for a moment?"

Chagrined, I make a show of turning back around, closing my notebook, and *not* apologizing. If pressed, my creative process sometimes needs input. "Sure, no problem."

I follow her out of the room and down the hall to her office, and only then do my palms sweat. Lelani won't be firing me, will she? No . . . I made a slam dunk out of the movie stuff—my work emails over the weekend confirm that they love my input. Okay, so what then? Another, worse, thought occurs to me. What if she and Ryan are having trouble and she's about to *ask for advice*? I can't really imagine this being the case, but . . . if I had to choose between being grilled on my social media usage at work and talking about relationships with the VP of my company, well, I'd choose to be castigated. Perhaps even publicly. Just because I'm now adult-ier, feeling-er, happier, MG does *not* a gal pal make.

By the time we reach her office, I've worked myself up into a few knots. Would I tell her to break up with Ryan? Should I tell *him* to break up with her? Tell her I haven't talked to him in weeks, hardly, so I have no idea what to say?

"Are you going to be seated?" Lelani asks, cluing me in to the fact that I'm still standing in her doorway, pondering who will get Ryan in the breakup. Me, obviously, but Lelani and I will still work together. Will she be cordial to him at work functions?

"Oh, yes, of course." I sit, bracing for work-inappropriate conversation.

Lelani is watching me like I'm some sort of sideshow act—like she can read my desperation on my face and doesn't know what to make of it. "I spoke with Mr. Casey about your second project idea."

"Oh. *Oh.*" *Ooooooh.* I'm an echo chamber of my own making and nearly smack my own forehead. *Of course.*

Lelani appraises me close to how one looks at an elderly aunt who has suddenly announced she needs help getting to the bathroom. Or that the sky is orange. In short, she's not sure I'm in possession of my sanity at the moment. I clear my throat. "Oh yes, of course this is what you'd call me into your office about. Proceed. Er, please."

"Yes, thank you." Cue the totally baffled look from Lelani that I answer with a benevolent smile. "As I said, I met with Mr. Casey as a follow-up to our green-light meeting. I have to say that unfortunately he didn't think that your second idea had as much market reach as the first, and he'd like you to proceed as directed in the meeting. I think it is a little closed-minded, but he has the final say." Her last words are colored with distaste. Though she doesn't elaborate, I read between the lines that she's not pleased by his decision. I feel grudging respect for her, going to bat for this project when we both probably knew it was doomed to fail.

She hands me back my sketches, encased in a neat manila envelope, complete with a label bearing my name and the words "Unnamed Project Proposal."

I hold the folder, feeling a bit like it's a coffin for my project. My heart project. The first project I've been excited about—truly and completely—since *Hero Girls*. Here it lies, the final stop for everything I dreamed it could be.

And yet.

L's words come floating back to me, along with this new calmer center I've found inside myself in the past few days. This realization that I can *be* complex and still a strong businesswoman. I can still go after what I want, even when I'm told no. That there may be ways other than *pushing* to get what I'm after.

It's time to weave a little. "Thank you for my sketches back; I'm sorry this project won't be at Genius." I steel myself. I can do this. I can go after what I want. "And I'd like to ask permission to moonlight and publish it myself, now that Genius has had the first right of refusal."

Lelani sits back a little in her seat. I've surprised her, and in a good way, if I take to heart the appraising look she's giving me. "I can certainly see if Mr. Casey will give his permission; it isn't a conflict of interest in my estimation."

I nod, terrified to even breathe. That's more positive than I'd dared hope. "Okay, great."

Lelani looks ready to dismiss me but leans forward again, over her desk. Her gaze is level and grounded. "I have to say, we've had some complimentary communication from the movie team, and it sounds like you're representing Genius admirably. I was nervous about making the exception to change your work role, but it's a pleasure to see your career benefiting from the change." There *may* have been a silent threat of "And be sure it continues to benefit," but I'm not sure. "I look forward to seeing your work on the previously approved pitch. Please let me know when you have finalized panels."

"Thank you." I stand and she nods, which I take to mean I'm actually excused. I make my way back to my desk. Everyone eyes me when I walk in the door—a class completely curious why their classmate was in the principal's office.

"Nothing to see here," I respond, sitting primly down in my seat. I pop my earbud in and scroll to *The Nerdist* in my podcasts. My own comic project. Outside of Genius. Feeling like a boss, I open my notebook to work on *Falcon*.

It's around dinnertime that I realize I'm the last one in the office. Andy must have peaced out at some point, but I've been in a bit of a zone. My half day in the office has turned into a full day of investigation, under the guise of work. After my meeting with Lelani, my work for *THF* actually flowed faster than it had in recent months, and I found myself itching to take a look at the journal copies Matteo had given me.

Since Saturday, Matteo's contact has been incredibly limited. He's made it clear that if I want to talk about *us*, it's going to take some effort on my part. If he contacts me at all, it's a real phone call—I *hate* talking on the phone—from the station number. And even then, my voice mail today was from Rideout. *Rideout.* I felt like I needed to scrub the inside of my ear out after that. Matteo had said Rideout was on probation and couldn't carry out case business by himself . . . I wonder, since he was the one calling, if the internal investigation exonerated him as the leak. *Pity.*

Mostly it's been the same: *Daniel's not talking, insisting he knows nothing. He has no ties to Muñez, no ties to police; his financials are clean, so no bribes or blackmail. We can't hold him much longer.*

Each time, it's clear they're interested in one thing and one thing only: *What is in that journal that might be of use to us?*

Right now, after hours of poring over the pages and then going to Genius's library to compare panels and characters and drawing styles and plot lines? My answer is, *Nothing.*

Honestly, I thought finding this half of the journal would be the Holy Grail. The panacea that would break this case wide open. Instead, I find much the same that I remembered seeing before. The story line about Falcon retiring. Half-started panels showing Swoosh's pledge of allegiance to always continue fighting the powers that would undermine the marginalized. The references to the story line with the safe in the wall—the story line I already followed to get to Sosa. There's not much else in the way of groundbreaking storytelling. So, the next time Matteo calls, I'm going to give him the hard news: other than being interesting from a fan's standpoint, I've got bubkes.

I've identified a few pages that have more personal notes on them to talk to Lawrence about tomorrow night. There are a few that look like handwritten schedule reminders or phone messages. One that I think includes a scribble about the party that Lawrence references, but all it is is a time and a note that says, "Costume party—card?" There are a few doodles in the margin of the next page, not unlike the kind I make while on a boring conference call: the axonometric for some sort of gadget that sprays water that Lawrence had tapped, and a few playing-card sketches—one of each suit. The pen work is slightly different on this page, so Lawrence's guess that it's someone else's hand is valid. My guess is maybe Casey Junior's, though I don't have any ready samples to compare it with. I'd gone looking for the very *few* issues of *THF* that bore his hand before he hired artists, and it's just hard to tell with such a limited sketch to compare it with. There are two pages that contain margin doodles that seem entirely unrelated to *THF*—again, something I do in my own journal, and something I'd usually just pass over if I weren't slaving over every detail, looking for some clue. The problem is, no doodle of men having a tug of war in a margin answers any part of this case for me. I see no note, no scribble, no panel, no matter how unfinished, that mentions a queen. No crowns, no tiaras, no nothing.

Really, the only good thing to come of this is that my ADHD's hyperfocus has kicked in, and time has flown. I've hardly been aware of time passing, which tonight I needed. It's so dark in the office that I have to hunt around for my keys and bag. I order an Uber and hope there's enough room on my credit card for this sort of existence while my car sits unused and unfixed in my driveway.

I'm making my way through the dark office just past sunset, trying *really hard* not to picture some sort of *Stranger Things* monster coming out from under the creepy abandoned desks in this dark building when my phone blares to life in my hand.

For the love of all Thor's hammers, I nearly throw my phone across the room. Despite having *just called* for the Uber, I wasn't prepared for the volume that one cell phone can have in a room lurking with potential monsters.

On shaking legs, I make it to the elevator lobby, press the down button, and get ready to answer the call. It's not Uber; it's Matteo. I waffle a bit, decide I don't want to have the "I don't have information" conversation until I'm home, and click the "Decline" button. At least he's deigned to call me himself this time, and not from the station number. He must figure if I think it's Rideout, I *really* won't answer the

phone. In the words of Sherlock Holmes, his deduction is correct—
"Elementary, my dear Watson."

Speaking of, Watson would make a good name for another corgi,
and that thought carries me into the elevator, where I press the "L" key
and am *again* startled by my phone dinging. This time a text message.
It's from Matteo, and it's a simple Call me when you get this.

"Keep your undies on, Captain." *Man*, when they want to know
about something, they want to know *right now*. A dark lobby greets
me with yet another veritable savanna for lurking monsters or predatory drug compatriots, so I hustle my way outside, hoping my ride has
arrived.

No such luck, but one quick glance at the app shows the car is only
about seven minutes away. Possibly enough time for me to call Matteo
and have an excuse to get off the phone before things get personal?
I'm still not ready to confront the new, leafier MG that has emerged,
and not sure what it means in the broader sense of what I'm ready to
commit to.

My waffling comes to a screeching halt when my phone dings
again. It's a text message from Matteo, and it's anything but business as
usual. Suddenly the car can't get here fast enough.

I know you're screening your calls, but please let me know
you got this. L is at Good Samaritan downtown, admitted with
multiple wounds. I'll be here when you arrive.

CHAPTER 27

It's like a scene from a movie. As soon as I am allowed to know which room L is in—cleared by no less than two LAPD officers in the lobby—I *run* like some lunatic through the halls. I can hardly see, my eyes are so filled with tears. My heart is still in my chest, frozen with terror. A burn in my throat tells me it's constricted, but I basically don't care.

My best friend has been stabbed.

My best friend is injured.

One third of my chosen family is dying in a hospital bed. I don't know if anyone's called Ryan yet.

The police are using terms like "critical condition," and what does that even mean? Can they just tell me if he's going to live or not? Am I running to a funeral? Will I make it in time for L to know I'm there before he dies?

The elevator seems too slow, so I climb the stairs. Sometimes on my hands and knees. I think I've gone up something like four or five flights before I even remember to look for the number four on a door. I'm in some sort of panicked trance.

Light spills with me out of the doorway of the stairwell and into a dimly lit corridor. I don't see gurneys or teams of people rushing around—that's good, right? Unless there's nobody alive to rush around for anymore? The thoughts war with me as I sprint down one hallway, jog over, and infuriatingly find myself back at the elevators.

I literally scream in frustration.

"MG!" I hear a voice, like a beacon, and I turn to see Matteo down the hallway I swear I just came from. I don't think. I just sprint, kitten heels slipping everywhere on the tile floors. I just need to get to Matteo. He'll make everything better. Maybe he can just make this all go away. Tell me it was a ruse for the case, a tactic to draw out a bad guy from hiding.

But I know as I near Matteo that it's no ruse. His face is chalky, his shirt rumpled, and . . . Oh God, is that *blood* on his shirt? I don't even try to stop, I just slam into Matteo, and I don't let go. I let him hold me up while I sag my weight against him.

"Whoa, whoa, whoa, MG. It's okay. He's alive. It's okay. It's okay."

I must be babbling semicoherent, hysterical nonsense, because as my senses return to me, the words that are spilling from my lips slow to a trickle. In pieces, I realize that Matteo is stroking my hair, murmuring over and over and over that it's going to be okay, that Lawrence is alive. His other arm is wrapped so tightly around me, I can feel him shaking. Whether it's from the strain of holding me up or the situation, I don't know.

I pull back, incredibly aware as I do so that I've left impressive snot-and-tears marks on his already stained shirt. I swipe a hand across my face. "He's alive? He's okay?"

"He's *alive*, yes," Matteo hedges.

"And he's okay?" I press again, hysteria rising afresh.

Matteo takes my hand and pulls me against him, then walks me to the window in the door of the room we're standing outside of.

There are so many wires. And tubes, and quite a few people bustle around the bed. I can hardly make out that there's a person *in* that bed, there's just so much *stuff* scattered around the room. Rolling tables, stands of blinking pump thingies. IV lines, and towels on the floor soaking up . . .

"Is that *blood?*" I ask for the second time, though this one is out loud. So much blood. On the floor, on the sheets. He's not okay, this will *not* be okay. There's no way Lawrence can lose that much blood and be *okay*. Matteo *lied* to me.

"I didn't *lie* to you," Matteo says, turning me to face him. I don't even know if I've spoken out loud, or if he's done his stupid mind-meld voodoo magic on me and just plucked it out of my head. "It was dicey for a while, but a doctor came out a few minutes ago and said they got him stabilized. They're waiting for blood to arrive for a transfusion. He's in critical condition for now, but the doctor thinks he'll make it. He's not *okay*, but it's going to *be* okay eventually."

The news sinks in slowly. And I know I've processed it when I stop stuttering and start blubbering. Big fat tears roll down my cheeks, and I sink into a chair placed conveniently in the hallway. "The—the police downstairs didn't know if he was still alive," I manage. I'm having trouble drawing breath properly.

"Hey now, it's okay, just breathe. Slow in, slow out." Matteo crouches in front of me, holding my hands between his. "They shouldn't have said that to you. I know this is scary, but I'm here, okay? We're both here for Lawrence, and I've called Ryan. As soon as he shows up . . . well, you can decide if you want me to stay or go. Your family, your call."

My eyes fly to his, and I grasp his hands. "Don't leave. No, don't you dare leave me."

Something fierce responds in his eyes, and he squeezes my hands back. "Deal."

But I don't mean just right now. I mean *don't ever leave me*. And there it is. Simple and pure, and crystal inside of me. The very essence, the culmination of my introspection. I love this man. It's not gooey or complicated, and everything's not folded neat and tidy inside that suitcase in my head, but it's clear. Sure, he's not a nerd like Daniel, but he *challenges* me to live outside my box without asking me to change who I am at heart. He's here for me, even when we aren't together. He's here for my friends and family. He wants the best for me, and brings out the best in me. It may not make sense on paper, but our two puzzle pieces just *fit*.

He sees it in my face even before I say it. "MG, it's okay. Now's not the time—"

I cut him off, not caring this isn't the right place, the right time, or the right reason. "I love you." It's a statement of fact.

His gaze burns into mine before softening slightly. He hasn't moved from his crouched position in front of my chair. The corner of his mouth turns up ever so slightly, and he says in perfect imitation of Harrison Ford, "I know."

It brings the smallest of laughs from me, and he leans in for a swift kiss. "And in the words of Mr. Darcy, 'I wish never to be parted from you.'"

Ditto. "Are you quoting *Pride and Prejudice* to me?"

"I went on a rom-com binge this week. Ate pints and pints of ice cream. Watched my telephone. Practiced my Mr. Darcy impression."

I love him all the more that I think he's probably telling me the truth. But the reality of the environment pushes back into our moment of levity. There will be time enough to explore our reunion later. "Okay, tell me what happened. I want all the details."

"I'll have to fill you in more later as the investigation reports come in, but it looks like someone stabbed him multiple times from the front. The wounds aren't typical—the doctors have commented several times on the bizarre nature of the lacerations. Maybe a custom butterfly knife, or, well—one likened it to a hunting injury. Specifically, possibly an arrow."

No way. I look around. "But . . . that can't be. Right?"

Matteo takes too long to shrug for my taste. "Truthfully, I don't know. Our suspect continues to insist that he has no knowledge of those items being in his house. And his alibi is shaping up to be pretty watertight. Unless he's a part of a duo, definitely something we're considering, I'm not sure we'll be able to hold him for this. He's already hired about the best lawyer in Los Angeles and has made arrangements to make bond. I'm waiting on the journal stuff before we make the call."

So many layers to think through. "There's nothing in the journal. Nothing I can find anyways. It's worth talking to Lawrence when . . . if . . ." Tears threaten to spill over, and Matteo shushes me again.

"He'll be awake soon. Then we can ask him what happened. Hopefully he remembers, and we can ask him about the journal."

"Do we know at *all* what happened?" My mind flashes directly to the homeless network and Lawrence's friend. Had it been a setup for the money?

Matteo frowns, then slowly says, "Well, we got a 911 call about a mugging. Bad neighborhood. He was taken to an emergency room not far from the Casey property, actually, and then transported here. His driver's license flagged our case, and I was notified as he was transported. Do you have any idea why he'd be in that sort of neighborhood?"

I nod slowly. "Lawrence has been trying to find that guy from the party. The one he thought he recognized from when he worked for Casey Senior."

Matteo's mouth compresses into a hard line. *Not pleased.*

"I know, but he basically said that none of these people would trust or talk to police. Or anyone they think is connected with police. So, he went to visit friends, told them a ridiculous story about how Casey Junior hired him to give out the reward, and today he got a text from one of those friends that they had information."

"So, let me get this straight: Lawrence went into a bad neighborhood, spread it around that he had access to a large amount of money, and then made a meeting with someone who thought he may potentially have money *on* his person."

"Well, when you put it that way, it doesn't sound so good."

Exasperation shows clearly on his face. "It wasn't a good plan *to begin with.*"

"Hey. If it had netted us a lead, you wouldn't be so upset—"

"Yes, I would."

"Okay, fine. You'd be upset, but you'd also be appreciative."

Matteo sits back and rubs his eyes with the heels of his hands. "You and your friends and your ideas about 'helping' may be the end of me."

We both glance at the closed door to the right of our chairs. It almost *was* the end of Lawrence.

Matteo clears his throat. "So, have you been okay? It's been killing me not to see you this week."

I know we haven't talked about where we're at yet, but that sounds promising enough to me. I lace my fingers through his, and relief floods through me when he squeezes mine back. "I haven't really been okay, but I needed the time to think. So, I guess I'm grateful. Plus, I've been crazy busy, as per usual. I have a lot to catch you up on."

Matteo nods. "Me too. The drug results came back, for one."

I sit up. "Really."

He nods, but his countenance doesn't lift. "Yeah. The drugs from the party were a partial match for Muñez's signature recipe."

"Partial match? How can they be a partial match?"

"Well, here's the weird part. In eight years as detective and a fair number of years on patrol, I've never exactly seen this. It's the same recipe, but it's in a different form. It's in a capsule. Or at least we assume so, since we found trace amounts of gel capsule in the mix, which can happen when someone opens a capsule by hand."

"Like the capsules I saw at the first party."

"Agreed. And more than that, the capsule fragments had LSD casing. It's essentially an epic high wrapped in a hallucination."

"That's insane."

"Dangerous is what it is; no wonder that kid overdosed. The hallucinogen skews even *that* part of the brain—people could take one, lose their inhibitions, and end up just taking a handful and OD'ing—they'd have no idea what hit them."

"So, this means . . . what?"

"It *means* that either someone got ahold of Muñez's stash, which is possible, or it means that this Queen of Hearts is somehow related to Muñez's business. All of our previous theories could still hold water: she could have stepped into Muñez's place because of the opening, or she could have been working with him the whole time. There's really no way to know, and as of now we're scouring Muñez and Sosa's case for any sort of unfollowed lead, but every known operative that is in our files is either in custody or is in another location right now. We also don't know at this point if the Queen is just the top dealer, or given the complex work at hand—this is no amateur-mix-with-flour sort of deal—the Queen could be the actual chemist and distributor. Like, maybe when Muñez was caught, the Queen just . . . kept going."

Well, none of *that* sounds like a good option.

We both fall silent as several nurses walk by, chatting about what they ate in the cafeteria for dinner.

Matteo is the first to speak again. "So, really *nothing* in that journal? I was so sure."

"Me too—"

"Are you the family?" A voice interrupts us; I hadn't even heard Lawrence's door open. I spin around so fast, I nearly topple off the chair.

"Yes," I answer automatically.

She casts a critical eye over my decided non-blackness.

"I'm as close to family as he has," I amend.

She looks tired and harried, and her long black braids are slipping from the netted cap perched on her head. After one more look at me, she turns her eye to Matteo. "And you're the detective?"

"Yes, ma'am."

She rolls her shoulders and then motions us up. "I'm Doctor Sholey, and it's past visiting hours, but I want to see if he'll wake to someone he knows." She turns a critical eye on Matteo. "You may ask questions *if* he wakes, but if he gets upset in any capacity, I'm excusing both of you. He'll be well enough for real questioning in a few days."

"Understood," Matteo agrees, and we push through the heavy wooden door and into Lawrence's room behind Dr. Sholey.

An astringent smell assails my nose as we walk through the pulled curtain, and our shoes squeak on the floor that's recently been mopped.

"Watch your step—one of his wounds reopened on the way to his room from the ER, and we had quite a bit of blood to clean up." Doctor Sholey catches my gaze where a small puddle of blood still sits under the side of the bed. "It's always interesting that people think the floors in a hospital are so clean. Operating rooms? Yes. The other floors? We clean them as we can, but . . . you wouldn't catch me using the ten-second rule around here."

I give a nervous laugh.

A few people file past, some of them carting several red biohazard bins with them, and suddenly we're alone in the room.

I haven't had enough courage yet to even look at the person *in* the bed. It steals my breath when I do. Lawrence looks *small*. Helpless. It's so different from my vibrant and constantly moving best friend that I wonder for a wild moment if we've got the wrong room.

But no, there's the small scar next to his eye that he got from an unfortunate eyelash curler incident his first year as a queen. The pitter pat of tears falling onto the bed alerts me that my faucet is on again, and I hastily wipe my face with my arm. This shirt is going *straight* in the wash when I get home, it's got snot and mascara *all* over it.

After a nod from Dr. Sholey, I tentatively grasp Lawrence's unmoving hand. Thank God it's warm and not cold, or I'm fairly certain I might have fainted.

"L?" My voice cracks, and it's hardly loud enough be heard above the beeping coming from the computer monitor of completely baffling, medical-graph things up on the wall.

Dr. Sholey reaches up and presses one of the areas on the screen, and the beeping stops. "Try again," she urges gently.

"Lawrence? Hey, it's me. Can you open your eyes?"

Nothing.

"Can you hear me? L, just let me know if you can—oh!" My hand flies up from the bed, and I turn to Dr. Sholey. "I think he just moved his fingers. That's good, right?"

She smiles encouragingly. "That's good. Keep talking. He's been drugged for all the procedures, so it might take him a little."

The beeping begins again, and she repeats the measure to silence the machines.

L's fingers move almost immediately after I grab his hand again, and I lean over his face so that if he opens his eyes, I'll be the first thing he sees. It's nearly ten minutes of talking and coaxing before one eye slides open, and even then, it's hardly enough for me to catch.

"L? Can you see me?"

Squeeze.

"He's responding," I say to the room at large, and the mania in my own voice echoes back at me off the block walls.

L's eye opens a little further, focusing on my face for several long moments before wandering around the room.

"You're in the hospital. Do you remember anything?"

There's a long pause before I feel his fingers squeeze mine again. I guess he tries to speak because he moves his head from side to side and makes several noises in his throat that end in a coughing fit.

An alarm on the computer monitor on the wall goes off, and Dr. Sholey regards it for a long moment before nodding at me to continue. She's less enthusiastic now, and I gather that the alarm wasn't a good one.

"Don't try to talk if it hurts," I offer. "We can stick with yes and no answers."

I swear Lawrence rolls his eye at me. Then he starts moving his head again, like he's trying to get his shoulders unstuck. IV lines pull taut, and Dr. Sholey leans down.

"Lawrence, my name is Dr. Sholey. I'm your attending physician for tonight. You're at Good Samaritan in the intensive care step-down unit. Don't move around much, you've got a lot of stuff attached to you, okay?"

Lawrence's eye rolls from her face to the screen up on the wall. His gaze moves back to me, and instead of relaxing, he moves his head again. More coughing. Another alarm.

"I'm going to have to ask you to leave," Dr. Sholey says quietly. "His heart rate is just too high; he can't handle a visit right now." She presses a button on his bed, and almost immediately a nurse shows up in the doorway. They discuss a pain med, and the nurse turns back to the hallway, presumably to go get a dose.

I turn to leave, but Lawrence's hand snakes out with a speed I don't expect from a man in his condition. He tugs at me, and I lean down over him.

"L, love, I have to go. They're going to help you with the pain, but I promise I'll be back the *moment* they say I can—"

Lawrence's lips are struggling with something. He's attempting to talk. The alarm on the wall is sounding continually, and it saws at my already frayed nerves. Would it kill the doctor to silence it again? We said we'd leave.

The nurse bustles back in, enters something on the computer and then administers the syringe into the IV line closest to the bed.

L's lips move again, and this time I'm sure he's trying to talk.

Matteo grabs my hand, trying to lead me out the door, but I shake him off, and instead lean over L so my ear is near his mouth.

Only one word is clear, and the rest sounds too much like whispers to make out.

"After?" I ask Lawrence. "Is that what you said?"

Lawrence gives the smallest of nods. He looks *exhausted* by the effort. His lips move, and this time no one stops me as I lean over again. Dr. Sholey thankfully silences the alarm so I can hear better.

There are a few words I can't catch, maybe something about a hat? Then "After the Arrow" is clearer. Lawrence labors.

"After the Arrow," I repeat back, my gaze flying to Matteo.

Lawrence's eyes are starting to flutter shut. The pain med is taking effect, and taking L along with it. His lips move again, and I basically plaster myself to him.

"MG," he says, squeezing my hand. I get the sense that he's just looking for comfort. His family.

"Love you, L." Tears prick my eyes again. "I'm here."

I think L's finished, but he doesn't let go of my hand. I lean over, and though his lips don't move, I make out the next three words. "Hat. Tell Ryan." And then he's asleep, fully quiet in the big hospital bed.

"I will. I'll make sure he comes as soon as he can," I promise, hoping L can still hear me.

Dr. Sholey hustles us out of the room and into the hallway. All around us the unit has a sense of sleepy productivity. The hallway lights are on half power, and nurses crowd around stations for some sort of change-of-shift meeting. Matteo and I make our way to the elevator, which opens on a harried-looking Ryan.

"Ryan!" I exclaim as he fairly spills out of the stainless doors. He looks awful.

"Is he okay?"

"He's sleeping, but he'll be okay," I say, and know exactly how it feels as I watch his shoulders sag in relief. Ryan pulls me to him. He's vibrating. "I was at the gym, so I didn't see my phone. I was so scared I was too late. I should have been here earlier."

"Ry, you're shaking. It's okay, you're in time. I had the same thought. He's not dead. He's going to be okay."

"Are you sure? Is it bad? How much blood did he lose?"

Matteo reaches out and grasps Ryan's shoulder. "He needs a transfusion, but they have a match. We just were in to see him for only a minute. The doctors say he'll recover."

Ryan's eyes blaze. "You saw him? Was he awake? Did he say who did this to him?"

"He isn't that with it yet," I answer. "All he wanted to know was that I was there, and that somebody told you he was here. He was just worried about us, Ry."

"Well that, and 'After Arrow,' whatever that means," Matteo says, watching Ryan closely. "Did *you* know about his insanely stupid project to find that guy on his own?"

Ryan straightens. "After Arrow? That doesn't make sense. And yeah, I knew." He straightens up a bit, when I'm expecting him to be sheepish. "I thought it was a good idea; the police can't be everywhere at once."

Matteo's mouth hardens, and he takes his hand off Ryan's shoulder. "It's likely what landed him here. The doctor who first admitted him said that several of the lacerations missed arteries by millimeters. Whoever did this meant business. It didn't look to the surgeon like a random stabbing; this person meant to kill Lawrence."

We all reenter the elevator in silence, and I bet we're all thinking about the same thing.

After Arrow.

The invention of a painkiller-altered brain? Or a message? If it's a message, obviously it has to do with the Golden Arrow. The question is, what does it mean, and was it worth nearly getting killed for?

CHAPTER 28

If anyone wants to know what a float-size bust of a drag queen looks like in their lives, they need wonder no longer. Lawrence's vision for the Halloween float is at once monstrous and somehow grand. Like the prow of a great ship, she hangs like a benevolent overlord to all of us peons slaving to finish her varnished wood hull. *Slay, Girl.*

Beside me, Paige tosses her paintbrush into a bucket and grimaces as dirty water splashes the wheels of her chair. Luckily, the concrete floor in this shop has seen worse, so I don't even worry about it. The dance studio's neighbor recently moved out and the landlord was open to renting the space to us at a low cost for float construction while he contracted for some upgrades. In fact, the ripped-out floors, ceilings, and walls really give the whole thing a *Hunger Games* post-apocalyptic kind of vibe that goes well with constructing a Halloween float.

"Thanks for offering to help with this," I say, trying not to sound desperate. With L still in the hospital and Daniel still in custody, Ryan and I had no choice but to divide and conquer this *massive* undertaking—one of which we have middling understanding of at best. Geek girl and gamer boy, putting the finishing touches on a drag-queen float? Probably one of the weirder things to happen in recent drag herstory. Ryan and I haven't talked much about exactly *why* we're doing so much work to see this through, but I think both of us want to uphold L's vision. His project to bring drag queens of all ages and backgrounds together, to strengthen community. To spread the message that is so prominently wired on the side of the float: LOVE

YOURSELF. Well, actually it says the S.S. LOVE YOURSELF, because the whole theme of the outside of the float is a boat, but close enough.

We have exactly one week to go until Halloween, and we're going to be scrambling to get things done. I even asked my coworkers if they'd pitch in tonight after work, rather than doing whatever normal nerds do on a Friday night. To my surprise, nearly everyone has come—only Kyle and Nina had existing plans. Paige surprised me by agreeing first, followed almost instantly by Simon. Andy waffled a bit but ended up saying something about "teambuilding" and actually ended up being an impressively dab hand at papier-mâché sculpting. His creation of her abundant cleavage was a pièce de résistance—oh, the things you learn about your coworkers if you hang out outside the office. I can't believe I missed years of this. And truthfully, our relationships have only improved for hanging out as friends. I don't respect Andy any less; I may even like him *more*. I still think him the human version of a suck-up fish, but baby steps.

Two of Ryan's gaming crew showed up, as well as Harrison, Daniel's business partner in the dance studio. And more than several of Latifah's queen gang are in attendance. We are a motley crew, to be sure.

Paige has finished painting the pink of the figurehead's dress bodice and starts attaching one of many feather boas that will provide an adequately ridiculous neckline for our masthead. She accepts my thanks for her attendance with her usual deadpan grace. "And miss all this? I wouldn't dream of it. It's the price I'm paying to look like a team player."

I laugh; I liken her to April from *Parks and Recreation*, only with much better makeup and hair. Prickly, but lovable once you understand she is mostly bark and probably only slightly prone to biting.

A short Filipino guy approaches me with a huge stack of orange-and-black, shiny garlands. I recognize him as one of the performers whose drag persona was onstage with Latifah in the superhero lip-sync-off. "Where do you think this goes?"

"That's a good question." I consult the sketch that I found in Lawrence's stack of Halloween Party *stuff* on his desk. It's woefully behind schedule, and I'm totally making it up when I tell him, "Ah, yeah, says here that it's going to wrap around the wiring for the letters on the side. Let's do 'Love' in the orange, and 'Yourself' in the black."

"Okay," he agrees, then looks down at the stack. "Do you think there's enough of it here?"

"Definitely." *No idea.*

He walks off, and I look up to find Paige watching me. "Such BS."

"Shh." It's uncanny how good Paige is at reading people. I look around to make sure the guy hasn't heard us. Luckily, he's off, staring at the wires on the side of the flatbed trailer that makes up the base of the float. I'll let *him* engineer how to get the garland on. Queens are nothing if not crafty and inventive, on balance. Far better as a breed than comic book writers, who definitely should *not* be put in charge of a house-size DIY craft.

Other than a minor squabble about our working music, everything has gone much better than I worried, if I am being honest. It seemed like a recipe for disaster, probably involving some enthusiastic-but-underqualified drag queens and artists, one flatbed trailer, enough papier-mâché to cover the Ark, and copious glue fumes inside an industrial strip mall.

Instead, the people who responded to my emergency email this week have been helpful, focused, and entirely concerned about Lawrence. I've told no less than fourteen people that no, we haven't been allowed in for more than five minutes, and that each time I've been in, he's been asleep. The doctors assure me he's making progress, but it's so terrifying, picturing this being *it* for Lawrence.

The smell of pizza breaks through my thoughts, and Paige and I both sit up at the same moment.

"I smell pizza," she says appreciatively.

"Me too. Who on earth thought to bring manna from heaven with them?" I was wrong when I thought my four boxes of Wheat Thins and sad veggie tray would be enough for the volunteers.

"I've brought dinner, you shady bitches," comes a singsong voice from around the largest stack of pizzas I've seen outside of a comic book. It's seriously maybe eight boxes high, and it must weigh a pretty penny.

My joy at seeing such a delicious and calorically dense vision is dampened only by my realization that I know that voice. It's Cleopatra.

A fairly curvy Latino man appears from behind the boxes, recognizable even out of character. His large eyes even still have lash extensions. He's wearing a black mock turtleneck and black leggings, so I decide I'm looking at Cleopatra Lite. Cleo sets the pizzas on one of the folding tables in the middle of the room, moving bags of random float-making supplies to make way for dinner, and the float-makers fall on it like a pack of hyenas.

Ryan surfaces from whatever mechanical endeavor he's been working on in the interior of the float. I don't even know what he's working on—that's our divvy. I take the exterior and the aesthetic stuff, Ryan is coordinating the vendors and necessities for the workings of the interior of the float where the people will actually . . . What does one do from inside a float? Preside? Exude pomp and circumstance? Princess-wave? In any case, Ryan is covered in dust and grease—I hope he's planning on staying or at least changing at Lelani's . . . I don't want it in our upstairs shower.

My feelings are at war with themselves. On one hand: hot pizza, starving body. On the other hand: Cleopatra. But maybe these are an olive branch. Surely eating free pizza isn't like signing a contract with the devil, right?

Paige suffers no such odds with her loyalty. She's already got a slice of veggie and a slice of meat-lovers balanced in her lap.

Hunger wins out, and I dive for the paper towel roll that serves as plates. While I'm picking up my two slices of Hawaiian—pineapple absolutely belongs on a pizza, and I will die on that hill—Cleopatra ambushes me from behind the stack of pizzas.

"MG, hey, girl, how's it going?"

"Good," I mouth around my first bite—the cheese is gooey and the perfect edible temperature without being cold. In short, it's perfection, and I don't want to waste my precious perfect-pizza-temperature time talking. "Thanks for bringing the pizza." Which sounds an awful lot like *thmm brng piz-hur* because my mouth is full.

"You're welcome. I told my benefactor I was coming tonight—well, never mind. I didn't want to win my little bet with Latifah this way. Consider this a peace offering from me, personally. When one in our community is hurt, we all feel it." The words *seem* genuine. Plus, she lost one of her own drag family just a few weeks ago; maybe it's made her more sensitive.

I reach out a hand impulsively. "I'm sorry about Louis, and I'm sorry I didn't reach out when it happened."

A cloud passes over Cleo's face . . . a flash of bitterness, sorrow, and something else waits just beneath the sunny surface of her persona. "We've had a tough week. You tell Lateetee that we're all living for her, okay?"

Something about her bearing cracks, and I furrow my brows. She looks close to *tears*. Which is so unexpected, tears prick my *own* eyes before I realize what is happening. I clear my throat. "I, ah—I will."

There's a long beat where Cleo looks like she's about to say something to me. Her mouth opens, and she closes it again, so I wait. Finally, she seems to settle on, "How is she? Really?"

All trace of Cleo's normal character has vanished, and beneath the concealer and carefully applied bronzer, I swear she's pale. And I *think* I can see circles under her eyes, artfully concealed with more stage makeup. This . . . *realness* throws me.

283

"Latifah—Lawrence—is alive. He'll recover, they think." I keep it vague, but I *do* want to put her mind at ease.

It seems to do just that, and her shoulders drop a little, though the tightness doesn't leave her face. It looks like she's trying *so* hard to keep her typical aloof countenance and failing. It's *eerie*.

She clears her throat. "I'm glad to hear that. Too many people have gotten hurt who shouldn't have."

Again, I have the gut reaction that there's more to her words than the surface. It's almost as if . . . there's ownership there. True, Louis was in her family, and it hits close to home. But is her ownership of Lawrence's attack purely from a shared-community place? Surely she couldn't have had anything to do with it. Drag queens may throw shade, but they generally prefer to slay on the stage. In the end, it's a competitive community, but they love each other.

Cleo seems nervous with my silence. "No one has come forward or anything? No one . . . knows . . . anything?"

Again, my warning lights go off. This conversation is just . . . off. Beyond mere concern I can't help but wonder if I'm hearing *guilt*. Maybe Cleo knows something about who attacked L and is afraid to share. I shake my head slowly. "No, no one has come forward claiming to know anything . . . do *you* know anyone who could help the police?"

My outright question seems to shake Cleo to her pointy-toed boots. She hastily shakes her head. "*I* don't. Certainly not. But, um"—she presses her lips together—"I'll keep my ears open, okay? I don't want anyone else to get hurt."

My truth meter pings this time. Cleo may be shifty, but she's being truthful. She's going to be looking out for the queens. I'm about to press further when Ryan settles in beside me, his plate *heaped* with pizza. He makes no excuse, just sits down with our shoulders touching, nods to Paige in greeting, and then starts shoveling food into his mouth like he's been locked in some foodless dungeon for a year.

I spare a glance for Ryan, wondering how much to say. "L's doctors have been amazing; I don't think we're clear yet on his recovery. We're going there tonight to visit; hopefully we'll know more soon."

I expect Ryan's appearance to scare Cleo off, but she seems to have regained some of her composure.

Instead of leaving, she grabs some pizza, skirts the table, and settles herself next to Ryan. Which goes over about as well as the reboot where Supes and Lois Lane aren't an item. Ryan tosses me a panicked "Help!" look and commences inching closer to me. I get it. This is L's nemesis. But there's something different about her tonight, something I'm not quite ready to write off so quickly as a game.

"Do they know what happened? Everyone's speculating wildly."

Ah. She's apparently after gossip. But . . . speculating wildly? Wouldn't a car accident or something be more plausible? I ask what craziness people have come up with, and purposefully shut my mouth to let her inner Gossip Girl go.

"Oh, you know queens, they love to talk. Someone said that Latifah went after the Golden Arrow to get the reward offered by police."

That's so uncomfortably close to the truth, I choke on my pizza.

Ryan gives me an alarmed warning look and schools his own features. He claps me on the back, and gives a big laugh like he's joining me in a joke. "Oh *man*, I agree, that's ridiculous."

I gain control of my esophagus. "People are just too inventive. It's much more mundane than that, I promise." Ryan and I haven't invented a cover story because our goal is to just *not* talk about it. "But I'll send along your well wishes."

Paige's eyebrows shoot up, and she studies me. I fear her BS meter has picked up on my falsehoods. Even more of a reason to move this conversation along.

I turn to Ryan as casually as I can. "So, how's the inside of the float coming?"

Thankfully following my train of thought, Ryan latches on to the change in conversation. "Pretty good, I think. I got the platform for the fountain secured and the lines in place to cycle the water."

"Fountain, what now? This thing has a *fountain*?" L had settled on the idea of a cruise ship—sort of a nod to Princess Cruises, where there's a prow of a boat, a wood-lined exterior, and all things nautical—navy-themed dancers, water-inspired costumes, everything.

Ryan tosses me a quizzical look. "Yeah, we have that fountain thing designed by one of the sponsors. There's that on one end, and then the fake catwalk at the other end with the railing so that we can have everyone who wears a tiara and a sash just stand and wave. The catwalk is provided by another sponsor, and the hair and makeup for everyone *on* the float is done the morning of by several sponsors. That's why we need all that room for signs on the exterior."

At my alarmed look, Ryan rolls his eyes. "You *are* leaving room for the sponsor signs on the side that doesn't have the words, right?"

No. "Of *course.*" I make a mental note to go unstaple the garland that I'd started putting up earlier. I'd wondered why one side of the float was completely blank.

"You all have a lot of work to do in a week," Cleopatra observes, watching Ry and me like we're some sort of tennis match.

"Yeah, well, we'll figure it all out," I say, pasting a smile on my face.

"How is the actual *event* planning going? I mean, assuming you get to that part." She looks pointedly at the piles of unused float decoration and the half-finished interior of the boat.

"Fine Totally fine." Waves of anxiety batter the walls I've put in place in my head to keep me sane. *One step at a time.* Losing *both* the people responsible for this event the week it goes off isn't exactly fine timing, and I feel like Ryan and I deserve a damn medal for not just canceling it.

At this lie, Paige just outright snorts. She covers it with a small cough and says something about going to throw away the trash, then rolls to the big trash can in the corner of the space.

"Yeah, okay, we're a little behind," I admit.

Cleopatra presses her lips together, oddly hesitant. She's dropped a lot of her regained bravado; her persona thins again, where I can glimpse the human beneath the character. "I thought that might be the case. It was always the plan, but I'd like to help out. For Lateetee. For myself."

I blink. Help us out? "Help, like how?" And what the hell does she mean, it was always the plan? There's no way to check right now, but I have a hard time picturing Latifah graciously accepting Cleo's help. And yet . . . I know almost nothing about this event; I suppose it could be possible. The event *is* all about presenting a united front for queendom kind.

"I'd like to take over planning the event portion for you, given the circumstances. You already know I throw a wicked party, and you know I'm the only queen who could pull this off."

It's true that her last party was epic. But her last party also was where I was thrown out and L thought he narrowly avoided getting beaten up. I decide against mentioning it. This has all the feel of a Scooby-Doo trap, but Cleopatra has a point. She *can* plan a mean party, and I *am* completely overwhelmed, putting together the float, much less getting the venue decorated and volunteers organized. And there's this . . . uncomfortable *realness* behind the offer. Perhaps Cleopatra is really shaken up and wants to reach out. I can't truly turn away someone's honest attempt at righting a wrong, can I?

Ryan is already shaking his head, and I can see the word "no" forming on his lips. He'd missed our previous conversation and probably one hundred percent suspects Cleo's motives to be questionable. Truth be told, I should too, but here I am, cutting off Ryan's answer with one of my own.

"We do need the help, and you *do* know how to plan a party."

Ryan throws me a look that suggests he thinks my brains have been eaten by the walking dead.

I look back, trying my best to communicate, *No, dude, we really need the help.* "Ah, Cleopatra says this was the plan all along, Ry."

Cleo looks decidedly uncomfortable, and the moment stretches into silence while Ryan and I have an eye duel. I win with a silent, *This is Lawrence's thing; let's not mess up his plans.* And Ryan throws up his hands like I've dealt the killing blow. "Fine."

"We'd appreciate your help, is what Ryan means." I hold up a finger and look around, finally locating my messenger bag over near the float. Within a minute I have produced one of my business cards and hold it out to Cleopatra. "Here's my contact information; can you email me how to get ahold of you and provide me with a list of questions you have? I'll forward everything I have on the event and venue."

Her smile falters but finally settles on genuinely pleased. "Sounds perfect. I have so many ideas."

God help me, but I believe her. And at the very least, this counts as "keep your enemies closer," I guess. "So, are you here to help beyond bringing food?"

Cleopatra gives a husky smoker's laugh that says she thinks I'm amusing. The old Cleopatra is back. "Oh, honey, I don't do manual labor." She eyes Ryan appreciatively. "Although maybe I should hang out and supervise."

"If you're here, I'll put you to work," Ryan says, pushing to his feet.

Cleopatra is there for the punch line. "Oh, I'd love for you to put me to *work*, honey—"

"O-kay." I interrupt Cleopatra before she can elaborate by clapping my hands and standing up. "Dinnertime is over. Let's all pile up our garbage so we can clean up."

Ryan picks up the stack of sketches for whatever monstrosity he's working on in the back of the trailer. Now that I catch sight of it, the shape of the fountain seems familiar to me. I snatch it out of his hand and study it, turning it this way and that. If I squint my left eye . . . It hits me. This sketch looks like that axonometric sketch in Casey's journal.

Ryan's gaze is questioning, but I just sit right back down to think, head in my hands, nail tapping my teeth. Why would a sketch of *this* be in Casey's journal?

"MG? Are you okay?"

Ryan's voice interrupts my thoughts.

Crumbs scatter onto the floor as I brush my hands off and turn to Cleopatra. "I think there's a dumpster out back; I don't think the dance studio will care."

One well-drawn eyebrow raises sardonically. "I do not do dishes or pick up garbage." She glances at her phone again, her brow furrowing. If I had to label her swing in demeanor, I'd say she was nervous about the message that just came through. "Actually, I have to run; I have to go talk to someone." She wiggles her fingers distractedly and heads for the door.

Well, okay then. I roll my eyes at her. I'm left no option but to call after her retreating figure, "We'll talk soon!"

"I'll help you with these," Ryan says, reappearing at my side. The look he's giving Cleopatra isn't a nice one. "I think we need to be careful about getting into bed with that one, if you don't mind the metaphor."

"Not my type," I say automatically. "But yeah, I know what you mean. Something's up, but I think she's really upset about L."

Ryan hesitates, then shakes his head. He reaches out and hands me several empty pizza boxes. "I'll take the rest; let's get these outside."

I grasp the pizza boxes, keeping them as far away from my graphic tee as possible, and follow Ry out the back door of the building and into the dark parking lot beyond. It's sketchy for sure, one flickering streetlight for three businesses illuminates an almost-empty expanse, with broken pavement and black puddles from the recent rain.

The big dumpster in the back has the padlock hanging open, thankfully.

"Here, do you think you can hold all these while I get this open?" Ryan motions to his larger stack of boxes.

"Yeah, no problem." *Unless it gets on my shirt and then: problem.*

Ryan deposits the pizza boxes on top of mine, and starts working the rusty padlock out of the metal loops.

I'm trying not to inhale too much of the "too many types of pizza in close proximity" smell that's going on, but there's no way of avoiding the receipt that is fluttering near my eyeballs. I'm nosy, so to kill time while Ryan works on the dumpster lid, I try and read the receipt upside down. I wonder how much Cleopatra dropped in order to look like the saving grace and earn my agreement to turn over the party to her.

"Huh," I say, shifting under the weight of the boxes.

"Huh, what?" Ryan parrots back. One of the lids is already open, the lock lying on the ground. Ryan stoops to inspect the lock, and it *looks* like it's been smashed. Hoodlums. This city is going to the dogs.

"Huh, Cleopatra even got these pizzas catered. She must be friends with the owner of that Hat Trick Entertainment, or something. Honestly, they were the best pizza I've had, so—"

Ryan appears around the side of the stack. "What? What do you mean?"

I try to point with my nose. "The receipt—it's a catering slip from Hat Trick. Cleo must really have wanted us to know she went the full mile. It looks like she drew a heart on the receipt and everything."

Ryan looks way more alarmed than I think is warranted. He snatches the receipt and stares at it. His eyes move from the top of the sheet to the heart drawn on it.

I don't like the look on his face, and a chill chases down my spine. "What?"

"Do you feel okay?"

"Er . . . yeah? Should I not?"

"This is the same company that served us those spiked drinks."

True. Oh man, I'm the worst police detective ever. I even go so far as to let my head fall forward into the pizza stack in defeat. *Wait.*

"Do you hear . . . beeping?" I ask, peering around. It sounds like a phone going off—maybe someone's dropped theirs.

Ryan measures me with one look, pauses, then stares at the dumpster in horror. We both glance at the broken lock, and Ryan lunges forward, shutting both of the industrial lids with an immense *clang* before turning and charging straight into me. The last thing I feel before an intense wave of heat and the conclusive jolt of an explosion is Ryan pushing me backward, onto the pavement of the parking lot, leftover pizza and boxes flying into a sky filled with a plume of dark smoke. The last thing I see before it all goes to black is my other best friend lying facedown in the parking lot beside me, a pool of blood spreading between us.

CHAPTER 29

Matteo is pacing the small bay in the ER. Again.

"Matteo, you've got to stop; it's making my head swim to watch you."

He stops, runs his hands through his hair, appraises me in the hospital bed, then starts pacing again. *At least this time he's not muttering to himself—ah, nope. There's the muttering.* He's saying something about how if he never gets a call from Good Samaritan Hospital ever again, it'll be just fine with him.

Soft beeping from my heart monitor and oxygen sensor fills our space. "We've got to be reasonable about this. I'm okay—"

"You *have* a minor concussion—"

"Okay-*ish* then—"

"That you got when your roommate pushed you out of the way of an exploding dumpster; you had shrapnel from a pizza box," he continues as if I hadn't spoken. "You're *not* okay."

I still have to fight back laughter. It's so *Ninja Turtles*, it's kinda awesome. A giggle escapes, and Matteo looks at me as if I've grown a second head. I shrug. "These painkillers are really good. I'm hardly scraped up. I'll be fine."

I hold up my one little Band-Aid on my hand. "It's Ryan who has all the road rash on his face and that wicked cut in his head from the—*do* you call it shrapnel if it's cardboard and pizza crust?"

"You are both damn lucky that Ryan had the sense to throw you out of the way. Are you ready to talk about what you remember? No one inside saw what happened, and Ryan's memory is fuzzy. That whole *building* could have caught fire; everyone is lucky the lid of the dumpster took the brunt of the force. It looks like there were smaller packets of fuel inside the dumpster, specifically designed to ignite on landing— presumably on the building."

I squint, my head throbbing when I try to do anything except laugh about exploding pizza. "The lids? I think it was open when we got there? No, that doesn't seem right. Wait. The lock was broken, I do remember that. Ryan slammed the lids shut before it blew up. I think it was just luck that we went out to throw away the boxes and shut the doors. Guess we're lucky no one else was hurt."

Matteo grumbles. "We're damn *lucky* there were people there to call 911." He starts pacing again. "We've told the media that it was a combustion explosion by improperly disposed-of spray paint. So at least we're not public yet, but we need a plan."

He stops pacing long enough to jerk the curtain open, look into the room where doctors and nurses bustle around, no one paying us any attention. Given that I'm just here until my IV saline drip finishes, I think we're low men on the importance totem pole.

"But I'm already getting reports from the bomb squad. This wasn't some can of spray paint you guys tossed in that combusted. Someone did this on purpose."

I sigh. "The only thing I remember is that Ryan and I were talking about something. The price of the pizza, or . . . the receipt. It was odd for some reason." My mind works like molasses, and it is hard to recall specifics. And then it gels, and I see it clearly. I sit upright in the bed, nearly pulling my IV out. "Oh! I remember! The receipt was from that catering company. Hat Trick."

"The same one who catered Cleopatra's party."

"The same."

One last detail emerges from the depths of my brain. "There was a heart colored on the receipt."

It takes almost no time for Matteo to make the leap that I've been toying with. "You think the Queen of Hearts is involved with the caterer."

I shrug. "It makes sense, right? Anyone connected with Muñez has a reason to want to see Lawrence get beaten up. Maybe it's a good cover to get into the parties where he'd be . . ." I trail off. And then I laugh. I'm not sure if it's the drugs or what, but it dawns on me. "Queen. Of Hearts."

Matteo eyes me. "Yeah?"

"No, you don't get it. Just think: *Queen* of Hearts. There's only one queen I can think of who would benefit from Lawrence being hurt, and she brought the pizzas."

"Cleopatra."

"Just so."

We both ponder this possibility for a moment, but Matteo nods, accepting my theory. "This is enough for us to take her into custody. She's tied to the caterer; she's tied to the other death, even if peripherally—it happened at her party. I'll have her brought in immediately." He pulls out his phone and dials the office, quickly describing our suspicions to Rideout. He clicks off and eyes me. "Not that I don't agree she'd benefit from harming L, but . . . why would she do all this? I never thought she seemed the murderess type."

I filter through everything that's a loose end for me in the case: the Queen of Hearts, the masked man at the party whom L thinks he knew, the note from the Golden Arrow to "follow the White Rabbit," the journal. Several of those things just fall together into a story line. So, if we throw out the ones that don't jibe with that story line . . . I let my writer's brain take over for a long moment, wandering down the paths of "what-ifs," doubling back, taking quicksilver detours that are instantly dismissed until I arrive at a theory.

"It fits for Cleo to be the Queen . . . but what if the Queen is *the Golden Arrow?*"

"Are these the pain meds talking?"

I throw my pillow at him. "Quiet. My brain is mushy, and I need to talk this out."

Matteo mimes buttoning his lips and motions me to continue.

"Okay, we know the Queen is the person who has essentially taken over Muñez's position in the community, and we have reason to believe that the Queen worked with Muñez directly. We also thought that the Golden Arrow may have been the Queen—except we caught Daniel, and he's definitely *not* a drug dealer or master chemist, right?"

Matteo shakes his head but stays wisely silent.

"So, we have to assume the GA at the parties is an imposter." I tap my head, willing my sluggish brain to work. *Why.* Why go to all the trouble of having an imposter GA, other than to make it look like you had celebrity friends? Especially when the Golden Arrow at the party wanted to hurt Lawrence. But there's the thread between Cleo and the parties, and the Golden Arrow imposter. "Maybe *all* of this has been about Lawrence." It's crazy, but in my drug-addled state, it's what makes the most sense. I put it all together for Matteo with the snap of my fingers. "The Queen of Hearts could be a *team*. The imposter is whomever L knew from his past. For whatever reason, he tipped his hand and L realized he knew him, went off and tried to find him . . . and bam, Lawrence in the hospital. The Queen is scared that Lawrence can ID him or"—I trail off for a moment, shuddering—"*has* ID'd him, and that's what got him stabbed. Lawrence is the key—one of the Queens is a part of his past. We've been barking up the wrong tree—the Queen isn't connected to this case through Muñez; she or *they* are connected through Casey." I snap my fingers. "In fact, right before the explosion, the fountain on the float reminded me of a sketch I saw on the pages from the journal. I'm positive now; the other person we're looking for worked for Casey Senior. Not Muñez."

"Who designed the fountain?" Matteo's frown is deepening. He believes me and he's worried.

My face is grim. "It's a champagne fountain."

"The caterer," we say at the same time.

"But why is a caterer after you and Ryan?"

While he's stopped looking at me like I'm in la-la land, Matteo doesn't look fully convinced.

Okay. Farther down this rabbit hole we go. "What if the reason the Queen is targeting Ryan and me is because Lawrence *is* alive? And they figure he's told us something—find that friend, and we find our would-be killer and Cleopatra's partner."

"It's so crazy it almost makes sense to me," Matteo says. He opens his notebook and starts scribbling. After a long stretch, he looks up. "One thing doesn't make sense. Why would the Queen—or one of them—pretend to be the Golden Arrow then? Why bring the GA in at all?"

I hesitate. "I guess because Lawrence, Ryan, and I probably couldn't resist attending a party where we might meet him? We've all been in the news. Maybe it seemed a good bait tactic."

Matteo nods. "And a good way to get to wear a cape and a mask without people asking questions. The problem is, we've scoured Muñez's contacts. We can't find this person."

"But Cleo can."

Matteo nods grimly. "We need to talk to Lawrence. See if he can think of anyone connected to Cleo who would stoop to murder, and who fits the profile of this mysterious person from his past. At least until we have Cleo in custody. Rideout is on his way over there right now, but no telling how long it will take to apprehend her."

I nod, hesitantly. "It's not like L made much sense the first time, but it's worth a try . . ." I start to think about what Lawrence said before, and yet another piece slides into place. Goose bumps rise on my arms. "Lawrence said something else, Matteo. He said 'After Arrow.' What if we're not the only ones in trouble? What if Lawrence essentially gave us a hit list, and the Golden Arrow is on that list too?"

"Daniel will be released tomorrow . . . we can't hold him any longer. His alibi checks out; we don't have DNA evidence, anything."

"But he had the journal."

Matteo slowly shakes his head. "We confirmed his bag is left in the open at the gym five days a week. Literally anyone could have put it in there and tipped off police."

"Brother-in-law?"

Matteo shakes his head. "Everything checks out."

Great. Now we possibly have a police leak, a person who framed my friends, and a real vigilante out there who might be in trouble. How are we going to find the *real* Slim Shady in this game of imposters? This pain medication may help with invention of ideas, but it sure doesn't help with fact recollection. And yet everything is just falling into place, and in my gut, I *know* I'm right. Cleo. The GA imposter, the caterer, and the would-be murderer.

Matteo's jaw works, and he resumes pacing the small space. He is forced to stop moments later when a nurse enters, checks my chart and blood pressure, then deems me ready to discharge. I'm given a sheaf of papers, my shoes, and told I can leave when I feel able.

Matteo helps me into my shoes, then stands me up before pulling out his phone. "Since we're still not clear about why you or Ryan—or possibly the Golden Arrow—would also be targets, we're going to put all of you under security surveillance immediately. And we've got to find an ID for Hat Trick's owner."

"Good luck with security. In about a week's time, Ryan and I are going to be hosting a party with thousands of attendees . . ." I cut off, my brain working again. "Wait. The party. Cleopatra offered to host the party." I thought she was genuine, but really, she was playing an angle.

"We're canceling that party," Matteo says dismissively, as if it's a done deal.

"Don't you dare," I toss back. A slow smile spreads across my face.

"What? No, absolutely not. Whatever it is, no."

"Let's check in on Ryan, and then we need to go upstairs and talk to L."

"Why are you smiling?" Matteo's suspicious side is showing now, as it should.

"Because, my dear, *I* have a plan."

Ryan's face is wrapped in gauze, and he looks rather like a mummy. Bonus points being that he'll not need much of a Halloween costume, I guess?

Matteo's eyes graze Ryan's bandages before settling on Lawrence. "Are you sure you want to use your best friend as bait?"

"Only *one* of them. The other one will be helping you."

Matteo is not taking too kindly to my plan. Why is he failing to grasp the brilliance despite the risk? "The Queen is after L," I state.

"I know." We've just been through this, so Matteo is understandably gruff.

We turn to regard L. He's been in and out of consciousness, but we haven't set off any alarms, so the doctor is allowing our visit. Or maybe she feels bad that three of the four of us are wearing hospital ID badges and bandages. A gorgeous arrangement of flowers sits on his windowsill, and I wander over to take a look—I'm trying to learn to appreciate flowers now, since Matteo is so into them, and these look particularly expensive. I go ahead and own my nosiness and look for a card, finally locating one that simply says, "W." My heart warms.

All the more reason to get L's attacker off the street. "*So . . .* if we say that L is going to be at his party, there's a chance the Queen will make a move."

Matteo rolls his eyes. "I'm pretty sure that the arrest of Cleopatra is going to tip off the other teammate—if that's truly what's going on."

I hold up a finger. "*Not* if we convince Cleopatra to help us."

Ryan snorts. "Like that would ever happen, MG—"

"Actually, it might—" I start to argue, but a small sound comes from the doorway, and we turn as one to regard the very person we're discussing lurking in the doorway.

We freeze. Well, the rest of us do, but Matteo springs into action, hands flying to his waist, where I assume he has a pair of handcuffs.

Cleo holds up her hands. "Look, I know this is unorthodox. I'm prepared to turn myself in, but if you'll permit me a moment, I came to offer a bargain in return."

"We can talk about it at the station," Matteo growls, advancing on her.

She stands her ground, and I just cannot get the *earnestness* of her tone out of my head. She allows herself to be handcuffed without argument.

"Matteo," I ask, "would it hurt to hear her out?"

"Yes," Ryan and Matteo answer together.

"My offer only stands if you hear me out here and now," Cleo replies. "Otherwise, you can just wait until my trial to find out what I know. And believe me, you want to know."

We all exchange glances, and finally Matteo allows her into the room, closing the door behind her. "You have five minutes."

Cleo nods. "I came here to find you specifically, after I heard about the explosion." She turns to me, and again I think I see tears in her eyes. "Too many people have been hurt. I know who set that explosion; I can't prove it, but I'll tell you what I know."

It's on the tip of my tongue to accuse *her*, but we all seem to decide to hear her out.

She looks around, gaze finally landing on L, and the rest of her resolve crumples. "It wasn't supposed to be like this. I was just supposed to gain followers, sell more tickets, rise to the top of the scene. Finally get the attention *I* deserve. He convinced me that Louis's death was an accident—"

"He *who*?" Matteo asks, and my stomach jumps.

"My benefactor, for a lack of a better term," she answers on a sigh. She looks completely defeated. "He approached me a few months ago and offered to sponsor my career. He was a fancy events guy; I figured he was the real deal."

That stops us all cold. *Benefactor?*

She continues. "I thought it was amazing. Someone to buy me costumes, fund my rise to the top, throw me elaborate parties. I wanted so badly to get ahead, to be famous, that I really didn't question *why* this person appeared, I just took the opportunity I thought I was due." She swallows, and again I fear tears are about to slide down her cheeks. "But. I should have questioned, because I've come to the conclusion that this . . . person . . . wasn't interested in me for *me*, but for who I associated with. I wasn't anything to him but a pawn."

Lawrence. Latifah. And apparently by proxy Ryan, me, and the Arrow.

Matteo and I exchange significant glances. Cleo is sounding less and less like the Queen of Hearts and more and more like a victim of circumstance.

"But Cleopatra is no pawn, and I decided, from here on out, I am queen of my own destiny. No more expecting someone else to make it for me." She turns to me. "I am so sorry you and your friends were hurt. I'm sorry Louis overdosed on the drugs being sold at my party. I want to help you catch this person, in exchange for leniency in my sentencing."

The way she frames Louis's accident isn't sitting right. "But you're the Queen. The Queen of Hearts, I mean. Right? That's what you came to confess?"

Cleo looks confused. "That's what he calls me, his 'Little Queen of Hearts,' but how did you know? I thought it was sort of a pet name." She looks between us. "There's something I'm missing?"

Uh-oh.

"Ah," I press, "so are you here to confess to being a drug lord?"

I can basically *hear* Matteo hitting his hand on his head. This is far from an official interview room. I probably shouldn't even be asking these questions. Ask forgiveness and not permission, I guess.

"Drug lord—no, I'm a *performer*. Now, I don't mind if people have a little fun, but I'm not spending my time dealing, if that's what you're talking about."

"Purveying is more like it." My lips thin.

Cleo looks alarmed now. "What?"

I eye Matteo, who frantically shakes his head, then adamantly ignore him. "The person who took Muñez's and Agent Sosa's"—I pause to make sure Cleo nods in recognition before I continue—"place in the drug community is known as the Queen of Hearts. And since Louis OD'd on those specific drugs at your party, and since Lawrence was pulled aside and threatened at another of your parties . . . well . . . you're the prime suspect."

"I had nothing to do with that," Cleo says. "I mean, I knew there were drugs there. There usually are a few people carrying, and a few using. But I'm not *behind* it."

"Not on purpose," I say, grimly. It seems to me that Cleo's *partner* probably meant to frame her for all this, and he's very neatly tied it all up. "This *person* funding your 'rise to the top'—can you give us a little more information? Name? Address?"

Cleo's face crumples. "I know you're going to think I'm stupid, but I don't even have a last name. He always contacted *me*, never the other way around. It felt like such a dream, I didn't question it."

More like a nightmare.

Matteo shakes his head. "This is all on your word, which will never stand up in court. I'm sorry you've been used, but if you can't even provide a name . . ."

"I can do something better. Halloween. He specifically asked me to get involved. To help plan, and to keep him informed about Latifah's status—"

"Ha!" Ryan breaks in, pointing at me. "I *told* you she was up to something."

Cleo holds up a hand. "That *was* the plan, but I told him the day I picked up the pizzas that I didn't want anyone else to get hurt. That I wanted to break ties. He threatened to tell the police it was me all along, and I was scared, so I agreed to help him." She looks pleadingly at me. "I swear I didn't know he was going to try and blow you up that night. I think I made him mad. He knows so much about me, it wouldn't take much to frame me. And I really meant it, I was going to help just out of the goodness of my heart. I wasn't going to tell him anything."

I snort, and Cleo's eyes cast downward. "I deserve that. But I promise it's true."

Matteo is all business. "This is all well and good, but *what* are you offering?"

"To finish planning the party," she offers.

"She's offering to be Severus Snape," I clarify for Matteo and Ryan. "We know, but the benefactor doesn't *know* we know."

"Exactly," Cleo agrees. "I'll tell him whatever you want. I'll get him there, to the Halloween party. I'll tell him Latifah is definitely going. I'll help however I can; I just want you to catch him to keep him from hurting anyone else."

No one says anything for a long time.

I clear my throat. "I think we should do it. It ties in perfectly with my plan."

"Your plan is *terrible*," Matteo quips.

"Do you have a better one?"

Matteo is silent.

I nod at Ryan. "You? Can you think of any other way to assure ourselves of a chance to stop this?" I need his cooperation too.

Matteo sighs. "Fine, I'll talk it over with Rideout."

"Tell him about my ideas for the costumes."

Ryan squints. "Yeah, remind me again why *you're* not in costume in this scenario?"

"Well," I say, drawing it out, "someone has to host, and everyone already knows me. Everyone already can recognize Matteo from TV, so this is the only way to have him close to the action without tipping off our suspect. There are queens coming from all over California. That's why this is perfect."

Neither Matteo nor Ryan looks enthusiastic, or sold on the idea.

Matteo eyes Cleo. "How do we get your benefactor to agree to attend?"

Cleo is prepared, it seems. "It's simple. Just release the news story that Lawrence will make a recovery and his first appearance will be at the party after the parade—a presentation or something. Announce the Golden Arrow is in custody and you consider the investigation finished. Then you go undercover and wait for him to try and attack Lawrence, catch him red-handed, and voilà. One crime, neatly solved."

In the bed next to us, L stirs, and we all sit up straighter.

"What the hell are you guys yammering about?" L says after a long moment of silence. "Can't a queen get her beauty sleep?" His eyes widen as they land on Cleo.

"We're planning how to catch the person who did this to you." The *other* one, but I don't want to stress him out with details.

L is silent a long time, and when he speaks, he sounds incredibly sleepy. "I'd rather you not."

I squeeze his hand. "It's okay. Matteo and Ryan have agreed to go undercover as queens to try and catch them." I ignore their looks of outrage. Okay, maybe *agreed* was a strong term. I nod toward the door. "We're just *leaving* to go to the station and iron out our plan."

Lawrence gives a wheezy laugh, is quiet long enough I'm pretty sure he's fallen back asleep, then speaks without opening his eyes. "You'd better take pictures. I want to see Hot-Lanta with boobs."

CHAPTER 30

Shwanda and Amy Blondoniss have done a bang-up job—even I barely recognize Matteo or Ryan. Matteo makes a sultry contemporary Ariel—Shwanda's homage to my bright red hair and a nod to the *princess* theme of the float. The entire past week, I've frantically thrown myself into costume construction—usually my favorite activity ever, but the time for these projects was so compressed I even did the draping *on* Ryan and Matteo. We plundered the entirety of L's costume closet—upstairs *and* down—for material for all the looks. Ryan has his navy-inspired look, which didn't take as much time as the *supersecret* look for the halftime of the lip-sync competition. If shit is going to go down, at least Ryan will look *amazing*.

Ryan and Matteo both needed themed looks to wear in and near the float, and I simply adore the man in front of me—comfortable enough to be rocking a green-sequined skirt, flared at the bottom to suggest a tail. The ruffles that line the skirt's layers hide Matteo's thigh holster, and I cleverly sewed in a kill switch—a rip cord of sorts so that if Matteo really needed to run, the skirt would essentially disintegrate around him.

"Is the clamshell bra really necessary?" Matteo asks. "And how does anyone ever see *anything* with these eyelash things on?"

"You'll get used to the eyelashes. I'd skip them except . . . no pageant queen would *ever* skip them. It would be a dead giveaway." Amy Blondoniss silences Matteo by applying another coat of green, glittery lipstick.

L's drag family is the utter best. "We couldn't have done this without you guys."

"No one hurts our family and gets away with it," Amy says.

Luckily, Ryan has submitted more willingly to his ministrations, and his buxom, navy-boy-inspired Sailor Moon, princess of the galaxy, costume, to be exact. This look has been easy to put together; the trouble is going to be *selling* it. I have to hope that Ryan has a strutting, dance-loving queen somewhere deep inside his gamer soul.

Shwanda comes over to check Matteo's makeup and gives a nod of approval before leveling her gaze on Ryan. "Okay, remember, your name is Camila Toe Parker. You're from Northern California, and this is your first year. It'll go fine."

I have my own doubts, but there isn't time to address them as Rideout arrives.

He eyes Ryan, then Matteo, and wisely keeps his likely less-than-complimentary thoughts to himself. "The undercover detail is ready to roll with the float."

Outside our little tent, the crowd has gotten louder and louder. It's time to take our place in line for the long drive to the venue. Matteo and Rideout have failed to find more than just the registered name of the catering company's owner. The address was empty, and no credit history exists for this person. Either they deal in cash only, which seems unlikely, or the identity is a fake.

We've baited our trap as best as I could figure out how—with Lawrence. We've told everyone we could think of that while Lawrence is still recovering, he plans on attending the lip-sync competition and making a special presentation.

"Okay, we need to go over all this again," Matteo says, then smacks his lips awkwardly around the glittery lipstick. "Ryan will keep a lookout on the float. Rideout and his crew will move with the float, and I'll be riding in the cab with the driver. We all are wired, so make sure to signal at the very first sign of trouble. We don't expect anything until the presentation, but . . . you never can be too careful."

We all nod. We have to hope that the Hatter is targeting Lawrence and will be drawn out by our bluff. So much hinges on tonight. Going in with only a hunch and a prayer feels rocky at best.

I mount the stairs to the finished float and take a seat near the back to operate the champagne fountain behind the dancers, all my senses on alert. Beneath my feet, the engine of the large truck pulling the float roars to life, and the ship's floor gives a shudder. In short order, we're rolling out to Santa Monica behind several pedestrian groups and a jazz band. Dusk is falling; throngs of people line the street, and up ahead somewhere, music blares over a sound system. My blue Alice dress swishes around me in the wind, and I take stock.

Cleopatra. She's holding court in the prow of the boat, wearing a pink-sequined gown shot through with gold. Golden wings sprout from her back, she carries a harp, and her sash says, "Miss(es) Heaven." Ryan joins several of the other dancers and loads up with Mardi Gras beads to throw. The music pumps to life, the lights on the interior of the float go up, I press the "On" button for the fountain, and we're live. Cleopatra's gaze connects with mine and she smiles. I return it as we roll forward.

Game on, bitches.

By the time we reach the venue, it's fully dark, and the number of costumed people on the street makes looking for the Hatter impossible. I'm hot and sweaty despite the chill in the air thanks to the motor for the fountain, and frustrated. The float is a huge success—the crowds of people love the dancers and the bubbles created by the frothing champagne, and wave to the princesses at the bow of the boat. That should be balm to my soul—step one is complete for L's vision—but all it does is amp my anxiety for the next step: the party, the lip-sync competition, and the presentation.

We disembark the float at the door of the bar, and about one hundred people walk in the doors with us—queens, friends-of-queens—everyone is in costume, and it's nearly impossible to identify anyone. I wade through a group of Club Kid–inspired queens and make my way into the emptier part of the venue. Halloween is my favorite holiday, mostly due to the costumes—I'm not disappointed tonight. Everything from a zombie Khal and Khaleesi to Dangermouse, and several convincing Supergirls. We also have our fair share of Golden Arrows, and several people running around in large hats. Any of whom could be our suspect, if my hunch about his costume is correct. I run right into Rideout, who is coming up from the back of the house.

"Did he show?" We'd been hoping the caterer would be easy pickings and show up when the food did.

Rideout shakes his head. "Someone from Hat Trick showed up, but he says the owner is coming later. Cleo *assures* us she's played it straight and convinced him to come."

Great. I resist the urge to wipe my hand across my eyes, given my carefully applied makeup. The general atmosphere is amping up, and I look around. My eye catches a familiar form—I blink twice to make sure it's really Daniel walking toward me.

"Daniel!" I call out. "Or should I say . . ." I take in his costume. He looks a little like a Korean *Fresh Prince of Bel-Air*, so I'm stumped.

"Tweedledee," Daniel answers, giving his beanie a twirl. "Harrison is . . . well, he drew the short straw. Ryan told me there was a theme when I called to find out if it was okay if I came. I almost dressed as the Golden Arrow, but figured that it might be a *little* soon for that joke."

I swallow as awkward silence descends. "I'm—ah—sorry about that whole thing."

Daniel takes a moment to meet my eye again, then sighs. "I'm just lucky it was my little girl's fall break with her mom and she has no idea

I was in jail. I suppose I can eventually take it as a compliment that you thought I was cool enough to be a superhero." He offers a hand, and I take it, giving it a firm squeeze. Things may not be perfect between us, but I have a feeling they'll return to normal eventually.

I turn to the corner where the deejay has already set up, a huge rack of lights ready to shine onto the oversize dance floor adjacent to the bar. I snag the microphone he has ready for us, and I mount the stairs to the catwalk that juts out into the space.

"Hello, everyone!" I paste on the brightest smile I can. *This is for L. This is for L.* I freaking hate public speaking. In fact, I'm shaking in my black Mary Janes. Hundreds of eyes turn to mine, and large groups shift into the space, surrounding the stage by degrees. Waiters, dressed all in black, mingle through the crowd holding platters of steaming appetizers; service has begun.

"Welcome!" I say again, trying to give the crowd time to settle.

I had anticipated it would be difficult to identify our suspect before the presentation, but I didn't know *how* hard. There are costumes of every make and model here. And more than several that involve *Alice In Wonderland.* It's our only guess that *perhaps*, given the Hatter's affinity for the work, he'll wear a costume related to it.

Matteo is also unnerved by the growing crowd. I can tell by the way he's pacing the front of the crowd near the stage, his hand drifting every now and again to his seashell belt to make certain his holster is in position. I keep an eye on him and Ryan from the stage as I make my way to the end of the catwalk. Time to get Operation Mad Hatter underway. I introduce myself and share L's vision for the evening to much applause. All the while, I'm watching the crowd. Eye contact from Shwanda, Amy Blondoniss, and Rideout. All shake their heads. It looks like we're going to have to flush our quarry.

Out of pleasantries, I motion to the decorated table to my right. "You'll see our panel of esteemed judges for our Lip-Sync Spooktacular, and let's make sure to mention that our winner gets a fabulous gift prize basket put together by our sponsors!" Our judges take their places, and the event begins just as Halloween festivities get into full swing outside.

The first half of the lip-sync goes off without a hitch. There is a *killer* MJ queen duel with the song "Thriller," and once or twice I'm so captivated that I forget I'm supposed to be watching for a would-be killer. All too soon, the lights come up, and the judges have their heads in a huddle over their score sheets. The thrum of my pulse sings in my ears as I realize that *this* is our moment. This is what our planning and scheming have brought us to.

My heartbeat matches my shuffle as I climb back up, standing to face everyone from the base of the catwalk.

I clear my throat, catching sight of Matteo. He's craning his neck around, pushing his red wig over his shoulder to allow better peripheral vision. At about my three o'clock, Daniel stands near the front—he doesn't know exactly what's going on, but I suspect he knows me well enough to read my unease. He's looking at me with mild concern—a good reminder to keep up my cheery onstage persona. I don't want to tip our poker hand too soon. Over his shoulder, I catch sight of another concerned face, and this one makes my stomach bottom out a little.

Lelani. Dressed in a gorgeous black leather jumpsuit and brilliant, ringed faux-fur tail, she's the Cheshire Catwoman. But she doesn't look self-assured and polished. She's watching me with so much anxiety written on her face that I *know* Ryan has told her enough of the plan that she knows he's in danger. Heck, her boyfriend got injured by flying food debris worse than I did. She's got a horse in this race too; as much as I wondered how Ryan and Lelani's relationship was faring, she obviously cares about him. To the task at hand. Deploy net number one.

"Before we get to our presentation, let's give our sponsors a round of applause. I'd like to invite them up on the stage so that we can thank them properly." I pull out a sheaf of notecards so that it looks official, even though this is part of our dragnet operation. In and among the local news station, makeup companies, party rental company, and hair products, I call the name of the catering company. It's a special kind of torture, not being able to crane my neck around to see what happens when I read the name "Hat Trick," but that's what Matteo and Rideout are here for. Soon there is a line of people behind me, and after I give a short description of each of their businesses, I invite the crowd to join me in a round of applause in thanks. It's nice for those vendors who *didn't* come here with murder plans to get recognition, *and* it gives me an excuse to turn around and survey the line of folks behind me. No one looks familiar, no one looks threatening. I chance a glance at Matteo, who is in obvious contact with Rideout through his wire—he offers me a small shake of his head and my shoulders droop. *Okay, step two.*

"And tonight's thank-you wouldn't be complete without recognizing the benefactress who stepped in so *magnanimously* to help us when Latifah was injured. Cleopatra, come on up here so we can all give you a special round of applause."

Net two: deployed. Everyone is supposedly present and ready for capture.

A quick glance at my bellwether, Daniel, confirms that I might look ill. He looks positively alarmed and ready to vault up on the stage. Okay. *You've got this, MG. Superhero up. This is earning you XP points, as Ryan would say.* Cleopatra climbs up onstage, waves to the crowd, and turns to me expectantly. Time for the pièce de résistance, and to put our suspicions to the test.

Cheery smile. Cheery smile. "While the judges deliberate, I know we promised you a very special visit and a presentation you wouldn't forget." My mouth is suddenly filled with saliva, and I nearly choke. My anxiety is out of control. It's scary being up here, so exposed, waiting to detonate what we hope is a catalyst for solving this case.

"Without further ado, I introduce our special guest who will kick things off!"

I sweep my arm to the side, allowing the violet velvet–clad figure to walk up the catwalk. Ryan's imitation of Gene Wilder's Willy Wonka is impeccable, and I have to say I had a dab hand on the costume imitation. I'm not a purist about many modern adaptations, but *Anne of Green Gables, The Hooded Falcon*, and *Willy Wonka and the Chocolate Factory* (sorry, Johnny Depp) are franchises that were done best first, and should never be done again.

Ryan limps up the catwalk, hat cocked totally over his face, just as in the movie. The purple velvet looks amazing under the lights, and all around us the crowd grows silent and watchful. I *know* everyone is expecting Latifah. It's what we've led them to expect, and we've padded Ryan to be a little bigger than his lean frame. The music cuts out, and the clink of Ryan's decorative cane on the catwalk echoes as everyone watches with rapt attention. It's dramatic perfection. Or it would be if I weren't nearly passing out from the pounding of my heart. My eyes are darting everywhere. Will the Hatter make his move now? Wait until he sees if it's Lawrence? Wait until Ryan's announcement? Maybe *nothing* will happen. Maybe this is all a gigantic setup with multiple police squads for literally nothing.

Near the top of the catwalk, I expect Ryan to stop and push up his hat in a jaunty manner, but he goes the full McGillicuddy. He drops into an impressive roll, dropping the cane to the side, and pops back up onto his knees.

The crowd. Goes. Wild. At least they do until a confused murmur ripples through the room, scattering the applause.

Ryan holds out his hands good-naturedly, then removes his hat. His large wig of frizzy hair—another nod to Gene Wilder—springs out, and a few people laugh, which he accepts with a cheery bow, top hat over his heart.

"Thank you, good people; I realize I may not be the droid you are looking for."

Another ripple of confused laughter.

"But let me assure you, I will be the best showman I can be while I let you in on a big secret."

I don't know how he looks so calm, so *natural* up there. I'm dying back here. It's all I can do to avoid reaching out and snatching Cleopatra's perfectly smooth arm next to mine, just as insurance.

Ryan continues, really yukking it up. "Good audience, you came to see a show, and I have to confess you're about to be a part of a spectacular piece of Halloween history. Because among us, we have not only those *dressed* as villains but real ones as well."

The crowd, which had been getting into the spirit of Ryan's monologue again, seems baffled.

"But we all have a chance tonight to be real superheroes by outing those who have hurt the very community you're here to support." Ryan starts to explain that earlier in the summer there was a tragic overdose death, a part of the speech that *seems* innocent enough but targets our suspect.

In front of me, Matteo straightens, waves slightly to get my attention, and nods over near Daniel. I pivot the merest degree and scan the crowd.

There.

A top hat. A top hat I've seen before. A vision of this hat from both the first party at the Zebra and then again at the black box theater comes crashing into my brain. I squint my eyes. If I picture a gold mask across his face, it *could* be the man from L's fuzzy picture. I give a definitive nod. My Spidey-sense says *it's him*. This is it.

CHAPTER 31

In front of me, Ryan is winding up for the pitch. "As senseless as that death is, it will shock you further to know that someone within your *own* community caused it. We have evidence to support that there is an individual, or individuals, present in this very room that contributed to the death of Louis."

The murmur that sweeps the crowd this time is shocked, and just about everyone side-eyes their neighbor.

Ryan continues. "You are all about to be a part of one of the biggest drug busts in our city's history. As we speak, we have two teams of police with warrants searching the known residences of these suspects—"

It's a lie. We don't even know the Hatter's name, or residence.

"And it may shock you all to know, one or both of them are on this stage. Please welcome Detectives Rideout and Kildaire of the Los Angeles Police Department, please. They will be taking both of these people into custody immediately." Beside me, Cleopatra is fidgeting. Positively vibrating. The pressure is getting to her, and I will her to *keep cool*. If she loses it now, she could jeopardize the entire setup. This was part of the plan. So that the person doesn't figure out that she's double-crossed him.

As planned, Rideout makes a big show of clomping up the stairs opposite of Cleopatra, and everything happens in an instant. My reality explodes into movement and chaos as Cleo loses her nerve and spins—a wave of blonde wig and wings—and bolts for the back door.

"She's making a run for it!" yells Rideout. I make a grab for her arm, and we grapple for a moment.

I have only the barest glimpse of the Top Hat melting quietly into the crowd before Ryan points with his canc out over the crowd, and everyone ducks and turns to follow where he's pointing. "Stop that man!"

In front of the stage, Matteo slings his boobs and bra over one shoulder, hand going to his holster, but I don't get to see what happens. Cleo knocks me off-balance, and I plunge off the side of the stage. Over my shoulder, I catch sight of Detective Rideout—tie flying as he gives chase, hand clamped over his ear in an effort to stay in contact with the team spread out all over the venue. I cartwheel my hands as I fall, closing my eyes for impact. Except instead of floor, I hit a very solid something. Something human.

I scramble up from a shocked Lelani as the crowd moves into a feverish dance, everyone craning their necks this way and that.

"Which way did she go?" I ask, and Lelani points to the back of the stage while climbing to her own feet.

"Sorry!" I yell as I barrel back toward the stairs. I'll confront the "I just landed on a Genius executive from a stage where we're chasing a criminal" later.

Up onstage, pandemonium has broken loose. Half of the sponsors stand around like sheep, turning this way and that, watching the commotion. The other half have joined in the chase, running off backstage.

"Where did they go?" a voice asks. "Are you okay? I saw you fall."

My knight in shining fish scale screeches to a stop at my side, one boob over his right shoulder, red wig askew, no green skirt in sight, shell bra around his neck like a necklace. I have the wildest urge to stop and mime having a cigar and say, "Hey, nice clamshells." *Focus, MG.*

"Kildaire!" a voice calls out. It's Rideout. "She ran that way." He motions to the group of people gathered around the back entrance.

Matteo doesn't waste time jumping back into the milling crowd. Rideout spins to me, and he and I share a thought. There's *three* of us in

314

pursuit of Cleopatra. Who is going after the Hatter? "You get back up on that stage and keep a lookout!" Rideout yells, pitching me a walkie-talkie. I catch it midair and nod as he and Matteo head back into the fray. I swear I hear him *growl* as he doubles back, dashing for the front door and, I assume, the Hatter.

I spin on my heels and run straight into Daniel. Without time to explain, I reach out, grab his hand, and yank him toward the stage. "Come on, ninja boy, we've got another suspect to catch!"

Daniel is much nimbler than I am and keeps up with me with ease. "I'm not a *real* vigilante, you know," he yells over the chaos.

"Pity!" I yell back as the stage comes back into view. "We could really use one right now!"

Onstage, the only one left at this point is Ryan. He's craning his neck, peering into the crowd, and yelling into his earpiece. My walkie-talkie squawks with whatever he says, but I can't make it out. So much good that does me. I chuck the walkie-talkie to the ground. I can only assume Ryan is directing . . . well, *who*, I'm not clear on.

A shout near the front door alerts the crowd to a new happening, and Daniel and I pivot as one to see Amy Blondoniss in hot pursuit of the Hatter. For a six-foot-tall guy in heels, Amy is remarkably agile. But the Hatter, impressively yet disappointingly, is more so. He does a neat tuck-and-spin move that looks like something straight out of *Swan Lake*. His coattails fly out. It's like he does a double axel skating jump on dry land and switches directions, right back the way he came—right over the top of Amy Blondoniss, who does an admirable imitation of a quarterback diving for a ball but missing.

Daniel and I suck in our breath as one; we watch as the unidentified assailant—Lawrence's would-be murderer—bursts right out the front door and into the crowd outside. Amy Blondoniss and Rideout follow, but the odds of finding him in this crowd have got to be abysmal.

We've lost him.

CHAPTER 32

I spin around, determined to throw in with Matteo, only to find the door to backstage hanging open too. A small group of people mill around it, talking and pointing.

I yell several expletives, grasp Daniel's hand, and *drag* him straight off the stage and through the backstage door. The parking lot is filled with cars and people, and I think I see Matteo's form dodging around the corner of the building, so I take off in hot pursuit. Daniel keeps up on my heels, and we screech around the corner only to be met with a literal *wall* of parade-goers. Floats filled with lights still make their way down the street, and costumed witches, goblins, and every fandom spook fill the space between floats.

I dodge a guy with a tuba. And nearly run into a seven-foot-tall Jack from *The Nightmare Before Christmas*.

This is literal insanity.

"There!" Daniel yells, pointing off to our left. I glimpse Cleo's form diving into a group of *Walking Dead* cheerleaders, and the oddly lumpy form of Matteo, boobs still flopping over his shoulder, diving in behind her.

Footfalls echo behind us, and I glance over my shoulder to see Ryan, Lelani, and several of L's friends skidding to a halt behind us.

I wave my arm, hoping Ryan sees it before plunging after Matteo, my ears filled with some creepy circus music piped from the nearest passing float.

Daniel dodges some dude on a bicycle, and I leap over several of the cheerleaders who have been knocked to the ground by Cleo's flight. It's only seconds before we catch up to Matteo, attempting to make his way upstream after Cleo, who isn't having much more luck. She gets stuck against the side of a float that has stopped, and I see our chance.

"I've got this," Daniel yells. "Hoist me."

"What?" I yell; I can hardly hear.

Daniel mimes me making a basket with my hands, and I throw him an incredulous look. "No way!"

"Come on!" He pulls me to a stop, and without thinking too much, I basket my hands, and he puts his foot in.

"On three!" he yells. "One! Two! Three!"

I have no idea what I'm doing, but I boost my arms up as fast and as hard as I can, and somehow Daniel flies upward like some magical rocket ship. I'm knocked backward onto my rear, but Daniel's sheer athleticism saves him. I have no idea how he manages it, but he does a slow flip through the air, landing literally on top of Cleopatra. Not a moment later, Matteo sprawls onto the pair of them, handcuffs already out.

Not even attempting to wade my way to them, I instantly turn to look for Top Hat, Rideout, or Lelani or Ryan. There's no way to know which direction they've gone. I'm temporarily blinded by two people walking by, covered head-to-toe in glow sticks, but when I open my eyes, I spot something familiar atop the float next to me. It's Top Hat, peering over the edge like he's trying to hide, watching the fate of Cleopatra.

"Matteo! Above you!" I yell, pointing up.

I tip Top Hat off, and he immediately disappears, but Matteo also thankfully hears me, and I see him press his hand to his ear. Please, *please* let Rideout be close.

I set off at a sprint, rounding the side of the float. Hoping I see *anyone* familiar. We can't let him get away, we—

That's when I see the literal *net* of people making their way up the street, led by none other than Lelani. She's cool as a cucumber, in the dead center of a line of people, locked at the elbows, that stretches from one side of the street to the other. The crowd has gotten wind that there's something up, and most people move out of the way or duck under as the chain passes.

It's bloody brilliant, is what it is. The net of people stops the fleeing Top Hat in his tracks, and he doubles back, hopping back into the float he'd just jumped out of.

Only now can I make out the man's face. He looks older than Lawrence, his dark face weathered with gray around his beard. The oddity nearly stops my forward momentum. Shouldn't all villains be young? This man looks grizzled. He looks like someone's dad. A nimble dad with ninja training.

The net of people reaches the float just as Rideout sprints up on my left. I'm about to suggest that we close the gap when another familiar, hatted figure joins our fugitive on the deck of the float. Ryan.

"LAPD business! Please exit this float!" he yells, and the inhabitants scramble to obey.

Hatter senses his impending doom, and suddenly, everything happens at once. Instead of fleeing with the costumed attendees, Hatter launches himself straight at Ryan.

Lelani breaks from formation and runs forward, her mouth open in a scream of warning. He's going to mow *right* over Ryan, and none of us are close enough to nab him.

Ryan, caught unawares by the leap, stumbles backward, badly off balance, obviously not wanting to engage a frantic would-be murderer. Can't say I blame him.

Ryan's cane flashes up, and I'm surprised he manages the effort, given how bumbling he appears right now.

Like a flash, the man's cane comes out to meet Ryan's, intending to knock Ryan aside.

But . . . it doesn't happen. Ryan parries the man's cane, which outright surprises me. When on earth had Ryan taken up sword fighting?

The two engage in a cane-to-cane duel for several seconds before the man realizes that this avenue, too, is fruitless. He glances over his shoulder at the uniformed police officers who have infiltrated the line, closing ranks behind him, and gives a laugh that sends chills down my spine and can be labeled only as *maniacal.* His gravelly voice is oddly audible over the shuffle of feet, its timbre so unusual it sticks out above the noise. "You think you're so smart."

He does something odd with his cane—gives it a little shake, and something shoots out the bottom. I'm full-out sprinting now, desperate to get to Ryan. Without any further warning, he lunges toward Ryan, the end of his cane having turned into a three-bladed knife.

Blood blossoms across Ryan's throat as the cane makes contact with his skin and—

An enraged *bull* of a man side-tackles the Top Hat maniac so hard it carries them both off the side of the stage and to the street in a series of sickening crunches. A bull of a man that looks an awful lot like Lawrence in the dim and creepy light afforded by the float. Around us, people scream and scatter, and in the distance, sirens wail to life.

"Lawrence!" Ryan screams at the same time as my thought. He launches himself off the float, and there is a scuffle on the ground as police officers, Lelani, and several queens descend onto the dog pile.

"Don't be dead, don't be dead, don't be dead," I chant, skidding over the edge of the float, looking where my best friend—who should be in the hospital—lies motionless on the ground. My other best friend is bleeding copiously from the neck as two policemen drag him to a sitting position. Lelani and one of the queens each take one of Ryan's shoulders from there, hoisting him up.

Someone screams—an animal scream. But it's not someone in the crowd. As the police around Ryan clear slightly, I see it's the man, being held against his will by Shwanda and Amy Blondoniss. In short order, several officers have joined them, and the man struggles anew.

My feet have carried me to Lawrence's side. Someone's taking his pulse. Someone with copper skin and tousled curls. I do a double take as I slide in next to Whalon. The distraction is short-lived, though, as my eyes move to Lawrence, relief washing over me as L opens his eyes and starts to sit up, woozily.

The Hatter points at us. "You stole *everything* from me. You deserve *none* of this. Casey would have been *nothing* without me. You got everything I was promised—a home, a job. And I was out on the street! And then when I came up with a brilliant business plan, you managed to sink that too." He gives a laugh that sets my teeth on edge. "You and that boyfriend of yours. Guess who threatened to tell his father about you two? All I needed was the capital to start my business, and I'd have been set. But no. You had to go and get Casey killed, and kill my plan along with it."

Lawrence sits up farther and levels a look at the man. "You've carried this with you your entire life. To what? Get even? This is *crazy*. I had nothing to do with your business." His eyes flash. I can only imagine that this man's meddling in L's relationship cuts deep. "Why would you do that to me—to us?"

The man laughs again, clearly off his rocker. "To get what's mine. Fame. Fortune. Everything Casey promised me. I want my reward. I want to be on the news. I want to be *known*, but instead *you* got it all."

Whalon takes L's hand and addresses DeWayne. "You were crazy back then, and you're crazy now. And I'm not going to let your threat hang over my head any longer. You convinced me the business world would never accept me—that my *family* would never accept me as I was. That I needed to prove myself. Well, I think I've done that, and I think it's far past time that the world knows who I am. And who was important in making me who I am today. You may have wanted to tear us apart as young men, but it looks like you failed in keeping us from finding each other again—in fact, we have you to *thank* for it, I think." He squeezes L's hand, and a murmur runs through the crowd.

Lawrence slumps down, clearly in pain or overcome by Whalon's declaration. My quick *awwww cute* is followed immediately by worry. "L, are you dead? Did he kill you? Are you bleeding? Wait, why aren't you in the *hospital?*"

"Shwanda drove me. I just had a bad feeling," Lawrence manages.

The police drag the man, kicking and screaming, through the crowd. He brandishes his finger one more time, pointing at where I sit right in front of Ryan, Lelani, and Daniel.

They're almost to the door when the Hatter laughs again. "I may be going down, but I'm taking you with me, *Golden Arrow*. What do we think Casey is going to say when he finds out he's been employing the very person he's been trying to find?"

Everyone goes still, even the police. Suddenly our little group is the center of attention. I start to laugh it off, but the man speaks again. "Oh yes, I have proof, and the police will be *so interested* in trading what I have to offer that I'll be back out on this street again before you know it. And *all of you* had better watch out." His smile is all razor teeth and no mirth. It's a promise.

"Shut. Up." Shwanda swoops in, snatches his cane, and snaps it in half.

This startles the man so much he stares for just a moment before grinning. "Don't believe me? Fine. I'll just out the Arrow right here, or should I say *arrows*—"

Ryan steps around our group, standing alone in the cleared circle on the floor, bleeding from his throat.

"Ryan, no," Lawrence says, a dry cough racking his body.

"Ry?" I ask. Surely this is a joke.

Ryan doesn't move. None of us move.

The police stare. I catch sight of Matteo and Rideout, a cuffed Cleopatra between them.

"He's right," Ryan says in a clear voice.

There's *no way*. This is my *roommate*. My nerdy, game-playing *roommate*.

And yet. Time stops, and I stare at Ryan. He's so *sure*, so calm. Almost noble. He's not faking it, and that leaves me terrified.

The man starts to talk again, but Ryan raises his voice above his. "Shut him up, and I'll tell you the truth. My work is done; my friend is safe—I'm ready to confess. I *am* the Golden Arrow. No one else, none of those imposters. And I have enough proof to share with the police that you'll be behind bars for the rest of your life."

Talk about a gut punch.

But.

Everything, *everything*, about this twist checks out in my gut. I don't want it to. I want it to be full of holes, but it sits like a pit in my stomach. Perfect. Holeless. Ryan's scrapes, his brushes with drug dealers. Skulking about in the dark. His obsession with CrossFit, his knowledge of the comics. Hell, even his move to save us from the explosion. I have no idea *how* he pulled it off, I just know . . . he *could* have.

I watch, with Lawrence shaking in my lap, as Ryan is cuffed by police—officially a vigilante superhero behind bars.

CHAPTER 33

"We'll have to go to the station," Matteo says gently, sitting next to me on the edge of the catwalk, where I'm kicking my one foot that lost its shoe. I haven't even tried to find it. My wig is a complete disaster, my dress covered in blood. Lawrence's, Ryan's, mine—I don't know. I declined the ambulance ride to the hospital, but I need to check in and see how Lawrence is doing since he went back.

"Yeah, I figured."

"Lelani went with Ryan, and I took L's statement before he headed back to the hospital."

This rouses me a little bit. "Did he say at all how he put everything together? How on earth did he appear just at the right time?"

"Well, he calls this guy the Hatter. And he said those journal pages you left just sort of clicked. The boy who Casey had worked with before him had helped Casey with gadgets and little concoctions for his crime fighting—remember, Casey saw himself as a real superhero. It was his place Lawrence took the night of the party thirty years ago."

I remembered Lawrence's story, saying all Casey had to give him to wear was a hat.

"We're not clear on all the particulars, but apparently DeWayne has been eaten alive by jealousy. First that Casey Senior chose to hire Lawrence instead of him, and then that Lawrence rose to fame not only for his drag but also because of the Casey Senior case again. He thought Lawrence was profiting off the death of Casey Senior—something he couldn't stand. So, he hired Cleopatra to be his front woman, and he systematically targeted L. By strengthening his competition, and by ultimately trying to keep him silent when he got too close. We suspect he joined up with Muñez after Casey dumped him and ultimately became his drug chemist. He just . . . kept going when Muñez was jailed, but he needed a new front person."

"Cleo. What on earth happened there?"

Matteo nods. "Lost her head; thought if she got away she wouldn't get jail time."

"That's too bad. What will happen to Ryan?"

Matteo sighs. "There will be an investigation, but since he confessed . . . he even confessed to breaking into the evidence room and stealing the drug samples to test."

I'm beyond glum. Slightly impressed that he pulled that off, if it was really him, but incredibly *glum*.

"We can always hope it's a mistake," Matteo offers, though we know it's an empty comfort.

I sigh. "Yeah."

Matteo picks up a glass from the table nearest the catwalk and holds it up to the light. "Well, at least he can rest assured that he accomplished his goal. Look how many people are behind bars thanks to his work."

"I guess, but this is a lousy price to pay."

Matteo shrugs and hops down to the floor. "He might not think so. The safety of your friends and family is worth an awful lot." He holds up the glass again and this time looks through the end.

"What are you doing?" I ask.

"Trying to see what Lewis Carroll saw."

I smile. "Alice through the looking glass? Did you just make a joke?"

He smiles and offers me a hand. "You're rubbing off on me."

I sigh and hop down too. "You're rubbing off on *me*. Literally. Let's go get you de-glittered."

"I thought you'd never offer. This stuff is stickier than tar."

He puts the glass down on the table, and we walk through the door out into a world that is suddenly much less exciting. Sure, there're no crazy drug dealers on the loose, but . . . now I live in a world where the Golden Arrow isn't out there watching over us. I know justice was served, but is life really better? I look into the dark sky of Halloween, sad the magic is gone.

"Do you think Casey will give the reward money to Ryan?" I ask suddenly.

Matteo's eyebrows rise. "Ah—I'm not sure, but I suppose Twitter is all over it."

"Number one trending topic in LA," I confirm.

Matteo is silent a minute but then shrugs. "I hope so. It would buy him a *hell* of a lawyer, and honestly, it's probably a story that will sell like crazy."

I snort, picturing Ryan penning a "tell-all," and then sober at the realization that he *has* a tell-all to sell.

My shoulders droop. Ryan doesn't belong in jail. "Let's go try and find a way to keep my roommate out of jail, okay?"

Matteo grabs his red wig, wraps his arm over mine, and guides me to the door. "I can't promise anything."

I sigh. "I know."

We link arms and walk out into the Halloween night, into a world where our vigilante hero no longer exists in anonymity. The world feels just a little less safe. Gotham without its Bat.

"I'll try, though." Matteo's tone is Captain America–level genuine, and I know he means it.

My mouth quirks to the side as we stroll, and Matteo must notice, because he stops us mid-stride. "What?"

Maybe he's afraid I don't believe him. "You know, there's an old Jedi Master that says something about trying—"

"Are you really going to quote Yoda right now?" Matteo pulls me forward again.

I'm impressed he can even guess what I'm going to say. The Padawan has become a Jedi Knight—a fitting title for Matteo. "I think it's applicable in this situation."

Again we stop, this time in a puddle of streetlamp light. Matteo turns me to face him, hands on my arms. "MG, I will *do* something, I just can't promise that it'll have much effect. All I can do here *is* to try. And I will." He leans forward and kisses my forehead before steering us once more toward his car.

I sigh. Maybe, held in that light, Yoda was wrong to be so cut-and-dried. Sometimes trying is all you *can* do.

ACKNOWLEDGMENTS

This book, more than any other I've ever written, was a community effort. I owe a debt of gratitude to every single person who kept me going and played a part in finishing 2018 and this book.

First off and foremost, thank you to my family for seeing me through this crazy year. Between the complicated pregnancy, the complicated delivery, and bringing home another human for our family—not to mention attempting to finish a book in a month with a newborn—it's been a wild ride. To my husband, Kent, for ceaselessly cheerleading my writing career, putting up with the late nights, and working for our dreams right alongside me while being the best dad ever. To my mother, who spent *so* much of her time with our family right after the baby was born: I couldn't have managed this second book without you. Thank you to my *other* mom and dad, and Bee and Duff, for unlimited support and questions about my book around the dinner table. These books wouldn't exist without you guys.

I'd be remiss if I didn't thank my plotting partner, Trisha, for the crash course we did while I was so sick—you even provided ice cream, as I recall. Here's to less hectic plotting in the future! And always a big thank-you to my girls: Erin, Vanessa, Ashley, and Kristi. There aren't enough words to express my gratitude for you all, and your willingness to hash out plot, read rough drafts, or just inspire me with your lives.

Secondly, but no less importantly, thank you to my writing crew. Ian, you've done it again as an amazing CP, and I will forever laugh that

I managed to get exploding pizza into this novel. These books would be dreck without your witty banter. Thanks too to Mike Chen for the cheerleading and the support of being debut authors together—your love of MG's world means more than you know! The rest of my writing posse is so vital to all this: my PW '16 #Amwriting group, Debut '18 and '19 groups, my Mom Writers group, and basically everyone on writer Twitter who has buoyed me when I thought I couldn't do this. Community is *everything* in this career. I have the *best* community.

A huge shout-out to my agent, Joanna, for being so kind, compassionate, and understanding during my year of so many personal Everests. To my editor Adrienne: my debut experience has been amazing, and I'll forever be indebted to you for your love and guidance of MG et al.! So many other people from 47North have made this process amazing. To Jaym, my ever-faithful developmental editor: you are my people, through and through. A huge thanks to Brittney of 47North and the Little Bird team for everything you've done.

As MG would say, onward and upward!

ABOUT THE AUTHOR

Photo © 2018 Julie Patton

Meghan Scott Molin is the author of *The Frame-Up* and *The Queen Con*, the first two books in the Golden Arrow series. After studying architecture and opera at college, she worked as a barn manager before becoming a professional photographer. An avid lover of all the nerd things—*Star Wars*, *Star Trek*, hobbits, *Doctor Who*, and more—Meghan also enjoys cooking, dreaming of travel, and listening to audiobooks in the barn. She lives in Colorado with her husband (and fellow zookeeper), her sons, two horses, a cat, and a rambunctious corgi. For more information about Meghan, visit her website at www.MeghanScottMolin.com or follow her on Twitter (@megfuzzle).